W9-CTO-920

TWICE

LISA MISCIONE

Twice

Lisa Miscione

Snowbooks

2

Proudly published by
Snowbooks Ltd.
120 Pentonville Road
London
N1 9JN
Tel: 0207 837 6482
Email: info@snowbooks.com
www.snowbooks.com

British Library Cataloguing in Publication Data
A catalogue record for this book is available from the British Library.

ISBN 10: 1-905005-28-8
ISBN 13: 978-1905005-28-4

Printed and bound in Great Britain by J. H. Haynes & Co. Ltd.

Also by Lisa Miscione

Angel Fire

The Darkness Gathers

For Frederick and Donna Unger

"Where there is love, there is life."

—Mahatma Ghandi

Acknowledgments

With every book I write, the list of people to whom I am thankful grows longer. If I were to name here all of those who have bolstered and helped me in the process of completing this novel, I'm afraid I could go on for pages. Or worse, in the listing of them, I would neglect someone crucial. So I'll just say that I have been blessed with an amazing network of family and friends without whom I would be pretty lost. They know who they are.

I am most especially grateful to my wonderful husband, Jeffrey Unger, for his love, encouragement, patience, and tireless efforts as first reader, webmaster, and publicist; my agent, Elaine Markson, and her assistant Gary Johnson for their unflagging support; Kelley Ragland for her brilliant editing; and associate editor Ben Sevier and all the people at St. Martin's who work so hard and achieve such wonderful results.

TWICE

PROLOGUE

It was night when he came back. His return was washed in bright moonlight, accompanied by the crackling whispers of branches bending in harsh cold wind. He stood for a while on the edge of the clearing, making himself one with the barren trees and dry leaves beneath his feet. Standing tall and rigid as the black, dead trunks around him, he watched. It stood like an old war criminal, a crumbling shadow of its past grandeur, the stain of its evil like an aura, the echo of its misdeeds like a heartbeat. It lived still. He couldn't believe that after all this time, it lived. He pulled cold air into his lungs and felt the fear that was alive within him, too. Like the old house, his dread had aged and sagged but would not be defeated by time alone.

He made his way across the once elaborately landscaped and impeccably manicured lawn, now a battlefield of dead grass, weeds, hedges that had grown wild then died from neglect. The branches and thorns pulled at his pant legs like an omen. Everything about the house, even the grand old oak that stood like a sentry beside it, warned him away. But he was a part of that house and it was a part of him. He was all about collecting the lost parts of himself now. It was time.

Memories flickered before his eyes, 8mm film projected on a wall. He could see her dancing and see her smiling, see her running. Her chubby little girl legs, her tiny skirts and little shorts. He could see her blond pigtails, her round blue eyes. As she grew older, grew beautiful, her hair and eyes both darkened, her skin looked and felt like French vanilla ice cream. He could see her in those last moments before everything went bad. He heard her laughter and her screams and both were music to him. His love for her was a ghost pain. Since they had been wrested apart, he felt as though someone had donated his organs to science without waiting for him to die. He lived with a prosthetic heart.

He stood on the porch and felt the old wood groan beneath him, threatening to snap. He heard skittering behind the door, and the branches from the great oak scraped the sides of the house, fingernails on the inside of a coffin. He was the damned in front of the gates of hell. He was terrified but knew in his heart that he was deserving.

The house was a caricature of itself, dilapidated, shedding splinters and shingles, with cracked windows and sagging eaves, every house in every horror movie ever made. As he pushed the door open, it knocked some beer cans and they rattled across the floor. The house seemed to sigh with relief as he stepped into the foyer and he felt its cold breath on his neck. The chandelier, made of a thousand crystal teardrops, blanketed in dust, was the central point for a million spider webs that reached across the grand foyer. The crystal jingled like tiny bells above his head.

The door blew closed behind him. He looked around at the havoc disrepair and neglect had wreaked. He felt a rush of anger. It was to have been maintained; instead it had been vandalized and looted. Sun damage had drained all the colors from the rugs and furniture, the portraits on the walls. Spray-painted obscenities screamed in black and red. He could see in the sitting room that a sofa teetered on three legs. But his anger passed quickly. It was nothing a good cleaning wouldn't fix.

"Or a good exorcism," he said aloud to himself. He was surprised at how old his voice sounded.

A cracked mirror framed in ornate gold-leafed wood hung lopsided on the far wall. Someone had spray-painted *Tracy Loves Justin TL4* on the glass. He startled at his own reflection there. His face was masked by a long full beard and straggling gray hair hanging in limp, dirty dreads. He wore a tattered denim jacket, filthy and stiff over layers of equally rank T-shirts and a once-red sweatshirt. He looked like the kind of man people avoided on the street, the kind people turned away from, holding their breaths against the inevitable stench. He raised a hand to his face and his beard felt gritty and stiff as steel wool. His fingertips were as thick and hard as stones, his nails black with dirt.

He stood mesmerized as the wind hissed through broken windows, rattled cans across the floor, fluttered the heavy drapes that hung in tatters in the study. He couldn't remember the last time he'd seen his own reflection. In his mind's eye, he always saw himself as a young man. Handsome and lean, with ice blue eyes and hair so black it sheened violet in the sunlight. But he was less shocked by what he saw in the mirror today than he used to be. At least now he was as wrecked on the outside as he was on the inside. It used to seem like nature's joke to him that his heart was such a black dead place while his skin flushed with youth and health, while his smile dazzled, electric and charming. The same infected, twisted DNA that made him what he was, that forced upon him his congenital legacy, also had made him exceedingly handsome, like the Venus's fly-trap that attracts insects with its scent and beauty and then snaps them within its jaws. At least now he was recognizable for what he was.

He heard the echo of laughter and he looked behind him at the sweeping staircase that led into the darkness of the second level. And he heard the house draw and release its foul breath. The bright full moon outside passed behind clouds and the room fell into darkness. He felt his heart rate elevate slightly and his belly fluttered with fear.

"I'm home," he said as he turned and walked up the stairs into the black, knowing as he did that there was no turning back. That the curtain had risen on the final act and that all the players would be pulled inexorably toward their end.

PART ONE

ONE

Lydia Strong ran. She ran in spite of the myriad reasons she shouldn't. She ran hard and fast in December drizzle, her face flushed with cold air and the heat that burned inside her like a furnace. She ran down Lafayette Street past the Gaseteria and the Puck Building, over broken sidewalks, bottles, and litter. Past a dark, dank alley, crowded with bulky shadows and a hundred pink shutters reaching into a sliver of slate gray sky. Into the chintzy chaos of Chinatown, all red and yellow, mobbed with men selling knockoff designer bags, buzzing with windup toys and statues of Buddha, smelling of crispy duck. Past the massive, grand, dirty-white Manhattan court buildings and on to the Brooklyn Bridge.

Lean and strong, with a fullness about her hips and breasts, Lydia was a graceful runner with perfect form, moving seemingly with little effort through the crowded city streets; abs in, shoulders back, heels connecting first with the concrete, her next stride drifting gracefully off her toes. She wove between slower-moving pedestrians on the crowded downtown sidewalks...lawyers, cops, slack-jawed tourists gazing up in awe at the impressive size of the stately court buildings. Her strong angular face and storm-cloud gray eyes were expressionless, if a bit drawn and determined, and offered only the slightest hint of the tension she carried with her this day. It was the tension of always being watched. Hunted, in fact, if she was honest with herself.

She quashed the urge to glance behind her as she crossed the street against the light and began to ascend the mild slope toward the center of the Brooklyn Bridge. She knew he was there. Maybe not right behind her, but nearer than she wanted him. She only hoped that he couldn't keep up with her.

She increased her effort against the incline and smiled to herself when the concrete gradation gave way to the wooden slats of the bridge. Something about the feeling of wood beneath her feet, the way it gave under her weight, made her feel safer than concrete, reminded her that there was a more innocent New York somewhere in the not too distant past and that part of its essence still existed on the bridge.

It had only been a few weeks since her worst nightmare came true. Since then, she'd struggled to maintain some semblance of normalcy. Not that normal for her was normal for anyone else. As a bestselling true crime writer, once-consultant and now partner in the private investigation firm of the newly minted Mark, Striker and Strong, Lydia got a daily dose of horror that would put most people in a sanitarium. She had devoted her life to understanding the criminal mind, wanting to know what drove a man to rape and kill, what was present or missing within him to make him a monster. In this quest, she had nearly destroyed herself and any chance she would ever have at happiness. She'd been pulled back from the brink before, but now she found herself dangling there again.

Jed McIntyre, the serial killer who murdered her mother, was on the loose after fifteen years behind bars. And he was considerably more insane and newly obsessed with Lydia. It had upped the chaos in her life to a level that she was having a hard time handling. Throw in the fact that she had just realized she was pregnant and that Jeffrey Mark—her longtime friend and mentor, and her live-in lover for over a year—was putting the pressure on her to marry, and some moments she felt like her head was going to explode.

Not that she put her love life in the same category as she put Jed McIntyre. But it was all part of the mounting sense that she had lost control of her once very orderly existence.

She came to a stop in the middle of the bridge under the first gigantic arch and walked over to the railing facing west. She felt the cold on her nose and her cheeks, her heart thumping the rhythm of exertion. The skyscrapers of lower Manhattan reached, gleaming monoliths against a flat slate sky, and the morning rush hour flowed beneath her, a slow, noisy river of tires whispering on wet asphalt, the occasional screeching of a sudden stop or the blast of an angry horn rising from the current.

All the answers were on the Brooklyn Bridge. It was the place she always came to when her mind wrestled with a thousand worries and the cacophony in her head made the city noise seem like an orchestra, composed and melodic. She wondered, not for the first time, what was wrong with her. Why she wasn't more euphoric, the way you were supposed to be, about the baby...Jeffrey's baby...and about the fact that he was gung-ho to get married. Isn't this what women were supposed to want? But she had never wanted what other people wanted. She had never understood the urgent desire some women feel to procreate. Or the happy blissful glow they displayed when they discovered they were finally pregnant. Don't you realize, she'd wanted to ask, what an awesome responsibility you have to this new life? That your actions from here on out will affect this child forever?

Lydia wondered how she could bring a child into a world

populated by monsters, monsters that she seemed to have an insatiable desire to chase and destroy, one at a time. Or vice versa. She worried that, at the end of the day, she didn't have enough to offer a baby. It seemed like so many people were concerned about wanting a child, while they never considered what they had to give. She didn't want to be one of those people. Maybe you should have thought about all this before you went and got yourself knocked up, she chastised.

Jeffrey, on the other hand, seemed to have a Zen-like confidence about the whole thing. "It happened now because it's time for us," he had said during one of their midnight conversations after anxiety had disturbed her sleep, and as a consequence his as well. "You'll surprise yourself. You're going to be a doting, intelligent, sensitive mother...with your own identity. Trust me."

Jeffrey was the only person in the world she did truly trust—with her life, her future. Lydia had met Jeffrey when she was only fifteen years old and he was a twenty-five-year-old FBI agent investigating her mother's murder. Over the next fifteen years, they stayed in touch and their connection evolved into friendship. They became colleagues on a number of projects and he became for her a mentor, confidant, and advisor. Somewhere along the line, he became much more. But it was only a little more than a year earlier that they both finally gave in to the feelings that had been boiling beneath the surface of their relationship.

The years before her life with Jeffrey seemed like a landscape of loneliness and isolation that she had crossed. While her career had flourished, her inner life had been a wasteland of fear and pain. She had felt permanently scarred by the loss of her mother, whose body she had discovered one autumn day when she returned home from school. Abandoned long ago by her father, Lydia was raised by her loving but elderly grandparents. In spite of the love and care she got from them, she grew up afraid to really care for them or anyone, afraid to trust because of a crippling fear of loss. After the death of her mother, she had clawed her way back from the abyss of grief and as a young woman she'd decided, albeit on a subconscious level, that she had no intention of ever being thrown back into that slick-walled pit again.

Loving Jeffrey had changed that, had helped her to trust the universe more, to trust herself, had helped her to embrace life instead of wasting it fearing the death of those she loved. Things had been more or less blissful until she invited the monsters back into her life...into their lives. Now Jed McIntyre roamed free. She reached down and felt the Beretta in the pouch she wore at her waist. It gave her some small measure of security.

From the corner of her eye, Lydia spotted a thick figure dressed in black making his way quickly through the smattering of people strolling up the wooden slats of the bridge's walkway. He was like a drifting mountain and people turned to look at him as he made his way past. Lydia moved quickly behind the stone ballast that stood in the center of the walkway dividing it in two, the bike path on the left and the pedestrian path on the right. She pressed her back against the cold stone and waited, her heart racing.

She knew it would happen just like this. When she was being careless, or worse, reckless, he would come on her in broad daylight in a throng of people. He wouldn't come in the cover of night, when demons were expected. He would move from the crowd, take her in front of bystanders. No one would make a move to stop him. She could imagine it all as clearly as if it were a memory. When the time came there would be a fight to the death and the odds were even as to who would walk away. She peered around the ballast to see the giant form almost on top of her.

Dax Chicago rounded the corner, breathless and clutching his side.

"Bang, you're dead," said Lydia loudly, startling him.

"Jesus Christ, woman. What is wrong with you?" his

heavy Australian accent making the words little more than a jumble to her. But she had learned to understand him better after three weeks of seeing him every single bloody day.

"I thought you were in better shape," she said with a smile.

"I'm trying to help you," he said, walking a circle, still holding his side.

"You're a mercenary, Dax. Let's not glorify your role here."

"Fuck off," he said miserably. "It's fucking cold out here."

Dax Chicago was six-foot-four of pure muscle and grit. He had the kind of strength that bulldozers envied, and the kind of graceful speed that seemed impossible in a man of his size—in the short haul. Lydia knew that over miles, he wouldn't be able to keep up with her. She did like to make him earn the money Jeffrey was paying him to be with her when he couldn't be. A fact she greatly resented. But Jeffrey could not be dissuaded...so Lydia made it as difficult as possible for everyone.

"Pregnant women who are being stalked by serial killers should not be jogging anyway," he added with a smirk.

She punched him hard on the arm and connected with flesh that felt more like a boulder than a man. She didn't really mind Dax, and even when she hated him it was the kind of hate reserved for family members, always threatening to bubble over with laughter and lined with affection. She had to admit he was a good man to have on the team. A former Special Forces agent for the British army, his knowledge of weapons, surveillance, and an almost supernatural gift for stealth had definitely been an asset in the past.

The other thing Lydia liked about Dax was that his whole life was cloaked in mystery. He revealed little about his past, how he came to work for the firm, how he came to live in a palatial home in Riverdale complete with a basement that put dungeons to shame. His basement was a maze of rooms—one a weapons armory filled with enough firepower to equip an army; one with a cruel metal table, complete with five-point restraints; yet another adjacent to a second room connected by a two-way mirror. Lydia never tired of probing Dax for details about himself that he refused to disclose. It was as if Dax Chicago sprang fully grown from the earth in a full set of body armor and carrying an AK-47.

"Come on, Lydia. Let's go," Dax said, a pleading look in his jade eyes. His pale skin was blotched with angry red patches from cold and exertion. A few brown curls snaked out of the charcoal wool stocking cap he'd pulled down over his ears. He was not bad-looking for a big dumb Aussie.

"Dax, maybe we need to get you a girlfriend," she said as they reached the bottom of the bridge and headed back into the court district.

He snorted his contempt as Lydia's cell phone rang. She unzipped the pouch at her waist and removed the tiny silver Nokia that rested against the not so tiny Beretta.

"Hi," she said, having seen Jeffrey's number on the caller ID.

"Where are you?"

"At home, on the couch, like a good little prisoner."

He sighed on the other end of the phone. "Are you with Dax?"

"I can't seem to shake him."

"Listen," he said, "why don't you two hop in a cab and come to the office? There's something I need to talk to you about."

They walked across Chambers Street, the sickly sweet smell of honey-roasted nuts from a vending cart carrying on the cold air. An angry cabbie leaned on his horn as a Lincoln Town Car cut him off and sped past them. Sharply dressed yuppies rushed along in a blur of navy and black on their way to important jobs, tasks, meetings, carrying paper cups of Starbucks coffee.

"What's up?" asked Lydia, hearing the lick of excitement in his voice.

"Did you see the news this morning?"

"No."

"Then I'll explain it to you when you get here. Half an hour?"

"About that."

Dax and Lydia jogged to Sixth Avenue and hopped a cab heading uptown to Mark, Striker and Strong.

TWO

Detective Halford McKirdy, Ford to his friends, liked the dark. Darkness formed a cocoon where thoughts could gestate into theories, theories into answers. The light beckoned a man outside himself, encouraged him to be distracted. That's why he always pulled the shades in his dingy, cluttered office so that only just the hint of sunlight leaked in between the blinds and the sill, between the slats, creating thin ladders of light across the files and photographs on his desk.

This morning there was a strange odor in his office. It could have been the half-empty coffee cup—or half full, as an optimist, which Ford was not, might note—that was perched dangerously on the corner of his desk. It could have been the pastrami sandwich that he knew still lay on the bottom of his wastepaper basket beneath a drift of discarded paper, forms, and message slips. Or the stale cigarettes in the ashtray that he kept in the upper right-hand drawer of his metal and faux-wood desk, so that no one would notice that he was still sneaking the occasional cigarette. Or maybe it was just that the smell of death had followed him from the crime scene he'd left an hour before. Likely, it was some combination of all of those things.

"He has come for me again," she'd said slowly with a nod, her pink silk pajamas stained with blood, clinging to her, her voice quavering, her eyes staring off into some horror only she could see. The horror right before her eyes seemed to elude her.

"I'll never escape him now. He'll eat my young...swallow them whole. And me as well. You can't stop him. No one can."

The words she'd spoken to him as the paramedics wheeled her away in restraints were echoing in his head now as Ford flipped through the crime scene photographs. They were up there with the most gruesome he'd seen in his twenty-year career. He sat quietly at his desk. Only the halogen lamp beside him lit his office as he slowly wrote notes in black ink on a yellow legal pad, trying to make sense of what he had seen this morning. This would be the second time he'd investigated the murder of one of Julian Ross's husbands.

He remembered the first time clearly, just as he remembered all the cases where the answers had never come clear. Something had haunted her that night ten years ago. He could see that behind her eyes, ringed horribly in black by the mascara she had wept from her lashes. But she is not innocent, he remembered thinking. Nor, however, had he sensed in her the capacity for the cold and calculating murder of her husband. He'd had the same conflict about Julian Ross again as he'd arrived at her Park Avenue duplex at five in the morning, called in to investigate the murder of her second husband. It was a good thing she kept her maiden name.

He shifted in his chair, leaning back and rubbing his eyes. He rolled his head from shoulder to shoulder, hearing the tension crackling there. He remembered Julian as a tiny woman, really frail-looking, with a fragile beauty that threatened to shatter with the passing years. For some reason he had always remembered her hands and her wrists vividly, so white that he could see the blue of her veins beneath the parchment of her skin. Every time he'd seen one of her paintings over the years, in a magazine or a SoHo gallery, he'd remembered those hands and the questions he still had about her years after she had been acquitted. Something about it had never rested with him. Here he was again. That was his karma; the sleeping dogs never did lie.

Julian Ross, still tiny, still frail-looking, had aged considerably since he'd last seen her, in spite of her wealth and success. To be fair, the fact that she was covered in her husband's blood and rocking back and forth on her haunches in the corner of her bedroom didn't do much for her. She had looked at him when he entered, and said, "You again."

When he'd walked through the front door of the duplex, the energy of rage and terror had raised the hair on his arms. Something wasn't right, he knew at once. Something wasn't simple. When he saw the room where the crime was done, all the feelings he'd had that night ten years ago came rushing back to him...the disbelief and the slightest notch of fear in the back of his throat. It was like when he took his wife to Egypt for their honeymoon and they saw the Great Pyramids, those gigantic monuments reaching into the sky so solid, so symmetrical. All he could think was, No human could have done this with the resources available at the time.

Julian Ross's second husband, Richard Stratton III, the father of her twins Lola and Nathaniel, had been stabbed repeatedly in their bed while she allegedly slept beside him. But stabbed was really too friendly a word for what had been done to Mr. Stratton. He had been disemboweled, nearly decapitated. His face had been bashed beyond recognition. His blood and innards had been spread around the room. There were long trails of blood along the floor and along the walls, as though he'd been dragged about by a poltergeist.

Just like Julian's first husband, Tad Jenson, his wedding ring and the finger on which he'd worn it had been removed.

Neither object was anywhere to be found.

It didn't seem physically possible that Julian Ross could have done what had been done to her husband. But at the moment, there was no evidence that anyone else had entered the apartment. Julian's elderly mother, Eleanor; Julian's six-year-old twins; and their young nanny were sleeping in rooms on the lower level of the duplex. Julian's claim that she had popped sleeping pills before bed and didn't wake during the violence wasn't exactly an airtight alibi.

On the other hand, there was nothing at the scene that could be easily identified as the murder weapon. Then there was the pure physicality of a 100-pound woman beating and bludgeoning to death a 250-pound, six-foot-four male and somehow managing to get his blood all over the walls and even on the twelve-foot-tall ceiling. There was something definitely spooky about it.

"You again," she'd said when he walked into the room. A smile played upon her lips. Shock or insanity...maybe a little of both.

"What is she still doing in here?" he'd asked the cop who stood at the bedroom door, supposedly guarding the scene until the ME and forensics arrived.

"I'm not leaving my husband," she said, her voice shrill with the hysteria he knew was going to hit like a tornado in a few minutes. The cop he'd addressed shrugged his helplessness.

"Ms. Ross, let's get you out of here, okay?" he said, holding out his hand.

"No, I'm not leaving him," she answered. Her eyes had started to glaze over and he could see that she was trembling. He looked around him at the bloodbath, trying to determine the source of a dripping noise he heard. Blood had soaked through the sheets and was collecting in a pool on the hardwood floor next to Julian. She didn't seem to notice as it grew and crept toward her.

It was the kind of room showcased in magazines—or

anyway it had been before the carnage. The bed was the size of some apartments he'd been in, with its dramatic four posts and plush mattress, at least ten brocade throw pillows. French doors opened onto a balcony revealing a breathtaking view of uptown Manhattan. Pictures of Julian and Richard or the twins, beautifully framed in sterling, wood, or crystal, occupied most of the available nooks and crannies of space on the dresser and night tables. A small alcove of bookshelves reached to the ceiling and a plush maroon chenille chair, matching ottoman, and standing lamp nestled in the space. Embers still glowed in the fireplace, above which was a large canvas that Ford recognized as an early work of Julian's. An entertainment armoire stood partially open, revealing a large-screen television, DVD player, stereo, and speakers. All of it was marred by blood splatter.

"Sir, the paramedics are here," said the other uniform on the scene, after jogging up the stairs and stopping at the bedroom door.

"Only one of them in here," answered Ford. "She needs to be sedated and removed from the room and then no one else will be allowed in here until the crime scene investigators arrive."

"You think I did this, don't you?" she asked him in one of her last moments of semi-lucidity.

He looked at her, knowing he should inform her of her right to remain silent.

"I took sleeping pills before I went to bed. I woke up and found him...like..." she said, as a sob took over her body and her voice. "Like this," she finished in a whisper. He looked over at the body of her husband face down and naked on the bed, one arm draping over the side, knuckles touching the floor. The body looked white and deflated, which Ford guessed made sense, as it seemed to have been drained of most of its blood.

"I wouldn't say anything at all right now if I were you, Ms. Ross," he said, trying not to sound as cold as he felt inside.

"Just be grateful you're not," she said as he walked from the room, passing by a paramedic who looked younger than seemed possible. Even the cops on the scene looked like babies to him. When did he start to feel so old?

He sighed, remembering, wishing he'd handled her differently, hadn't let the anger and emotion he'd felt at the scene get the best of him. With Julian totally incoherent now, he couldn't expect to get anywhere with her for a while. She talked so softly, like a child...seemed so delicate, just like the first time. He remembered how surprised he'd been ten years ago when he'd seen her canvases. Halford McKirdy didn't know much about art, but he knew rage when he saw it sure enough.

She painted on gigantic canvases in rich, bold lines—heavy on the blacks, reds, and yellows. She painted scenes of rape, murder, and carnage. Some were intricately detailed murals of mass violence, with bleeding, writhing figures in fields of gore and fire. Some were close-up images of mutilated female genitalia, broken flesh and bones, faces contorted in fear or anger or both, women fleeing from some unseen hunter. Other works were just angry slashes of color, amorphous figures in black or gray, lines and shadows. When he first investigated her, she was already a successful artist, a darling of the SoHo gallery scene. Now she was an international sensation and a very wealthy woman. This type of scandal would only make her work worth more, he knew. The world was populated by bloodsuckers that loved the taint of violence as long as it didn't come too close.

He'd headed down the stairs and toward the sitting room, where he knew Julian's mother, her children, and the nanny were waiting.

Eleanor Ross was a regal woman in a black silk dressing gown, her silver hair pulled back into a braided bun. She possessed an eerie calm, sitting on a plush red velvet sofa in front of a fire she must just have made. A twin lay on either side of her, each with a head on her thigh, each with blue eyes wide open staring into the flames. She had a hand on each twin's head.

The nanny, a young girl with skin the color of caramel, weighing in at maybe a hundred pounds on a fat day, sat weeping in a chair close to the fire. It was a mournful and helpless sound, kind of weak. Ford turned to look at her, but her head was buried in her hands, a lush mane of black curls falling almost to her lap. Her shoulders trembled, her feet barely touched the floor.

"We heard nothing and saw nothing, Detective," Eleanor said before Ford sat down on the ottoman he'd pulled in front of them.

He didn't look at her as he pulled out his notepad. "Is that so?"

A moment of silence passed between them before Eleanor turned her gaze on him.

"Surely you don't think my daughter could have done such a thing," she said imperiously.

"At this point, ma'am, I'm not sure of anything."

"Don't just take the easy way out like you did last time. You decided right away it was Julian and never even looked for who really killed her first husband. Whoever killed him got off scot-free," she said with a disapproving shake of her head.

"You can say that again," he answered, thinking of the day Julian had been acquitted and the mix of emotions he'd felt. Tonight he felt like Julian had had ten years of freedom she hadn't deserved and now someone else was dead.

She snorted at him, picking up on his sarcasm. "That jury of teachers and mechanics had better sense than you and the whole police department. They could see. Julian doesn't have the strength to do such a thing. She doesn't have the nerve."

The way Eleanor said it, it sounded like an insult. He looked at her. There was a coldness in her eyes that was mirrored in the eyes of the twins on her lap. Her mouth was a hard straight line in a landscape of lined and sagging skin. Her stubborn chin was a dare to argue with her, to defy her. It occurred to Ford that this woman did not seem even remotely upset that her son-in-law had been brutally murdered, probably by her daughter just upstairs from where she sat. Seeing the three of them there like that, the knowledge of the scene above their heads, the weird aura of togetherness that seemed to surround them, he felt a cold finger of dread trace his spine.

"I'd like to take your statement now, Ms. Ross."

"I'll come to the station around noon with my attorney. Leave me your business card so we know where to find you."

He gave her a look that he'd hoped would be intimidating but clearly wasn't. They stared at each other for a moment and he saw that she was not going to budge.

"You're not a suspect at this time, Ms. Ross."

"The Ross family does not speak to police officers without the presence of an attorney. Remember that, children."

"Yes, Grandma," they each said softly. Ford's creep-meter went off the charts. Nice family, he thought.

"Have it your way," he said, pulling a card from his jacket pocket.

"I always do," she said with a bitchy smile that was more a grimace and a narrowing of her eyes.

He heard raised voices from the second level. Eleanor got up and scooted the children toward a door on the far end of the sitting room. Julian's thin and piercing voice carried down the stairs, ranting something incoherent that ended in a heartbroken wail.

"I'm taking the children to their rooms."

Ford nodded as she disappeared, and wondered briefly who would take care of Julian. He wasn't sure why he cared.

When Ford turned to the nanny, he saw that she'd looked up from her hands at the sound of Julian's voice, and now sat wide-eyed, peering toward the landing of the second floor as if awaiting the approach of a demon.

"Miss?" he said, walking over to the girl. She looked at him, startled, as if she'd only just realized he was there. "You're the nanny to Lola and Nathaniel."

"That's right," she said. Her voice was oddly level for someone whose eyes looked so wide with fright, someone who'd been weeping moments before.

"Your name?"

"Geneva Stout."

Ford scrawled her name in his notes. "Do you have identification?"

"Why? You don't believe me?"

He looked up from his notepad and saw a flash of what might have been anger, might have been fear. "It's routine, Ms. Stout. That's all." He made his voice calming.

She narrowed her eyes suspiciously and then rose to disappear through the same door where Eleanor had taken the children. If she was a little edgy, Ford was willing to give her the benefit of the doubt. One of her bosses had just been brutally murdered, the other was ranting like a madwoman, and now she was left with the Wicked Queen as her sole employer. Who wouldn't be out of sorts? Julian's wails continued to waft down the stairs, raising the fine hairs on his arms and the back of his neck. Talk about overkill.

Geneva returned and handed him a New York State driver's license and a New York University student ID. He wrote down the numbers and handed the hard plastic cards back to her.

"Any other addresses?" he asked her. He'd noticed that she listed the Rosses' address on each piece of identification.

"No," she said with a quick shake of her head. "I'm a live-in nanny. I take care of Lola and Nathaniel full-time."

"When do you go to class?"

"I manage," she said, averting her eyes. "Part-time."

"Family?"

She looked at him blankly like she wasn't sure what he

was asking. A little too blankly.

"Do you have any family? Where do they live?" he said slowly, looking at her full on now.

"Nope," she said, again with that quick, certain shake of her head. "I don't have any family."

He was going to ask her to clarify her circumstances, but another cry rang through the apartment and Geneva closed her eyes and rubbed them hard with her fingers.

"What are they going to do to her?" she said, her voice tight with anguish.

It seemed like a strange question. Of all the possible things someone would be wondering about at a moment like this, she wanted to know what would happen to Julian.

He sat down on another ottoman that was near her chair and pulled himself next to her.

"Are you very close to the family?" he asked gently. She looked at him like he was some kind of an idiot.

"Well, yeah. I live with them. Take care of their kids. What do you think?"

Then her tough-chick mask split and she started to sob again. "I—can't—believe this," she said, barely able to get the words out. He put a hand on her knee and felt her body shaking.

"Okay, Ms. Stout. Take a moment. You can come tomorrow with Ms. Ross and give your statement to me when you're calmer."

"My—statement?" she said, looking at him in horror. "I didn't see anything or hear anything until Julian started to scream. My bedroom is at the other end of that long hallway." Her words came out between the sharp drawing and releasing of her breath and she pointed unsteadily toward the door she'd gone through earlier.

"Okay," he said, writing down what she'd said. "We'll talk more tomorrow. Unless you want to talk sooner. Call me anytime." He handed her his card and she grasped it in her hand, gave a small nod. Here she looked at him with those wide dark eyes and he had found himself wondering what it was he saw churning in their depths.

Then he'd heard movement on the stairs. He and Geneva watched as the paramedics brought Julian down restrained on a stretcher. She had stopped screaming and had started to sob her husband's name in a desperate, keening tone. When she saw Ford at the bottom of the stairs, she looked at him with a pleading in her eyes and said, "He's come for me again. I'll never escape him now. He'll eat my young... swallow them whole. And me as well. You can't stop him. No one can."

THREE

The temperature in the offices of Mark, Striker and Strong seemed to drop ten degrees when Eleanor Ross pushed through the glass doors. Even from a distance, she had the stern demeanor of a warden and about as much charm. Her long, black cashmere coat was buttoned to the neck and its hem skirted the floor. Dark red lipstick made her face appear paler than a live woman should want. In her proud chin and unsmiling mouth, she carried with her the air of authority that money afforded and the attitude that any deviation from her wishes would result in a beheading.

She was familiar to Jeffrey Mark and he watched her with interest through the glass wall of his office, through which he could see out but those in the waiting area could not see in. It took a few seconds to place her. He had just figured it out when the intercom buzzer on his phone sounded.

"Jeff, there's an Eleanor Ross here to see Lydia," announced Rebecca, the firm's receptionist, who was also a student at John Jay College studying for her master's in forensic science. "I told her Lydia was out and she asked to see you."

“Give me a minute. I’ll be right out.”

He had just turned off the television in his office after watching the footage of Julian Ross being rolled out of her Park Avenue building in a stretcher. He remembered her well from ten years ago, and he was not surprised to learn that she was under suspicion again. The only surprise was that it had taken so long. He spun around in his black leather desk chair and looked out over the city, trying to stitch together the fragments of his memory.

The murder of Tad Jenson, Julian’s first husband, was never solved. Even after Julian Ross had been taken into custody and arraigned, Jeff’s good friend Ford McKirdy, the Ninth Precinct homicide detective working the case, couldn’t let it go. It wasn’t that Ford was crusading for her innocence as much as he’d just had a sense that there was more to it, that there was someone else involved. Ford’s superiors considered the case closed. So Ford had contacted Jeffrey and asked for his help, unofficially...not as an investigator but as a friend.

The night her first husband was murdered, Julian claimed that she had been painting in her studio at the far end of the loft, with the door closed and the music blaring. She claimed that she had come out of her studio around six o’clock to see what her husband wanted for dinner and found him brutally murdered. She dropped to her knees beside him in shock and picked up the knife that lay next to him. When the police broke down the door, responding to an anonymous 911 call, that was how they found her.

Ford had arrested Julian Ross because she had been found hold-ing the murder weapon, covered in her husband’s blood, and there appeared to have been no one else at the scene. Only her prints were found on the weapon. The building doorman claimed that no one but Julian and Tad had entered the apartment that night. But something about it had never rested easily with Ford. He was convinced that there was another piece to the puzzle. So, even as Julian went to trial, he and Ford had tried to track down another suspect on Ford's own time. For a number of reasons, Jeffrey and Ford both agreed that Julian at least had not worked alone. Turned out they were the same reasons that gave the jury enough reasonable doubt to acquit her.

A twenty-three-year-old heroin addict, Jetty Murphy, who had been shifting through the building garbage four floors down from Tad and Julian's apartment, said he heard three voices, two male and one female. At one point, he heard an inhuman roar come from the window and a woman's desperate scream. Then, minutes later, as he cowered behind the Dumpster, a giant figure with long hair looking like "some kind of homeless dude on steroids, man, like a real giant but super fast like Speed Racer," burst from the building's back door. Jetty claimed to have followed the figure to Prince Street, where the man just disappeared.

There were several long brown and gray hairs found at the scene. But they were never able to match those hairs to anyone Julian knew...friends, associates, neighbors. There were places in the gore where it appeared that someone had wiped something away, possibly foot- or handprints, and the cloth used to do so was never found.

Most compelling of all was Julian's physical size. It seemed unlikely, if not impossible, that such a small woman would be capable of overpowering a man who outweighed her by a hundred pounds and was nearly a foot taller. Yet the beautiful NoHo loft had been nearly destroyed in the mortal struggle that ended in Julian, allegedly, overpowering Tad and stabbing him to death with a serrated kitchen knife. From the newscast he'd just heard, it sounded like Richard Stratton had met with a similar end, nearly decapitated, parted from his insides.

There had been enough evidence to suggest that someone else had been present; but not enough to figure out who it was or how he got in and out of the apartment that night.

Ford was a good man, with the instincts and tenacity

of a bloodhound. He'd been given his nickname, short for Halford, by the other guys at the Ninth Precinct because he was solid and reliable, made of steel, and never said die. Jeff knew that over the years he'd never stopped asking questions about the Julian Ross case. It always came up on the rare occasions they managed to get together for a drink at McSorley's on Fifth Street. The same place they used to get together nights and talk about the case when it was on, it seemed like the right place to have a beer and talk about old times.

"Remember the Tad Jenson case?" Ford would say with a shake of his head, filling the lull that followed after they'd talked about the job or his kids for a bit.

It was too romantic to say that the case haunted Ford, that it was the one that he never got over. But it was something Jeff knew Ford's mind turned back to often enough that it niggled at him on those nights after he'd happen to read about Julian Ross in the paper or see her interviewed on television.

Jeffrey swiveled back around in his chair, picked up the phone, and left a message on Ford McKirdy's voice mail. He called Lydia, then rose to usher Eleanor Ross into his office.

"Do you know why I'm here, Mr. Mark?" asked Eleanor as soon as Jeffrey had closed the door and she had seated herself in one of the two leather Eames chairs that sat across from his desk. Her voice was thin and shaky, with the rasp of a smoker. But he noted that she moved with the grace and strength of a dancer.

"I just turned off the news. I am sorry for your loss," he said, leaning back on the edge of his desk in front of her, keeping his voice neutral but courteous, compassionate. "How can I help you?"

"I want you to find out who murdered my son-in-law," she said, turning a cool stare on him.

He turned away from her and felt her eyes on his back

as he walked around his desk and sat in his chair. He could smell just the lightest scent of her perfume. It was airy and floral and reminded him of a scent that Lydia wore.

"Which one?" he asked, placing the tips of his fingers together and finally returning her gaze. He had sensed that she was a woman accustomed to giving orders and he wanted it straight at the outset that he was a man not accustomed to obeying them.

She narrowed her eyes and seemed to be assessing him, taking in the details of his face, his clothes, like a boxer sizing up an opponent.

"Ten years ago, the police failed to do their job," she said slowly, her voice flat. "I want to see that the same thing doesn't happen again here."

"Have you considered the possibility that it was the jury that didn't do their job, Ms. Ross?"

Eleanor Ross's face lost some of its hardness, seemed to crumble a bit as if she might cry. But Jeffrey had a hard time imagining that kind of emotion from the woman, would have been less surprised if tears fell from the eyes of the Statue of Liberty.

"I know how it looks, Jeff. Can I call you that?" she said, her voice suddenly becoming softer as she leaned toward him in her chair. When he nodded, she continued.

"But I know my daughter and I know that she is not capable of this. If you're familiar with the case of Tad's murder, you know there was sufficient evidence to suggest there was someone else at the apartment that night."

"Do you have any idea who that person might be?"

He thought he saw a flicker there; something that passed in front of her ice blue eyes but was gone as quickly as it came. "No," she said, raising a hand to her throat. "I can't begin to imagine."

"But you believe that the person responsible for Tad Jenson's death is the same person responsible for Richard Stratton's?"

"I don't know what to think," she said, looking away from him. "I just know that it wasn't Julian."

It was in these moments when Jeffrey most needed Lydia. Jeffrey was a facts man. He lived for the empirical, the provable, the trail of evidence that led to an undeniable truth. Lydia believed that the truth sometimes left only a scent on the wind. She got a sense of people, their hidden selves, their secret motives, sometimes in just a few moments. Her instincts were usually dead on. He called it "the buzz." The tingling of the senses she got when something was not as it seemed, when something was off or needed investigating. Looking at Eleanor, he saw a woman in distress, needing help for her daughter. He wondered, though, what Lydia would see.

He knew Eleanor couldn't be aware of his involvement in the case ten years ago. No one knew about that except Ford. It seemed like a strange coincidence that she would wind up in his office. He didn't like coincidences.

"Who's working the case?" he asked, already knowing the answer.

She pulled a card from the pocket of her coat that she'd unbuttoned but not removed.

"Detective Halford McKirdy. Do you know him?"

"Yes, I do. He's a good detective, Ms. Ross. You might be wasting your money."

"Don't you think I know how it works?" She shifted forward on the chair, her eyes widening in desperation. "The police will go for the easiest suspect. Right now, that's Julian. I'm her mother, and even I know she looks as guilty as sin. But there's someone else out there, Jeff, someone who murdered Tad and now Richard. He'll go free again."

She pulled a tissue from her pocket and dabbed her eyes, even though Jeffrey had not actually seen any tears. He could see that she had been a beautiful woman once. Even now, with her silver hair, fair skin, and searing blue eyes, she was remarkable. Her face was a map of fine lines, but they communicated depth and character to Jeffrey rather than old age, beauty faded.

As Eleanor made a show of wiping her eyes, Jeffrey looked up and saw Lydia walk through the glass doors of the office, feeling the familiar lift in his heart that he did every time he saw her. She was shadowed by Dax, and looked tiny next to his large frame. He could see the flush of her skin, her black hair pulled back into a tight, high ponytail. He watched her stop at the reception desk and then stride toward his office, all attitude, dressed head to toe in black except for her white Nike running shoes and socks.

Lydia entered Jeff's office without knocking, bringing with her the scent of cold air outside. Eleanor startled a bit and looked up from her tissue. Then she rose, extending her hand.

"I'm an admirer of your work, Ms. Strong," she said. "That's why I've come here."

"I'm a great fan of your daughter's. I was sorry to hear of the tragedy that your family suffered today," answered Lydia, taking Eleanor's hand in both of hers. Jeffrey wondered at how she had gathered so much information in the half hour since he'd spoken to her, as he watched Lydia focus all the energy of her attention on Eleanor. He'd watched people shrink under that gaze, as if sensing that she could see all the facets of themselves they strove to hide.

Eleanor only nodded at the compliment and sat down again, lowering her eyes. Lydia sat in the chair beside her, leaned back, and crossed her legs. Jeffrey could see the flash in Lydia's eyes as she sized up the woman next to her before Eleanor raised her eyes again.

"How can we help you, Ms. Ross?" asked Lydia.

"Ms. Ross would like us to find out who killed her son-in-law," said Jeffrey.

"Which one?" asked Lydia, and Jeffrey suppressed a smile. "I mean, the case ten years ago was never solved, was it?"

"No. That is why I am here today," answered Eleanor,

barely concealing her annoyance at having to repeat herself. "I don't want the same thing to happen this time."

Jeffrey noticed that she'd dropped the frightened, desperate-mother persona she had employed in her conversation with him and that her imperiousness had returned.

"Where's your daughter now?" asked Lydia.

"She's at the Payne Whitney Clinic, where she's being treated for a psychotic break she suffered this morning. Quite a natural response to the trauma she's suffered, I'm told. Especially for someone so emotionally...fragile."

"Shouldn't she have gone to Bellevue?" asked Jeffrey, knowing that the Midtown hospital was the standard place to bring what the police referred to as EDPs, emotionally disturbed persons.

"Our lawyer was able to see that she was taken to the hospital with which her psychiatrist is affiliated."

"Is that to say that she's had mental health issues in the past?" asked Lydia.

"Julian has suffered severe bouts of depression in her life. But since the birth of the twins, she's been quite stable. Now...this. Well..." Her voice trailed off and she didn't finish the thought.

"Can we talk to her?"

"She's not lucid."

"Still..."

"I'll arrange it, if you think it will help."

Lydia looked closely at Eleanor, wondering how she could be so cool and unemotional in light of the events of the day. Eleanor had appeared to be wiping her eyes when Lydia entered, but Lydia didn't sense any genuine sadness from the woman. She seemed more like a CEO at an emergency board meeting than a mother whose daughter's life was unraveling. Some people hid a tumult of emotions beneath a serene façade. But Lydia had the sense that Eleanor's chill went straight to the bone.

Eleanor looked at her watch suddenly and rose.

"I have to collect my lawyer and see Detective McKirdy to give my statement," she said, turning to Jeffrey. "I'm sure you'll recap our conversation for Ms. Strong and contact me to let me know if you'll accept this case. You realize, of course, that money is not an issue."

"We'll contact you by the end of the day today," answered Jeffrey.

Lydia stood and shook Eleanor's hand again, saying nothing. The older woman's hand was as cold and hard as a corpse. She turned toward the door with a sweep of her coat.

Jeffrey escorted Eleanor to the elevators and Lydia watched as they exchanged a few more words while they waited in the lobby. She could hear the cadence of Jeffrey's deep voice even though she couldn't understand his words. The elevator doors slid open and Jeffrey held them as Eleanor stepped on. Lydia always admired the way Jeffrey treated people, with a kind of courteous distance. He wasn't cold, but he wasn't falsely intimate. There was a quality about his manner and his voice that communicated authority. There was something about the gaze of his hazel eyes faceted with gold and green that could be in turn withering or understanding, loving or just plain dangerous.

When Eleanor disappeared behind the stainless steel, Jeffrey turned to face Lydia, raising his eyebrows and giving her a small smile. She knew he couldn't see her, but that he was aware of her watching, observing them. The thought made her smile.

In the cab on the way up, Lydia had checked the news headlines on her cellular phone. Remembering Jeffrey mentioning the Julian Ross case of ten years ago to her more than once, she had deduced immediately what was up. Though she certainly hadn't expected Eleanor Ross would be sitting in his office when she arrived.

She hadn't been blowing smoke up Eleanor's ass, not that

she was above it. She truly had been a fan of Julian Ross's work for quite some time. It was grim and violent, alive with a raw passion that moved Lydia. She'd thought more than once of buying an original piece but could never quite bring herself to part with the small fortune it would cost. Besides, there was enough violence and passion to be found on the landscape of her own inner life to keep her occupied.

Eleanor Ross made quite an impression herself. Lydia could tell that she was a formidable woman, strong and domineering, intelligent, and not to be fucked with. But she could also see Eleanor was hiding something, something that frightened her very much. Lydia could sense that by the way the older woman's hands were ice-cold and shook almost imperceptibly, by the way she shifted her eyes quickly between Lydia and Jeffrey, by the way she slipped behind a queenly façade when Lydia mentioned the first murder case. The buzz was so loud it sounded like blood rushing in her ears.

Jeffrey returned to the office and shut the door behind him. He wore a thin black Armani sweater with three bold horizontal gray stripes across his broad chest, over charcoal wool flat front pants. A pair of black leather boots was the perfect finish. His sandy brown hair was cut short with a stylish bit of length on top. He was the only straight man she knew who loved designer clothes and good hair as much as she did.

"What did you think of her?" he asked, knowing by the look on her face that she'd already formed an opinion.

"Freaky," she said with a smile. Lydia stood and Jeffrey pulled her in to him. She took in the scent of his cologne, feeling his warm hard body against hers and the stubble on his chin against the soft smooth skin of her face. She wrapped her arms around his waist.

"How's everybody?" he asked, pulling back from her and patting her still-flat belly. Then, not waiting for her to answer, "I really don't think it's a good idea to be running, do you?"

She bristled a bit, never liking much the suggestion that he knew better than she what should and should not be done.

"Maybe not, but it's not even a month yet," she said with a shrug, moving away from him and heading toward the couch.

He smiled and said nothing, knowing by now the futility of trying to tell Lydia what to do. He pulled a bottle of water from a small refrigerator under the bar on the far wall of his office and tossed it to her. She pulled it from the air and they sat on the cream chenille sofa arranged to look out onto his spectacular view of downtown Manhattan. She put her feet up on the glass top of the chrome-and-bleached-wood coffee table and hugged a rust-colored pillow to her chest as he filled her in on the rest of the conversation with Eleanor and some of the more relevant details of the earlier case.

"What about those hairs? Any chance they're still floating around somewhere? DNA technology has come a long way."

He shrugged. "Anything's possible. I left a message for Ford McKirdy."

"So what do you think?"

He drew in a deep breath and rubbed the bridge of his nose. "I'd like another crack at this," he said thoughtfully. "There are too many unanswered questions. I know Ford feels the same way. At least, if we get involved, we know we can count on his cooperation."

"You really think there was someone else there that night...you know, back then?"

"I really do. I'm not saying she was entirely innocent. But there was definitely someone else there. There's more to what happened than we were ever able to piece together. I just have a strange feeling that what happened last night will shed some light on the past."

He got up and walked across the elaborately patterned Oriental rug to the window.

"Just one thing, Lyd. Don't get pissed." His voice was tentative as he watched her from across the room.

"What?" she said, looking up at him with a frown.

"I only want your brain involved in this. You leave the legwork to the other people on the team."

She nodded, since they'd already agreed that she'd do nothing to put herself in danger while she was pregnant and until they had captured Jed McIntyre. But the resentment she felt was already a stone in her heart. It pulled down the corners of her mouth and creased her brow. He walked back over and sat down beside her, putting his arm around her shoulder.

"I know this is hard for you. But it's not forever."

"Is there any word?" she answered, not wanting to look at him, not wanting to reveal how constantly she wondered where Jed McIntyre was.

"There's no sign of him. The FBI has people watching us, watching your grandparents on Kauai. There's an alert at airports and at bus and train stations. If he makes any kind of a major move, chances are we'll know about it. He's going to have to take a risk sometime."

She nodded, knowing he was right. But the waiting was like a physical pain, invading her sleep, keeping her from peace and comfort. The sense of something dark and angry at her heels was always with her.

"How are your grandparents doing?" he said, trying to lighten the subject that was casting a pall over their days.

"Great," she said with a forced smile. "They love it there. They're looking forward to seeing us."

They had sent Lydia's grandparents on a "vacation" indefinitely to Hawaii after their brush with Jed McIntyre early last month. There they would stay under FBI surveillance until Jed McIntyre was behind bars again. Or until he was dead.

"Did you tell them?" he asked, and she knew he was talking about her pregnancy.

“No, I’ll tell them when we go to visit in February,” she said, leaning into him. She looked into his eyes and smiled, running her fingers though his thick hair. “It’s too soon. And I want them to hear it from both of us...together.”

She got up and walked toward the window, looking out onto the cityscape, leaning her head against the cool glass. After a tense minute, she gave a little laugh.

“What?”

“I was just thinking, at any given moment I could be watched by the FBI, Jed McIntyre, and Dax Chicago...all at once.”

“I resent being lumped in with that crew, I’ll tell you that,” said Dax, appearing at the door on cue like a bulky apparition. He walked into the office and stood next to Jeff.

“Not very good company, is it?” said Jeff, patting Dax on the back.

The buzzer on the intercom sounded.

“Jeff, there’s a Detective McKirdy on the phone for you,” Rebecca’s voice announced over the speaker.

“I got it,” Jeff said as he moved toward his desk and picked up the line.

“Hey, Ford. Rough night?” he said into the phone. He laughed lightly after a pause and said, “Well, you’ll never guess who just stopped by my office.”

Lydia looked at Dax and said, “Let the games begin.”

FOUR

The woman was afraid, small, cowering in the shadows. Lydia could practically see her chest heaving, could almost hear her ragged breathing. The woman, her skin gray, her face bleeding from a gash under her eye, clung to the tatters of her clothes as she tried to look around a concrete wall, tried to see without being seen. But she couldn't quite commit herself to the action, as though she'd really rather not know what was on the other side of the cinderblocks. Maybe it was just as well, because on the other side of the canvas world was carnage. The sky was painted a churning of red and black, the streets were washed in blood. Bodies writhed in pain, disemboweled, decapitated, clawing at the earth. Some figures were engaged in violent sexual contact, others in the throes of death and murder...and it was hard to tell the difference. The detail was intricate, a screaming mouth, a bleeding eye, a man inserting a blade between a woman's legs, a woman ripping the heart from her own chest. Reigning over it all, two towering black wraiths, the shadows of their ghoulish fingers leaking in the black clouds in the sky, the blood on the earth. The canvas was gigantic, nearly seven feet tall and ten feet long. Julian Ross called it a self-portrait.

Something about Julian Ross's artwork had always resonated with Lydia. Standing now in front of the giant canvas in the white SoHo gallery space, the sounds of light traffic carrying in through the open door, the sunlight washing through floor-to-ceiling windows onto the bleached wood floors, Lydia was moved again by what she saw. What hung before her was the work of a victim, someone haunted, someone hunted. Whether she was chased by demons inside her mind or by demons that lived and breathed in the real world, Julian Ross was on the run. Lydia could relate.

"That's bloody awful," said Lydia's shadow.

"It's art," said Lydia briskly, annoyed with him for always being right behind her, invading her space and her thoughts. Dax was so close she could smell the peppermint on his breath.

He snorted. "Art...as if any hack that puts a brush to canvas is an artist. That's rubbish."

She ignored him, hoping he would go away and let her think. After a moment he walked a loop around the gallery and found a place standing outside the door, legs apart, arms folded. My bodyguard, Lydia thought, wanting to scream and throw things at him like a toddler having a tantrum.

"Why did you want to come here?" asked Jeffrey. She'd persuaded him to come with her to the gallery that displayed Julian Ross's most recent work on their way to meet Ford McKirdy at a diner on West Fourth Street.

"I just wanted to get a sense of what she'd been painting recently. This one," she said, pointing to the tag beside the giant canvas, "was finished about two months ago."

"It's intense," he said, regarding the painting before him. "Not the work of a stable person, if you ask me."

Lydia nodded. "But not necessarily the work of a murderer, either." She pointed toward the cowering figure behind the cinderblock wall. "Julian Ross sees herself as a victim."

"Maybe so, but her husband is the one spread all over the bedroom walls."

Lydia nodded again, not quite sure how to respond to a statement like that.

"Can I help you?" asked a smooth male voice from behind them.

They turned to see a suave, tall, dark-skinned Latino with a slick of black hair that flowed to his shoulders. His lips were a warm, full pink and his liquid brown eyes spoke to Lydia of salsa dances under a full moon, scandalous assignations, and sangria. He wore a pair of black linen pants that draped elegantly from his thin hips and a white silk shirt unbuttoned to reveal a hairless chest. He extended a manicured hand to Lydia. "I am Orlando DiMarco and this is my gallery," he said, looking straight into her eyes.

Lydia smiled and shook his hand but didn't offer her name. He released her hand a moment later than was appropriate and glided past her. He removed the information tag from the wall beside the painting and replaced it with one that read sold.

"Unfortunately, this piece was sold this morning."

"Bad news travels fast," said Jeffrey.

Orlando gave Jeffrey a cool smile. "But there are many more interesting pieces in the back I can show you, if you like."

He was handsome and sexual in a very effeminate way, not as though he were gay but in the way of European men. As if he were more in touch with his emotions and less afraid to show them than an American man. She could sense that he was highly temperamental. It was something in the shape of his eyes, the warmth of his hand, and the sway of his hips that communicated to Lydia that he would be an earth-shattering lover.

"Are they recent?" Lydia asked.

"Yes, of course. One of them she turned in just a few days ago. Of course, it may be her last for a while. So, it's particularly valuable," he said matter-of-factly. "Follow me."

She turned around to tell Dax they were going in the back, but he was already right behind her.

The room behind the gallery space was bigger than Lydia had expected. There were hundreds of shrouded canvases leaning against the walls like ghosts. The lighting was dim and the air cooler than it had been in front, she imagined to preserve the artwork. A light and not unpleasant scent of paint and linseed oil permeated the room. In the back she saw a large black lacquer desk with a computer, a credit card machine, and stacks of files. She also noticed a framed picture, a close-up of Julian Ross smiling radiantly, her cheeks flushed from the sun, a wisp of dark hair blown in front of her eye. She looked happy, in love. Lydia glanced over at Orlando DiMarco as he climbed up on a chair to remove a shroud from the largest canvas in the room, and wondered.

"You carry Julian Ross's work exclusively?" she asked, as he struggled with the far corner of the sheet. Jeffrey moved in to help him, but Orlando waved him away.

"Well, mostly," he said. "Though recently I have started to feature other artists. There has always been enough demand for Julian's work, but she hasn't been as prolific in recent years."

"Why is that, do you think?"

"She was happy," he said almost sadly, and the shroud dropped to the floor.

A monster stared out at them, trapped in Julian Ross's canvas. It was a face divided in half. On the right, the canvas was dominated by the features of a handsome young man, his mouth drawn into a twisted sneer. He had a shock of blue-black hair and one clear green eye, in which there was the reflection of a beautiful woman. The figure posed in the reflection of his eye, naked, her arms bent lifting her hair off her neck, her breasts pushed forward. On the left, it was the same face but age had warped the features, the hair had grown long and gray, twisted into shabby dreads, his teeth brown and sharp. His mouth was drawn into the same sneer, but a trickle of blood trailed from the corner of his mouth. In his eye, the reflection of the same woman, mutilated, her body opened and innards escaping, hung from the black branches of a great oak tree. The detail of the face and the images dancing in his eyes was exquisite, every line, every shadow, every muscle defined by the deft hand of a gifted, accomplished artist. It was remarkable.

All four of them stood there looking.

"What did she say about it?" Lydia asked finally.

"Nothing. She had it sent by messenger. I called her and she never returned my call," he said, and sounded bitter.

"Who is it?"

"Look closely."

She examined the detailed facial features of the man and at the woman reflected in the green pools of his eyes.

"It's her," said Lydia. "It's Julian Ross."

"The woman?" asked Jeffrey, looking more closely at the reflection in the monster's eyes.

"Both," answered Lydia. She walked over to the desk and picked up the picture she had seen there. Orlando looked uncomfortable but didn't protest. She held the picture up for Jeffrey and the features were undeniably similar to the man in the painting.

"What did she call it?"

"He Has Come for Me," he said, shaking his head. "I think it's her most disturbing work. Though I can't say why. There's just something so fearful about it."

"How well do you know her?" Lydia asked.

Orlando reached out and took the photo gently from Lydia's hand. "Who are you?" he asked, suspicion creeping into his voice. "You're not here to buy art."

"No," said Jeffrey, holding out his private investigator's identification. "Eleanor Ross has asked us to find out what happened to Julian's husband. I'm Jeffrey Mark and this is Lydia Strong. This is our associate Dax Chicago."

Orlando nodded, as if he weren't surprised. Most people would have been at least annoyed, but he looked suddenly tired. Lydia saw him retreat into himself. He got that glazed-over look that people get when their thoughts have turned inward. He walked back over to his desk, placed the frame back in its place, and sat in the chair behind his desk.

"We have worked together for over twenty years. We were...we are friends," he said, still looking at the photograph, and Lydia saw so much more than feelings of friendship there in his face.

"So you knew her when her first husband was murdered," said Lydia.

He nodded. "She was acquitted," he said, a little defensively. "She's innocent...of that and of this. I'm sure of it."

"How can you be so certain?"

He sat forward and looked directly at Lydia. She walked closer to him, while Dax and Jeffrey hung back a bit. Lydia sat down across from Orlando, returned his gaze. He sounded positive, as though there were not a doubt in his mind. But Lydia had to wonder, wouldn't even the most loyal friend have his suspicions after the second murder?

"Because I know her," he said, sitting back.

"So then, any thoughts on who would be motivated to murder Julian Ross's husbands?" she asked, keeping her voice light and even. Here she saw his eyes shift, as if he were remembering something. Whatever it was, he didn't share it.

"Someone who was stalking her, someone who wanted to hurt her, an enemy?" Lydia pressed. "Was there anyone she feared?"

Orlando shook his head slowly. "No," he said, his voice harder, more certain than his eyes.

Lydia nodded now, thoughtful. She was reaching, probing, looking for something that might give her a map of Julian's life, something that might lead her eventually to find out how it had fallen so horribly apart.

"You said she was happy. She was happy with her husband?" said Lydia. "She loved him?"

He shrugged. Again the shade of something across his face.

"Yes, she loved him. He gave her the thing she wanted most in life, her children," he said quietly. "Lola and Nathaniel—she loved them more than her art. She would never do anything that would take her away from them."

It was an interesting answer. Interesting because of what he didn't say. She had expected to hear how wonderful Richard and Julian were together, that she loved him more than life, that she could never hurt him. But he didn't say any of those things.

"Was there trouble in her marriage? Were they having problems?"

He raised his hands and stood. His face had flushed and now there was anger in his eyes. "That's enough. What you are looking for here, you will not find. She's innocent. This I know for a fact."

"You could only know that for certain if you know who killed Richard Stratton."

Orlando looked stricken for just a second. But then he just shook his head and grew quiet.

"I don't need to know that. I know Julian."

Lydia looked back at the monstrous face on Julian's canvas.

"But her art is so violent. Is it possible that there's a side of her you never saw?"

He followed her eyes to the canvas and didn't answer for a second. "I suppose," he said, looking from the canvas to the photo in his hand. "There's a side to all of us that no one ever sees."

The basketball courts on West Fourth Street were packed as

usual with mostly young black guys and a couple of white guys either playing hard or hanging on the fence watching. Most of the players had their shirts off and were sweating like it was July even though the air was cool going on cold. The bouncing ball and the short shrieks of rubber soles on the asphalt echoed off the concrete buildings and an occasional cheer rose up like a wave over the traffic of Sixth Avenue. Jeffrey watched a young man fall hard on the concrete with a groan trying to block another player's shot and then bounce right up like he was made out of rubber. He was back on his feet and running across the court.

"I remember what it was like to be young and in shape like that," said Jeffrey.

"You're not ready for life support yet, Grandpa," said Lydia, patting his hard, flat abs.

"I'm just saying...you don't get up from a fall like that and run a mile after forty, you know."

"I wouldn't know," she said with a smile. She liked to rub in their ten-year age difference whenever possible. He gave her a look.

Dax had left them suddenly after he received a mysterious call on his cell, so Lydia and Jeffrey proceeded to their meeting with Ford McKirdy alone. They entered the Yum Yum Diner on the corner and found a table toward the back of the converted trailer that stood next to a playground under the shade of trees. They slid into the same side of a red leather booth and Lydia started to flip through the mini-jukebox at the end of the table. The smell of coffee, grease, and cigarettes had worked its way into the walls and the leather seats. Lydia was suddenly ravenous, lost interest in the jukebox, and eyed the pie case, where cakes and pastries rotated enticingly on plastic shelves. The Yum Yum Diner was the kind of place that was just as packed at three a.m. when people were heading home from the clubs as it was on a weekday at lunchtime.

Jeffrey waved to Ford as he watched his old friend make

his way through the crowd that was forming for lunch. Jeffrey stood up to shake Ford's hand.

"It's been too long, man," Jeffrey said. "How're you doing?"

"You look good, Jeff. You, too, Lydia. How are you?" said Ford, taking Lydia's hand.

He sat down across from them, and placed on the table a manila envelope he had carried in his left hand. Ford McKirdy looked soft and pasty to Lydia. She knew him to be a little over fifty and he looked every second of it. The late nights, high stress level, and bad diet of a cop's life were taking their toll. He had a light sheen of perspiration on his forehead and she noticed that his belly grazed the edge of the table as he slid with effort into the booth.

"How was your meeting with Eleanor Ross?" asked Lydia.

"Chilly," said Ford, wiping his brow with a napkin. "That woman is a real piece of work. She was supposed to come with the nanny. But she claimed not to have anyone else to leave the children with; I'll have to catch up with Geneva Stout later."

"She give you anything?" asked Jeff.

"Claims she didn't see or hear anything until Julian started screaming."

"What did she tell you about their marriage?" asked Lydia.

"Said they were happy. She'd been with them three weeks and said they didn't have so much as a tiff that she saw."

"Where's she visiting from?"

"She lives in Boca now part of the year, part of the year here with her daughter. Said she would have been with them through the holidays and then back down to the condo after the New Year."

"So what was it like? The scene, I mean," asked Jeffrey.

"You know, you asked me the same question ten years ago. My answer is the same. It was a fucking mess. Not the same struggle as last time, but Richard Stratton was taken to pieces, just the same as Tad Jenson. I brought you copies of the crime scene photos and my preliminary findings and notes," he said, sliding the envelope over to them. "You guys are taking the case, right?"

"I haven't called Eleanor Ross yet, but I think so. I want another shot at this and I know you do, too."

"You're damn right."

"You think there was someone else there this time?"

"I don't know...doesn't look like it. On the other hand, it doesn't look like she could have done it alone. There was blood on the ceiling...a twelve-foot ceiling, for Christ's sake. The doorman said no one came or left from the front door. But we got no murder weapon. From the preliminary findings of the ME, he said it was a serrated knife, just like the last time. One other thing...don't tell anyone about this. We're keeping it from the press. Richard Stratton's ring finger, and his wedding ring with it, are missing. Unless she swallowed the knife, the ring, and the finger or hid them very, very well, someone else took them from the scene. When I got to her, she was in no condition for a lucid action like hiding evidence."

"Or so she'd have you believe," said Jeffrey.

Ford shrugged, gave a quick nod. "Yeah. Tell you what. She's faking it? Then she's one hell of an actress."

"Tad was missing his ring and ring finger, too," Jeffrey explained to Lydia.

"Nice," said Lydia with a shake of her head.

Lydia turned it over in her mind, what a thing like that might mean. Was it a symbol? Was she freeing herself from the bonds of marriage? Or was someone else freeing her from it?

"You said she wasn't lucid when you found her?" asked Lydia.

"She was losing it. She wouldn't leave the room where her husband had been killed. When the paramedics took her away, she was ranting. She said, among other things, 'He's come for me.'"

Lydia and Jeffrey exchanged a look.

"What?"

"We just came from her gallery. A couple of days ago she turned in a painting to Orlando DiMarco, her rep there. She'd titled it He Has Come for Me."

Lydia described the painting to Ford. He took notes as she spoke, she could see him taking the information in, plugging it into the equation that was growing in his mind.

"I'll head over there and check it out," said Ford. "I remember Orlando DiMarco from the investigation ten years ago. He was a big cokehead then. Rumor was that they were lovers, on-again off-again...nothing serious. But I was never able to place him at the scene. Anyway I had him pegged for a lover...not a murderer. Bet he wouldn't want to mess up all those pretty clothes."

"It looked to me like there were some hurt feelings there. I would have put money on him being in love with her," said Lydia.

He nodded and looked at her without seeing her. It was a look she recognized from Jeffrey and even herself. He was moving pieces of information around in his head trying to see what fit where.

"So, what's the game plan, kids?" he said after a moment in thought and coming back to the present. "I think I'll pay a visit to Mr. DiMarco. Take a look at that painting."

"I think we'll pay Julian Ross a visit," answered Lydia.

"Good luck. She's gone, baby, gone. You're going to need a decoder ring to get anywhere with that one right now."

"It's worth a shot," Lydia said as the waitress approached. She looked ridiculous and unhappy in a pink-and-white-checked uniform with matching cap, someone's idea of what a fifties diner waitress would wear. Her name tag read buffy. She was clearly over fifty years old, and her enormous breasts hung down to the top of her apron. Buffy looked at her customers beneath layers of blue eye makeup and mascara.

"What can I getcha?" she said.

"I'll have a bacon double cheeseburger with fries and a large chocolate milkshake," said Ford as the waitress scribbled in her pad.

Lydia looked at him with worry, hoping that he wasn't going to have a heart attack right there at the table.

"I'll have the same," she said.

FIVE

Urine, Lysol, and misery were the odors that assailed Lydia and Jeffrey as a strapping orderly buzzed them through a heavy metal door. They stepped into a gray, dimly lit hallway with speckled Formica floors, brightly clean and polished, with a flat wooden railing running the length of each of the walls. Lydia could hear the sounds of someone sobbing and someone laughing.

"Is this your first visit to a psychiatric facility?" asked Dr. Linda Barnes, a bright, pretty young woman whose deep, sultry voice seemed incongruous to her petite frame. Lydia and Jeffrey had met the doctor down on the street in front of the clinic. It was clear from her clipped attitude that the doctor was not pleased with the visit Eleanor Ross had insisted upon. She had the drawn look of someone acting against her better judgment, offered nothing but a quick polite greeting and then an escort up to Julian Ross. She walked quickly and quietly, her rubber-soled shoes not making a sound on the floor. Lydia and Jeffrey had to pick up their pace to keep up with her.

"No," answered Lydia, "We've both seen our share of places like this."

"I ask because the first time can be pretty rough on the uninitiated," she said.

"We are fairly well acquainted with insanity," said Jeffrey.

The doctor shot him a look. "We prefer 'mental illness' in my profession."

"Call it what you will, Doctor," said Jeffrey.

A large man with a larger brow and a badly shaved head shuffled past them. His lids were purple and heavy, his eyes stared off into the distance intently as he clenched and unclenched his fists. He muttered something unintelligible as he moved past.

"Normally, we wouldn't allow Ms. Ross any visitors at all," she said. "It is not advisable to her recovery at this point. But since there are special circumstances and her mother insists, I'll allow it. But I am going to ask you to keep this visit as brief as possible."

"I understand," said Lydia. "How is she?"

"She's had a psychotic break. It's a state that occurs, usually, when the mind has sustained a shock that it is not equipped to handle. Julian has more or less shut down. She is incoherent...sometimes ranting, sometimes nearly catatonic. This is more than likely a temporary condition...but I couldn't hazard a guess as to how long it will last."

"Could she be faking it?" asked Jeffrey.

"If she is, she's a very convincing actress," said Dr. Barnes. "Generally, Mr. Mark, people don't try to fake their way into a place like this."

"It's better than prison."

"I'm not so sure about that," answered Lydia.

An elderly woman in a pink smock holding on to a walker with one hand pounded on a door at the end of the hall. "Let me in!" she yelled, frantically looking around her with eyes wild and red-rimmed at her invisible pursuers. "Let me in!"

An attendant in green scrubs ran over to her and gently ushered her down the hall, whispering to her. A crowd of patients, all wearing the same pink smocks, crowded around a window where a nurse was handing out tiny paper cups filled with pills.

Looking around her, Lydia felt some combination of pity and dread. She couldn't imagine a more grim place in which to find yourself. She felt the fear and suffering radiating off the walls and wondered what it would be like to wake up and go to sleep in this place haunted by the delusions of your own mind, searching for the road back to sanity.

"How long have you been Julian's doctor?" asked Lydia.

"I've seen Julian on and off for about the last eight years," she said. "Until about a year ago."

"What happened then?"

"She came to her appointment and told me she would no longer be continuing our sessions."

"Did she say why?"

"She said something very odd. That she'd realized that ninety percent of her problems were due to the fact that she hadn't been true to herself. That she'd decided to surrender."

"Surrender?"

"That was the word she used. She wouldn't expound. Just thanked me, wrote me a check, and left. I didn't see her again until she was admitted here."

Lydia turned the connotations of the word over in her mind. Surrender...to give up, to admit defeat. What within herself had she been fighting?

"Her mother told us that she's suffered with depression. Any indication that there might be something more seriously wrong with her? Did she ever discuss with you the murder of her first husband?"

This time Dr. Barnes didn't bother to hide her annoyance.

"Naturally," she said officiously, "I am not at liberty to discuss my patient's condition or the things we discussed with you. But if you're asking me if I had any indication that she might be a threat to herself or to others, the answer is no."

"Did she mention to you at any time that she was afraid of someone, that she had any enemies who might wish to harm her or her family?"

The doctor didn't answer Lydia. She pulled her mouth into a tight grimace as if she were physically trying to prevent words from flying out.

Lydia stopped walking and the doctor turned to face her. "Look, Doctor. I'm not trying to infringe upon your professional ethics. But a man is dead and your patient is the prime suspect—the only suspect. We're trying to help her. Maybe you can do the same."

"I can't help you. And the only way I can help Julian is by treating her illness and protecting her patient-doctor privilege."

Case closed. Dr. Barnes was a tough nut and Lydia could see that they'd gotten as far with her as they would today.

After a number of twists and turns down long gray hallways, they reached another metal door and were buzzed through into yet another hallway that had six closed doors on each side and ended in a large, barred window. Sunlight streamed in through the grating and a uniformed police officer sat in a green metal chair reading a copy of the New York Post outside the last door.

"This is the wing for patients who are not stable enough to mix with the others. Ms. Ross is being kept here for obvious reasons," said Dr. Barnes.

The cop at the door checked his list for Lydia and Jeffrey's names and found them. He stood up and stepped aside as the three of them entered Julian Ross's room.

Julian Ross was a ghost of the woman Lydia had seen in the photograph back at the gallery. She sat on the small twin bed in the corner of the room, leaning against the wall, hugging her knees to her chest. She was pale, her eyes glassy and wet. All the light had drained from her. Lydia imagined that she could be picked up and tossed to the floor like a rag doll.

Lydia tried to reconcile the frail woman before them with the gruesome images in the crime scene photographs Ford had given them. She tried to imagine Julian's tiny, delicate hands wielding a serrated knife and committing the carnage that had been wrought in her Park Avenue duplex. It didn't work for her. Physically it didn't seem possible. But more than that, Lydia just couldn't envision it, though she couldn't say why. Lydia pulled up a metal chair beside Julian's bed and tried to look into her eyes. But they were like the eyes of a cat, flat and without depth. It was as if her soul, the essence of who she was, had floated away, leaving only a breathing human shell.

Lydia was not uncomfortable with mentally ill people. She'd interviewed more than one in the past. In fact, she was more comfortable with them than she was with most "sane" people. There was often a logic to their thoughts that made a kind of sense if you listened carefully. There was no artifice to their personalities, nothing put on. It was crazy but it was real.

"Julian," said the doctor as if she were talking to a child. "This is Lydia Strong and Jeffrey Mark. They are here to see you at your mother's request."

There was no sign that she had heard.

"Julian," said Lydia, "we want to help you."

She turned bright green eyes on Lydia. Lydia felt a little jolt of shock inside as she saw clearly the eyes from the portrait in Orlando DiMarco's gallery. She wondered if, as in the painting, there was another side to the wispy woman before her, another side that only Tad Jenson and Richard Stratton had seen. Someone that she had hidden from others and maybe even from herself. In the hard fluorescent light of the room, Lydia could see that Julian's pupils were dilated. Her long dark hair was highlighted with strands of red and was pulled back into a loose ponytail. Several strands had escaped and hung listlessly around her frail shoulders and in front of her eyes.

"You can't help me," she said softly, her voice thick and slow. "No one can."

"Is she heavily medicated?" asked Lydia, looking at the doctor.

"Oh, yes," answered the doctor. "She was hysterical, a danger to herself."

"We can help you, Julian," said Lydia softly, leaning in slightly. "If you can tell us what you remember."

The doctor sighed, agitated suddenly behind Lydia. "I don't think you're going to have much luck, Ms. Strong. She's not going to be able to remember anything at this point."

Jeffrey held up his hand. "Just give her a minute."

Julian held Lydia's eyes. "My children," she said, her tone not quite a question, more a musing.

"They're fine," answered Lydia. "They're with your mother."

Julian gave a little laugh and rolled her eyes dramatically. "Oh, well then...they'll be fine," she said, her voice suddenly tight with sarcasm and anger. "Look how well I turned out."

She scribbled something in the air with an invisible pen and looked at Lydia with a wink, as if she thought Lydia were in on some private joke. "My mother, the queen. The queen of the damned. Evil bitch."

"She's ranting," said the doctor.

"I can see that," said Lydia, turning to look at her with annoyance.

"Why are you so angry at your mother?" asked Lydia. Julian didn't answer. She just kept writing in the air furiously.

The room was so silent, Lydia could hear the buzz of the

fluorescent lights above their heads and Julian's quick and shallow breathing. A moth fluttered above them, knocking itself into the light with a succession of soft taps.

"Julian, do you know where you are?"

"Do you know where you are?" Julian answered with a childish giggle. "Does anyone?"

"Some of us have a pretty good idea," Lydia answered gently.

"I'm hiding," she said with a vigorous nod, as if this answered everyone's questions.

"Who are you hiding from?" asked Lydia.

Julian slid down on the bed suddenly, as if invisible strings that had been holding her upright had snapped. She curled up into a ball facing Lydia, holding herself tight. She was so thin that Lydia could see her shoulder bones poking through her pale skin.

"From my other half," she said, closing her eyes. Lydia thought of the painting again, the man's face divided into two parts, the two women.

"What do you mean, Julian?"

But Julian turned her back on them. She lay facing the wall, her breathing becoming slow and heavy. Lydia asked her question again but got no response.

"I'm going to have to cut you off, Ms. Strong," said the doctor. "You can see how exhausted she's become. You can try again in a couple of days."

Lydia looked reluctantly at the small form of Julian Ross. From behind she looked like a child. She got up to leave, pushing the chair back to the place where she'd found it. She'd seen something dancing in Julian's eyes, something reachable. Lydia thought if she could only come up with the right trigger, she could rescue Julian from her own mind. The three of them walked toward the door.

"Lydia?" said Julian, without turning around.

"Yes, Julian."

"He's come for me, again. No one can stop him now."

Lydia stood staring at Julian, remembering again the canvas, that monster's face. As the doctor put her hand on Lydia's arm and led her from the room, she felt a chill move down her spine. She felt an odd connection to the artist. Maybe it was because Lydia felt hunted, too.

From above his copy of the New York Times, he saw them leave the Payne Whitney Clinic on West Sixty-eighth Street. He could smell the honey-roasted cashews from the vending cart on the corner and it made his stomach rumble. Lydia hadn't eaten yet and neither had he.

She was radiant today, truly glorious, and it filled his heart with love just to be near her. There was something so flushed and creamy about her skin. He would do anything to reach out and touch it. But she was surrounded, always. If it wasn't Jeffrey Mark, it was that other monkey, the burly Australian. Just the thought of him made his blood pressure rise, caused a tightness in his throat. He wouldn't forget the way he had been treated by Dax Chicago.

Jed McIntyre wiped the newsprint from his fingers onto the long black wool coat he'd picked up for ten dollars at a thrift store in the East Village and adjusted the plaid golfer's cap.

Today he was an old man reading a paper at a bus stop. Yesterday he had been a homeless woman pushing a cart down her block. Tomorrow...well, who knew? Every day was a creative challenge. The world was looking for him. He was hiding in plain sight. People never really saw what was right in front of them; you could always count on that.

Luckily for him, before Dax Chicago had put a major kink in his plans, he'd stowed the duffel bag given to him by Alexander Harriman, Esq., in a locker in Grand Central Station. The key hung on a chain around his neck. So he was flush. No money worries, though he had lost his vehicle. Anyway, in the city, a car was more a pain in the ass than it was worth.

He watched her, through the round gold rims of his glasses that had no lenses, as she stood on the corner with Jeffrey. He watched the way she draped a hand casually on his arm as she talked. She was animated, leaning into him, her eyes bright. Jeffrey Mark hailed a cab and then opened the door for Lydia. He slid in behind her and then they took off.

Jed stood and watched until the cab was out of sight. The cross-town bus hissed to a stop in front of him and he got on, slid his card through the slot, and took a seat at the back. He saw a white van pull from its spot on the street, though he was sure there hadn't been a driver in there a minute ago. It headed downtown after the yellow cab. Those FBI guys were everywhere. Yet they saw nothing. He laughed a little too loudly and the elderly woman sitting next to him glanced at him warily. He gave her a bright smile.

"It just doesn't work for me," said Lydia, flipping through the photos Ford had given them. The cabdriver wove between and around cars, racing up the West Side Highway as if the cops were chasing him.

"Can you slow down, please?" Jeffrey said to the bulletproof glass that separated them from the driver. But the driver seemed not to hear...or maybe more likely not to give a shit.

"I admit the logistics are a bit hard to put together," he said, finally giving up on trying to get through to the maniac cabdriver. "But right now it doesn't look like there was anyone else there."

"More evidence is going to turn up," she said. She had a way of sounding so sure of herself and her intuition that Jeffrey was always inclined to nod in response to what she said, even if he didn't necessarily agree with her.

"You know, there have been cases where a person is so pumped full of adrenaline that he takes on superhuman strength."

"Usually brought on by fear," said Lydia, thinking of the painting again.

"Or narcotics."

"Ford's notes say that her blood alcohol level was only slightly elevated and that there were no narcotics present at all."

"Or rage," suggested Jeffrey, bracing himself as the cab made a sharp fast exit from the highway at Ninety-sixth Street and headed across town. It was the street that divided the city. Ninety-sixth separated the richest people in Manhattan from the poorest, the safest neighborhoods from the most dangerous. The city was segregated like that all over, but nowhere more starkly than here. If you followed Madison Avenue or Park Avenue from midtown up to the Bronx River Expressway, you saw the city change before your eyes. Luxury high-rises, trendy cafés, exclusive shops morphed into stark projects and dark doorways, abandoned buildings with boarded-up windows and marred by graffiti, empty lots filled with garbage.

"I guess the most pressing question at this point," said Jeffrey, "is whether there was another way into the building."

"There are a lot of questions," said Lydia, feeling the buzz tingling in her fingertips. "Like who does Julian believe has come for her? Is it someone real? Or is she delusional?"

"Well, she's definitely delusional."

"Something's not right," she said, looking out the window.

"If I had a nickel for every time you've said that..."

"You do," she said with a smile.

"True enough."

Jeffrey and his partners Jacob Hanley and Christian Striker had started their private investigation firm nearly seven years ago, now. All former FBI men, they'd grown tired of the politics of the bureau, tired of the paranoia about public perception of the organization, and they'd decided they'd be more effective investigators on their own.

They'd started out with small cases—insurance fraud, husbands checking up on wives, some employee screening. Then they'd started working with the FBI and NYPD on cold cases, or cases where the police felt their hands were tied...in those cases, the firm's involvement was strictly confidential. But it was Lydia and Jeffrey's first case together, the infamous Cheerleader Murders, that put them on the map. Now the firm that started out of Jeffrey's one-bedroom East Village apartment employed over a hundred people and filled a suite of offices in the West Fifty-seventh Street high-rise. They'd been hugely successful, in large part due to Lydia, her contributions as a consultant, and the publicity that surrounded the books she wrote on some of the cases they'd worked. When Jacob died last year, Jeffrey and Christian Striker had asked Lydia to come on as partner.

"True enough," he repeated, taking her hand.

The cab came to a halt in front of an attractive brownstone off of Central Park West. Jeffrey paid the cabdriver through the small flip tray in the glass and tipped, even though the guy had practically killed them all. But they had made good time, and he couldn't complain about that. He did make a mental note of his name and ID number—Abdul Abdullah, number 689GHT2—for what purpose he didn't know. The driver never acknowledged them at all except to take the money.

Lydia slid out of the cab behind Jeffrey and looked at the door to the ob/gyn office with trepidation.

"Maybe that test was wrong," she said, hesitating at the sidewalk.

"Maybe," answered Jeffrey, reaching out his hand. "That's why we're here."

But he hoped that it wasn't wrong. He wanted this and he knew in his heart that she did, too. She was just afraid. But he was sure that everything was just as it should be and that they were going to be fine...all three of them.

SIX

The past was immortal. Maybe it slept, but it never died. It had been creeping up upon them all this time. Without sound and without odor, like the most skilled predator, it had stalked them and suddenly it was upon them. In her two-bedroom suite at the Waldorf-Astoria on Fifth Avenue, Eleanor Ross poured hot water from a hand-painted porcelain pot into a matching teacup. The scent of oolong tea rose potent and savory as she put the lid in place with a delicate clink, and replaced the pot on the tray. She sat on the plush sofa and drummed her long fingernails on the dark oak surface of the coffee table.

She regarded her hands for a moment with their long manicured fingers, their loose white skin and veins like ropes beneath the nearly translucent surface. They were the hands of an old woman. She brought a hand to her hair and touched the rough, brittle strands that were pulled back tightly into a bun. The hair of an old woman. It was funny how the external changed so dramatically but the internal remained much the same. Her perceptions, her concept of herself had not changed all that much since she was a young mother. Even though the shell of her was virtually unrecognizable. She'd been beautiful once, so beautiful. Tall and voluptuous, with a long, thick red hair, almond-shaped eyes that blazed green, perfect breasts, magnificent white unblemished skin. But that was all in the past now...the only part of the past that was dead and gone. Beauty had faded, but the horror lived and breathed.

It seemed so silly now that she had imagined they could all escape their legacy. She thought of her daughter in that awful place, the twins sleeping in the bedroom across the suite. They were still innocent, but she saw it in them, too. In their too-old eyes, in the way they looked at each other, in the way they communicated without speech. She had tried to ignore it, but she had seen it too many times. Eleanor still missed her own brother, in spite of everything. In spite of the fact that he'd been dead now nearly twenty years. There was a connection there that no one and nothing could sunder. Not even time. Not even murder.

She looked into the facets of the magnificent emerald in its antique platinum setting on her left hand. Her engagement ring, given to her by the only man she had ever loved enough to marry. Gone now, too. Before she could stop it a tear traveled down her cheek and she quickly wiped it away. She got up and walked to the window, looked down to the street, where people hustled about their ordinary lives. Steam billowed from a manhole cover, its plumes rising into the air and dissipating in the cold before they reached the sky. The day was gray and felt like snow. The people, coming home from work, or running to do some shopping for Christmas, or meeting friends for dinner, filled Eleanor with envy. What must it be like not to live under the shadow her family lived under? But then she imagined, maybe just to make herself feel better, that they were all haunted by something, weren't they? There was something that they didn't want to be. They didn't want to repeat the cycle of their family legacy, become an alcoholic, an abusive parent, the victim of a congenital disease, an old woman living alone with no one to look in on her. Everyone lived under the shadow of some fear or dysfunction, didn't they?

The phone was ringing softly on the end table beside the couch, maybe twice, maybe three times before she noticed it. She moved over to it quickly and picked it up.

"Hello?" she said warily, anxious that it might be more bad news. The phone was cold and heavy in her hand.

"Ms. Ross. It's Lydia Strong. We wanted to let you know that we're going to be taking on your case."

"I'm so glad," she said, and she was. Relief washed over her like a wave.

"There's paperwork you'll need to fill out. Would you like us to messenger it to you, or would you prefer to come by?"

"You saw my daughter today," she said, not answering the question. "Do you think she's guilty?"

There was a pause on the other end of the phone before the girl answered. "No. I don't."

Eleanor was glad to hear it, though she wasn't sure she believed Lydia Strong. "I'll come by the office tomorrow around noon, if that's all right."

"That's fine. We can talk some more then. I have some more questions for you."

"Very well," answered Eleanor. "Good-bye." She hung up the phone and sighed. They could ask all the questions they wanted. But there were only so many answers she could give.

Lydia folded Jeffrey's cell phone and handed it back to him. He took it from her and held her hand in the warm pink waiting room. Everything was pink and roses, smelling of potpourri. Even the bulbs behind the sconce lighting were pink, the reception desk a rose-colored Corian. A very pregnant woman sat across from Lydia reading a copy of Parenting magazine. She looked so young and serene, her cheeks glowing with health and color. She had her arm looped with the arm of a young man, who was reading a copy of Money. She stared at them in wonder. Aren't they terrified? She was ready to get up and run screaming from the doctor's office, and these two just radiated peace and joy. The young woman looked up at her, must have felt Lydia's eyes on her. She gave Lydia a happy, shy smile, and patted her belly. "I'm huge, aren't I?" she said, her blue eyes shining, "Just a couple more weeks."

Lydia smiled back at her. "You're beautiful," she said, and meant it. The man smiled at them and returned to his magazine. After a few more moments, a nurse came out and escorted the young couple in to see the doctor. Lydia noticed a soapstone sculpture that sat beneath a lamp on the end table next to the couch where the woman had been sitting. It was the impression of a woman, her head a stone atop her belly, which was a circular nest with another tiny stone nestled in the curve. Motherhood.

"Oh, God," said Lydia, squeezing Jeffrey's hand.

"I'm right here," he said with an indulgent smile.

"You damn well better be," she said. "You're stuck now... shotgun wedding and all."

He laughed and released her hand, put his arm around her and pulled her close. "You couldn't get rid of me if you tried," he whispered in her ear.

SEVEN

Ford McKirdy pulled his green Taurus into the narrow driveway beneath his Bay Ridge row house. He didn't bother pulling the car into the garage, but he attached the Club to his steering wheel, took the bag of Chinese takeout from the passenger seat, and locked the doors. Nobody wanted his piece-of-shit car, anyway, which was part of the reason why he drove it.

He felt heavy and tired as he pulled himself up the red brick steps to his front door. His neighbors in most of the other houses had hung their Christmas lights and decorations, making the block a tacky visual cacophony of multicolored bulbs, plastic Santas, reindeer, snowmen, and nativity scenes. Ford's house looked grim and neglected by comparison. He held the screen door open with his back, looping the bag around his wrist as he fit the key into the knob. The air was cold outside, a biting winter chill moving in for the first time in a season that had been unusually mild. The house was dark inside, empty.

A lifetime ago, his children, Katie and Jim—or James, as

he liked to be called now—and their golden retriever Max would have raced each other to the door in a messy, happy tumble to greet him. He could hear the echo of Max's deep barking, the kids' yelling. His wife would be standing in the archway between the living room and the dining room, the look on her face telling him if he was in trouble or not for however he'd fucked up that day. The smell of whatever she was cooking reaching him as he embraced her. But tonight the house was quiet. Max was long gone, put down nearly five years ago now. Katie, a kindergarten teacher, lived with her husband and two kids in Houston. Jimmy was a Wall Street broker living in Battery Park City—"working like a slave and partying like it's 1999," as he liked to say; Ford saw even less of him than he did Katie, though he was only a few subway stops away.

His wife, Rose, hard to believe she was gone more than a year now. All the difficult times they'd faced together, all the hell he'd put her through, all the fights and late nights she spent worrying about him, all the canceled dates and missed anniversaries because he'd "made a big collar." After thirty years together, she'd finally had enough.

"I have good years left, Ford," she told him one night, when he'd come home to find her sitting at the kitchen table, her coat on and an overnight bag by her feet. "I don't want to live them like this. Our children are grown and happy. I did my job, taking care of my family."

She'd put some money away, wanted to travel.

Turns out no one ever told him that all the things that make you a great cop make you a shitty father and husband. He missed her every night when he came home to the quiet, cold Brooklyn house where he'd lived for twenty-five years, twenty-four of them with her. But when he thought of her, he realized he didn't know certain things about her that a man should know about his wife, like her favorite color, the perfume she wore, what made her laugh. He'd paid attention to every detail of every case he'd ever investigated, had a catalog of professional memories, remembered things about cases twenty years ago like it was yesterday. But when it came to Rose, he was ashamed to admit, he didn't even know her dress size.

Ford flipped on the light in the hallway and hung his coat in the closet. He looked at himself in the mirror that hung behind the door, the mirror where Rose had always combed her curly black hair and applied lipstick to her full, soft mouth before leaving the house. He looked old, with blue smudges of fatigue under his eyes, a five o'clock shadow on his jaw. His salt-and-pepper hair was in serious need of a trim. He was fat and pale. Shit, he didn't even get on the scale anymore. He didn't want to know.

He turned out the light and walked over the red shag carpet of the living room and onto the speckled Formica of the dining room and into the kitchen.

When Rose left, he realized he didn't know how to run the dishwasher. That he couldn't remember the last time he'd washed a stitch of clothing or been inside a grocery store. He was virtually helpless. Thank god for Chinese takeout and Laundromats. If it weren't for the Asians, he'd be dirty and hungry all the time.

The aroma of sesame chicken wafted from the bag as he dropped it on the counter by the sink. He washed his hands and pulled a plate from the cupboard. It was funny, not in a ha-ha way but in a pathetic and miserable way, that he'd spent his whole life trying to be different from his father and his life was turning out just exactly the same way—alone, a heart attack looming in the not-too-distant future. He turned on the television that sat on the stand by the table to the eleven o'clock news, brought the bag and the plate over to the table, and sat down.

Ford's father, a first-generation Irish American, had been a mean bastard of a drunk who'd never held down a job for more than a month. Living off welfare and the meager salary Ford's mother earned as a clerk at Macy's, his father had systematically terrorized and tried to ruin the lives of his wife and each of his children. He'd beaten Ford and his older brother Tommy, nearly killed his mother before she got the strength to leave him and move them all away. His father died alone in a room at the YMCA, a heart attack at the age of fifty-six, with no one to mourn him.

In his life, Ford had worked to be exactly the opposite of the man his father was. He'd learned the value of discipline and hard work from his mother and promised himself that no children of his would want for things the way he and his brother had. He'd worked long hours of overtime to make sure his family had everything they needed and more. He'd never had more than a beer or two in a sitting. Even with all of that effort, always sure he was doing the right thing just because it was the opposite of the way his father had done it, now he was alone.

Ford had never touched his children in anger; in that way at least he had not lived his father's legacy. Nonetheless, Katie and James were distant, polite strangers who made the obligatory calls on Sunday night and visited every few months. He couldn't blame them...he hadn't been the best father. He hadn't really been a father at all. But they were good kids because of Rose.

He reached over to turn up the volume on the set when he saw himself on the screen. He looked even worse than he thought. He stood beneath the maroon awning of the Park Avenue building where Richard Stratton had been killed, with the reporter he'd agreed to answer some questions for when he'd been ready to make his statement to the press.

"At this time," he was saying to the pretty blond reporter, "no charges have been brought against Julian Ross."

He cringed to hear himself talk. Just a month ago, his partner Frank Benvenuto would have talked to the press. A good-looking guy, charismatic, funny, Frank had always handled the press with ease, knew how to use his relationships with reporters to the department's advantage.

But Ford had no such expertise. Now, with Frank retired and no new partner assigned to him, Ford had to deal with the vultures himself. He tried not to think about the fact that his chief had hinted at a reluctance to assign Ford a new partner, the assumption being that Ford, too, must be considering retirement.

"Does this murder make you doubt the jury's decision to acquit Julian Ross ten years ago?" the television reporter asked, her smile and perky voice seeming inappropriate to him.

"There's nothing at this time to connect the two events," he said, curt and non-committal. Why did I keep running my fingers through my hair like that, Ford thought, hating the way his voice sounded.

But Ford wasn't thinking about retirement. He had no idea what he would even do with himself. It was fine for Frankie, now sailing around the Caribbean in a fifty-foot sloop with his wife Helen...his dream for as long as Ford had known him. Ford kept getting postcards from exotic locales: "The emerald water is calling you, my friend! Come meet us in St. Bart!" Yeah, right. And do what? Sit on my ass and sip cocktails?

"Where is Julian Ross now?" asked the reporter.

"She's under psychiatric care at an undisclosed location," he answered.

"Are there any other suspects?" the reporter pressed.

"There are no suspects at this time," he said, moving away from the reporter and toward the unmarked Caprice that he drove while he was on duty. "That's it. I have no further comments right now."

As he watched himself get into his car, the camera still following him, Ford noticed that he had a huge bald spot on the back of his head. He sighed and served himself some of the sesame chicken, started eating with a plastic fork. The fact of it was that, without a partner, he'd been lucky to catch this case at all. If he hadn't worked the first Julian Ross case, he'd be doing peripheral work for people like Piselli and Malone, a couple of junior guys assigned to work the case with him.

"As you can see," the reporter concluded, "the police have no leads in the murder of Richard Stratton, husband of world-renowned artist Julian Ross. But inside sources say that the arrest of Ross is imminent. We'll keep you apprised of all breaking news on the case. This is Betsy Storm, ABC News."

The newscast was enough to switch his focus from the misery of his life back to the Julian Ross case. His visit to Orlando DiMarco had led him nowhere. The guy wasn't about to admit that he and Julian were lovers. But Ford did get a good look at the painting Lydia Strong had described. It reminded him of the description Jetty Murphy had given him ten years ago, the mysterious man who'd left through the basement back door and disappeared into the night. He could track Jetty down easily enough, but getting him to remember might not be so simple. After Jetty raped and murdered an elderly woman in Tompkins Square Park a few years ago, he'd been diagnosed as a paranoid schizophrenic and sent to the New York State Facility for the Criminally Insane. It was an awful place...made Payne Whitney look like Club Med. People who went there didn't usually get better. So he didn't expect Jetty's mental health to have improved much. But it might be worth a trip up there with Lydia and Jeff, to see if there was anything they'd missed the first time.

He looked down at his plate and was surprised to see that he'd polished off all of the sesame chicken and the white rice that had come with it. He'd barely even tasted it. He pulled himself up from the table, threw the containers in the garbage, rinsed the plate off, and placed it in the dishwasher next to the plate from last night. He walked over to the refrigerator and popped a Michelob Light and headed down the stairs to his basement office. He walked past the groaning old furnace and through the laundry room.

His office was a converted walk-in pantry; it was in this small space where he had pored over the Julian Ross case, among others, over the years. It was this small space that he had chosen over the love and company of his wife and children. It was here where he had spent every ounce of his energy and his free time going over the cold cases where the answers had eluded him. It was here that he had given everything of himself over the course of his career. So it was fitting, he supposed as he reached up to pull the string and turn on the light, that it was all he should have left.

The bent old man carrying a Balducci's bag, wearing a long black woolen coat and a plaid golfer's hat, shuffled off the bus at Astor Place. He moved slowly with his head down, moving against the crowds of people still pulsing along the streets though it was nearly midnight.

He made his way down the stairs to the subway and walked to the end of the nearly deserted platform. He could hear the street noise from the grating above his head. When the downtown 4/5 arrived, a screeching, hissing metal bullet, the few passengers waiting on the platform got on. But the old man waited, seated on the wooden bench against the tiled wall. "Stand clear of the closing doors," the conductor yelled, and in a rumble and flash the train was gone.

The old man walked to the edge of the platform, looked once over his shoulder, and then jumped with the strength and grace of a younger man onto the tracks, careful to avoid the third rail. He made his way along the edge, watching for the circle of light that would warn him of an oncoming train. In the darkness, small forms skittered, their tiny razor-sharp nails scratching against the concrete. They didn't bother him anymore, the rats. They didn't bother him at all.

He felt more than heard the roar of the approaching train before it turned the bend and he saw the glow of the light looming ahead of him. He picked up his pace to a jog, moving faster as the light approached him. The sound was louder now as the train grew close and he broke into a run. His heart rate quickened and his breath came harder in the dank and soot of the tunnel. As the train bore down on him, a frenzy of light and sound and metal, Jed McIntyre ducked into a doorway and the train went rushing past in a blaze. He leaned against the concrete for a moment to catch his breath, and then pushed through the entrance and made his way down the corridor. Water dripped from the ceiling, dropping rhythmically to the ground, collected in shallow puddles. Ahead of him, he could see the blaze of a fire and hear the echo of voices.

Beneath the streets of New York City there was an entirely other world. He'd heard of it when he'd been locked up. A paranoid schizophrenic had told him about the tunnels. But he'd never actually believed it...after all, the other people at the New York State Facility for the Criminally Insane were insane. But his unfortunate circumstances had compelled him to investigate the matter for himself.

The homeless were the invisible population of New York City. They staggered through the streets, ranting, reeking, begging for change, and yet they were barely acknowledged by even the most compassionate New Yorkers sharing the sidewalks. People didn't want to acknowledge their existence, as if to do so were to admit that they themselves were only about a paycheck away from the same fate. The homeless were filthy and crazy, to be ignored and avoided at all costs, just like the city rats. Worse...because rats could be poisoned. He had always felt that way himself until by his circumstances he became one of them...well, in that he had no place to go.

In a small park on Rivington Street he'd met a man called Charlie, an aging Vietnam vet with a bad case of halitosis and a mean heroin addiction. Charlie approached Jed at a moment when Jed was feeling quite lost. The city was crawling with cops and Feds with his picture on their dashboards and he'd been moving in the darkness, through alleys, dressed as a homeless man for two days and nights, sleeping in subway stations. Truth was he had enough cash to stay at the Waldorf or to go anywhere in the world, but he didn't dare go near a hotel, an airport, or a train station. Jed had been slumped on a park bench, pretending to sleep, when he heard the clattering of a shopping cart pushed over concrete and detected a dreadful odor...some combination of urine and foot rot. He looked up to see the watery brown eyes and dirty face of his savior.

"New at this, huh?" Charlie had said, sitting beside him, pulling his cart possessively to his side.

Jed had just nodded, eyeing him suspiciously. He couldn't remember the last time anyone had spoken to him of his own accord. He wondered briefly if Charlie was an undercover cop. But decided he was just too disgusting; he smelled of years of being on the street, irregular bathing. No cop was that good.

"I'm Charlie," he said, offering a moldy hand, his long fingernails caked with dirt. Jed didn't offer his in return. Charlie withdrew his without emotion.

"Well, it's gonna start to rain soon," he said with an air of authority. "Soon it's gonna get real cold. You got a plan?"

Jed shook his head.

"I know a place where you could go and be safe...well, safer than the shelters anyway. You could find a little place to call your own, you know? Got any money?"

"A little," said Jed, curious.

"Can you help an old man out?" asked Charlie, looking like he was jonesing a bit, his foot tapping, his mouth moving as though he were chewing an invisible piece of gum.

So they made a deal...though it didn't quite turn out for Charlie as he had expected. After Charlie told Jed about the tunnels, how to get in, who to see when he got there, Jed pretended to reach into the pocket of his coat for money and instead took a blade and plunged it deep into the old man's throat. Charlie never made a sound and Jed thought the old man had looked at him with relief, as if he'd been done a favor. Jed sat beside him until the life drained from him and his eyes stared off into the world beyond. You could never trust a junkie.

So Jed had finally found a home, a place where he could be safe in the mad world that loomed above him. Catacombs, webs of tunnels that stretched for miles, wound down into the earth some said ten, some said twenty levels deep. There were nooks, rooms, bridges, ledges, catwalks, a million places where you could make yourself a nest, free from the hassles of the city above. He'd been a little afraid at first, a little uneasy. But then the dark and the silence had seduced him...and really, of whom exactly should Jed McIntyre be afraid? Who was sicker, more evil and twisted, more homicidal than himself?

He turned off into another tunnel before he reached the group of bottom-feeders that were gathered around the fire under a vent that led to the street. There was a community under here that Jed did not wish to be a part of. He only participated enough to be connected to the information web when he wanted, directions, secrets of the tombs. He had a few things they did not. Money, for one; intelligence, for another. Then there was the fact that people knew somehow to be afraid of him. Those who lived down here hadn't survived without a certain kind of animal instinct. They smelled his evil like an odor. All these things had served so far to get him what he needed. That was how he had figured out a very important thing about the tunnels.

He would rest awhile in the little space he'd created for himself and then he'd continue his exploration of the catacombs, as he liked to call them. It reminded him of Paris and the networks of tunnels lined with bones beneath Denfert-Rochereau in Montparnasse. Comte d'Artois, later Charles X, threw wild parties in the catacombs just before the revolution. He, like Jed, must have been very comfortable with the idea of death—other people's deaths, of course.

It was totally silent by the time he'd reached home. He climbed the metal stairs with a light jog, removed a key from his pocket, and unlocked the padlock he'd bought at the Big K up top. The door creaked loudly as it opened, and the echo sounded in the tunnels like a human scream.

Inside, he lit one of his battery-powered lanterns, placed the padlock on the interior latch, and left the key in place, in case he needed to get out in a hurry. It was the only door in or out of his cozy little space, so he felt relatively safe. But one could never be too careful.

He'd also purchased an AeroBed from the same Big K where he'd picked up the padlock and lanterns, along with some lovely sheets, blankets, and pillows from the Martha Stewart Collection. The floor along the wall was lined with books, Lydia's books, books about the history of New York City and its subway system, computer manuals so that he could keep up with his trade. He kind of liked his little nest.

He sat on the floor and removed his foie gras and Carr's Water Crackers from the Balducci's bag. He had other little treats in there, too, but he'd save them for later. He spread the foie gras on a cracker with a plastic knife and savored the spicy, meaty taste on his tongue while he gazed up at the wall. Taped up on the wall were long sheets of brown paper towels that he had drawn upon in charcoal pencil. It was here that he was making maps of his wanderings in the catacombs, charting how the tunnels and levels connected to each other, and what corresponded on the streets above. By his calculations, his little nest was almost directly below Lydia and Jeffrey's Great Jones Street loft.

The rumor of the tunnels was that some of them led to concealed entrances to buildings, passageways created during the Prohibition Era so that bootleggers could move their product to the city's speakeasies beneath the sight of the law. He'd yet to find any of these entrances, and he wasn't a hundred percent convinced that they even existed.

But he liked the romance of the idea, the idea of a dark netherworld connected by secret portals to the world above, small unguarded spaces where demons could move from hell into the light and back again, carrying their prey on their backs. He fairly shivered with the thrill of it.

Dax Chicago loved Lydia Strong. Not in any kind of romantic or sexual way. She'd drive him absolutely insane. But in the way of friendship, which for Dax was the most powerful love of all. He loved Jeffrey Mark in the same way, with a fierce loyalty and deep affection. Because they were threatened, because their lives and their happiness were in danger, he felt threatened and very much as though he'd let them down that night in Riverdale when Jed McIntyre had gotten away.

Jeffrey had been right when he'd warned Dax. "Don't underestimate him," he'd said. "He's not as stupid as he looks." Dax hadn't listened. Of course, Jed McIntyre had some help that night. But still, if Dax had been a little more cautious, Lydia and Jeffrey wouldn't be in this mess. Dax considered it his personal responsibility to fix it up right. And fast.

He drove his Range Rover slowly down Tenth Avenue. The night was turning frigid and the cold had crawled in beneath his sleeves and down his collar and he felt it in his bones, in spite of the fact that heat was blasting from the Rover's vents. He felt badly for the prostitutes and she-males that strutted their stuff in fishnets and miniskirts. He'd always had a soft place inside himself for the strays of the world, the broken, the damaged. Some people, he knew, just never had a chance.

He watched as they gyrated and preened underneath the orange glow of the streetlights. Their sparkling and brightly colored clothes were a garish contrast to the dark, gray buildings and empty doorways. Some of them looked okay from a distance, but they were skanks, every last one of them, dirty, looking ten years older than they actually were, covered in track marks, wreaking of sex. But there was no one who knew the streets like these people, knew what was going down when and on whom.

He fiddled with the heat, adjusted the vents, though he knew it couldn't blow any harder; he couldn't stand the bloody cold. His thick, strong hands gripped the wheel as he scanned the women and wanna-be women, looking for one in particular. They catcalled him as he drove by, walked slowly toward his vehicle. A tiny woman with orange hair and red leather pants gave him the finger when he didn't stop for her. He couldn't tell how old she was and he tried not to think about the fact that she looked like an adolescent. He'd been moving slowly enough and she'd come close enough for him to see her eyes. There was the deadness there of someone lost, someone who'd already been marked for a tragic end.

He saw her, finally, huddled by a Dumpster with a long bleached blond wig hanging to her thin waist, long, shapely legs in red tights and black patent leather platform shoes and matching hot pants, a big pink faux fur cropped jacket unzipped to reveal a leather bustier. He pulled the car over to the sidewalk and rolled down the widow. She sauntered over and leaned her arms on the door in typical ho fashion.

"Dax. I missed you," she said, her voice deep and husky.

"You got a little bit of a five o'clock shadow going there, Dan-ielle," said Dax, with a smile, unlocking the door.

"It's been a long shift," the transvestite complained, sliding her six-foot frame into the Rover with the grace of a duchess. Dax handed her a hundred-dollar bill, which she immediately stuffed into the little pink clutch she was carrying.

"Oh, honey," Danielle said. "You shouldn't have."

"It's the least I could do," answered Dax, not quite making

eye contact with her. Danielle made Dax uncomfortable; she was a black hole of need and misery and Dax knew there was only so much he could do for her. He needed to keep his distance.

"You got that right, cowboy," she said, her voice growing hard. She sensed his unease and it insulted her. "What I have is going to cost you more than that."

"Tell me what you've got first and I'll decide how much it's worth."

She laughed a deep, hearty laugh...a man's laugh. Then she moved to get out of the vehicle.

"Okay, okay. How much?" he said.

"Five hundred," she answered.

He took the money from the breast pocket of his leather jacket and handed it to her, watched as it disappeared into her bag. He could feel hard calluses on her hands as she grabbed the bills from him. It was what he had expected to pay her anyway. She settled into the passenger seat and got comfortable, held her hands up to the heat coming from the vents and rubbed them together for a minute.

"All right, Danielle, enough fucking around," he said, losing patience. "Tell me what you know."

"Um-hum, I just love that accent. It's so sexy. Take me to McDonald's, Daxie, and get me a Big Mac and fries, huh? I'm starving. I'll tell you everything over a hot meal."

Her face was a mess. Her nose had been broken and never healed right, leaving a large bump on the bridge. Her violet contact lenses looked ghoulish in combination with her dark, scarred skin. Dax noticed that her lip quivered and her hands shook slightly. As he looked at her, his impatience gave way to pity. He started the Rover and moved away from the sidewalk. It was going to be a long night.

EIGHT

Lydia had never been so acquainted with her toilet bowl as she had become over the last few days of morning sickness. She felt like her insides were being ripped open by some alien creature trying to get out. She was weak and tired, sleep having eluded her the last few nights. She'd dreamed of Julian Ross and the painting they'd seen, but she couldn't remember the content, just that she'd awakened sweating and with a feeling of restless unease. She rested her head on the rim, bracing herself for another round, but was grateful when the nausea seemed to be subsiding.

"You all right?" asked Jeffrey, entering the bathroom, kneeling beside her, and placing a hand on her head.

"I'm okay," she answered, trying to smile at him. She looked into his eyes and saw how happy he was, and it made her happier, too.

She pulled herself together and got up from the marble floor, leaned against the sink and inspected her face closely in the mirror. He stood behind her and smiled at her reflection. He was dressed already, wearing a royal blue Ralph Lauren oxford and charcoal pants, a black Italian leather belt with brushed chrome accents and matching buckled boots.

He put some of her Sebastian gel in his hair behind her as she brushed her teeth and pulled a comb through her jet-black hair.

"Come have a cup of coffee with me before I go?" he said, hugging her from behind.

"Sure," she said, and trundled downstairs behind him still in her purple silk pajamas. She had a few hours before she had to meet Eleanor Ross at the office, so she planned to do a little exploring on the Internet, see what she could find about Julian Ross and her past. Dax was sitting on the couch with his feet up on the coffee table watching The Today Show as they came down the stairs.

"When did you get here?" asked Jeff.

"A couple of minutes ago," he said, not looking up from the screen. "I made some coffee."

"He has a key?" asked Lydia.

"I thought it was a good idea," answered Jeff with a shrug.

"God, why doesn't he just move in here and start paying rent?"

"Katie Couric is really hot, you know. She's got this whole sexy girl-next-door thing going on," said Dax.

"So where did you go yesterday, Dax?" asked Lydia, grabbing two coffee mugs from the cabinet. They'd just left the gallery and were walking toward the Yum Yum Diner when Dax's cell phone rang. He had about a thirty-second conversation, which seemed to mainly consist of grunts. Then he had hung up quickly and said, "I gotta go. I'll see you in the morning." He had walked away without another word, disappearing around the corner.

"None of your bloody business," he said gruffly. "Christ, you're nosy."

"All of a sudden you get this call and then you just disappear like James Bond on a mission."

"I have other clients, you know," he said, standing up and walking over to them, pouring himself some more coffee and then handing the pot to Lydia. "You are not the center of my universe," he continued, patting Lydia on the cheek. "A concept that I know is difficult for you."

"Oh, come on, Dax," she pleaded, "give it up. You're too mysterious. I can't stand it." Her curiosity about him, his life, and his past was like an itch that she couldn't scratch. She placed the cups on the counter, poured some coffee in each, and put the pot back in the machine. She was about to press Dax further when she was struck by yet another powerful wave of nausea. She turned and ran to the downstairs bathroom, slamming the door behind her. When she was gone, Dax turned to Jeff and said quietly, "I got a lead on him."

Jeff raised his eyebrows. They'd agreed that if they got a handle on Jed McIntyre, they'd take care of it themselves, without the FBI...and without Lydia.

"Is it reliable?"

Dax shrugged. "I think so. We'll need to check it out. Sooner rather than later."

"Lydia has a meeting at the office in a couple of hours with Eleanor Ross. Let's talk then."

Dax nodded as Lydia waddled back into the room, holding her stomach, looking gray and sweaty. She threw herself on the couch with a groan. "This kid is kicking my ass already."

"You know," said Dax, sitting beside her and dropping his arm around her, "you don't have that healthy glow so many pregnant women seem to have." He gave her an affectionate squeeze.

"Oh, fuck off, Dax."

Lydia's office, which had been more or less transplanted from the home she'd sold last year in Santa Fe, took up the greatest square footage on the first floor of their apartment. The south wall faced Great Jones Street and was comprised largely of four ten-foot windows. The east wall was floor-to-ceiling bookcases, containing the intellectual clutter of most of the books she had read and all she had written in her career. Across from her desk sat a large sienna leather couch and matching chair, between them a mahogany wood table, which had once been the door of an eighteenth-century Spanish castle.

It was a peaceful place, a cocoon, and as she settled into the black leather chair at her desk and booted her laptop, she listened to the hushed street noise that only just barely made it through the thick glass of the windows. A scented candle beside her gave off a hint of jasmine, though it wasn't lit. On the wall behind her hung a clutter of awards, her Pulitzer chief among them. Several black and white photographs accented empty wall space: an adobe church against a darkening sky threaded with lightning, a photograph of her taken by Herb Ritts during a shoot for a Vanity Fair feature in which she looked a pleasing combination of haunted and mysterious, mischievous and wise. It had surprised her then that she looked so utterly together, when she was really just lost inside. She had been relieved that it didn't show.

Here, in her office, she was free. She didn't have to think about Jed McIntyre, or about her pregnancy. She only had to focus on the case at hand, give in to the buzz, and search for the pieces of the puzzle. It was like a drug she used to escape her reality, even as she was chasing someone else's.

When her computer was up and running, her fingers danced across the keyboard as she logged in to her powerful search engine. She entered Julian Ross's name and came up with over a thousand entries. Lydia wasn't necessarily interested in the accounts of Julian's first husband's murder. She had more details from Ford McKirdy's old files and Jeff's memory than she would find online. She wasn't sure what she was looking for exactly. She was just looking. She would know she'd found it...when she felt the familiar jolt of electricity course through her veins.

She scrolled down through the gallery reviews, the publicity pieces, the gossip columns, the wedding announcement. Lydia marveled at the photographs...the radiant, photogenic woman captured laughing, dancing, or serious, with searing, intelligent eyes, giving interviews, walking in Washington Square Park with a child on each hand, her husband close behind.

There were several images of Julian with Richard Stratton. He looked more like her father than her husband, an elegant man with graying temples, high forehead, and a cool, distant gaze. There was a photo of them in tennis whites on the lawn of a sprawling Hudson estate, one of them in formal wear arriving at a Guggenheim event, and a candid shot captured as the family shopped on Fifth Avenue. Three different moments in time, but their body language in each was similar. Richard with a possessive arm around her shoulders, hand on her arm, or holding one of her hands in both of his. Julian leaning away or looking away. In the candid, she seemed to shrink from him and he had a wistful look on his face as though even when they were close, she eluded him.

Still, the Julian Ross Lydia saw cataloged before her in snapshots, moments, some posed, some honest, seemed content if not exactly happy, in command of her life, a mother, a wife, an artist. But she was a specter, in no way resembling the shattered, wretched woman Lydia had met at the Payne Whitney Clinic.

"What happened to you?" she wondered out loud, her voice just a whisper.

She clicked on a New York Times piece, at home with julian ross. Here a color picture of Julian showed her delicate beauty lit in natural sunlight that gleamed in from a tall window in her Park Avenue duplex, as she reclined on a red velvet sofa. Her small twins, tiny reflections of each other, sat on either side of her. They were her image, delicate features, green eyes, wise and deep. There was nothing of Richard Stratton apparent in their faces. They stared at the camera as if hypnotized by it. The little girl Lola sucked her thumb. Lydia felt a little twist of something in her stomach as she looked at the photograph. There was something so ephemeral, something otherworldly about the twins. They were almost...spooky.

She read through the article, which was a valentine about Julian Ross, how wonderful, how talented, how resilient to bounce back from personal tragedy. It contained no questions about who might have murdered Tad if she did not. Just a story about her struggles with an uptight art professor at New York University Tisch School of the Arts, her studies in Paris, in Florence, an art teacher who recognized her talent in grade school in the small upstate New York town where she was a child. A town called, of all things, Haunted.

Nice place to raise a family, she thought, images of dead trees and dilapidated cemeteries playing in her mind.

She looked at the clock on the lower right-hand side of her screen and realized she had lost track of time, scrolling through the numerous articles. She'd have to jet if she was going to make her appointment with Eleanor Ross. There was just one more thing she wanted to check. She entered "Haunted, New York" into the search engine. There weren't that many entries, so it didn't take her long to find what she was looking for. She sat back when she saw it and inhaled sharply with a shake of her head, the buzz electric inside her.

"Did you know that back in 1965 when Julian was five years old, her father Jack Proctor was murdered? And that Eleanor was accused, tried, and acquitted for the crime?" said Lydia to her cell phone in a cab headed uptown. Jeff and Ford McKirdy were conferenced in on the line.

There was silence on the other end of the phone before Ford said, "Uh—no. Is that true? Where did you hear that?"

"I found it online, a periodical archive search engine I subscribe to. I printed up copies so that you could see for yourself. Did anybody look into Julian Ross's childhood during the last murder investigation? Or did you focus primarily on the physical evidence and witness testimonies?"

"Yeah, I have to admit," said Jeff. "We focused pretty much on the present tense."

"How was he killed?" asked Ford.

"In much the same way that Tad and Richard were killed. Taken apart at the seams. Eleanor was acquitted for many of the same reasons Julian's jury found her innocent. No one could believe that a woman, especially a woman of that size, was physically capable of it."

The cabdriver leaned on his horn pointlessly as they crawled through midtown crosstown traffic. Other cars jammed on the street followed suit.

She heard Ford let out a loud sigh. "God...how could we have missed that?"

"So what are you suggesting?" said Jeffrey. "That nearly thirty-five years later the mysterious killer strikes again?"

"I'm suggesting that it bears looking into. The murder took place in a town called Haunted, New York."

"Haunted?" both men asked simultaneously.

"Yes."

"Actually, Lydia," said Ford, "I think I know where that is. It's north, near the New York State Facility for the Criminally Insane...."

Lydia's stomach lurched at the mention of the place that had housed Jed McIntyre for so long and had failed to keep him where he belonged.

"I was planning on heading up there this afternoon," Ford continued. "Feel like taking a ride?"

"Why do you need to go up there?"

"To talk to Jetty Murphy. You remember him, Jeff. The witness who saw the man leaving the apartment building."

"He was a junkie, Ford."

"Yeah, and he's a murderer and a rapist. But he's got eyes. Won't hurt to interview him again. You never know."

"I'll go with you, Ford," said Lydia. "If we can stop in Haunted, too."

"Lydia," said Jeffrey, "are you sure that's a good idea?" She could hear enough concern in his voice to visualize him frowning and tapping his pen on his desk.

"Jed McIntyre isn't there anymore, Jeff. Anyway, that's probably the one place in the world he won't follow me."

"Oh, shit, Lydia. I'm sorry," said Ford, embarrassed at his carelessness.

"It's fine," she said, annoyed at being handled like a porcelain doll. "Pick me up at the firm at one."

"See you then. Don't worry, Jeff. I'll keep her safe." She heard him click off.

"Are you sure you're all right with this?" asked Jeff.

"I promised you I won't put myself in any danger and I meant it. So trust me to take care of myself, okay?" she said briskly.

"I do. You know that," he said. But she didn't believe him. She knew he thought her reckless and stubborn. And maybe, sometimes, she was both of those things.

"I'll see you in a minute."

She hung up the phone feeling restless, caged. She didn't like the limitations being imposed on her...don't go here because of Jed McIntyre, don't do this because you're pregnant. Beneath the claustrophobic sense of being shackled and helpless was a tiny flame of rebellion. She was starting to feel a headache creeping up on her.

"Don't worry, Lydia," said Dax beside her. He was so quiet sometimes that she forgot he was right next to her. She looked at him and he had earnest eyes on her. "It'll be over soon. I have a feeling."

She knew he was talking about Jed McIntyre. He had a way of knowing what she was thinking that revealed about him a surprising amount of intuition. She looked at him and gave him a sad smile.

"You're right," she lied. "I feel it, too."

When Lydia and Dax arrived at the office of Mark, Striker and Strong, Eleanor Ross was already seated at Lydia's desk, filling out the firm's paperwork...payment contract, liability disclaimers, etc. It occurred to Lydia that this was the first case she'd had that actually involved a paying client. Usually she was drawn into cases by something else...a hunch or a feeling. Something would pique her interest and she'd wind up tripping into a whole big mess and bringing Jeffrey along with her.

She pushed her way through the glass doors, wearing a long black cashmere coat, black stretch jeans, and a red Calvin Klein ribbed wool sweater with a cowl neck. A big leather bag over her shoulder contained her "life"—everything from her Palm Pilot to her Beretta to her hairbrush.

As Lydia was about to enter her office, she turned to Dax and said, "What are you going to do with yourself for the next hour or so?"

She was not-so-subtly suggesting that he entertain himself elsewhere while she conducted her interview with Eleanor Ross. She didn't need him skulking in the corner of her office like a gargoyle while she tried to extract more information from the old woman.

"I dunno," he said innocently, looking behind him at Jeffrey's office door. "I'll go talk to Jeff."

"Fine," she said, shutting the door behind her.

Eleanor looked up from her documents.

"I hope I haven't kept you waiting long," said Lydia. She approached Eleanor and waited for her to relinquish the spot she'd chosen at Lydia's desk and move over to the chairs clearly designated for visitors. The fact that Eleanor had chosen to seat herself behind Lydia's desk in the first place was extremely annoying, a clear violation of Lydia's personal space. She certainly wasn't going to sit on the couch or in one of the chairs opposite her desk, allowing Eleanor the power position. After a long moment, the woman got up, looking at her watch.

"For all the money you charge, I'd imagine you'd be on time," she said, moving past Lydia.

Lydia smiled politely, reminded of the reason she hated being on somebody's payroll. She seated herself at her desk and took a cursory glance to see that nothing had been disturbed.

"I'll just take a moment to establish a few ground rules, Ms. Ross," she said sweetly. "First of all, you pay this firm for the service of finding the answers to your questions. Those answers may not always be the answers you wanted. Second, I am not your employee. This firm may choose to walk away from your case at any time, should we feel that your demands exceed our resources or that you have been dishonest with us in a way that hinders our ability to meet your goals. Is that understood?"

The woman began to bluster. "I don't appreciate—"

"Do you understand my terms, Ms. Ross? If there's a problem, we can terminate this agreement before you've inconvenienced yourself further with the paperwork."

There was a moment when Lydia expected Eleanor to get up and walk out. She had drawn herself up and sat rigid and tall, her eyes blazing indignation and anger. But the moment passed and Eleanor's attitude softened. "I understand," she said finally, though the words seemed to choke her.

"Good. Now, with that said, I'd like to know why you didn't consider it relevant that you were tried in 1965 in Haunted, New York, for the murder of your husband, Jack Proctor. Particularly when the manner of death was so eerily similar to the murder of both of your late sons-in-law."

Eleanor Ross went quite pale. She seemed to swoon a bit, but Lydia didn't rush over to her to see if she was all right. Eleanor Ross was a strong woman and Lydia knew it.

"Can I have some water?" the old woman said quietly. Lydia rose to walk across her office, passing the large windows that offered an expansive view of uptown Manhattan and to a small refrigerator that sat behind a large black leather sofa. Her office was almost as large as Jeffrey's and decorated in the same warm colors, cream, rust, browns, and greens. She took a small bottle of Evian and handed it to Eleanor, who cracked the top and took a delicate sip. Lydia walked back over to her high-varnished mahogany desk and waited.

"I didn't kill my husband, if that's what you're thinking," Eleanor said without looking at Lydia.

"Who did?"

"I don't know," she answered, and the grief that shadowed her features and darkened her eyes suggested she might be telling the truth. But Lydia wasn't quite convinced.

"But you believe that the three murders are connected."

"Doesn't it seem likely?" asked Eleanor, turning her gaze to Lydia.

"So why didn't you say anything about it?"

"It's a chapter of my life, as I'm sure you understand, that I was not eager to reopen."

"It seems as though it has been reopened for you. I guess the question is, Eleanor, by whom?"

They sat in silence for a second, with Eleanor looking down at her hands and Lydia watching her intently, looking for some sign of the inner workings of her mind. Eleanor's arms were folded across her body and she hugged herself tightly. She's protecting herself, thought Lydia. Lydia knew that it was often the furtive gesture, the nervous tick, the tapping foot that communicated the most about a person. Words were chosen, but the body never lied.

"You never remarried," said Lydia, breaking the silence.

"No...." said Eleanor.

"Why not?"

Eleanor stood up and walked over toward the windows. "I loved enough for one lifetime. My husband...no one could have compared to him. It was a rare love; we were lovers, friends, and partners in this life. It's a hard thing to replace. I never tried."

Her words struck a chord inside Lydia. It reminded her of Jeffrey and how she loved him. Reminded her of her old fears of losing him to death, how she knew that if he was gone all the light would drain from her life. She shuddered inside, pressed the feelings down.

"Who do you think killed him, Eleanor?" said Lydia, her voice softer now.

"I don't know," she said again, her voice catching and dropping to a whisper. Her eyes seemed to look into her past, flip through a catalog of bad memories. There were things there she didn't want to look at again and things she didn't want to share.

"You suspected no one, Eleanor?" Lydia pressed. "You were in the house when it happened, weren't you? Just like Julian."

"I was in the garden, tending to my roses. I was far from the house out by a gazebo near a lake on our property," she said, defensive now, raising her voice. "I saw nothing and heard nothing."

The woman was shaking and Lydia backed off for a second. She took a breath and let Eleanor move back to the couch and sit for a minute, sipping her water and sifting through the past. People clung to denial like a shield in a hail of arrows. Convincing them to put it down and face the truth was like convincing someone to commit suicide.

"I'm not sure why you've hired us. You believe that the murders of Julian's husbands are connected to the murder of your own, but you failed to reveal that to us. Did you hire us because you want answers? Because from where I'm sitting, it doesn't really seem like you do."

"I hired you because I want the killing to stop," she said with a sudden ferocity. There was real emotion on her face now, her careful façade slipping to reveal the true woman. "Because I want someone in this family to grow up without tragedy."

She looked up at the ceiling and clenched her fists. "I begged her not to marry again," she hissed.

Eleanor sat on the couch and put her head in her hands, anger and frustration coming off her in waves. Lydia sat forward on her chair, confused and intrigued.

"Why, Eleanor?" she asked, shaking her head. "Why shouldn't Julian have married again?"

"Because for generations," Eleanor said, looking up from her hands, tears falling now unattractively down her face in black rivulets, her mouth quivering, "someone has been killing our husbands."

Her words hung in the silence and Lydia looked at Eleanor Ross, wondering if there was a history of mental illness in the family.

"My husband, my father, my grandfather before him. Probably further back. Every generation, every woman thinks that she will be the one to escape it. Every time, she's wrong. I need you to find out what's happening to our family...and stop it. Enough is enough."

NINE

The sky had turned from bright blue to gunmetal gray and the air smelled like snow as Lydia and Ford McKirdy sped up I-95 toward the New York State Facility for the Criminally Insane.

"She didn't have any idea who might be behind these multigenerational murders?" asked Ford, not bothering to keep the disbelief out of his voice.

"She claimed not to have the faintest idea," said Lydia, looking out the window at the gray trees, some brightly colored leaves still clinging to their branches. The road and the foliage had taken on a kind of silver tinge in the sunlight pushing through the thick cloud cover. The world was cast in the eerie light that portends a storm.

"So what is it? Some kind of Black Widow curse?"

Lydia shrugged. "I don't know." Her mood had turned foul since her interview with Eleanor Ross, not that it had been so great leading up to that.

"What's the matter with you anyway? You're all punky."

"Where are Dax and Jeff?" she asked, not answering his question.

"I don't know," he answered, eyes intent on the road ahead. "They were gone when I got there."

"Yeah, right," said Lydia.

Ford pretended not to notice her sarcasm.

Her interview with Eleanor had ended abruptly. The woman had just stood up and left. As she was clearly at the end of her rope, Lydia just let her go. They'd talk more later, she was sure of that. Eleanor had more to tell. The past was insidious that way; you could only press the horrors down for so long. Once the lid on the box in your heart had been opened a crack, the demons rushed forth. You could never close that lid again.

She had walked across the hall to tell Jeff what she had discovered and he was gone. So was Dax. Ford McKirdy sat in the waiting area reading a copy of National Geographic.

"Jeff and Dax had to run out," said Rebecca, her Brooklyn accent thick, drifting out over cotton candy pink lips. She had a round pretty face and a sophisticated layered blond bob. Her face was dominated by bright, deep brown eyes.

"Jeff said he'll call and to stay with Ford McKirdy until he does."

"Was that an order?" Lydia asked, directing her annoyance at Rebecca, who really didn't deserve it. She noticed how Ford kept his nose in the magazine during this encounter, not even looking over at them.

Rebecca lifted up her hands, cool and unflappable as she always was. "Don't shoot the messenger. They were out of here like their pants were on fire."

"Where did they go?"

"I swear, Lydia, I have no idea."

Lydia had the distinct impression that she had been "handed off" to Ford, and the thought filled her with resentment and a fierce need to bust away from all of them. But what bothered her most of all was wondering where Dax and Jeffrey had gone and why they hadn't told her where they were going. It was totally out of character and she felt a swell of anxiety that she couldn't quash. A hard twinge in her lower right abdomen caused her to inhale sharply.

"You okay?" asked Ford, glancing over at her. But the pain passed as quickly as it had come.

"I think so," Lydia said, though in her heart a tiny seed of dread was blooming.

Dax and Jeff walked down the stairway that led to the long-closed Lafayette Street station. As they rounded the bend past the staircase, they faced a locked metal gate. A bright hard shaft of light shone in from the street above them, but on the other side of the gate a tunnel led into such blackness that it looked as though a curtain had been drawn. The walls around them were covered with the work of graffiti artists, and the single bulb that lit the tunnel buzzed and dimmed, threatening to go dark. Jeff watched as Dax removed a key from his pocket and fit it into the lock on the gate.

"Where'd you get that?" asked Jeff, pointing toward the key.

"Apparently, when the city retires subway stations, they put these special locks on the gates. They make about four hundred keys for transit workers. But my contact told me about a hardware store in Brooklyn that actually sells copies of the key, if you can imagine. I thought she was full of shit, but here you go." He removed the padlock, unraveling the chain and opening the door.

"Leave it open in case we need to get out of here in a hurry," said Jeff. Dax nodded as he wrapped the chain back through the metal bars and hung the padlock from the last link.

Dax jumped down on the tracks and Jeffrey followed. They made their way through the dank and dirty tunnel, the rumbling of trains audible in the distance, the stench of urine and mold heavy in the air. Beneath the streets of New York

City was a labyrinthine network of subway and train tunnels, gas and water mains, sewer lines and cables. There were layers of lines for phone, cable, and electric, street and traffic lights, then gas mains on top of water mains. There were over a hundred miles of steam mains, below which lay the sewer lines and tunnels. The organization of this vast network was pure chaos. No cohesive map of the underground network existed. Over the years so many different companies had been responsible for the installation of lines and networks that even the workers responsible for upkeep and repairs now never knew what they would find when they entered the tunnels. Jeffrey had read that a merchant sailing vessel from the eighteenth century was found under Front Street, part of the landfill when Manhattan's lower tip was being extended. Wall Street was named for a three-hundred-year-old wall that still stood beneath the street, presumably designed to keep out intruders, probably Indians.

Below all of that were miles of abandoned subway tunnels and stations. Here thousands of homeless people were rumored to live, creating communities and social networks beneath the streets. Most people considered the idea of people living under the streets to be an urban legend, too fantastical to be true. But working with the NYPD for so long on so many different cases, Jeffrey had learned that this was a sad and certain fact. One that the police tried to keep as quiet as possible. The burgeoning homeless population was one of the department's greatest challenges and the fact that thousands of displaced people now lived beneath the city didn't make the situation any better.

"Why does your contact think he's down there and how did she know to tell you?" Jeffrey had asked Dax back at the office. Dax had looked reluctant to reveal how he got his information.

"I put the word out there with some of the people I know on the street and this is what came back," he said with a shrug. "It's going to cost you, too. I had to pay five hundred dollars for it. Plus another seven at McDonald's."

"Just put it on your expense report," said Jeff absently. "What do you mean, you 'put the word out there'?"

"You know, there's this network aboveground and belowground. Information is passed from one person to the next."

"So it's about as reliable as a game of 'Telephone.'"

"It's all we have, mate. Let's check it out," Dax said sensibly. "We've got nothing to lose."

Maybe you have nothing to lose, thought Jeff.

So they'd waited for Ford to arrive, filled him in on their plans, and asked him to stay with Lydia until they got back. Then they slipped out before her meeting with Eleanor was over. He knew she wasn't going to be happy. But there was no way he was going to allow her to tag along on this errand and there would have been no way to stop her if she knew where they were going. So he'd take his beating later.

"According to Danielle, the entrance should be coming up here on the right," Dax said, his voice low. A moment later they came upon an opening in the concrete wall. They could hear voices in the distance. Dax and Jeff exchanged a look. "After you," said Jeff with a smile, and Dax disappeared into the hole. Jeffrey followed him into the darkness.

The New York State Facility for the Criminally Insane rose like a beige monument to misery against the horizon. Lydia and Ford had driven for miles through heavy trees without passing another car or seeing another building, and a light snow had started to fall. Whether it was the stark lines of the structure, or the bars on the windows, or just the knowledge of the hell within its walls, Lydia went cold inside as they grew closer. The place had always existed in her imagination as a house of horrors...where patients suffering from disease of the mind, and maybe the soul, wandered about trying to sort out reality from delusion. She imagined flickering lights, wet gray hallways, somewhere the sound of someone scraping, someone moaning. A place where the cures—shock therapy, lobotomy—were more horrifying than the disease. She wondered if the walls of the structure soaked up the nightmare visions of its residents, she wondered if their fantasies lived somehow in the concrete and gates—if that's why the sight of it filled her with dread.

She was glad there was still a half an hour of distance to cover; she was almost sorry she had come at all. What good did it do for her to come to this place, former home of Jed McIntyre? It was like she was always trying to prove something...how brave, how strong, how able she was to handle any situation.

"So how's Rose?" asked Lydia, trying to make idle conversation. Billy Joel sang "The Piano Man" on the easy listening station and

his tune crackled and sounded tinny on the cheap car speakers. The moment of silence that followed her question told Lydia that she'd said the wrong thing.

"Better than ever, if you ask her," he said with a small laugh. "She left me about a year ago."

"I'm sorry," she said, looking at him. He tapped his finger on the steering wheel and she watched his jaw work. Instead of letting it drop, she asked, "What happened?"

She'd only met Rose a couple of times, once at a Christmas party the firm threw and once when the four of them had dinner one night at Burrito Loco on West Fourth Street more than two years ago. She wouldn't have said that Ford and Rose looked overly happy together, but they had seemed like a set of people, like bookends, one less of itself without the other.

"What happened? I don't know...what happens to people? I was an asshole and she put up with it for thirty years. Then she stopped wanting to put up with it. Said if she couldn't be the center of my attention, then at least she could be the center of her own."

They were both quiet for a second. Lydia thought he would go silent, but he went on as though he were glad for the release.

"She said when the kids were home it wasn't so bad. She felt needed, loved. She was busy. But when they went away to live their lives, she realized that we didn't have a life together. She saw the rest of her life stretching out ahead of her and she wasn't sure she wanted to live it with me. Not the way I am, a workaholic, always putting the job first. I can't really even blame her."

"So she packed and left?"

"Pretty much," he said with a shrug, remembering her there, waiting with her suitcase and her coat on.

"Did you try to stop her?"

"She didn't want to be stopped."

"Maybe she wanted you to go with her?"

He was silent, like it was a possibility he hadn't considered.

"Well, its too late now," he said finally.

"It's never too late, Ford. Not after so many years. Not if you still love her. You should retire and go after her."

"Yeah, right. What am I if I'm not a cop?"

"Maybe it's time to find out."

More silence as the hospital grew closer and loomed before them. Ford glanced over at her. She wondered if she'd stepped over a line with him. But she'd never been very good at staying inside the lines or keeping her opinions to herself.

"Sometimes, you know," he said, "you're so busy being yourself, so selfish, that you forget about the people who depend on you, who love you. You just walk through your life creating damage. By the time you notice, you feel too old, too tired to undo the mess you've made and there's no turning back anyway."

Lydia looked at the road ahead thinking what a sad way to have to look back at your life. She wondered if he was right.

"But you can always move forward," she said. Ford shrugged and gave a polite nod as if he weren't convinced but wanted the conversation to end. The conversation withered between them, leaving them both feeling a little worse than they'd felt before it started.

Ford took a right onto an access road. The snow was falling more heavily now, lightly blanketing the trees that surrounded them as far as she could see. They were in the middle of nowhere, which Lydia guessed was a good location for a place that housed dangerously insane criminals. She looked out the passenger window into woods and saw a high metal fence topped with razor wire running along the side of the road, almost invisible through the trees.

Of course, the reality of the hospital was nowhere near her twisted imagining of it. Originally built in the late 1800s, the New York State Facility for the Criminally Insane sat on nearly three hundred acres of heavily wooded land. The first mental hospital in New York and one of the first in the country, NYSFCI was remarkable for its history and its architecture. The main building, closed but still standing on the grounds, was designed by Captain William Clarke. The 550-foot-long edifice with its immense Doric columns was still imposing and grand, meant to exude an aura of authority and stability. And the rest of the buildings were a hodgepodge of different architectural styles, all unified by their gated windows and aura of pain.

Over the years the hospital endured a number of different incarnations. Initially it housed only civil commitments, people who were mentally ill but not necessarily dangerous. When violent and escape-prone convicts began to arrive from local prisons there in the 1950s, the institution became overburdened and a new building was erected on the same grounds for insane convicts. But even with the additions, the hospital became dangerously overcrowded.

It was closed briefly in the 1970s due to budget cuts and allegations of patient abuse and administrative corruption.

But the prison systems became so overwhelmed with mentally ill prisoners that the hospital opened again in 1985. Just in time to provide a bed for Jed McIntyre. This was not a place people went to get well. It was a place intended to warehouse and manage people too ill for prison or society, though, of course, no one would ever officially admit that.

Two armed and uniformed guards manned the booth beside the mammoth metal gates that separated the hospital from the rest of

the world. Lydia could see another in a tower high above them, the silhouette of a rifle visible from the ground. The younger of the two guards approached the car and Ford handed over his ID and shield. The man returned to the guardhouse and could be seen picking up a phone and briefly speaking into the receiver.

"Proceed to the visitors' entrance," the guard said when he returned to the car, handing back Ford's identification.

The giant gate slid open and Ford drove forward, pausing before a second gate. The first gate closed with a heavy clang and Lydia looked behind her. She took a deep breath as the second gate opened and they drove up the road.

The odor in the tunnels was hard to describe except that it smelled so strongly of human rot and dank earth that it made Jeffrey's eyes water. The two men forged their way through the darkness, behind the beam of Dax's Maglite. Jeffrey held one hand over his mouth and nose against the odor and kept his other on the wall to his right. A strange crunching suddenly beneath their feet prompted Dax to shine the flashlight beam to the floor. Cockroaches the size of hamsters formed a writhing, skittering carpet on the ground.

"Holy Christ. I fucking hate bugs," said Dax. "Ah, God. I wish I'd just left the light off." They picked up their pace a bit and Jeff fought the urge to scratch every inch of his body.

"Do you have any idea where we're going?" asked

Jeffrey, glancing behind him at the fading shaft of light that marked their entrance. He tried not to think about the fact that if anything happened to them down here, they might never be found.

"There should be a stairway coming up," said Dax. "Someone is supposed to meet us."

"Another one of your mysterious contacts?"

"Something like that."

"And what does this person know?"

"Well, we won't find that out until we talk to her, will we?" said Dax.

In the distance, the acoustics of the tunnels making it impossible to tell if noise came from above or below, from in front or behind, they could hear the sound of voices. Briefly, Jeffrey swore he heard the sound of someone playing a flute. The tune was mournful and slow, melodic. Some diffused light made its way down from the gratings above them, enough so they could make out doorways, shapes in the darkness but not enough to really see. The wall was cool and wet beneath Jeffrey's hand. A dripping could be heard from somewhere and twice something had brushed past his shoe. The Glock at his waist gave him no sense of security at all. They were underneath the world and reality felt suspended. Bullets couldn't stop shadows.

"This is worse than I imagined it would be," said Dax.

"No shit," said Jeff.

"Figures an animal like Jed McIntyre would make a lair in a place like this," said Dax. "I couldn't think of a better place for him."

"I can," said Jeff.

Dax turned around to look at Jeffrey but saw only a shadow behind him. "Here we go," he said after a moment, shining his light into an opening in the wall that led to pitch-nothingness. "Just where she said it would be."

A flight of metal stairs took them into a new layer of darkness where whatever brightness had carried in from the streets above was extinguished by a damp and utter black. The silence was so total that Jeffrey could hear his breath and Dax's, too. The stairs had led them to a narrow walkway, and at the end in the beam of Dax's flashlight they could see a metal door with no handle. Jeffrey felt like they were in a tomb. They approached the entrance and stood for a moment.

"What do we do?" said Jeffrey.

"We knock," said Dax, raising a big fist to the metal and banging hard.

Jetty Murphy reminded Lydia of nothing so much as Golem, the creature from The Hobbit that dwelled in darkness guarding his precious ring. Bent over and twisted like an old branch, he was so thin that his elbows looked like knobs and his collarbone stretched against his skin. His overlarge head seemed to bob on the end of his neck as if he didn't possess enough strength to support it. Black oily curls hung past his shoulders. He cupped his hands together over his mouth and his fingers were long and ghoulish, with nails bitten to the quick, his eyes black saucers set in gaunt features. He rocked on his haunches in the chair across from Ford. An armed guard stood by the door and Lydia stood beside him.

"Do you remember me, Jetty?" asked Ford. He'd seated himself across from Jetty and sat relaxed, leaning back in the chair. Lydia noticed how he'd molded the expression on his face to a look of benevolence, of understanding.

"Of course I remember you. I'm crazy, not stupid," Jetty said bitterly. He dropped his feet to the floor and pulled himself upright so that he was sitting with a straight back. He raised his chin in a gesture that seemed to mock dignity.

"It was a long time ago," said Ford gently, running his fingers along the edge of the table. "Even I have a hard time remember that far back. How long ago was it now?"

"Ten years or so," Jetty answered with a shrug. "What do you want?"

"Something's come up, Jetty. I think you can help me."

"Help you?" he said, laughing a little, as if such a thing were beyond imagining. But Lydia saw a brightening in his expression, like he had something someone wanted and it was a new feeling for him.

"I want you to remember that night for me again. Tell me again what you saw."

"What's in it for me?" he said, looking over at Lydia quickly and then back at Ford. "Can you make me a deal?"

He leaned forward quickly on the table and Lydia felt the guard twitch at her side.

"Sit back, Murphy," he barked at Jetty. His voice boomed off the cold walls and filled the room. Murphy jumped back as if he'd been shocked.

"It's okay," said Ford, looking at the guard. "Me and Jetty go way back. Right, Jetty?"

"That's right. Way back," said Jetty, relaxing and casting a smug smile at the guard.

"I can't make you a deal, Jetty. I won't lie to you. But I might be able to get you a few privileges, put in a good word at your next review. I'll tell you straight that you don't have to help me. But I'd really be grateful if you did."

Something about the way Ford had softened his voice to a conspiratorial whisper, the way he leaned in slightly toward Jetty, seemed to have an impact. Jetty looked less hopeless, a little less edgy. Lydia had to remind herself that she was looking at a rapist and a murderer, but it was hard not to have compassion for someone who just seemed so weak, so desperate. Ford lifted a bag that had been sitting by his feet filled with candy bars and a carton of cigarettes.

"I remembered that you used to have a sweet tooth, Jetty."

"We're not allowed to have that stuff here," he said, casting a sidelong glance at the guard and a longing look at the bag.

"I'm sure I could get them to bend a few rules if you help

me today, Jetty. What do you say?"

Jetty shrugged, trying and failing to look nonchalant. "What do you want to know?"

Ford took a Baby Ruth from the bag and slid it over to Jetty, who grabbed it up, ripped the wrapper off, and shoved it in his mouth in one movement. He pressed the bar into his mouth, chewing at it frantically, smearing chocolate on his face, as if he were afraid if he didn't eat it fast someone would snatch it from him. Lydia looked away. It was pathetic. She wondered what had to happen to a person in his life that he wound up here, like this.

Ford took a photograph from his pocket and slid it over to Jetty, waiting patiently for him to finish eating. When he was done, Jetty wiped his hands on his jumper, leaving long streaks of chocolate up his leg. He reached for the photograph and stared at it.

"It's a painting. But does this face look familiar to you?" asked Ford.

"Yeah...yeah. It's the man I saw that night. The one I told you about."

"Tell me again what you saw that night."

"I was behind this building looking through the garbage. I was a junkie then and I was always looking for something to sell, you know. I heard voices up above me...loud, scared. It sounded like two men and one woman." He was talking fast, the sugar making him hyper.

"Try to remember now, Jetty, did you hear anything that you could understand? Did you hear what they were saying?"

Jetty closed his eyes as if trying to transport himself back to that night.

"I heard the woman. I heard something she said."

Ford looked surprised. "You did? You didn't mention that ten years ago."

"Didn't I?" Jetty shrugged. Then, "You don't believe me?"

"Sure I do. What did she say?"

"She said, 'I don't love you. Not like that. I never did.' She screamed it. I mean, she was screaming her lungs out. And then another voice, said, 'You're lying. It's time to surrender.' He was yelling, too. That was all I could understand."

Lydia caught the word and remembered what Julian had said to Dr. Barnes, that she'd chosen to surrender.

Ford looked at Jetty and couldn't decide whether the guy was full of shit or not. Jetty had given a statement and testified in court ten years ago and had never mentioned those words before. But why would he be lying now?

"Then there was a, like...I don't know how to say other than it was like a roar. It was scary, man. I almost bolted, but there was a lot of good garbage. Then I didn't hear anything for a while except a sound that could have been the woman crying, like a low wailing. And then, when I thought it was over and started looking in the trash again, the back door of the building came slamming open and a giant man with long gray dreads, just like this," he said, lifting the picture, "came out. He turned, but I was behind the Dumpster, he didn't see me. It was dark, but I saw part of his face. Then he ran. I don't know why, but I followed him. But he just disappeared...he rounded the corner of Prince and Lafayette and he was gone. That's it. That's what I saw."

Ford was impressed that this man who was so fried from drugs and medication remembered anything at all. Except for the conversation he claimed to have overheard, the details of the story hadn't changed much in ten years, though Ford didn't remember Jetty telling him that he'd seen the man's face. He would have remembered that; they would have had a sketch done or something. As far as he knew, the man in the painting was a figment of Julian Ross's twisted imagination and Jetty was just embellishing his story to make himself feel important.

"And you're sure that this person in the photograph is the person you saw?" asked Ford.

"You wouldn't forget that face if you saw it," said Jetty, and Ford could see Jetty believed it to be the truth.

"You sure you didn't see anything else when you rounded the corner? Think back. A cab speeding off, a door closing... any hint of where he could have gone."

"There was a subway station."

"When we went down into that subway station, there was a metal gate. It was locked up. He couldn't have gone any farther."

"Well, that's not true. I know things now about those entrances that I didn't know then," said Jetty with a sly smile, tapping his foot rapidly on the floor. Lydia could see that some of his teeth were brown and jagged, some of them missing entirely.

"What's that?" asked Ford.

"People live down there, man. In the tunnels. The mole people."

"Give me a break, Jetty."

"No, for real. There's, like, a whole society under there... mainly psychos and junkies, but they're under there. They make whole, like, towns...with mayors and 'runners,' people who go topside for stuff. I'm not making this up. You can check it out for yourself."

"I'll do that," said Ford. He wasn't about to engage in an argument with a prisoner in a mental institution. It was a story he had heard before but never quite believed. The thought of people lurking beneath the ground, living their lives out there, was just too weird to be true. A lot of cops he knew believed it, but he'd never seen any evidence of it. Anyway, anybody who was willing to go down there to investigate the possibility had a screw loose, as far as he was concerned—Jeff and Dax included.

Jetty seemed to have fixated on Lydia after he finished talking. He couldn't take his eyes off of her and Ford couldn't blame him. It must have been a long time since he'd seen a woman like Lydia.

“I know you,” he said suddenly, pointing a bony finger at her, his mouth widening into a jagged grin.

“I don’t think so,” said Lydia with a polite smile.

“Yeah, I do,” he said, nodding vigorously. “You’re Jed McIntyre’s girlfriend.”

The sound of Dax knocking on the metal door reverberated on the concrete around them and sounded like thunder. Silence was the answer and the two of them stood holding their breaths, waiting. Jeff was half hoping that no one would respond to the knocking so that they could get the hell out of there.

After a moment, they heard a shuffling inside and then a thin tentative voice whispered, “Who?”

“Danielle sent us. She said you could help us find someone,” Dax answered, sounding as casual as if they were selling Girl Scout cookies door-to-door.

The door opened slowly and Dax and Jeff entered a small, tidy, warm space that was lit with hurricane lamps. The ceiling must have been sixteen feet high and the floor was actually carpeted. Large cushions and beanbag chairs were scattered about the floor, and a wooden table leaned against the far wall covered with a black crocheted tablecloth and topped with silk flowers in a blue and white vase, a chair on either side. A futon mattress was covered with sheets and quilts and plenty of pillows. A small refrigerator hummed in the corner and a kettle sat on top of a hot plate.

“There’s electricity here?” said Dax, incredulous, looking around him.

“Of course, young man. Just because we’re houseless doesn’t mean we’re uncivilized,” said the woman who let them in.

“Of course,” said Dax, throwing Jeff a look.

“My name’s Violet,” she said. Her voice sounded like coins dropped on tin, her white hair stuck out like wires.

Her eyes, sunken and misshapen, were an unnerving shade of violet, hence her name, Jeff imagined. And it only took a second to realize that her fixed stare meant she was blind. Short and round, with hunched shoulders and a shuffling gate, she took Jeff's hand as he and Dax introduced themselves with a strong confident grip. She wore a gray bathrobe over a pilled, stained green sweater and navy blue sweatpants. Her feet had been shoved into too-small black Chinese slippers. Using a cane to move across the room, she seated herself stiffly on a pile of cushions.

"Have a seat and tell me, what can I do for you boys?" Violet asked affably.

Jeff and Dax seated themselves across from the old woman and told her who they were looking for. Jeff wondered if it was impolite to point out at this time that he was unsure how a blind woman could help them to find Jed McIntyre.

"Just like topside, there is good and evil under here," the old woman said as she stared off at nothing. "The balance is the same, just some people up there hide themselves better. Down here, all pretenses have been dropped. The one you are looking for is down here. He's a different kind of bad."

"I don't want to be rude," said Dax, "but you're blind. How could you know that?"

"If anything, I'm at an advantage," she said. "You two stumbled through the tunnels, not used to the dark. I heard you coming ten minutes before you arrived. Darkness is my natural habitat. I've only got these lights on for visitors. Besides, I've been down here longer than most. People come to me for advice, with gossip. I know everything that goes on."

Jeff and Dax exchanged a look. Jeff's disbelief was palpable, but Dax shrugged. Jeff stared at the woman, who he thought looked a little bit like Yoda without the ears. He didn't question her sanity; he could tell by the way she spoke that she was as sound as either of them, educated, intelligent.

"Well, then...where is he?"

"I'll have to take you there myself. If you don't mind following behind an old blind woman," she said with a raspy noise that was somewhere between a cough and a giggle.

"And what do you want for your help?" asked Dax. In his experience, people like this never did anything for nothing. It was the way of the streets.

She cocked her head a bit. "Young man, I just want him out of the tunnels. People are afraid of him. The call him The Virus because that one's no good for anyone. No one's safe with him down here. People start coming after him, and we're all gonna be in trouble. It starts with you two, next thing you know it will be the police, the FBI. This hole," she said, waving her cane, "is the only place I have in the world. I lose this and I have nothing."

Dax nodded. "Well, let's go, then."

The three of them exited her nest and continued down the tunnel that had led them to her home. Violet led the way and Dax trailed behind them. The going was slow and the darkness and stench became less and less tolerable the deeper they got. The flashlight Dax carried created a narrow beam of light, but there were so many edges and corners it didn't illuminate that it didn't make the blackness any less menacing. After a while, Jeff lost track of the turns and stairways they had taken and said a silent prayer that this woman could be trusted enough to lead them back.

Though she walked with a limp and a cane, Violet didn't stumble and grope in the darkness as Dax and Jeff did, didn't seem startled by the sounds of rats or voices in the distance. She was home and they were not; she could see and they were blind.

"How did you wind up down here, Violet?" asked Jeff, after they'd been walking awhile. She'd pushed off the offer of his arm and lumbered up ahead of him. She sighed lightly as if she'd been expecting the question but was reluctant to answer it.

"How did you not wind up down here, Jeffrey?" she

asked in return. "There's no easy answer to that question, is there? How many decisions little and big did you make every day of your life, how many factors known and unknown to you, within and out of your control, led to your life being what it is today?"

"I never thought of it that way," he answered, chastened.

"Why would you? You don't seem like the kind of person that has a whole lot of reason to question your decisions... and maybe not a whole lot of time, even if you had reason. Me, I find that I have plenty of both. Reasons and time, that is," she said without bitterness, her voice little more than a whisper.

"So what did you come up with?" Jeff could sense Dax moving in closer to hear the answer.

"Short version: I was born blind, like I told you, in the late thirties. Part of a large Irish family living in a railroad flat in the East Village. I grew up, got married, was a teacher at the Helen Keller School for the Blind. My husband, Patrick, worked in the Bowery sweatshops making men's shirts. He handled all our finances and I trusted him to do it, even though he was a drunk and a gambler. I thought that all our lives we were putting money away for our old age. I had a pension, insurance. But when he died about ten years ago, I learned that he had drunk and gambled away every penny, even going so far as to take a loan against my pension. It was only a matter of months after his funeral that I was on the street."

"No family?" asked Dax.

"None I could turn to," she said quietly.

"But there have to be programs set up to help—" Jeff began.

Violet held up a crooked hand. "I won't live in a shelter or a hospital where they treat me like an invalid. I need my own space. This is not so bad...for a blind person. At least it's quiet. I got people who bring me everything I need, a comfortable place to sleep. I'm safer down here than I would be up there."

"I could help you, Violet," said Jeff. He thought of his own mother, who'd died five years back from pancreatic cancer surrounded by loved ones. If she had to die, he was happy she'd died like that, knowing that she was loved, that her life had meant something. He would rather have died himself than imagine her like Violet, living in a coffin.

"You're a nice boy," she said, not turning around to face him. "But I'm like one of those recidivists. You know, those guys in jail that bitch and moan about how bad they want out of prison. But then they get out and they don't even know what to do with themselves. They go right back. I don't think I could live another life."

"Well, you get in touch with me through Dax and Danielle if you change your mind. You help me get Jed McIntyre and I'll owe you my life," he said, putting a hand on her shoulder.

She shrugged him off. "I don't like to be touched," she said sternly.

"Sorry," answered Jeff, turning around to look at Dax, who lifted his hands with a grin. He pointed a finger to his temple and made a circle in the air mouthing, Crazy. Jeff shook his head.

"We're coming into Rain's territory now," she said. "Stay close to me and keep your mouths shut."

"Who's Rain?" asked Dax.

"Someone down here that you don't want to fuck with."

Dax gave a smug little laugh and Jeff checked the Glock at his waist.

"What did you say?" asked Lydia as the ground and the room around her seemed to disappear. She looked at the wretched man before her and he looked back with a lascivious leer. She wanted to leap across the room and strangle him, but she kept her place by the guard. The room suddenly felt hot and small and she wanted nothing more than to leave—except to know why this little psycho thought she was Jed McIntyre's girlfriend.

"What are you talking about, Jetty?" asked Ford, the sweet lulling tone he'd been using to coax information out of Jetty gone, cast off like a bad disguise. His voice was a fist poised to take care of Jetty's few remaining teeth.

Jetty turned to look at him in surprise, the smile he wore flickering into a worried frown. He looked sadly at the bag of candy and cigarettes that Ford still had under his hand.

"J-J-J-Jed," he stammered, "had pictures of her. He talked about her all the time. Said she was waiting for him to get out."

"When did you have the opportunity to talk to him?" asked Lydia, who had always imagined Jed like Hannibal Lecter, bound, isolated, with a mask over his face. At least that's how she liked to think of him.

"During art therapy," said Jetty quietly. "He only drew pictures of you."

Lydia had to suppress a laugh, even though there was nothing funny about any of it. The ridiculousness of allowing Jed to have

art therapy where he fed his obsession by drawing pictures of her was a testament to the idiocy of the psychiatric profession in general and this hospital in particular. No wonder he'd been allowed to get away. "You bastards," said Lydia under her breath.

"You said a bad word," admonished Jetty. Lydia shot him a look and he cringed as if he thought she'd strike him. She felt bad for a second. Then the feeling passed as another thought occurred to her.

"Jetty," she asked, moving toward him and sitting in the free chair beside Ford, "did you tell Jed McIntyre about the tunnels beneath the street?"

Jetty nodded. "He didn't believe me."

Ford looked at Lydia guiltily with a shake of his head.

"What?" she said, a frown creasing her forehead and dread burrowing what seemed to be a permanent home in her belly.

As they approached a rag tag group of men sitting around a lopsided card table playing poker by candlelight, Jeff decided that they had entered the twilight zone. They appeared to be playing for bottles and cans, using caps and metal tabs for chips. A few sacks filled with cans and bottles lay scattered on the floor around the table. Engaged in a loud, slurred argument over who had won the last hand, the card players did not acknowledge Violet, Dax, and Jeff as they passed until Dax accidentally shone the flashlight beam on their table.

"Hey, brother," barked a beefy guy with a red baseball cap. "Mind your own business."

Jeffrey braced himself for Dax to flip out but he just raised a hand in apology. "Sorry, mate."

They passed a row of tents that seemed to lean against each other and go on forever. They were lit from inside, and Jeff and Dax could see shadows moving within, heard the occasional voice. Jeff thought he caught the scent of meat cooking.

"Track rabbits," said Violet.

"Track rabbits?" said Dax with a grimace. "Dare I ask?"

"People down here are hungry. And the rats get pretty big," she said with a shrug. "It's not half bad. The concept is harder to swallow than the meat."

"That is fucking disgusting," said Dax.

"Spoken like someone who's never gone hungry," said Violet indignantly.

"Whatever," he said, not liking the old lady's attitude. Jeff rolled his eyes; Dax didn't even know how offensive he could be sometimes. But his honesty, even when it was inappropriate, was one of the things Jeff liked most about him. There was no artifice to Dax. He didn't give a shit what anyone thought, and that made him one of the most trustworthy people Jeff knew. Dax was just like Lydia in that way, which was probably why the two were always butting heads.

Jeff felt Dax's hand on his arm just before he noticed a tall form appear before them on the track, taking up the height and width of the tunnel. Violet seemed to hesitate for a second as though she had sensed something, but then she kept walking.

"There's someone ahead of us," whispered Jeff.

"I know."

Jeff heard Dax click the safety off his gun. As they drew closer, Jeff could see that there was a light source behind the form, creating a shadow that was much bigger than the man who waited in their path.

"You brought cops down here, Violet?" asked the shade, his voice deep and resonant. He stood about six feet tall and seemed to be draped in robes, but the light was dim and Jeff couldn't make out his clothes or his face. He just looked like a wraith, a dark shadow in a land of shadows.

Violet had instructed Dax to turn his flashlight off a while back and it didn't seem like a good idea to turn it back on, though Dax was itching to do so. But he had his hands full with his Magnum Desert Eagle, a nasty Israeli gun that had more stopping power than a freight train.

"They're not cops, Rain. They're friends of Danielle's."

There was a pause and then a deep, cruel laugh. "That crack ho doesn't have any friends."

"Yes, she does," said Dax, offended. He didn't like it when people insulted his friends, even if what they said was true.

They stood silent for a moment and Rain was so still that he looked as though he could fade into the black and be as gone as if he'd never been there at all.

“What do they want?” he asked finally.

“They’re here for The Virus.”

As they talked, Violet continued to move forward slowly toward Rain and she was dwarfed by his height and size. Jeff and Dax hung back, waiting to see how the standoff would go.

“We’re the cure,” said Dax, his voice quiet but resonating against the concrete.

Rain nodded but kept his ground. “And then what?”

“And then we leave and never come back,” said Jeffrey.

“And you never tell anyone that you came here.”

“Sounds like a deal.”

“Leave the body. We’ll take care of it. No one will ever find it.”

And with that he seemed to meld into the darkness and was gone. Jeff was left with a chill down his spine and a feeling of dread in his heart. They’d be murderers when this deed was done and he wasn’t sure that rested well with him, no matter the reason. It was justice, of that he had no doubt. It was whether they had the right to dispense it that worried him. He knew how Lydia felt about it; they tried to take care of it her way...the “right” way. They’d failed, and now Jed McIntyre was free, uncontained. And that was unacceptable to him.

The three of them started walking again in silence. He didn’t want to talk anymore, to just pretend the bizarre unreality of this made it all a bad dream. If he hadn’t been one hundred percent certain that he had no choice, they wouldn’t be here at all. As it was, he’d willingly trade his soul for the woman he loved and the child she carried in-side her.

TEN

"What are they thinking?" said Lydia at the wheel of Ford's Taurus, speeding back to New York City. Ford had let her have the keys because he knew her head was going to explode if she didn't have something to do on the way back to town. Now he regretted it as she pushed the old car beyond its limits, driving it as if it were her small tight Mercedes. Which it definitely was not. Ford heard an unfamiliar noise from the engine.

"Look...there's no point in overreacting and there's no point to racing back there," said Ford. "We should just proceed to Haunted as planned. They'll call when they're done."

"Done with what?" she asked. "Even if Jed McIntyre is lurking in the subway tunnels, what exactly do they plan to do?"

"That's not information I need to have. And you should just let it go, too. They're big boys, they can take care of themselves and anyone who tries to fuck with them. What are you going to do when we get there? Race into the tunnels and try to find them? Sit at your apartment, wringing your hands?"

Lydia pulled the car over to the side of the road and put her head on the wheel. He had a point. But her whole body was electrified with the need to get back to New York. What if something happened to them down there? The thought of Jeffrey crawling beneath the streets looking for Jed McIntyre made her sick with anxiety. How could he do this? Without telling her? When she knew he was okay, she was going to kill him.

Ford put a warm, callused hand on the back of her neck and she sat up, taking a deep breath. He had a kind, fatherly face, even if it was a little hard around the edges. She'd seen it change from warm to cold in under a second. Brown eyes communicated a depth and a sensitivity that Lydia found rarely in career cops, told her that he

still had a humanity and compassion that were often casualties of the job. A thin smile disappeared into deep creases around the corners. A seemingly permanent five o'clock shadow made him look a little tough, a little unkempt. He smelled of Old Spice and sesame chicken.

"Pull it together, girl," he said. "Let's go to Haunted."

She was about to agree with him when his cell phone rang. He removed it from the inside pocket of his lined beige raincoat.

"McKirdy," he answered. "Oh, yeah?" he said after a second, his eyebrows raising in interest. Another pause, then, "What do you mean, 'unusual'? He tapped an impatient finger against the dash. "Well, I'm more than an hour away."

He looked at his watch and then at the sun hanging low and white in the sky, the sky growing dim as night began to fall. "Okay. I'll be there as soon as I can."

"What's up?" she asked as he put the phone back into his pocket.

"Turns out there's a surveillance tape from the Ross building."

"Really? What's on it?"

"They can't tell. One of the junior detectives I got working with me says they can't make sense of what they're seeing. The camera was in the basement of the building, in the laundry room. They see something strange around two-thirty in the morning and then it goes black."

"Huh," said Lydia. "So...what?"

"So looks like it's back to NYC after all. Haunted will have to wait until tomorrow."

She pulled out onto the road and headed back toward the city. Relief and anxiety fought it out in Lydia's stomach. Part of her wanted to head toward Haunted and away from everything that was happening in her life, as if to lay distance between her and the possible outcomes of Dax and Jeffrey's mission were to make it less real. And the other part of her wanted desperately to be there, to be present, as if just being in the city would prevent the worst from happening. It was the helplessness that she couldn't handle, that tied her up inside, that caused a dull ache in her head. She gripped the wheel and forced her foot down on the gas. The car struggled in response, but she kept pushing as if going faster would speed up time.

"This is as far as I go," said Violet. "I'll wait here to take you back."

They stood at a point where two tunnels met. About a hundred yards away they could see in the beam of Dax's flashlight a metal staircase leading to a landing and a narrow catwalk that led to a door.

"Is he in there?" asked Dax.

"I know he lives just past this divide," she said. "I don't know if he's in there or not."

"Let's wait a bit," said Jeff to Dax. "Turn out the light and let's just see if there's any activity."

"Come on, man. Let's take this fucker. We've waited long

enough. I'm getting fucking claustrophobic down here," said Dax, cracking the tension out of his neck.

"There's no point in just busting in there if he's out and about. We'll just give ourselves away and lose our chance. Patience."

Dax turned out the light and Jeffrey motioned for him to follow as he made his way toward the staircase. Beneath the metal landing there was a narrow break in the wall that looked like it had once held an emergency phone. There was enough room for both of them to stand side by side. There they could see anyone coming from either direction and were just below the doorway.

Dax sighed and crouched down on the ground. He pulled the Magnum Desert Eagle from the holster at his shoulder and examined it, clicking off the safety. Jeffrey removed his new Glock from his waist. He'd never recovered the gun he'd lost in Albania a few months ago, and this one had never been fired off the range. He liked the semiautomatic and generally carried one, but it always seemed like a wild card compared to the revolver. Revolvers were workhorses, they never jammed; semiautomatics were less reliable but had more rounds.

He tried to get a feel for their situation, but it was as if being in the tunnels had dulled his senses. He had always believed as a young FBI agent that you knew when you were walking into a mess, when the house that was supposed to be deserted, wasn't; when a bust was going to go wrong; when a negotiation was about to fail. But he'd learned over the years that there was no way to tell how bad things were going to get, even if you had the instinct that things weren't going to go your way.

He leaned against the wall and ran his free hand through his hair, which was damp with sweat and the moisture in the dank air. He regretted walking out on Lydia without saying good-bye. He felt it now in the form of an ache in his solar plexus; it had been arrogant to assume he'd be back before she knew he was gone. He wasn't sure how much time had passed, or how long it would be before he saw her again. He would have strangled her if she tried to pull something like this over on him. The only comfort he had was in knowing she probably would have done the same thing.

"I heard something," said Dax.

"From where?" asked Jeff.

"From inside the door."

Jeff listened carefully in the darkness and then he, too, heard a shuffling from above them. "Let's move," he said quietly.

The metal staircase was surprisingly strong and didn't creak under their weight even slightly. They climbed carefully and then edged their way along the catwalk, backs flat against the wall. At the landing, Dax stood on the far side of the door examining the hinges. He was glad to see that the door opened in; it made for a much easier and more surprising entry. The heavy gray metal door had a latch for a padlock but was unlocked from the outside anyway. Dax touched it with his finger and it moved just slightly. It was open.

Jeff held up one hand and counted to three on his fingers, and before he'd reached go, Dax had pushed open the door with one hand and was moving in with his gun aimed in the other.

"Get down on the fucking floor," yelled Dax at no one, as Jeff followed him in, gun in one hand, flashlight in the other. His booming voice echoed against the walls.

The room was empty except for a large rat rustling through a Balducci's bag. The rodent looked up resentfully at the intrusion. Beside the bag lay a copy of Lydia's first book and a piece of notebook paper on the floor.

"Motherfuck," said Dax, feeling his face flush. He picked up the piece of paper and held it up for Jeff. It read, "You didn't really expect it to be that easy, did you?" Then he crumpled it in his fist and threw it against the wall. The rat moved past them slowly, unafraid.

"Looks like that game of 'Telephone' goes both ways," said Jeff, staying in the doorjamb in case someone was looking to surprise them from behind.

"He's slippery. I'll give him that," said Dax, trying to keep his voice light but unable to control the tight line of his mouth. Jeff saw the anger in his eyes, how it turned his normally affable face cold and hard.

"Let's get out of here," said Jeff, the walls suddenly closing in on him. He took a last glance at the room, shining the light onto the walls and up onto the ceiling. There was no other exit from the room. Jed was gone before they had arrived. Just as Jeff was about to turn around and leave, he caught sight of something on the wall...pieces of masking tape with shreds of paper stuck beneath. It looked as if something had been affixed there and then ripped from the wall in a hurry.

"What's that?" asked Dax.

"I don't know," Jeff answered, moving in to examine the pieces. He could see the edges of some type of drawing, but couldn't begin to make out what it might have been.

"Shit," he said, the frustration of Jed McIntyre slipping through their fingers raising his blood pressure.

As Dax and Jeff moved down the stairs, Jeff shone the flashlight over to where Violet had been standing, but he didn't see her there. He wanted to call out her name but thought better of it, not sure who was skulking in the darkness. He suppressed a feeling of panic when they rounded the corner and Violet was nowhere to be seen. They stopped and looked at each other.

"Oh, bloody hell," said Dax quietly, grabbing the flashlight from Jeff and shining it down into the tunnel they had come from. The light seemed like the tiniest thread in a field of black.

"Violet!" Dax yelled, his voice bouncing all over the tunnels. They were answered by a low laugh that seemed to come from everywhere. Then a giant form melted out of the tunnel walls and into the beam of their flashlight. It moved slowly toward them, seeming to glide rather than walk. Jeff and Dax held their ground with guns drawn.

"Freeze or I'll blow your fucking head off," yelled Jeff, in his best stop-'em-in-their-tracks voice, leveling the Glock against his target, though his heart was racing in his chest.

"This is no time for bravery, boys," came a voice behind them suddenly. "Run. Follow me."

The Midtown North Precinct was a circus of activity, phones ringing, perps yelling, civilians waiting to file police reports, as Lydia and Ford entered through the tall wooden front doors. The desk sergeant with a unibrow and a permanent scowl buzzed them through the gate. Both Lydia and Ford checked their weapons with the rookie who sat guarding the lockers. It was over warm in the precinct to combat the dropping temperature outside and a large, sloppily decorated Christmas tree wilted in the corner of the room. They were buzzed through another door and they began the climb up the stairs to the third floor to homicide.

The homicide office was dark and quiet in comparison to the cacophony that followed them up the stairs. Computer screens glowed green in the dim light and somewhere a phone was ringing. Lydia glanced at the window and noticed that the last moment of light had passed from the sky and it was officially dark, officially night, with no word from Jeffrey. She checked her cell phone again to see if she'd maybe missed a call. She fought a feeling of dismay that lingered, waiting to push its way through as soon as she let it. Walking toward the back of the offices behind Ford, she focused on the task at hand, knowing anything else was pointless.

Two men sat in the audiovisual room, which was really just an interrogation room where they kept a television, VCR, and tape cassette player on a metal cart that could be rolled out if the room was required for its original purpose.

"What have we got, guys?" said Ford, entering the room and shedding his raincoat. Lydia kept her cashmere coat on, wanting its warmth around her in the chill that had nothing to do with the temperature of the room. She sat at the table after being introduced to Detective Joe Piselli, a short, dark-haired man with girlishly long eyelashes, a bright smile, and a strong handshake, and Detective Al Malone, an awkward man with bad acne scarring and stooped shoulders. Neither of them looked older than twenty-five, and if they'd seen any kind of action at all, Lydia would have been surprised. They still had that bright and eager look in their eyes, the shine of idealism about the job they were doing.

"We've watched it over and over and we can't figure out what we're seeing," said Piselli as he walked over to the television. He pressed play, then fast-forward, and Ford took a seat beside Lydia.

The tape showed a row of ten washing machines that faced a row of dryers. The camera, which must have been mounted over the door, captured most of the large laundry room. The room was washed in a harsh fluorescent light and as the time-elapsed play progressed, a short, plump woman in a maid's uniform skittered in, threw in a load of wash, and left in under a second, her fast-forward movements making her look like a windup doll. She returned and changed the wash to the dryer a few minutes later.

"Can we speed this up?" said Ford impatiently. "It's a laundry room. If all you have is a bunch of people doing laundry—"

"Just a second—" said Malone. "There." He reached over and put the machine back to play. Lydia leaned in closer and saw the ghost of a movement, the edge of something that was just out of reach of the camera's lens. Then the screen went black.

"Is there another entrance to that room?" asked Lydia.

"Not that we saw," answered Piselli. "It's just that one

door. And the super says there's no other way in."

"How much of the room can you see on the tape?" asked Ford.

"I'd say about seventy-five percent. You can't see under the camera and the far back of the room. And apparently there's an area to the right of the camera that's out of range."

"So someone familiar with that could have come in the door and stayed to the right, out of range of the camera?" asked Lydia.

Piselli gave a nod and a shrug.

They rewound the tape and Lydia watched it again, leaning in close to the screen. The fluid nature of the movement and the faint pattern Lydia saw on second look made her think it was fabric.

"It's a hem," she said, putting her finger on the screen. Piselli rewound the tape again and they all leaned in. "It's the hem of a dress. See...it's a dark color with tiny hearts."

"So why would someone be skulking around the laundry room at two-thirty in the morning? And why would they be purposely staying out of range of the camera?" asked Ford, thinking aloud.

"It would have to be someone pretty small to be able to stay out of sight," said Malone.

"And how did the camera get turned off without our seeing who did it?" asked Piselli.

"So maybe it's down here where we'll find our missing murder weapon and Stratton's ring...not to mention his finger," said Ford.

"Well, we'll find something down there," said Lydia, getting up and moving toward the door. "Let's go."

"With a cure like you guys, who needs disease?" said Rain with a short disdainful laugh. "I thought you boys had an edge, were going to take care of the problem. Instead I have to save your sorry asses."

"What was that back there?"

He didn't answer, just kept moving on ahead of them. Rain was

an older man with smooth chocolate skin and a full white beard. His liquid eyes were clear and sober, but his face was etched with the lines of struggle and pain. Without the robes, he was just a stooped old man who walked with a limp. Most people didn't live to be his age in a place like this, and Jeffrey wondered what his story was but declined to ask. Ahead of them, he could see some kind of light; it looked like the glow from a street lamp shining through a grating. They couldn't get there fast enough as far as he was concerned.

"Now he's on the move and it will take time for us to locate him again," Rain went on. "You boys have made a mess down here."

"You didn't answer my question," said Dax testily. He'd just about had his fill of street people and their tirades.

"And I'm not going to," answered Rain, stopping and turning to Dax with a frown and a pointing finger.

"How did he know we were after him?" Jeff cut in.

"Someone tipped him off. I can't be sure who. But I'll find out and I'll deal with it, believe me."

"What are you, like the Mayor of the Tunnels or something?" asked Dax with a smirk.

"Something like that. I don't like your attitude, boy," said Rain. If Bill Cosby were dirty, very crabby, and lived below the streets of New York City, he'd look like Rain.

"What happened to Violet?" asked Jeff, moving between Dax and Rain.

"I don't know," he answered, looking away from Dax, concern darkening his features. He shoved his hands into the pockets of his pants and looked Jeff in the eye.

Then he turned, casting a warning glance in Dax's direction, and started walking again. Soon they stood at the opening in the wall that would lead them out the way they had come in, and Jeff had never been so happy to see a subway track in his life.

"Remember your promise," said Rain to Jeff, moving away from them.

"Wait a second. We didn't get what we came for."

"That's not my problem," he threw behind him as he continued on his way with a thug's saunter.

"I think it is," called Jeff. "All we have to do is tell the FBI that we know he's down here somewhere and they'll tear this place apart."

Rain stopped in his tracks and Dax smiled. "Won't be much of a mayor without your city, will you?" he said.

"What do you want from me?" he said, turning around. "Goddammit, I knew that one was going to be trouble the minute I heard about him."

"Then why didn't you take care of it yourself?" asked Jeff.

"Because that's the code down here, man. Everybody gets a chance to be a part of this community. Up there, they're losers—drug addicts, prostitutes, criminals, nuts. They got nothing and no one to give them respect. Down here, there's a place for everyone, as long as you obey the rules, don't hurt nobody, and don't ever talk to the police or anyone topside about what goes on down here."

"This man is a murderer, Rain," said Jeff. "He's going to hurt more people. All we want is a line on him and we'll take care of the rest. When you know where he is, let us know. That's all we ask."

"And you're gonna take care of it? Like you did today?"

"You have a week," said Dax. "If we don't hear from you, we come down here with the Feds and you can kiss your little kingdom good-bye. You'll be in a shelter or a nuthouse or wherever it is that you belong."

Jeff shot Dax a look that was lost on him in the darkness and probably would have been anyway. They had different ways of dealing with people. Jeff believed that all people, regardless of their circumstances, deserved to be treated with respect until they proved themselves unworthy. Dax felt exactly the opposite. Dax was fiercely loyal to a few people and everyone else could just go to hell as far as he was concerned.

"Look," said Jeff, hoping to soften the blow of Dax's words—but Rain was walking away. "Rain, let's talk about this."

"Don't worry about it," said Dax, moving through the opening and stepping onto the comparatively bright track on the other side. "He'll get in touch with us."

"Fuck," said Jeff, watching the only lead he had on Jed McIntyre disappear into the darkness of the tunnels.

"Trust me, mate," said Dax with the winning smile that always made Jeff forget what an asshole and a wild card he could be. "I know these people. If he'd promised to get in touch with us, then I'd be worried. Let's get topside so we can call Lydia. She's going to kick your ass back fifty feet underground. And I want to be there to see it."

ELEVEN

There were few things Lydia hated more than arguing in front of other people. She hated the feel of eyes on her at the best of times but least of all when she was angry and vulnerable. People were judgmental and she didn't want the baggage of someone else's energy in her personal life. It was for this reason and this reason alone that she kept her voice light and measured as she spoke to Jeffrey on her cell phone. Her whole body had felt electrified with relief when she'd seen his number on her caller ID. When the relief drained her, anger and dread filled her back up.

"Hi," she'd answered. She was conscious of Ford sitting next to her and Detectives Piselli and Malone riding in the backseat. In the dark silence of the car all ears were on her.

"Hey, how's it going?" he said, voice tentative, guilty. The line crackled and he sounded like he was on the moon. And he might as well be, for as close as she felt to him right now.

"Fine. What's happening with you?" Her voice lilted, but the words felt like rocks in her throat.

"Not much," he lied. "Are you with Ford?"

"Yeah. Are you with Dax?"

"Yeah. Can we meet up with you guys?"

"Sure. We're heading over to the Ross building. We saw something on a surveillance tape and we're going to check it out. Meet us in the laundry room."

"The laundry room?"

She tried a joke, but it came out sounding harsh and angry. "Is there an echo in here?" She never was any good at hiding her emotions.

"You're pissed," he said.

"Why would I be?" Her voice sounded crisp and sarcastic even to her own ears, and she saw Ford turn to look at her out of the corner of her eye.

"We have a lot to talk about later."

She let his words hang in the air, tried to tell from his tone how things had gone.

"Is it settled?" she asked finally. There was a pause during which the specter of hope that had been lurking beneath the negative emotions swirling inside her faded and was lost.

"No. It's not."

"I'll see you in a bit."

"Lydia—"

But she hung up. She wasn't really angry at Jeffrey. She wasn't really angry. She was scared and tired. But anger was always easier to deal with because anger was power. Anger made you do something, made you act. Anger made you strong. Fear made you weak, made you cower, made you a victim. And that was just not acceptable to Lydia. It just wasn't an option at all.

"Everything all right?" Ford asked as if he were sticking his hand into the lion's cage at the Bronx Zoo.

She didn't even know how to answer that question anymore. So she just nodded and looked out the window as they pulled up to the building on Park Avenue.

"Hardly anybody ever uses this laundry room, you know," said the doorman as he took them down in the service elevator. His Yonkers accent was thick and he seemed out of place in the maroon tails with gold piping on the cuffs and collar that were the uniform for the building. It was probably the only suit he owned and even this was too short in the legs and wrinkled. He was affable and a little on the goofy side and his name was Anthony Donofrio.

"These people got the cash, you know," he said, quickly rubbing the fingers on his right hand together. He smiled, revealing crooked, yellowing teeth. "Most of them have washers and dryers in their apartments. Some of the old-timers, too cheap to buy their own, still come down here. But mostly the maids and nannies, if they have more than one load to do, they run down here to save time. I got the monitor in the office behind the front desk and I can count on the fingers of one hand the times I seen the actual tenant down there. But I work the night shift, mostly."

Ford could tell that Anthony was enjoying this a little bit. Ever since those cop shows had started to make it big on prime time television, people were a lot more cooperative. They felt like they were part of something when the police came to ask questions—unless, of course, they had something to hide. Anthony Donofrio impressed Ford as the kind of guy who visited his mother, had a hard time with the ladies, and still hung out with the same guys he went to grade school with. If he had something to hide, maybe it was that he jerked off every night with a copy of Hustler. And who didn't?

"So how did the camera get turned off that night, Anthony?" asked Ford, taking out his notepad.

"I don't know," he said with an exaggerated shrug. His eyes were wide and innocent, but Ford saw it. A quick shift of the pupils. "I never noticed it go off. Only when you guys looked at the tape did they find that it had been turned off and back on."

Ford didn't say anything for a minute, just looked down at his pad as if deep in thought. He let the silence grow thick and uncomfortable between them.

"Yeah, I don't know," Anthony said again, this time with a nervous chuckle. Ford cocked his head to one side and gave Anthony a thoughtful frown. Suddenly he sensed Anthony wasn't enjoying himself as much anymore.

"That's the only place where the camera could be turned off, from behind your desk?"

Again the shift, and an uncomfortable stepping from side to side.

"Uh, yeah, behind the front desk."

"Did you leave your post at any time? To take a leak or take a smoke—whatever?"

Anthony looked down at his feet and was quiet for a minute.

"Yeah, maybe," Anthony said. "Yeah."

"What was it?"

"A leak, I guess."

"You guess?"

"Hey," he said, moving in close to Ford and giving a quick look around him. "I'm not supposed to take breaks. I could lose my job."

"Anthony," said Ford. "You're not straight with me and your job's gonna be the least of your worries, man."

Anthony let out a long slow exhale and shook his head. "Every so often," he said, with his eyes down, "I'd, you know, step outside for a smoke."

"So the equipment was left unattended a number of times throughout the night. Someone could have walked in, turned it off, and turned it back on while you were outside?"

"I guess. Yeah, its possible."

Ford gave a hard look at Anthony. Maybe he had more to hide than that Hustler after all. "What else, Anthony? If there's something you're holding back, now's the time to let it out."

"No, that's it. I swear," he said, casting an earnest look at Ford.

Ford nodded but gave Anthony eyes that said he wasn't a hundred percent convinced that they were finished talking.

"Listen," Anthony said, lowering his voice. "I really need this job."

"You probably should have thought about that before, huh, Anthony?"

The laundry room looked like every other laundry room Ford'd ever seen—fluorescent lights, cinderblock walls painted a light gray, Formica floors. The scent of detergent and that unmistakable smell that comes from dryer vents was heavy in the air. Only one dryer rumbled and through the glass Ford could see rose-colored sheets and blue and white towels tumbling. A bulletin board held building announcements, a page printed from a computer printer offering babysitting services and some inspection documents. The room looked clean, innocuous. That would change. He looked at his watch; forensics should be joining them any moment.

"Nobody touch anything," he reminded Lydia and the other detectives.

"It's a laundry room, Ford. This place'll be covered with prints. You gonna have everyone authorized to use this room fingerprinted so that we can compare?" asked Piselli.

"Hey, you volunteering to head that up?" said Ford with a scowl. Piselli rolled his eyes.

"Fucking rookies been on the job less than five years and they think they know everything. It's not out of the question. Not easy, but not out of the question."

Lydia looked around the room. It felt like a dead end; there was nothing to see but washers and dryers, bland walls, white floors.

"How often is this room cleaned?" she asked.

"Maintenance comes in here once a week to dust and

mop the floors," Anthony answered, pleased to be helpful.

"Have they been here since Richard Stratton was murdered?"

"No, they come on Fridays—day after tomorrow."

Lydia walked along the edge of the dryers, tracing the path that the person caught in the video camera must have taken. She walked to the end of the row where there was a small space between the last dryer and the wall. Here she dropped to the floor and peered under the dryer.

Ford walked over to her. "What do you see?"

"I'm not sure," she said, standing up and wiping the dust from her nose. "We need to move the dryer." Piselli and Malone removed surgical gloves from their pockets and easily slid the dryer forward. The four of them crowded in to peer behind the dryer.

"Well, will you look at that," said Malone.

"What's going on?" asked Jeff as he and Dax walked into the room.

"Christ, you two smell like a couple of sewer rats," said Ford when they got closer.

"It's a trapdoor," said Lydia, not looking up at Dax and Jeff. She was too fascinated by their find. And besides, she hated both of them at the moment.

"Yeah. But leading where?" asked Piselli as if he didn't really want to know.

It was a wooden door with a wrought-iron ring for a handle. It appeared to have been nailed and painted shut at some point, the Formica laid over it. But the flooring had been cut away, the nails had been pried out, and the paint chipped through around the edges. Ford moved in and lifted the lid. A ladder led down into a pitch-black hole. A foul dank odor of mold and rot wafted from the darkness. It was a smell that Dax and Jeff recognized all too well.

"Just when I thought I was out, they pull me back in," said Dax in a bad impression of Al Pacino. Nobody laughed.

TWELVE

It's the dark spaces, the secret passageways, the hidden doorways that the demons use to enter your life and rip it to pieces. It's where the light doesn't shine that they dwell and breed like bacteria in a warm, moist wound. The hole in the floor they'd discovered opened a similar blackness within Lydia. Someone had crept through this trapdoor in the floor to visit death on Richard Stratton and horror onto Julian Ross. Julian's bogeyman, her worst nightmare, was alive and well and moving with stealth beneath the city streets. So was Lydia's. She was more kindred to Julian than she had imagined and wondered how far she was from sharing Julian's fate.

When Lydia had faced Jed McIntyre in the flesh, she felt sure that she would burst into flames. He had always been a ghost in her life, shadowing any peaceful moments, growing large in times of pain and sadness, and, in many ways, the reason behind most of her drive. If he hadn't murdered her mother, she wasn't sure she'd even be the person she was today. Certainly the pain that had always impelled her to understand the minds of madmen—her hopeless and relentless effort to pick up the pieces they left behind them, sort them, name them, make them understandable—had been visited upon her by Jed McIntyre. But actually, he had become almost theoretical. He was the face of fear, of pain, evil, grief. He was every murderer, every sin. And in being all these things he had become over the years a concept rather than a man. To see him real and alive, breathing, flesh and blood, had felt to Lydia like the animation of her darkest, most secret inner fears. To imagine him lurking, shadowing the edges of her life like a wraith, was too much for her mind to absorb. A sad numbness had wrapped itself around her. And every day he was at large, it pulled itself tighter and she was starting to suffocate, finding it hard to draw a breath.

The hole yawned beneath her and everyone around her had disappeared. She felt like she was standing at the gates of hell, about to be pulled from the solid earth into a place of misery. And its pull was almost magnetic.

"Lydia." She heard Jeffrey's voice as if through glass. She felt his hand on her shoulder and she spun around to face him.

"Easy, tiger," he said with a smile, and the world came rushing back. "Are you okay?"

"Why is everybody always asking me that?" she snapped, walking away past them and out of the room into the cool gray basement hallway. She leaned against the wall and rested her head against the stone wall. The pain throbbed again in her side. Slight but definitely not a good thing. She put her head in her hands and rubbed her eyes. When she looked up again, Jeffrey was standing before her.

If Jed McIntyre was the embodiment of all things ugly, wrong, and bad in the universe, then Jeffrey was all things good. Since the night they met, he had always been to her something just shy of a superhero. When he'd nearly been killed after taking a bullet in pursuit of a child killer on a Bronx rooftop, she realized he was just a man. But instead of that making him seem less to her, it had made him more precious. It had also allowed her childhood feeling of hero-worship for him to mature into love. Part of her still believed that he was faster than a speeding bullet, able to leap tall buildings in a single bound. Part of her would always believe that.

"We're going home," he said.

"What? No. I want to see where the doorway leads."

"Dax will stay. He'll call with any developments."

"But—" she protested. It sounded weak even to her own ears.

She let him put his arm around her shoulder and lead her toward the elevator. She leaned into him, accepting the warmth and comfort that washed over her. She was going to kick his ass, for acting like a vigilante, for scaring the life out of her, for just being a cowboy. But that could wait a little while.

Her head was twisted unnaturally to the right, her eyes were wide, and her mouth had frozen in a circle of surprise and fear. Her arms were flailed out to her sides and her legs were bent as though she were jumping for joy. Her eyes seemed to glow even in the darkness. Lying there on the cold dirty ground, she looked as though life had just left her, discarded her as if she'd never been worthy of drawing breath.

Rain stood over Violet's body and was sorry. Sorry that she'd led such a hard life and sorry that it had ended in such an ugly way. Some people had heard him scream in anger when he found her body lying broken and bleeding not far from where The Virus lived—or had lived. He could hear them now, shuffling up behind him, gasping as they saw Violet on the ground. Someone started to cry, but mostly they were silent. Tragedy struck here almost every day; people didn't live long lives in the tunnels. No one was surprised to stumble upon a dead body.

They came to call him Rain because of a line that De

Niro said in Taxi Driver. "Thank God for the rain to wash the trash off the sidewalks." He'd done that in a small way down here, he knew that. People depended on him because they needed order. Even in this place, people wanted to feel safe.

He felt them crowding in behind him and knew they were waiting for him to say something, to make it okay somehow. But he was momentarily at a loss for words. He'd depended on Violet as much as anyone else down here had, for motherly advice, encouragement, or just a sounding board. And now that she was gone, he felt true grief. More grief, in fact, than when his own mother, a junkie and a whore, had died what seemed like a lifetime ago. He fought tears, kept his back turned to those that had gathered around him and Violet.

He blamed himself for this. He should have taken care of the problem right away. Now they were all in trouble. Whether it was The Virus or the cure, they were in danger of having the world they created exposed and shattered. To hell with the "rules." Who were they kidding anyway? There were no rules down here. It was as lawless a place as existed on earth.

He turned to the people that gathered behind him and felt their eyes on him.

"We'll find who did this," he said, his voice deep and resonating with conviction. There was a murmured noise of agreement. Rain thought of Dax Chicago and Jeffrey Mark and the threat they made. He shrugged inside. If you can't beat 'em, join 'em.

THIRTEEN

The silence between them was heavy as Lydia lay on the couch staring up at the ceiling and Jeff made a salad in the kitchen while they waited for their pizza to arrive. From where he stood at the counter, he could see into the sunken living room and he watched Lydia idly twirling a strand of blue-black hair, looking up at the tiny halogen track lights that ran the length of their Great Jones Street loft. He wondered, as he tossed tomatoes, avocado, onions, and cilantro over baby greens, what was going on in that head of hers. They'd hopped a cab home and had been skirting the events of the day, agreeing on dinner and saying little else.

Lit by the orange glow of three pendant lamps hanging over the black granite island, the terra-cotta tile floor, the wood cabinets with their stainless steel fixtures, the kitchen was a warm and cozy room. Like everything in the apartment they had designed it together, paying attention to every detail of the home they would share. When they bought the duplex last year, they got rid of most of their old furniture and belongings, keeping only what meant most to them.

"New beginnings demand new objects," Lydia had declared. And Jeffrey had agreed. He'd never developed attachments to things anyway. He'd never had much of a home life, so he'd never spent much time on the East Village apartment he'd owned since he left the FBI. He'd started his private investigation firm from there, sleeping on a pullout couch in the back bedroom. In all the years he'd lived there, his apartment had remained almost empty of furniture. He found the only possessions that meant anything to him were his mother's engagement ring, his father's old service revolver, and a closetful of designer clothes.

Lydia's apartment on Central Park West had looked like it belonged on the cover of House Beautiful. Sleek, modern, impeccably decorated, but, Jeffrey thought, totally cold and impersonal. "You live in someone's idea of the most gorgeous New York apartment," he'd commented once. She'd sold it as is, furniture and all, to some software designer, just months before the dotcom bomb. Jeffrey sold his apartment, too, throwing in the pullout couch and rickety kitchen table and chairs. They both made a killing and then bought the three-bedroom duplex.

A metal door with three locks opened from Great Jones Street into a plain white elevator bank. A real Old New York industrial elevator with heavy metal doors and hinged grating lifted directly into the two-thousand-square-foot space. By New York standards it was palatial. The cost was exorbitant, of course, as it was New York City ultra-chic, shabby-cool. But Lydia had declared it home the minute they stepped off the elevator onto the bleached wood floors. The private roof garden, which was at least a story higher than most of the other downtown buildings, sealed the deal. From the garden, they could see the whole city. At night it was laid out around them like a blanket of stars, which was a good thing, since you can't see many actual stars in New York City. Now it was home, the place in the world they shared.

"So," he said, putting the salad on the table and walking

over to her. "How did you figure out where we were? Ford told you?"

"Not exactly," she said, looking at him. He lifted her feet and sat on the end of the couch, placing them on his lap. She told him about their interview with Jetty, what he'd told her.

"Ford just looked so white, so guilty when Jetty mentioned the tunnels, that it just clicked for me that's where you were. I can't believe you guys took off on me like that. How could you, Jeffrey?"

He shrugged and looked over at her. "I didn't see another way. Would you have been okay with it? With us going down there?"

"Hell, no. You were insane to do that. What if something happened to you down there? I should have been with you."

"Exactly my point," he said, his blood pressure rising at her stubbornness. "You're pregnant. Will you get that through your thick head?"

"I'm pregnant," she said, pulling her feet from his lap and sitting up. "I'm not made of glass." They regarded each other for a moment and then she said, "Fine. You shouldn't have gone down there, either. You should have let Dax go. Or called the FBI. But you shouldn't have gone off like that, not even telling me anything. It's not fair."

He nodded. She was right and he was sorry he'd frightened her. But he couldn't say he wouldn't have done it the same way again. So he said nothing at all, just looked down at the floor.

"I mean, what were you going to do when you found him? Bring him in?"

Again, there was nothing he could say. They both knew he and Dax had had no intention of cuffing Jed McIntyre and putting him back into custody. It was as if, because he'd managed to escape once, Jeff would never be able to sleep again until Jed McIntyre was dead. As long as he lived, Lydia would be in danger. And Jeffrey just couldn't live with that.

"No matter how you look at it, Jeff, it's murder. Are you a murderer?"

The word sounded as harsh and as ugly as it was and something inside him lurched. He looked at her face and she was pale and drawn. Her eyes shone with a wetness that licked at her lower lashes. That word on her lips felt like an indictment and he felt a sick shame inside.

"Not yet," he answered, not meaning it to sound as glib as it did.

She looked at him with an expression that was somewhere between worry and disappointment. The buzzer rang and Jeff got up to answer it. "Who is it?" he called, depressing the talk button.

"It's me," came Dax's unmistakable voice. "And I've got a pizza here. Though I don't know what you two are gonna eat."

"The tunnel went down about twelve feet, then out another two hundred, and then split into three separate passages. It's going to take a couple of men and a lot of man-hours to follow each of them and see where they lead. Not a fun job, as you well know," said Dax between gigantic bites of pizza. Lydia counted, and it took him a total of four mouthfuls to finish one slice. Jeff had called to order another after Dax polished off three pieces in under ten minutes. "And there was no bloody way I was going down there again. Not after our little adventure today."

"So why don't you tell me about this little adventure?" said Lydia, looking at Jeff. "I never did get to hear all the details."

"It was bloody awful," said Dax. He ran down the highlights as Lydia watched him, eyes wide. She managed to nibble at her salad a little as he talked, but she'd lost her appetite. She'd been ravenous just minutes before Dax arrived.

"If I didn't know better, I'd say you two were full of

shit," said Lydia, when he'd finished. "Did this Rain ever tell you who you saw down there?"

"No," said Jeff, remembering the specter that had seemed to melt from the tunnel walls.

"I can't believe people live like that," said Dax, as though he resided in a clapboard house with a white picket fence, two kids, and a dog.

"It seems like there's more than one gator in the sewers," said Jeffrey, thinking about how strange it was that the tunnels beneath New York City held Jed McIntyre and possibly some of the answers to the Ross case, as well.

"So now we know how someone else could have gotten into the building the night Richard Stratton was murdered," said Lydia, shifting the pieces around in her head.

"Yes and no," said Dax.

"Right," answered Jeff, knowing where he was going. "Someone from the inside had to move the dryer, otherwise whoever wanted in couldn't open the trapdoor."

"So it had to have been either Julian or Eleanor on the tape," said Dax.

"I'm not so sure about that," said Lydia as though she'd already given it some thought. "The person who snuck in there had to be really small to avoid the camera. And someone else had to turn it off from behind the desk upstairs. If the camera was still on, it would have captured the dryer being slid forward."

"So two people, then?"

"Definitely two people."

"Eleanor and Julian in on it?" said Dax.

"Or maybe—" said Jeff, looking at Lydia.

She finished his sentence. "The twins."

Sometimes in love, arguments are better dropped. No resolution is in the offing and to continue belaboring the point inevitably causes more damage than understanding.

Lydia and Jeffrey had allowed their disagreement to come to bed with them, and though Jeffrey slept soundly, Lydia lay awake staring at a small water stain that had just made its debut in the ceiling above them.

After Dax left, they'd tried to continue the discussion they'd been having before he arrived. But there was no understanding to be reached. Jeffrey apologized for frightening her, but that's as far as he went, leaving Lydia with the uneasy feeling that if the opportunity presented itself, he'd do it again. She looked over at his sleeping form and felt an odd distance from him. She felt angry at him, and helpless. She quashed the urge to nudge him awake and fight with him until she felt better.

She was conscious of the street noise from Lafayette below them, cars speeding, the general hum that was a million conversations, electricity through wires, trains rushing through tunnels, whatever combination of myriad sounds. She'd never imagined the parallel universe that existed beneath them. Naturally, she'd heard the stories somewhere in the periphery of her consciousness. But it had never seemed real to her. Now she had to contend with the idea of a netherworld just a few feet beneath her, like the first layer of hell where her nightmare—and Julian Ross's as well—stalked. The thought made her shiver.

The hem she'd seen in the video, a dark color patterned with little white hearts, had impressed her as something a child would wear. That was how it came to her mind that possibly the twins had let someone into the building. It seemed a little far-fetched, after she'd thought about it, but not out of the question. The how and why would take some figuring out. She'd see Eleanor and the twins tomorrow. Ford had said he'd work on a warrant to search the children's rooms and find the nightgown. He couldn't remember what the little girl had been wearing the night their father was killed. He'd promised to think about it and swing by in the morning to take Lydia up to Haunted.

She thought about getting up and searching the Internet for more information on Haunted. But she felt sleep tugging at the back of her eyes and the thought of putting her bare feet on the cold wood floor beneath her was enough to deter her. She shifted to her side and moved in closer to Jeffrey, his body heat a magnet she couldn't resist. She closed her eyes and curled up tighter beneath the covers. She hadn't felt the pain in her side again since earlier in the evening and she'd done a good job convincing herself it was gas or something. She closed her eyes and sleep came for her.

It took her off into a warm blackness. She dreamed that she was on a tiny wooden rowboat with only one oar. In a narrow stone tunnel, the current of a bloodred river swept the boat along and she had to hold the sides to steady herself. All around her she could hear screams, but she saw nothing except the walls of the tunnel and the river beneath her. She placed a finger in the water and pulled it back to find her hand dripping with blood. And at the sight of it, she was torn with the ache of a loss so profound that she felt she might die from it. She didn't know what was gone, only that it had been so precious and she so unworthy. And then there was the mocking laughter of madmen, echoing against the walls. It surrounded her and she couldn't be sure whether she was moving toward its source or away.

FOURTEEN

Haunted, New York, was every bit as bleak and even uglier than Lydia had imagined it would be. The gray sky seemed committed to gloom and the trees here had already shed their leaves. Winter branches reached gnarled and high and the ground looked as cold and dead as a grave. Even the weathered and beaten old sign that read welcome to haunted looked as though the sun had never shone on it. Someone had spray-painted run while you can across the top. Lydia wondered if anyone would bother to repaint or replace it.

Lydia sat in the front seat beside Ford, with Jeff in the back of the old Taurus.

"Ford, why don't you get a new car? This is a piece of shit," said Lydia when he had picked them up on Great Jones Street a few hours earlier. In spite of a restless sleep, she was feeling stronger than she had last night. The daylight made the events of yesterday seem surreal and far away. And she left them there, temporarily putting Jed McIntyre out of her mind.

"I take offense at that. Just because something looks

like shit doesn't mean it is shit," he replied, looking in the rearview mirror and tamping down an errant hair as they climbed into the car. "Meanwhile, I'm lucky it's running at all the way you drove it yesterday. I'm surprised the engine didn't fall out."

"You let her drive?" asked Jeff. "You shouldn't let her drive when she's angry."

"I'm a very good driver," said Lydia indignantly.

"Yeah, I'm sure that's what the monster truckers think, too."

She gave him a look to let him know he was still on her shit list and would be there until further notice.

"So, what happened last night?" she said, turning to Ford.

"Not much after you left. Forensics showed up, did their thing...obviously, there were a lot of different prints, fibers, hairs down there. No way to know if any of it will mean anything. However, no prints on the ladder rungs or on the door handle. Wiped clean. We got men down in the tunnels seeing where they lead. At least we know now that someone could have gotten into the building without anyone seeing. That's good news for Julian Ross. Of course, it raises a lot more questions for us."

"What about blood evidence?"

"Nothing visible. We're going to do some Luminol later tonight. So we'll see. Meanwhile, Eleanor Ross is expecting us at four, says we can speak to the twins then...with her lawyer present, of course."

"Of course," said Lydia and Jeffrey in unison, exchanging a look in the sideview mirror.

"I didn't tell her about the warrants I'd be bringing to search their belongings at the apartment and at the hotel. I gotta admit, though, Lydia, it seems a little crazy to think those kids had anything to do with it."

"Stranger things have happened. People use kids as pawns in all kinds of games. Some sicker than others."

She could think of a number of cases she'd come across where children had committed or been used in the commission of heinous crimes. Roger Jeffers, a middle-aged New Orleans tax attorney, used his ten-year-old son to lure other young boys out of community pools and parks, then made him watch while he sodomized and then murdered them. Even the Cheerleader Murders case, the first that Jeffrey and Lydia worked together, had involved a teenage girl. Fifteen-year-old Wanda Jane Felix, who'd been tormented and humiliated by the victims, helped her mother to abduct and mutilate the girls in retaliation...though Mrs. Felix had done the actual murders. Then there was twelve-year-old Randy Crabtree, who sold raffle tickets door-to-door to raise funds for his school soccer team. When one eleven-year-old boy who was home alone claimed not to have a dollar to buy a ticket, Randy forced his way into the house and beat the child to death with a coaxial cable. Kids, they were growing up so fast these days under the careful tutelage of sick adults. True, the twins were young. But they were old enough to follow orders. Children made loyal and diligent little soldiers, eager to please, their only knowledge of right from wrong hand-fed to them. Okay to murder, bad to tell anyone about it.

They pulled off the smaller highway that they'd been on since they'd exited the Interstate and followed the signs to Main Street. Unlike some upstate New York towns that prided themselves on their quaint, gentrified downtown areas lined with pretty, well-kept buildings, sweet cafés, and trendy boutiques, Haunted looked as though someone had dumped it on the side of the road in the seventies and forgot to come back and pick it up. It wasn't dilapidated as much as it appeared to be the victim of determined and persistent apathy.

The Taurus cruised up a street riven with potholes. An old woman hobbled along the sidewalk and took a turn into a bakery that didn't have a name-bearing sign. The word bakery was painted in a fading baby blue on the storefront window. There was a hardware store and a barbershop, complete with the requisite red, white, and blue pole beside the door. The Rusty Penny was a diner that from the street looked utterly empty except for a bored-looking waitress reading a paperback at the counter. All the buildings were painted the same slate gray and seemed to blend into the sky around them. Some hardened and brown snow edged the sidewalk, though most of yesterday's snowfall seemed to have melted away. They stopped at a light, though there was no other traffic except a decrepit red Chevy pickup behind them. It felt like they waited an inordinately long amount of time before the light changed again.

"Cheerful little burg," said Ford. "Where should we start?"

"Let's find the library," said Lydia. "Drop me off there, then you and Jeff can go off and talk to the local police. See if anyone from 1965 is still around and willing to talk."

"Sounds like a plan."

The librarian at the Haunted Public Library was as leathery and dusty as an old unabridged dictionary. Directed there by a gas station attendant who looked like he was high on something, they'd found it about ten minutes north of Main Street. As luck would have it, the local police station was just a quarter of a mile down the same road, visible from the parking lot of the converted old Protestant church-cum-library. Lydia would have expected to be treated with distrust and suspicion in a small backward town like Haunted; anyway that's what she'd always heard about small towns. But the few residents they'd encountered, the kid at the gas station, the waitress at the Rusty Penny where they'd stopped to pick up some truly vile coffee, had seemed to barely register their existence. In fact, they seemed to barely register their own existences. The librarian was another story.

Lydia had been inside a few small town libraries. She'd expected a few shelves of bestsellers, some back issues of Reader's Digest, and the archives of the local paper. She'd expected a gray institutional place with faux-wood shelving and bad carpet, fluorescent lights and the sour smell of apple juice spilled during a particularly riotous story hour. What she found was a musty old place, dimly lit. A heavy oak information desk with a gold-plated sign reading welcome to haunted public library, marilyn e. woods, head librarian seemed to act as a sentry against entering. Two banker's lamps with rich green glass shades sat atop the desk, casting a warm yellow light. Behind the desk, Lydia could see row after row of richly varnished oak shelving, stacked high with what looked like leather-bound volumes with gilt-edged pages. A staircase led to a gated loft, where more volumes could be seen behind glass. Off to the right was a cozy sitting area, where red brocade overstuffed chairs stood imperiously beside a long table the same varnished oak as the shelves. It was the kind of library Lydia would have expected to see at an Ivy League university or in some Gothic mansion.

"Can I help you?"

Marilyn E. Woods looked as though she had been born to be a librarian. She was a tiny woman, frail about the shoulders but with a long, graceful neck. Her graying hair flowed in thick curls down her back, a few strands pulled back from her face with a barrette. Her skin was as pale as moonlight. Wire-rimmed spectacles sat atop a beakish nose; the eyes beneath were dark and searing, wrinkled at the corners but glittering with intelligence and curiosity. She wore a simple black long-sleeved empire waist dress, and a jade amulet hung from prayer beads around her neck. She had an aura of belonging where she was, as if she were as much a fixture of the library as the oak shelves.

"This is a public library?" Lydia asked stupidly, the sign right in front of her.

"That's what the sign says," the woman said with a

courteous smile and interested eyes.

"It's just that Haunted doesn't seem like an especially wealthy town. And this is a beautiful library."

"It's a public library funded by a private trust, actually," said Marilyn, her smile widening as though Lydia had just said she was beautiful. The smile took about ten years off her face.

"Mind if I take a look around?"

"Not at all," she said, hitting a button under the desk. A soft buzzer sounded and a low gate to the side of the desk opened. "Is there something I can help you find? I'll warn you, most of the books you'll find are reference materials that don't leave the library. Some first editions of local New York writers, historical texts, old maps, genealogies of some of our more prominent families. I do have some shelves towards the back with some 'popular' titles." The word popular seemed to stick on her tongue and then get spit out as if it tasted bitter. "And I can order most anything you need from one of the larger libraries if you have a library card. But I don't think you do, do you?"

"No, I don't."

The whole place smelled like wood and leather and Lydia walked up and down the shelves looking at the beautiful volumes there. She traced a finger along the bindings and thought she caught the slightest scent of lemon, as if the books had been dusted with Pledge.

She came to a narrow staircase that crept along the wall, the mahogany banister polished until it gleamed in the light. A small plaque at the bottom of the stairs announced that Haunted historical texts and genealogies were kept above and were for reference only, not to leave the library. Lydia looked around, expecting the librarian to leap out from the shelves and forbid her to go any farther. But she didn't and Lydia jogged lightly up to the next landing. It was hard to believe that a town so small and innocuous could have so many volumes dedicated to its town history and the people who lived there, but there were at least ten floor-to-ceiling shelves lined across the room and stuffed with leather-bound volumes. Lydia looked around for a light switch but didn't find one. She made do with the low light that traveled up from the floor below and scanned the shelves. She went to the shelf marked q–t to see what might exist on the Ross family and walked along that row, squinting her eyes and leaning in close so that she could read the bindings. Toward the end of the shelf, she found a book entitled Hiram Ross: Son of the Founding Fathers. She pulled it from its place and moved over to a table close to the landing where the light was a bit better.

She sat and opened the book. The book was in pristine condi-tion and the now-familiar scent of lemons seemed to waft from its pages. She perused the table of contents and found a chapter entitled "Descendants," then flipped to that page. What she found was a careful chart, dating back to Hiram's great-grandparents, continuing through his marriage to a woman named Elizabeth Rye in 1856, who died early, before her twenty-second birthday, just a few years later in 1859. Less than a year later, Hiram remarried to a woman named Eleanor Hawthorne, who bore him a son and a set of fraternal twins, one boy, one girl. The chart covered several pages, reaching all the way to three generations later, to Eleanor and Paul Ross, twin son and daughter of Hiram's great-great-grandson. The chart ended at Eleanor's marriage to Jack Proctor, with no mention of Julian's birth or Jack's death. Lydia scanned back through the marriages and saw that Eleanor had been telling the truth, that the husbands of the Ross women seemed to die all within a few years of the birth of their children.

"What are you looking for exactly?" said the librarian, poking her head up from the stairs and flipping on a light from someplace Lydia couldn't see. Lydia's heart leapt, but she managed not to show it.

"How long have you worked here?" asked Lydia, not looking at her.

"Just over thirty years," she said.

"Did you grow up here?"

Marilyn seemed taken aback by the personal nature of her questions. She hesitated, then answered.

"Why—yes."

"Does the name Ross mean anything to you?"

Marilyn laughed a quick, uncertain laugh and seemed to back away a few steps. "The name Ross means something to everyone in this town. Something different to everyone." Lydia turned her eyes from the book. Marilyn looked as if she might turn and scurry away, but she didn't.

"Who are you? What do you want?" Marilyn asked finally.

"I'm looking for information on Eleanor Ross and her murder trial back in 1965. And anything else you can tell me about the Ross family."

A strange expression crossed the woman's face, some combination of conspiratorial pleasure and fear, the desire to talk and the knowledge that she shouldn't.

"I know the librarian can be the hub of almost any small town," Lydia flattered, remembering how well Marilyn had responded to the compliments to her library. "And I can see I wasn't wrong in coming here before going anyplace else."

"Who are you?" asked Marilyn again, moving in closer to her.

"I'm Lydia Strong. I'm a writer interested in the case."

"Oh, of course," the librarian said, covering her mouth and the smile that bloomed there. "I should have recognized you. I've read every one of your books."

Lydia smiled. The librarian had climbed the rest of the steps and now stood beside her, glancing at the book open in front of her on the table. Lydia held out her hand, which Marilyn grabbed and shook enthusiastically.

"Will you help me, Marilyn?"

The woman could barely conceal her excitement, but she recovered well and took on her previous air of authority.

"Well, it depends on what you'd like to know. I'll tell you what, there's a lot you won't find in these books."

Lydia followed Marilyn back to her office behind the information desk and sat in a plush sofa. Marilyn offered tea, and when Lydia accepted, she walked from the office and was gone for a time.

Lydia looked around the small space, made smaller by the heavy wood paneling and large oak desk lit by the same style banker's lamp that had sat on the desk out front. Marilyn's degrees hung behind her desk: there was a bachelor's in English literature, a master's in library science, as well as a second master's in American history, all from Syracuse University. Lydia stood up to inspect them more closely.

Marilyn's desk was predictably spotless and impeccably organized. A small pile of manila folders was stacked flush against the far corner of the desk, ten identical Uni-Ball black ink pens stood in a leather cup: A cup of tea, still steaming, sat on a coaster. A small, sectioned tray contained rubber bands and paper clips. An unfinished game of computer solitaire when Lydia accidentally touched the mouse. She must be bored to tears, thought Lydia as the librarian returned with a cup of dark oolong tea with cream and sugar.

"You said this library was funded by a private trust?" asked Lydia, sitting back down on the sofa and placing the tea on the end table. Marilyn jumped up to place a coaster beneath the cup and then sat back down.

"Yes, from the estate of one of the original settlers of this town, a man named Thomas Hodge. He is the ancestor of a woman who still lives in Haunted, a woman named Maura Hodge."

She paused a second and then took a sip of her tea.

"Does your visit have something to do with the recent murder of Richard Stratton?" Marilyn asked.

"It does," Lydia answered simply, not offering any additional information.

Marilyn nodded and a look of uncertainty crossed her

features, as if she were unsure now that she wanted to offer Lydia what she knew. But after a moment, she began to speak. "The Rosses' ancestors, originally from Holland, settled Haunted back in the 1700s. The land, obviously, was virtually wrested from the Seneca Indians, who are just one of the tribes that existed in this region before colonization. Mainly trappers and farmers, the settlers flourished here in the 'New Netherlands.'"

Lydia smiled politely, not exactly interested in a history lesson. The woman must have read it on her face. "I know it seems like I'm starting a long way back, but I think it's relevant to what you want to know," she said.

"Please, go on," said Lydia. "It's fascinating."

"By the beginning of the early 1800s the Rosses were by far the wealthiest farming family in the North. They also owned the largest number of slaves. In fact, before slavery was abolished in 1865, New York had the largest number of slaves of any northern state."

She paused here and took another sip of her tea, looking at Lydia over the rim of the mug, gauging her reaction.

"The Rosses were notoriously brutal to their slave workers. In particular, Hiram Ross, Eleanor Ross's great-great-great-grandfather, was rumored to have beaten and even murdered his slaves. Beatings, of course, were not unusual. But actual murder was more rare than you might think because slaves were extremely valuable. A strong young male could be worth as much as twenty-five hundred dollars, which in that day was an extremely large sum of money—as odious as it is to talk about human life in such a way."

Lydia nodded her agreement and understanding. She felt cold suddenly and had the sense that the history lesson was about to get ugly.

"Anyway, Hiram Ross was hated and feared by just about everyone who knew him...his slaves, his fellow farmers, even his family. He was a thief, a liar, and, if rumor was to be believed, a rapist and murderer. He was believed to have fathered a great many children by his female slave workers; children who grew up to be his slaves, as well."

Marilyn was by this time leaning forward on her chair toward Lydia, her face animated by the story she was telling. Lydia's interest was piqued, as well.

"Now, Elizabeth Ross, Hiram's wife, was not exactly a saint herself. In fact, she herself was carrying on an affair with one of the slave workers, a man named Austin Steward. They were both young, no older than twenty-seven or twenty-eight, and they were supposedly truly in love. Hiram was no fool and he learned soon enough about the affair. The story goes that one night, while he was supposed to be away selling the season's crops, he came home early to find the two in the throes of passion on the parlor floor."

Lydia could imagine the two lovers entwined on the floor of a grand parlor, the light from a full moon bathing their naked bodies. She could see a man enter and stand at the doorjamb, watching, his face contorted in anger, rage flowing through his veins.

"Hiram was obviously enraged," Marilyn went on. "And Elizabeth, whether out of terror or cowardice or both, claimed that Austin Steward had raped her."

Lydia could see the young woman, moving away from her lover, maybe gathering her clothes around her, hiding her naked body from the gaze of the two men...her lover and her husband, the circumstances having made them both hostile strangers to her.

"Austin was also married, to a young Haitian slave named Annabelle Taylor. Of course, that was her slave name. There are no records of her true Haitian name that I've been able to find. Hiram took Austin and Elizabeth out to the shack where Austin and Annabelle lived with their five children. He pulled those children out of their beds and asked Elizabeth again if she was having a willing affair with Austin or whether he had raped her. He promised to kill a child each time she lied. She lied five times. And Hiram killed all five children with a shot to the head while Annabelle and Austin looked on, restrained by Hiram's slave drivers. Naturally, Austin was arrested and hanged. And Elizabeth, it's said, went quite insane. She died of the flu the next winter."

Marilyn had told the tale as though it were a ghost story, something that was heinous and terrifying but not real. And she spoke with a kind of alacrity that Lydia found a tad inappropriate. Lore was like that; the years drained the horror from it, leaving just an echo over time. But in Marilyn's telling, Lydia had been transported and was left with a cavity of sadness in her chest at the cruelty and harshness of the story. She could imagine vividly the scene that night, see the bloated full moon, hear Annabelle screaming for the lives of her children, hear Elizabeth lying again and again as the children were slain, see their small bodies fall lifeless to the ground, smell the gunpowder in the air as the shots rang out. It was one of the worst stories she'd ever heard. And she'd heard some bad ones.

"That's an interesting piece of folklore, Marilyn. But I'm not sure what it has to do with—"

"There's more. Annabelle lived to be a very old woman. It's said that the only thing that kept her alive was her hatred for the Ross family. Some people believed that in Haiti Annabelle had been a voodoo priestess. And on the night her children died, she created a curse against the Ross bloodline. A curse that could only be kept alive by herself and her daughters, and her daughter's daughters—a kind of legacy of hatred."

"And what was the curse?" asked Lydia.

"That none of the women descended from Hiram would know a natural love. That if they fell in love and married, a horrible fate would befall their husbands."

"What about the children? Hiram killed her children. Wouldn't she want revenge for that?"

"No, supposedly she would not wish harm to children,

no matter what the crimes of their ancestors."

"So I take it Annabelle's bloodline is still alive and well."

"And residing in Haunted. Annabelle remarried and had more children some years after the tragedy. She was just nineteen when her children by Austin were murdered."

"Really," said Lydia, less a question than an exclamation. "And how did you come by all of this information?"

"In addition to being the librarian, I'm also the town historian," she said with pride. "And Annabelle's descendant is the woman I mentioned whose trust funds this library. It's Maura Hodge. A descendant of Thomas Hodge, Benjamin Hodge married a descendant of Annabelle Taylor, Marjorie Meyers...a very controversial marriage in its day, since Marjorie had Haitian blood in her veins. Maura was their only child. Her ancestors settled and worked as slaves on this soil. She knows everything there is to know about the history of this town, the Ross family, and especially the curse."

"So when Eleanor's husband, Jack Proctor, was murdered, people believed that it had to do with the curse?"

Marilyn lowered her eyes for a second, then raised them to meet Lydia's gaze.

"I suppose it seems silly to someone who's...not from here."

"No one other than Eleanor was ever suspected? No rumors?"

Marilyn looked thoughtful, but shook her head. "In a place like this where so little goes on and so little ever changes, the past just seems closer. Superstitions, ghost stories, they seem more real, I guess. When Eleanor was acquitted and no one else was ever charged, it almost seemed like proof that the curse was alive and well."

Lydia looked at Marilyn and she seemed suddenly strange and innocent. Haunted was only a couple of hours from New York City, but it might as well have been on the moon, it was so removed.

"Anyway, like I said," Marilyn went on, "Maura knows a lot more about the curse and the Ross family than I do. But I'll warn you that she's not overly friendly. And she's suspicious of outsiders. Since her ancestors settled this town, she kind of thinks of it as hers. There's not much left to it, but she'll protect it with her life."

Lydia thought of the roads riven with potholes and the crumbling neglected Main Street. She thought of a land wrested from the Native Americans and tilled by slaves that worked and bled and died on it. She thought of Annabelle Taylor and the souls of her dead children. She thought maybe there was never a more fitting name for a town.

"There's a lot of blood in the ground," said Lydia, half thinking aloud.

"Indeed there is."

"Frankly, Detective, I don't see what my mess, from nearly forty years ago, has to do with your present situation." Police Chief Henry Clay was a fat, sour man with a big belly and a face that was as wrinkled and dirty as an old potato. He was bald except for a few determined silver strands that were currently being blown every which way by the heat coming from the vent above his head. His hands were thick and pink, reminding Jeffrey of nothing so much as wads of Silly Putty.

"Well, sir," said Ford, trying his level best to use honey instead of vinegar, "it might have nothing to do with it; it might have everything to do with it. But we would sure be interested in your thoughts on the '65 case."

The old man made a noise that was somewhere between a grunt and a belch as he pushed himself up from the chair behind his desk. He walked past them and opened the wood and opaque glass door that bore his name and said to his secretary who was seated outside his office, "Can you go down to the archives, Miss Jean, and see if you can't find the Ross file?"

There was a moment of silence, and the woman, who was at least as old as the police chief, sounded incredulous as she repeated, “The Ross file, Henry? Eleanor Ross?”

“Well, goddammit, woman, you heard me,” he answered, and closed the door.

“The case was never solved, is that right, Chief Clay?” asked Jeff.

“That’s right,” he said with a sigh as he sat back in his chair, which groaned in protest of his tremendous girth.

“Who were the other suspects?” asked Ford.

“Well, there were no other suspects, officially. No one we could ever charge.”

“But you had someone in mind,” led Ford.

“There had always been bad blood between Eleanor Ross and another longtime resident, a crazy old woman named Maura Hodge. It was something ancestral, some kind of family feud that went way back to when their people settled this town. But that was just a lot of gossip. Maura’s always been an angry woman, very bitter. And she had a well-known hatred for Eleanor. Jealousy, I always thought. You know how women are.”

Jeff said a silent thank-you that Lydia was not with them. She really had a distaste for misogyny and could not be counted on to hold her temper when faced with men like Henry Clay.

“Oh, yeah.” Ford laughed in a complicit man-to-man kind of way.

“She’s still alive?” asked Jeff.

“Yeah, that old bitch is too mean to ever die,” he said with a laugh that ended in a rasping cough. “She lives just up the road a piece in a big old house. Gorgeous old mansion from her husband’s estate. Heard it’s gone to disrepair over the years, though. She doesn’t keep it up the way she used to. Doesn’t let anyone on her property to help her. Like the Ross estate. Now, there’s a piece of property that’s gone to shit.”

“The house where Eleanor’s husband was murdered?”

"The same. The Rosses still own it, but it's sat empty some fifteen years. They still pay taxes on it, though, so it stands as they left it. Furnished and everything. We have lots of trouble with kids up there, breaking in. They claim it's haunted, course."

The chief was loose and talking now, so Ford kept pumping. "Anyone else you thought at the time might be a suspect?"

The old man leaned back even farther in his chair and lifted his arms, folding his hands behind his head. He looked above them with his small blue eyes and squinted as if he were looking off into the past.

"Well, Eleanor's brother was always trouble when they were growing up. Something wrong with him...you know, in the head. He was never right. There were always rumors about him and Eleanor. That their relationship was..." He stopped before finishing his thought and looked at them. He seemed angry suddenly, as if they had tricked him into talking about things he hadn't wanted to discuss. "But that's all ancient history."

"Where's Eleanor's brother now?

"Paul? He disappeared more than thirty years ago. Most people think he's dead," he said, looking at his watch. Just then there was a knock at the door and Miss Jean pushed in before waiting for an answer.

"Sir, I just can't find those files for the life of me," she said, looking at them apologetically. Ford didn't believe her for a second. "I'll keep looking, though, and let you know if they turn up."

"All right, then, Miss Jean," the chief said with a nod. "Well, gentlemen, if you leave your card, I'll give you a call if those files turn up."

Ford handed him a card and the chief regarded it suspiciously before stuffing it in his breast pocket and standing. "If there's nothing else..."

"Actually, Chief Clay, I'm just curious," said Ford,

leaning in and lowering his voice to a low, just-between-us-cops tone. "Do you think that Eleanor Ross killed her husband? Did she get away with murder?"

He looked at Ford and an ugly smile split his face. "Tell you what. You were thinking of marrying one of those Ross women? I'd tell you to think again."

FIFTEEN

Word was that he wasn't welcome in the tunnels any longer. But that was just too damn bad. Word was that Rain, the omniscient, omnipresent Rain whom the bottom-feeders had deified into their lord and savior, was angry over Violet's murder and was planning to make him pay. Jed couldn't give a shit less. He didn't fear the wrath of Rain the way Horatio the Dwarf seemed to when he'd found Jed and delivered the news.

"You better leave, and leave soon," he'd said, shifting nervously from foot to foot and wringing his hands. Jed handed him a black and white cookie for his warning. Horatio was funny that way. He didn't care about money or drugs; he didn't even drink. But he had a sweet tooth and kept Jed in the loop for fresh cookies and pastries from some of the fine food purveyors in the city. Horatio didn't like packaged foods; only freshly baked would do.

"I'm not going anywhere, Horatio," he'd said, patting the little man on the head.

"That's what you said before. Where would you be now

if you hadn't listened?" he asked, his mouth full of cookie.

It was true. When Horatio had pounded on his door yesterday to warn Jed about the approach of intruders, he'd had only twenty minutes to pack his belongings and disappear deeper into the tunnels. He'd loaded Horatio up like a pack mule and sent him off while he waited in the darkness. When Jeffrey Mark and Dax Chicago burst into his hovel, he quickly and easily killed their guide, so they would have no choice but to turn around and go back. He'd thought about going after them, too, when they were trapped with no exit in his space. But Dax Chicago stood at the door, never turning his back. And he had the biggest handgun Jed had ever seen. That one couldn't be trusted to go down easily; he was crazy. Not to mention incredibly strong. So Jed slung Violet's body over his shoulder—she was surprisingly heavy for such a short woman—and disappeared. He dumped her where she would be found. He wanted the twisted corpse to be a warning to those who might think about trying to lead anyone to him again.

Now Horatio was the only one who was aware of his new location. The sudden move had been inconvenient at the time, but in the end he found himself a much better spot, closer to an exit. Closer to Lydia. The map he'd begun was lost, but he'd committed it to memory, had started to draw it in a notebook that he carried with him.

Horatio, who was not very bright and resembled nothing so much as a shabbily dressed, down-on-his-luck Umpa Lumpa, was the closest thing Jed had had to a friend since he was in grade school. With scraggly long black hair, a long, wide face covered with patches of hair that should have been a beard but didn't really seem to grow in right, and bright blue eyes, he seemed more like a creature from Grimm's than he did a man. He wasn't much, but he'd proven useful and loyal.

"You're the only one who knows where I am, right?" said Jed, turning his gaze from his notebook to Horatio, who seemed to jump a bit.

“Of course,” he said eagerly.

“Then we don’t have anything to worry about. Do we?”

“Rain knows these tunnels better than anyone. If he wants to find you, he will,” Horatio said, his brows knit, the rest of the cookie forgotten in his hand.

“You’ll have to make sure that doesn’t happen.”

“How?”

“I have every confidence that you’ll find a way to lead them away from me.”

“I don’t know—”

“Find a way, Horatio. You wouldn’t want Rain to know that you’ve betrayed him. Then it will be back up topside for you, doing little dances on the subway to make money.”

Horatio had made the mistake of telling Jed how frightened he was of the streets, how much abuse he’d taken as a homeless dwarf, how he’d almost been killed more than once. Rain had given him a home and community where he felt safe. Now Jed used the information to control him. The dwarf looked sadly at his cookie as if it were the reason for the predicament he found himself in and nodded.

“Good,” said Jed. “I have to keep a low profile for a few days. I’m going to need some help with a few things.”

SIXTEEN

The food was worse than the coffee at the Rusty Penny, where Ford, Lydia, and Jeffrey sat at a booth toward the back. New Yorkers never realized how spoiled they were when it came to eating out until they left the city. Even the worst greasy spoon in Manhattan usually had something to offer, a personality, a history, something. But the Rusty Penny was like a boil on the buttocks of Haunted, nothing you'd want to look at too closely and certainly producing nothing you'd put in your mouth.

Lydia picked at the sesame bun on her chewy and grizzled hamburger. Ford, however, hadn't seemed to notice and was eating as if he hadn't had a meal in a week. Jeffrey had pushed away his turkey club and ate potato chips from a small bag.

"I think it's better if we're not there when Ford interviews the twins," said Jeffrey, taking a swig from a bottle of mineral water. "After all, we're supposed to be on Eleanor's team. It wouldn't look good to show up with the cops, especially given her opinion of them."

"Not that you should be showing up with me anyway. As far as I'm concerned, you guys don't even exist," said Ford, looking at his watch.

Lydia nodded. She had been curious to hear the interview, but she was more interested in meeting Maura Hodge.

"How are you guys going to get back?" asked Ford.

"Dax is on his way," said Jeffrey. "He's meeting us with the Range Rover." Dax had been tied up that morning with one of his other "clients."

"What does that guy do exactly?" asked Ford. Then he held up a hand. "You know what? Don't tell me."

They were quiet for a second. Lydia couldn't stop thinking about what Marilyn Wood had told her.

"What do you think about the librarian's story?" she asked Ford.

"What," said Ford, with a laugh. "You mean the curse."

"You think it's funny?" asked Lydia, leaning in to him.

"I wouldn't say funny, exactly," answered Ford with a smile, his amused skepticism wrinkling his eyes and turning up the corners of his mouth.

"It's possible, isn't it, that this Maura Hodge is making sure her ancestor's curse is fulfilled...one way or another?"

"What do you mean...like she's killing the husbands?"

"Or paying someone to do it. Or she has some kind of accomplice."

Ford shrugged, looked up, and seemed to be considering the possibilities. "Seems a little far-fetched," he said finally.

"What's so far-fetched about it?"

"How old is this woman?"

"In her sixties, according to the librarian."

"So that would make her in her late twenties around the time of Eleanor's husband's murder."

"About that. What's your point?"

"Nothing. Just that all these murders have been overkill. You know, rage killings. A killer for hire isn't going to rip someone to pieces. And as for Maura Hodge, how much anger could she muster up for someone else's two-hundred-year-old gripe?"

"Gripe? A woman watched her five children murdered before her eyes and then her husband was hanged. All because Elizabeth Ross didn't have the courage to tell the truth. I'd say that's a little more than a gripe."

"Whatever you call it, it's Annabelle's gripe. Not Maura Hodge's gripe. See what I'm saying? Whoever killed those men was filled with rage right now," he said, tapping his finger hard on the table in time with his last two syllables. "Not a hundred and fifty-some years ago."

She was there again on that night, inside Annabelle's skin. She could feel the rage, the pain, the immense sadness that must have threatened to burst out of her chest, turn her mind toward insanity. She could imagine her powerless fury, hear her screams that must have sounded like an animal's howl in the night, carrying all the panic and terror into the air. What if rage like that, pain like that, left an imprint on your DNA? What if over generations it became like a congenital disease that was passed down from one soul to the next? And what if, over time, that rage grew stronger instead of weaker? But these were things she wouldn't say aloud to people like Ford McKirdy. He was so grounded, so flat to the earth; he would think she was insane. She couldn't tell him that the buzz was louder than it had ever been. That she sensed an evil in this broken-down town and she couldn't be sure whether it lived and breathed or whether it was just a part of the ground on which the town sat, that it had sunk into the water and poisoned the whole damned place.

She moved her hand to her belly. It was an unconscious gesture, but when she'd done it, felt the denim beneath her hand, she acknowledged a feeling that had been growing, fluttering in the periphery of her consciousness since she'd discovered she was pregnant. It was the sense that she was no longer alone in her skin. That everything she felt and thought, everything she ate, even the air that she breathed was being shared by another being. All of this, of course, she knew intellectually. Sitting there in the Rusty Penny, she experienced a palpable moment when the information reached her heart. And in that moment, she just felt so real.

She wasn't sure why this feeling had come to her now. Maybe

it was thinking of what people passed on to their children. How

the baggage people carried was unloaded onto the most innocent among them; how the generations of two families since that awful night long ago might have been impacted by hatred and revenge, one way or another. And maybe it made her think of her own baggage and how she was going to try like hell not to pass it along to their child. She looked up then and saw both Ford and Jeff looking at her.

"What?" she said. "I wasn't listening."

"What's going on in there?" said Jeff, looking at her with a little worry and putting a hand on the back of her head.

"Nothing," she said. She looked into his eyes and smiled.

"Well, curse or no curse, I gotta head back to the city," Ford said, wiping the grease from his mouth. He threw ten dollars on the table. "No offense, Lydia. I can't handle this hocus-pocus bullshit. I have to deal with the facts, find out who crawled up through that hole, if anyone, who let him in, which of them killed Richard Stratton. We're not going to figure that out digging into some town legend."

"And what about Eleanor's mysterious missing brother? And the town recluse, Maura Hodge? What if the answer to your question is right here in Haunted?"

"Call me on my cell. But watch out for the Headless Horseman, will ya?"

"Very funny."

"Seriously, keep me posted. I'll call you when I've finished with Eleanor and the twins."

"Ford, what about the autopsy results? When do those come back?" asked Jeff.

"Should be today; they've been a little backed up. Busy homicide month. But they pushed mine up because its high-profile. There's a meeting in the morning, ME, crime scene technicians, junior detectives, ten a.m. Midtown North. You guys can drop by afterwards if you keep a low profile. I'll fill you in."

"We'll be there," said Jeff as Ford slid out of the booth. He stopped a second before walking out the door. He regarded them with a frown and pointed a paternal finger at them.

"You two be careful," he said, thoughtful, as if his mind were already on something else. "Call me if you run into anything tangible."

Lydia watched him as he muddled out the door. With his worn old beige raincoat and bad navy blue suit, he looked like a sad cliché of himself. Run-down middle-aged cop, nothing in his life but the job. Anything tangible...she thought. As far as she was concerned, the information the librarian gave her was the most tangible thing they had.

"I say," said Dax with a wicked smile from the backseat, "we go in, guns blazing. Ask questions later."

The three of them sat in the Range Rover in front of a giant elaborate wrought-iron fence, its bars formed to look like a network of vines and thorns. A sign was posted to the right of the gate explaining that the owner was legally entitled to shoot anyone who set foot on her property. It also warned that trained Dobermans roamed the property and that the owner was not responsible for the actions of said animals in the event someone decided to trespass. However, the gate was ajar. It felt oddly to Lydia like a dare.

"As much as I appreciate your input, Dax," said Lydia flatly, "I think we'll try a more civilized approach."

She pulled her cell phone from the pocket of her black leather blazer.

"I've seen Chiclets bigger than that thing," Dax said,

pointing to her tiny cell phone. "I'd have to have a six-pack of them. I'd crush one a day at least."

Lydia smiled in spite of herself. She was trying to treat both of them with a disdainful distance for their actions of yesterday. But they were hard to stay angry with, especially since she knew they were motivated only by concern for her.

"There," said Dax, catching her smile in the rearview mirror and issuing a triumphant laugh. "I knew you wouldn't be a bitch all day."

"Just keep talking. You'd be surprised how long I can hold a grudge," she answered, turning away so he wouldn't see her smile widen.

"I wouldn't," said Jeff, with his best henpecked sigh. Lydia smacked him on the arm with her free hand.

A small Post-it that she'd tacked to the back of her phone had scrawled on it Maura Hodge's number. Lydia dialed and waited while it rang three times before a machine picked up. "Leave a message," said an angry voice. "Though there's no guarantee I'll get back to you."

"Ms. Hodge, my name is Lydia Strong. Marilyn at the library said you might be willing to speak with me. I'm in Haunted, at the bottom of your driveway, to be exact, and I'd like to take a little bit of your time. Please call me when you get this message. And by the way, the gate is ajar. Thought you might like to know." She left the number and hung up.

"Now what?" said Dax.

"We wait a few minutes."

"What makes you think she'll call back?" asked Jeff, skeptical.

"Because she's lonely. Lonely people always like to talk. Especially when they think they have a cause."

"Maybe we'll get points for not busting in even though the gate was open."

"My thoughts exactly."

They waited a few minutes in silence before the phone rang and Lydia picked up.

"Hello?"

"What do you want?" came the same voice from the machine in even less pleasant tones. She knew she'd have exactly one chance to enter the property with Maura Hodge's permission. Otherwise it was going to be B&E, with the possibility of either getting shot or mauled by Dobermans.

"I'm writing an exposé on the Ross family. Marilyn told me that you know a lot about their history. I was hoping you would share the truth about them with me, Ms. Hodge."

There was a moment of silence during which Lydia held her breath. Then, "Come up and make sure the gate is closed behind you."

"Okay," Lydia said, and hung up the phone. She looked at Jeff. "Let's go up."

Dax jumped out to open the gate, waited until the Rover was through, then closed it behind them. Closed it mostly, anyway. There was no way he was going to lock the only exit he knew of from the property. When he was back in the car, they headed up the narrow drive, shaded by a canopy of trees so thick that after a few feet it seemed like all the light had faded from the sky. Jeff turned on his headlights, wondering why they always seemed to be headed into the dark unknown.

Maura Hodge was a goddess with a sawed-off shotgun. She stood on her porch waiting, the gun cradled in her arms like an infant. Her hair was as black and wild as a storm cloud, reaching out every which way and down her back nearly to her waist. In a diaphanous patchwork skirt and long black wool tunic, she was a large woman, with big soft breasts and wide shoulders, legs like tree trunks, arms like hams. She looked at them as they approached, with a withering stare that probably turned most people right around. Luckily, they weren't most people. Though Lydia was starting to wish they were.

"Those your bodyguards?" asked Maura, nodding toward Jeff and Dax as Lydia exited the vehicle.

"They're my associates," said Lydia vaguely, but looking Maura straight in the eye. You couldn't give an inch to a woman like Maura Hodge, otherwise she'd bulldoze right over you. Anyone could see that. Lydia could also see that she was mostly bark. Though she couldn't speak for the Dobermans lying on the porch behind Maura, their black and rust coats gleaming in the rays of sun that sliced through the tree cover like fingers reaching down from heaven. They looked a little lazy, though. They hadn't even raised a head at her arrival.

"Now, I've had two calls. One from Marilyn telling me you are a writer interested in the Ross case. And one from Henry Clay telling me that your 'associates' here are investigators. Which is it?"

"A little of both," said Lydia.

If Lydia had to imagine what the descendant of an angry voodoo priestess might look like, Maura came pretty close. Generations of mixed races had lightened her skin to a coffee-and-cream color, but her eyes were as black as rage itself and they fairly glowed with intensity. The burden of a lifetime of bitterness seemed to have bent her back into a permanent slump. Her mouth was a hard cold line that looked as though it might never have smiled or spoken words of love.

Lydia approached the woman and reached out her hand. In a heartbeat, the dogs were on their feet, teeth bared, emitting low growls of warning.

"Easy, boys," said Maura lightly, and the three resumed their reclined positions, reluctantly. Lydia began to breathe again. "Now call your dog off," said Maura. Lydia turned to see that Dax had managed to draw his gun. How he'd done it so quickly, she couldn't imagine. Jeff hadn't even managed to get out of the car yet. Jeff and Dax looked more scared than she was.

"Easy, tiger," said Lydia to Dax.

"I hate fucking dogs," said Dax, lowering his weapon, staring at the beasts with suspicion.

"I'm sure they feel the same way about you," said Maura. She turned and walked into the old house, her dogs at her heels. The three visitors stood for a second. Jeffrey looked to Lydia and she shrugged. The air was growing colder and Lydia could feel her cheeks and the tip of her nose going pink from the chill.

"I'll stay with the car," said Dax, getting into the driver's seat and starting the engine as though he thought they might need to make a quick getaway. Lydia thought he was just afraid of the dogs.

"He just doesn't like things he can't intimidate," Lydia whispered to Jeff.

"Who does?" answered Jeff with a shrug.

There was something rotten about the inside of Maura Hodge's home. There was an air of neglect, visible in the dingy walls and dusty surfaces. Bits of grit crackled beneath Lydia's feet as they stepped onto the creaking floorboards of the foyer. A chandelier looked a bit less stable than it should. The gilt frame on a mirror across the entranceway was chipped, the glass foggy. And there was an odor. Or maybe a mingling of odors...mold, dirt, moisture trapped in wood. Lydia couldn't place the smell exactly, but her sinuses began to swell and a headache debuted behind her eyes. By the time they'd followed Maura in through the front door, she was nowhere in sight. They followed the sounds of the dogs' collars and their nails scratching on the floor through a dim hallway. Lydia looked around for a light switch but saw that the fixtures were bare of bulbs. Above their heads they briefly heard what could have been footsteps, but the sound was gone as quickly as it came. Lydia wasn't positive it wasn't just the house settling.

"Does someone else live here with you, Ms. Hodge?" asked Lydia as they entered a large sitting room where a fire burned in the hearth and Maura sat on a high-backed dark wood chair, her gun across her lap.

"I thought you wanted to talk about the Rosses," she said, looking at Lydia with a kind of sneer that may have been her natural expression.

Lydia sat on the couch across from the woman, though she hadn't been invited to, and Jeffrey stood beside her. "Police Chief Clay claims that there's bad blood between you and Eleanor Ross. Is that right, Ms. Hodge?"

The woman laughed a little. It was kind of a verbalization of her permanent sneer, accompanied by a shake of her head. "I sincerely hope you have not come here to talk about that stupid curse," she said.

"In fact—"

"Because I'll tell you right now that it's pure bullshit."

Lydia felt like they were sitting in Dracula's parlor, as Gothic manor was the general decorating theme of the room. A dark red wall-to-wall carpet was badly in need of a vacuuming and steam clean. The gigantic fireplace was topped by an elaborately carved maple mantel where a wrought-iron candelabra sat, its many white candles nothing but melted wax that had been allowed to drip carelessly on the wood and on the hearth below like stalactites. The feet on the overstuffed red and gold brocade sofa and chairs, antiques that Lydia couldn't name, were lion's paws. A beautiful rolltop desk made of a highly varnished wood nestled in a dark corner and was covered in ledger books, letters, all manner of papers. Lydia's fingers practically itched to rifle through the piles of documents.

"Marilyn didn't seem to think so," said Lydia.

"It's a ghost story, Ms. Strong. An urban—or maybe in this case a small town—legend."

"Most legends have some element of truth to them," said Jeffrey.

"I'm not saying the history is false," said Maura, reaching to a standing ashtray to her right and retrieving a pipe that rested there. She tapped out some stale tobacco from the bowl. "I'm saying that the matter of the curse is merely town gossip."

She removed a velvet pouch from the pocket of her skirt and pinched out some tobacco. She put the pipe to her lips and lit it with a small gold lighter. Lydia could see that her fingers were yellowed and the nails short and cracked.

"And yet the men that marry the Ross women do seem to fall on some bad luck, don't they?" said Lydia flatly.

For the first time, Maura Hodge smiled. "I'm afraid I can't explain that."

"But it amuses you?"

"They reap what they sow," she said, leaning back in her chair. Lydia could see that Maura Hodge was not a kind woman, that the heavy burden of hatred she carried had made her cold. The tobacco was a pungent cherrywood and the smell was making Lydia nauseous. Or maybe it was the company.

"So there's no curse. But you do hate the Ross family? Why?"

Again there was a noise from upstairs. She saw Jeffrey look up at the ceiling from the corner of her eye. Even one of the Dobermans, who had settled themselves at Maura's feet, pricked up his ears and then emitted a small whine.

"It might be hard for someone like you to understand," Maura said to Lydia in a mildly condescending tone, smoke filling the air around her, dancing like thin ghosts in the light shining from a lamp beside her. "But when you come from a family of slaves, generally you don't find yourself overly fond of people who descend from a family of slave owners."

"But, according to Marilyn, you descend from both."

A look of annoyance flashed across Maura's face, as if she resented someone trying to talk her out of her hatred.

"My father and mother loved each other, Ms. Strong. But any white blood in my mother's veins got there through rape, slave owners raping their female slaves. That kind of crime, that kind of injustice...let's say you don't just forget it."

"So that's why you disliked Eleanor Ross?"

"That and the fact that she's a bitch and a liar and a damn jezebel," she said, but without the heat of anger. There was no passion in her voice, just an old hatred, long hardened. Lydia thought of what Ford had said about the overkill, about how the murder was a rage killing. Maura Hodge was a big, strong woman, but there was a lethargy to her, like she might be as hard to move as a piece of the heavy old oak furniture. Time to see what her temper looked like.

"You grew up together in this town," said Lydia, more a statement than a question. Jeffrey heard a little flame of mischief light up in her voice.

"That's right."

"So what was it then, really? She stole your date to the prom? She took your clothes while you were skinny-dipping in the creek with your boyfriend? She wrote your telephone number on a bathroom wall? Or is it just that she was beautiful and rich and you were not—just jealousy, plain and simple? Why do you hate Eleanor Ross?"

There was a flash in the woman's eyes, her jaw tightened. But Lydia didn't get the reaction she was hoping for.

"It's an inherited hatred," Maura said easily, taking a long puff on her pipe. "Woven and handed down by Annabelle Taylor."

"Is it a powerful enough hatred that it would drive you to murder?" Obviously, she wasn't expecting a confession, just a reaction she could read, something to move the investigation forward.

Maura Hodge chuckled and the chuckle evolved into a full belly laugh. "You think I'm murdering the husbands of the Ross women?" she said when she'd finished.

Lydia said nothing, just sat with her eyes on Maura, waiting.

It took a little more than laughter to rattle Lydia's cage.

"Look," Maura said, turning a hard gaze on Lydia, "the Ross family doesn't even need a curse. They are so fucked up in so many ways that they curse themselves."

"What do you mean by that?"

"Karma, Ms. Strong. Bad karma."

"But how are they fucked up?" pressed Lydia.

"That's a question best answered by Eleanor. Only she really knows the answer. The rest of us can only imagine what went on in that house after Eleanor's husband was killed. Most of us weren't old enough to remember Eleanor's father's murder. But when Jack was killed, in the same house, no less—you can imagine the frenzy, the scandal in this town. For most people, it was as if the Headless Horseman himself had ridden into Haunted. Of course, people never looked at me the same after that, either. As I am the daughter of the daughters of Annabelle Taylor, naturally they believed that I had something to do with it—mystically or otherwise. As if I were sitting in my living room casting spells."

"And did you have something to do with it?"

"Please," she said, shifting her girth in the seat and rolling her eyes.

"Do you have daughters, Ms. Hodge?"

"Stillborn," said Hodge brusquely. "I've never been able to carry a child to term."

Here Lydia saw the anger she'd been looking for—anger and sadness laced with a mammoth disappointment. Always a volatile mix.

"I'm sorry," Lydia said.

"Maybe it's for the best. Then this business of the curse will die with me."

"What do you know about Eleanor's brother?"

"Most people think he's dead," she said, her tone indicating that there was more to come. Maura was silent for a minute, chewing on the end of her pipe. Lydia could see she had something more she wanted to say and was debating whether to continue. The keen desire to gossip was clear in her black eyes.

"Some people say he loved her," she said finally, her voice lowering a bit. "Not in the way a brother loves a sister. They say it tortured him, drove him mad."

"What happened to him?"

"I was told his family sent him away. Some people believed he joined the army, but the popular rumor always was that he was sent to an asylum, where he killed himself. And others..." she said, pausing dramatically, "others believe he escaped—either the army or the asylum, depending on who's telling the story—came back, and killed Eleanor's husband because he couldn't stand another man touching her. They say he ran off, leaving her to take the rap to punish her for not loving him."

She shook her head. "But I never believed that. Paul was a quiet boy, gentle, maybe even a bit on the slow side. He didn't have it in him. Just more stories for the bored little minds in this town."

Lydia was quiet.

"He was the only one of them that wasn't rotten at the core," Maura said, looking off over Lydia's head. She opened her mouth again, then clamped it shut as though to keep trapped whatever was about to escape. Her face grew harder and she looked at Lydia. Lydia could sense that they'd outworn their dubious welcome, but she pressed on.

"So who do you think is killing the husbands of the Ross women?"

A smile at once mocking and victorious spread across her face. "Well, it's always been my hope that it is Annabelle Taylor herself, come back from the grave to do the job."

"I thought you didn't believe in curses," said Lydia, fighting a chill that had raised goose bumps on her arms.

"I don't," she said, expressing streams of smoke from her nostrils like a dragon. "But I never said I didn't believe in ghosts."

SEVENTEEN

Sitting quietly on the couch, sunlight streaming in from the large window overlooking Fifth Avenue, Lola and Nathaniel Stratton-Ross looked less like children than they did tiny adults. But they were children and interviewing them was a delicate matter. It had occurred to Ford on the way back from Haunted that maybe he didn't have the finesse, the delicacy it might require. He didn't want to fuck it up, so he put in a call to a woman he knew, a child psychologist by the name of Irma Fox.

He and Irma had worked together a couple of times in the past five years. Most recently when his only witness to a double homicide was the six-year-old son of one of the victims. He remembered Nicholas Warren as he'd found him that night, in his Toy Story pajamas, holding tight to a wilted stuffed dog, freckled with blood splatter.

They'd found him crouched in the bedroom closet, where he'd clearly had a front-row seat as his father and his new stepmother were shot to death while they slept in their bed. He told Ford that night that he'd come to his father's room to wake him after a bad dream but hid in the closet when he heard something on the stairs. He'd not closed the door, he said, but he'd covered his eyes, so he hadn't seen anything. Ford knew that Nicholas had seen it all and believed he could identify the killer. But he wanted the information without traumatizing the kid further.

It took Irma to bring Nicholas to a place where he was able to reveal the truth about that night. After two hours behind closed doors with Irma, Nicholas revealed that he'd let his mother into the house that night, as he'd promised her he would. And that she'd killed his father and his father's new wife. "So that I could live with just Mommy again." Nicholas's mom was doing two consecutive life sentences and Nicholas was living with his aunt and uncle in a Brooklyn Heights townhouse. Ford hoped the kid was getting some good therapy and didn't wind up on the FBI's most wanted list sometime in the future.

Irma had a way about her and everyone responded to it, not just children. She was a careful person, careful with her words, her tones. She had a way of focusing all her attention on you when you talked, a way of turning her warm green eyes on you with such understanding, compassion, respect, that you just couldn't help but pour out your soul into her hands. Ford knew this truth about her well, having confessed more to her over the years than he had to his own wife.

She was pretty, not beautiful, with a kind face, her skin smooth and pink like a peach. She was small but not what he'd call thin, with a motherly fullness about her breasts and hips. She was always well dressed but was not exactly what he'd call stylish. It was as if she'd been carefully constructed to be pleasing without being threatening. As if she wanted people never to notice her so much that they forgot about themselves.

He called her from the car and by the time he pulled up in front of her Central Park West office, she'd cleared her afternoon for him. She owed him a favor big time. He'd managed to get her eighteen-year-old off the hook on a DUI that was going to cost him his license and possibly some jail time, and into a special AA program instead. Shrinks' kids were always the most fucked up, he'd noticed.

There were some small fireworks upon their arrival at the Waldorf suite when Irma insisted that she speak to the children alone, without Eleanor and without the attorney present. She did agree to a video camera, so that they could all watch on a closed-circuit monitor from another room. It took a while before a uniform showed up with the equipment.

As the interview began, Piselli searched the children's room in the suite, while Detective Malone was back at the crime scene, working their bedrooms. Ford felt confident that something was going to turn up, one way or another. Either that or he was going to lose his job. Eleanor Ross was pissed and she wasn't going to be quiet about it. He could feel her eyes boring into his temple as Irma introduced herself to Lola and Nathaniel, as they watched on the small black and white monitor.

The twins had different energies. While Lola's face was cool and expressionless, Nathaniel's was open and guileless. Lola sat upright, legs crossed like a little lady, leaning elegantly on the armrest. Nathaniel slumped, pumping his legs back and forth, fidgeting in his suit.

"Do you know why we're all here today?" Irma asked the children, her voice light but firm.

There was silence for a moment during which Nathaniel looked at Lola. Irma waited, not pushing them along.

"Someone killed our daddy," said Lola softly. Nathaniel nodded.

"I'm sorry, Lola," Irma said, and Ford could hear the sympathetic half smile on her face, though she was mostly off camera, just a triangle of her shoulder visible on the screen. "Yes, that's right. You're both very brave to talk to me today even though you're feeling sad. Is that how you're feeling?"

"Our daddy's with the angels," said Nathaniel with a vigorous nod. Again silence, and Ford could imagine Irma nodding, a look of quiet understanding on her face.

Then, "Do you remember the night your father died?"

Nathaniel seemed about to say something when Lola spoke up, casting a look at her brother. "We were sleeping," she said with finality.

"Okay," said Irma. "Tell me what you remember about that night before you went to sleep."

Again Nathaniel looked to Lola "We went to a restaurant with Mommy, Daddy, and Grandma," said Lola.

"That sounds nice. Where did you go?"

"Twenty-one. I had a hamburger and a Pepsi."

"And Nathaniel, what about you? What did you have?"

Ford rolled his eyes and tried not to be impatient. He didn't want a rundown of every item on the menu at 21. He reminded himself that his impatience was precisely why he'd called in Irma to handle this interview. He tried not to sigh as Irma and the children talked more about the dinner, about the story Grandma read to them before bed, and other inane details that were intended to relax the children, get them remembering and talking. Ford started to tune out, listening to the rhythm of Irma's soft voice, the lighter, higher pitches of the children's voices responding.

"Let's try a little game," said Irma, her voice bright. "Let's see how many little things you can remember about that night."

"Like what?" said Lola suspiciously. Something about her, the way she talked, even her facial expressions, made her seem so much older than her twin. She had a gleam of intelligence and a composure that Nathaniel lacked but made up for in a kind of lovable sweetness.

"I don't know..." said Irma, her voice coaxing. "Just anything that comes to mind. Like, what stuffed animals did you sleep with that night?"

Nathaniel's face lit up. "I had Pat the Bunny," he said

with a smile, then looked around as if to see if he could find it for Irma.

"I don't sleep with stuffed animals," said Lola imperiously, casting a disapproving look at her brother. Nathaniel looked at her with a sad shyness that made Ford's heart twinge a little. They were silent for a moment, looking at each other, Lola frowning, Nathaniel with a little worried wrinkle in his brow. There was a dynamic at play between the two of them, something unspoken, a meta-communication. Ford noticed that Irma remained quiet, waiting to see what would develop. Even on the monitor, Ford could see Nathaniel's eyes start to glisten.

"I want my bunny," he said suddenly, his little face threatening to crumble into tears.

"You're such a baby," said Lola, disgusted.

"It's okay, Nathaniel. We'll get your bunny for you," said Irma, turning and looking into the camera lens.

"It's not here," snapped Lola. "It's in his room at home and we can't go there."

"That's okay, Nathaniel," said Irma again, her voice light and happy. Nathaniel looked at her and smiled at whatever he saw in her expression. He sniffled a little, but the threat of a tantrum seemed to pass. "We're still playing the game," Irma reminded him, "and you're doing so well. What else can you remember?"

Lola was sulking now. He'd seen the look before—a frightened and sad child who used anger as a shield. Ford was reminded that, in spite of her composure, she was just a little girl who'd endured a shattering trauma.

"Ummm..." said Nathaniel, an exaggerated look of concentration on his face.

"I know," said Irma enthusiastically, as if the thought had just occurred, "what were you wearing?"

"Oh! I was wearing my SpongeBob SquarePants pajamas," Nathaniel said happily. "I wear those every night. Want to see?"

"That's wonderful! I can't wait to see them as soon as we've finished talking," said Irma. "What about you, Lola?"

"I don't remember," she answered sullenly.

Nathaniel looked over at his sister and seemed to be affected by her mood. He reached out a hand to touch her leg and she took it in hers. Ford saw the closeness there that he'd seen the first night. Nathaniel slid in closer to Lola.

"I remember," Nathaniel said. "You wore your red nightgown with the hearts. Remember?"

Bingo, thought Ford. Neither child seemed to feel that they had anything to hide about their attire. He'd half worried that Lola was smart enough to understand why they wanted that information. Ford cast a glance at Eleanor. But if she was having a reaction to what Nathaniel had revealed, she hid it well. She stood with her arms folded, her eyes fixed on the monitor. Her lawyer sat on the sofa watching, as well, and taking notes.

"So let's go back to that night. Close your eyes and think hard for me, okay, guys? Your grandmother read The Night Before Christmas. Then your mommy put you each to bed. What's the next thing you remember?"

At this, Nathaniel's eyes widened. Lola looked over at him with a severe glance as he started to sniffle.

"What, Nathaniel? What is it?" asked Irma, her voice coaxing.

"Nathaniel—" Lola said, her tone a warning. He looked over at her and his little mouth curled, his eyes filled with big tears.

"The bogeyman," said Nathaniel. "The bogeyman came." And he released a wail that raised goose bumps on Ford's arm, that was at once heartbreaking and frightening.

"Roaches, tunnels, curses, dogs—now ghosts. Give me good old hand-to-hand combat any day compared to this shit," said Dax from the back of the Rover. The sky had turned to blue velvet outside and stars began to glitter in the night. They had the heat on full blast and Lydia still didn't seem to be able to warm up after their visit with Maura Hodge.

"What's the matter, Dax? Chicken?" she said.

"Not bloody likely," he said, snorting his contempt. "But that woman and her beasts gave me the shivers. Who else was in the house?"

Lydia looked over at Dax. "She said no one. But I heard some movement upstairs, or thought I did."

"Well, I saw someone in the window upstairs. There was definitely someone up there."

"Man, woman? What?"

"What do I have, a fucking bionic eye? It's dark; I couldn't tell." Then, "Where are we going now?"

"Haunted house," said Jeff, looking in the rearview mirror. "No pun intended."

"Naturally."

They'd left the Hodge residence with the uneasy feeling that Maura was either crazy or deceitful or both. Lydia was unsatisfied with the interview; it felt like a tease and that they had left with more questions than answers. Lydia had the distinct impression that Maura had talked to them only because she knew they weren't going to take no for an answer. And that she'd carefully evaded giving any actual information about anything. Or maybe she really didn't know anything. Maybe she was just an old woman, alone with her bitter and crazy thoughts, and that was all she had to share.

Once they were back in the SUV, Jeff had a brief conversation with Ford in which they'd exchanged information about their respective interviews.

"So you got ghosts and I got the bogeyman," Ford had said with a laugh.

"That's about the size of it. Now what?"

"I'm going to head back over to the laundry room and

watch the forensics team. If someone did that crime and then left through the laundry room, there has to be blood evidence. Even if it was wiped clean, the Luminol has a chemiluminescent compound that reacts to the iron in the hemoglobin and glows under a blue light. If nothing else it could prove someone else was at the scene that night.

"The other thing I wanted to tell you was that we have about twenty guys down in those tunnels trying to find a trail to follow...the Luminol might help with that, too. I learned, however, from this New York City architectural historian that I located at Columbia University that tunnels like this are not at all unusual in older buildings. They were blasted out during Prohibition, made quick getaways for speakeasy proprietors and bootleggers. Interesting, huh? I never knew that before."

"Me neither."

"Anyway, they're all over the place, especially in the East Village. Most of them have been sealed up, though."

Jeff was silent a minute, thinking of the whole network of passages beneath the street connecting to buildings. It added another dimension in his mind to the city he thought he knew. With Jed McIntyre crawling around down there, it made him more than a little uneasy.

"Jeff?" said Ford.

"Sorry. We're going to head over to the Ross estate," he said, snapping back to the conversation. "Apparently it has sat empty and untouched for years. Lydia thinks we'll find some answers there."

"Good luck. See you in the morning."

Breaking and entering just didn't seem like that big a deal anymore. Lydia remembered a time when it seemed very exciting in its grayness, in the way it walked the line between right and wrong. But tonight it took Jeff about fifteen seconds to pick the lock and they were into the Ross home as easily and with as much a sense of entitlement as if they'd had a key.

"That lock is new," commented Jeff as the door swung open, creaking on its hinges. They'd bickered briefly in the car about Lydia waiting outside in the event that floorboards and such in the house were unstable. She, naturally, wouldn't hear of it. So Jeffrey guessed that their agreement about her not involving herself in the more dangerous aspects of the investigation was little more than a sham. It was his turn to be angry now. Angry that she was so stubborn; angry that his concerns for her safety—completely natural concerns, given the circumstances—were ignored. She made him feel like a Neanderthal for wanting to protect her and their child—and he was starting to resent the hell out of it. He wondered when she was going to start acting as if she cared about her own safety...and if she was going to start acting and feeling like a mother at some point.

The three of them stood in the grand foyer and looked about them at the havoc time and neglect had wrought. Their Maglite beams cut through the darkness like tiny kliegs, circles of light falling on graffiti across the walls, beer bottles on the floor. Spider webs glittered and swayed from the chandelier above their heads. In a drawing room off to the right of the foyer, the stuffing had been ripped from an antique sofa and chairs, a fireplace was filled with trash. The wind was picking up outside and it blew through the house with a moan.

"What are we looking for?" asked Dax.

"I'll know it when I find it," answered Lydia as she walked down a hallway that led deeper into the house. Dax headed off to the right toward the staircase. After a second, they could hear the steps creaking dangerously beneath his weight. Lydia half braced herself, waiting for him to come crashing through the wood until she heard him reach the landing above.

At the end of the hallway, she and Jeffrey reached a set

of double doors that led to a library, where every inch of wall space was covered with books on rich oak shelves. With high ceilings, an elaborate Oriental rug over dark wood flooring, a cavernous fireplace across from a leather sofa and matching wingback chairs, a low, wide cocktail table, the room was elegant in a masculine way. Everything was covered by a thick layer of dust, had the aura of decay and abandonment.

Lydia walked over to the books and observed leather-bound volumes of all the classics, full collections of Tolstoy, Dickens, Milton, Lawrence, Hawthorne, Shakespeare, pretty much every major author Lydia could imagine. She also noticed medical and law texts, volumes on botany, biology, psychology. She reached up and extracted one of the books, Wuthering Heights by Emily Brontë, and opened it to realize by the stiffness of the binding and the pristine condition of the pages that the book had never been read. But written on one of the endpapers was a note:

To Eleanor

We will never be apart.

Paul

It made her think back to what Maura Hodge had said about Eleanor and her brother. There was something so final in his assertion, almost as though it were more of a threat than a declaration of brotherly love. Really, there was nothing brotherly about it, and looking at it written on the page in the faltering hand of a younger person, dark wonderings about the Ross family started to dance in Lydia's mind like haunting specters.

Glittering particles hung in the beam of Jeffrey's flashlight like stardust as he shone it toward Lydia. She turned to smile at him and showed him the inscription.

"Weird." He nodded, taking the information in and wondering what it meant to the investigation at hand.

She placed the book on the shelf and walked behind a gigantic desk that stood before a bay window. The leather chair creaked beneath her weight as she seated herself and started opening drawers by their gilt handles. She looked like Alice in Wonderland, sitting in furniture that had clearly been made for someone much larger than herself. Jeff was just about to sit on the sofa across from her when he noticed a used condom there. He decided to stand.

"Let's think for a second," he said, walking behind her and glancing out the window behind him into blackness.

"Okay," said Lydia. "What do we know for a fact?"

This was their ritual. To line up the facts like cans on a wall, then shoot at them one by one with logic, intuition, evidence, or just plain guesswork. The last can standing was the winner, or the loser, depending on how you looked at it.

"That both of Julian's husbands, as well as Eleanor's husband, were brutally murdered in very similar ways. And that all three of those crimes are as yet unsolved."

"We know that Eleanor Ross has a twin brother who may or may not be dead," said Lydia. "And we know that she never revealed this fact to us. She also never revealed that her husband was murdered, until I cornered her with it. So what does that tell us about Eleanor?"

"That she's hiding things."

"So why did she hire us, then?"

"Because she doesn't know who's killing these men, either?"

"Or because she's afraid?"

Jeffrey shrugged, the question hanging in the air while Lydia rifled through what looked like old letters. He walked over and sat on the windowsill behind her, glancing over her shoulder.

"Afraid of what?" he asked.

"Or afraid of who?" She put the letters back into the drawer, apparently not finding anything that interested her. Then she opened another that was filled with old photographs jumbled together in a pile so large that she had to struggle to pull the drawer out all the way.

"The question is...and it nearly always boils down to

this...who had the most to gain from Richard Stratton's death?"

"Julian Ross," answered Lydia simply. Ford had done a pretty thorough job looking into Richard Stratton's business dealings and personal life. There was no one else who had as much to gain from his death as his wife.

"What about Eleanor Ross?"

"What about her?"

"Well, Julian is in a mental institution right now. If she's at some point judged incompetent...Eleanor will likely become her executor. She'll have access to all that money and the children, as well."

Lydia nodded thoughtfully. "Which takes us back to why she'd hire us in the first place. But let's stick to what we know for a minute. We know that there was another way into the building," she said. "So at least there's the possibility that someone else was there that night."

"And we know that someone from the inside had to let him in. And that it looks like it might have been the twins."

"Why 'him'?"

"It seems logical. After all, we're saying that Julian didn't have the strength to kill her husband. Wouldn't that hold true for another woman, as well?"

"Maura Hodge is a fairly big woman. Strong, too."

Lydia spoke without looking up, sifting through images. A young and gorgeous Eleanor with flame red hair in her rose garden; Julian as a toddler on Christmas morning peering into a gigantic dollhouse; Eleanor again in an embrace with a man Lydia assumed to be her husband. Beautiful people, all the images representing an idyllic life of affluence, their happy smiles never hinting at the tragedies in their past, nor foreshadowing the future. The Ross family lineage was rotten at the core and you'd never know it to look at them. Beauty was so often a trick of nature, a careful camouflage.

"Are you saying you consider her a suspect?"

Lydia held a photograph in her hand, looking at it closely

beneath her flashlight's beam. "Not necessarily. What about this mysterious brother of Eleanor's? Is it possible that he's been lurking around all these years waiting for the chance to kill again?"

"Living in the tunnels below New York City, hiding in the woods of Haunted? Possible. Not likely."

"How about living in the basement of this house?" said Dax, appearing suddenly in the doorway.

They both looked up at him.

"Follow me," he said.

The door down to the basement might have easily escaped notice, if Dax hadn't lost his footing, tripping over a spot where moisture had caused the wood floorboards to rot, one piece bending and curling up. He'd felt the wall give a bit beneath his weight when he used it to catch himself and thought it odd for an old house to have such shoddy construction. At closer glance, he discovered that there was a door fit to look like part of the oak paneling on the wall. A lock was hidden beneath a flap that had been cleverly camouflaged to look like a knot in the wood.

Now Lydia and Jeffrey followed him down as he shone the way with his light, his gun drawn. They were all quiet. The stench of mold and wet earth rose up to greet them and something about the smell made Lydia think of fresh graves. The dark space seemed to stretch on into infinity, the beam of their lights not revealing the far wall once they'd reached the bottom. All that darkness and something electric in the air made the hairs on the back of her neck stand up.

"Look at this," Dax said, leading them beneath the stairs.

Someone had made a little nest within a large blue nylon tent. Jeffrey got down on his hands and knees and Lydia followed. Together they poked their heads in through the tent flap. The smell was the first thing to hit her...the foul stench of body odor and semen, strong and ripe. It seemed to linger in the fabric of the tent and in the pilled brown blanket that lay atop an air mattress. Candy wrappers, empty potato chip bags, and a half-eaten can of kidney beans with a plastic spoon still in it were scattered about the space. Mingled with the other aromas, Lydia could vaguely smell salt and vinegar.

"Holy shit," said Jeff. Lydia wasn't sure whether he was reacting to the smell or to the fact that every inch of the walls and ceiling of the tent was covered with pictures of Julian Ross—photographs, newspaper clippings, magazine articles.

It was moments like this when she was glad she thought ahead, which didn't happen often. From the pocket of her coat she removed two plastic bags, surgical gloves, and a pair of tweezers.

"Nice," said Jeffrey with a smile.

In a rare moment of foresight, she'd taken them from her bag before they got out of the car. She slipped one of the gloves on, picked up a Milky Way wrapper with the tweezers, and put it in a baggie. Then she ran her finger across the blanket, shining the flashlight beam and looking closely at the surface. She found what she was looking for, strands of hair. Long and gray. She lifted them with the tweezers and put them in the second baggie, then stuffed them both into her pocket. She looked at Jeff, remembering what he'd said about the hairs they'd found at the scene of Tad's murder.

"Guys," said Dax. Lydia paused at the sound of his voice. Dax was constantly fucking around, cracking jokes; his voice was almost always edged with the promise of laughter. Except when he was worried. Then he was dead serious. And Dax didn't worry often.

"This space heater, right here?"

"Yeah?" they answered in unison, turning to look at him.

"It's off. But it's still warm."

They didn't have time to contemplate what that might mean because out of the darkness like a freight train came a blur of gray and red accompanied by an inhuman roar. The monster, because that's what it looked like to Lydia, knocked Dax to the floor before any of them knew what hit him. Lydia and Jeff scrambled to their feet, Jeff reaching for his gun, Lydia remembering that she hadn't taken hers from her bag—as usual. She raised the Maglite over her head to strike the creature and get him off Dax, who she couldn't even see beneath the gigantic mass of whatever it was that was on top of him. But she never made contact because the monster turned, as if by instinct, and swung out with an arm as heavy as a two-by-four. In the seconds before she took a blow to the head that put the lights out, she saw a flash of green eyes, a bared mouth of yellow, jagged teeth, a mask of pure rage and malice. It was a face she recognized.

The offices of Mark, Striker and Strong were dark and quiet. Everyone had gone home except for Rebecca, who was packing her bag and closing down the computer system from the main unit at the reception desk. Security was very tight at the firm and that included their intranet. Craig, their self-proclaimed cybernavigator, had built a firewall that was more secure, he claimed, than that of the FBI. And he should know, having been the most wanted hacker in the world until he was finally arrested just after his eighteenth birthday, for precisely that...breaking into the FBI databases and fucking around. Now, as he liked to say, he used his powers "for good and not for evil." Lucky for him, Jacob Hanley, his uncle and one of the firm's original partners, along with Jeff and Christian Striker, all former FBI agents, managed to get the kid a deal. Now he was plugged into the Internet more or less day and night, more or less legally working for the firm. Lydia called him The Brain behind his back and joked that one day they were going to look into his windowless office and find that he'd been sucked into his computers like a character in a William Gibson novel.

There was a whole elaborate shutdown process that was linked to the office security system. Rebecca was just about to initiate the final sequence that would give her precisely fifteen minutes to exit the front door when she heard the elevator. She looked at her watch—8:15. Rodney, the second messenger of the day, hadn't arrived at his usual time. Rebecca had been trained to watch out for little things like this. So she called the service and the dispatcher said, "It's been a crazy day. Two of my guys got into accidents today. He or someone else will get there tonight, I promise."

Christian Striker was waiting for photos back from the lab they used down in SoHo and she knew it was important he have them for tomorrow even though he was already gone. So she fixed her makeup, peering at her flawless pink skin in the Clinique compact mirror and waited, watching the elevator climb by the tiny numbers alternately lighting green as it climbed to their floor. She quickly pulled a brush through her silky blond hair and applied a berry shade of Princess Marcella Borghese lipstick to her full lips.

The stainless steel doors opened and a wiry bike messenger with long curly dark hair pulled into a loose ponytail, dirty, tattered bicycle shorts, and a tight white T-shirt with just do it emblazoned in orange across his chest walked into the elevator lobby and headed toward the door. A large messenger bag was slung across his shoulder and she noticed he was wearing soccer cleats when he pushed through the glass doors.

"Speedy Messenger?" she asked.

"You got it. Sorry for the delay," he said, removing a bundle of packages from his pouch.

"Last stop of the night, I hope," she said, looking down on her desk for a pen to sign his clipboard.

"Not quite," he said. There was something in his voice that made her look. She looked into ice blue eyes and caught sight of a few wisps of red hair peaking out from beneath the black. She realized too late that she was looking at Jed McIntyre.

EIGHTEEN

Before Jeffrey could react to Lydia flying back and hitting the ground hard, he saw a bright white flash and heard the unmistakable sound of the Desert Eagle firing off rounds. The basement exploded with the sound, as loud as a bomb, followed by a sharp report. The smell of gunpowder filled Jeffrey's nose as the assailant roared in pain or terror or maybe both. Jeffrey dove for Lydia as the monster got up and ran for the stairs, moving impossibly fast. Dax, a large cut bleeding on the side of his face, got up in a heartbeat and gave chase.

"I missed! I can't fucking believe it. He was right on top of me," he yelled as he disappeared into the darkness. Jeffrey heard the sound of the gun again as he pulled Lydia into his arms. His heart lurched with relief when she moaned. A line of blood trailed from her nose, and the light shadow of a bruise that he could see would flower into a deep purple and cover most of the right side of her face was already making its debut.

"Jesus," he said, filled with anger, fear, and a painful love for her. He wanted to lock her in a padded room for the rest of her life. He hated himself a little for it...and hated her for not allowing him to do it. He had known it would come to this if they weren't careful. And they hadn't been.

"Dax," she said, opening her eyes when more shots rang out upstairs. "I'm fine. Go. He needs help."

She sat up and gave a smile to show she was all right. Her head throbbed and the room seemed to lurch and blur.

"Don't move," he said, kissing her on the top of the head. Then he raced after Dax, taking the stairs two at a time, the Glock in his hand. When he was out of sight, Lydia leaned over and threw up the coffee and bad food she'd eaten at the Rusty Penny. It tasted even worse the second time around.

When she was reasonably sure that the room had stopped spinning, she reached for the flashlight that had rolled away from her and turned off. She pressed the black rubber button beneath her thumb and the beam sliced into the darkness. She could hear Dax shouting in the distance outside and she tried to struggle to her feet, but the floor wouldn't stay solid and she figured she'd be more a liability than a help to them in her present condition. It was probably the first smart decision she'd made all day. Another shot rang out, and she made herself believe that as long as she could hear them, they were okay.

Her mind was doing cartwheels, her heart racing, and her hands were still shaking from the adrenaline coursing through her veins like an Indy 500 race car. She reached into her back pocket and pulled out the photograph she'd been looking at upstairs. What she had seen in that photograph right before Dax entered the room was a young boy and girl standing side by side under a glade of trees. They were so alike, their features narrow and refined, the same bright green eyes, the same slight smile. The boy was much taller, much wider through the shoulders than the girl. He draped a protective arm across her shoulder and glanced at her, a mischievous glint to his expression. The girl was Julian Ross, the boy, Lydia deduced, her brother, possibly her twin. Why she hadn't thought of it before, she wasn't sure. If Eleanor was a twin, and Julian's children were also twins, it was very possible that Julian could be a twin herself. Lydia would put money on the fact that they'd just met Julian's other half...in the man who'd attacked them tonight.

She tried again to stand and the room did a little dance, a weird up-and-down, side-to-side kind of action, and Lydia braced herself for another bout of nausea.

"I'm sorry," she said to the baby, without thinking, patting her stomach and grabbing one of the steps to try to haul herself to her feet. It didn't quite work and she sort of hung there halfway between standing and falling. She tried not to think about the damage she might have done to herself; she just willed herself to be strong and solid, to walk it off. And as soon as she could stand, she was going to do that.

Thunderous footsteps broke the silence as Jeff and Dax ran down the stairs like a herd of buffalo. Lydia felt the sound on every nerve ending in her rattled brain.

"What happened?" she asked as Jeffrey helped steady her.

"Gone. Into the woods. I think I hit him, though," said Dax.

"You can't shoot a fleeing suspect, for Christ's sake," said Jeffrey, his face red from exertion and his brow knitted with concern for Lydia and anger at Dax.

"I didn't shoot him for Christ's sake," Dax shouted. "I shot him for my sake. He scared the shit out of me. He practically killed me. He hit Lydia. I'm not the fucking cops. I play by my rules." The adrenaline was clearly making him more aggressive and less reasonable than usual.

Jeffrey shook his head and rubbed his eyes.

"Let's put our philosophical differences aside, shall we, and get the fuck out of here before Julian's evil twin comes back?" said Lydia.

"Julian's twin?"

She handed the photograph to Jeffrey. “More information not provided by our client,” he said, handing the photograph back to her.

“Sounds like it’s time to fire the old hag,” said Dax.

“I want to make one more stop before we do,” said Lydia.

“My thoughts exactly,” said Jeff, taking her arm. “The emergency room.”

At first glance, Dr. Franklin Wetterau had the look of a man who had swabbed a million throats, delivered a thousand babies, and listened to endless lists of symptoms and ailments ranging from the common cold to stomach cancer. He looked as though he’d offered countless words of comfort, advice, and reprimand with the same gentle smile and knowing eyes he now turned on Lydia as she sat bruised and tired on his examining table. Dr. Wetterau was an old-fashioned country doctor, with his small office in the back of his old Victorian home on Maple Street.

The nearest hospital was over thirty miles away, so Dr. Wetterau was apparently the man to call with minor emergencies day or night, or so they were told at the gas station where they stopped for directions, the very same gas station, in fact, where they’d stopped earlier. There was a different slack-jawed attendant now on shift. The young man—Hank, if the embroidered name on his striped uniform shirt was to be believed—gave them the good doctor’s number. Of course, the earlier attendant had also worn a shirt with the name Hank embroidered on it. Were they both named Hank or were they sharing a shirt? Lydia wondered pointlessly, as “Hank” stared into the Rover at her and Dax, whose bruised and bloody condition was definitely notable.

They’d walked a narrow path along the back of the house as per the instructions the doctor gave Jeffrey over the phone and the old man was waiting for them at the door. Lydia saw him look them each up and down, his expression betraying neither shock, wonder, nor judgment, just a mild curiosity. Inside, a woman in a neat red dressing gown, trimmed with white, looking like nothing so much as Mrs. Claus with a wide pink face framed by graying hair in a bun on the crown of her head, sat primly at a small reception desk and took their names and addresses, entering the information into some type of logbook. She offered them water or tea and, when they declined, retired through a door marked private that Lydia assumed led to their home.

Alone with the doctor now, Jeff and Dax sitting out in the waiting room, Dax's cut newly cleaned and stitched, Jeff she assumed sinking into a foul mood and plotting ways to keep her locked up forever, Lydia sat stiffly as the doctor shone a light into each of her eyes.

"Mrs. Smith," he said, "what kind of an accident did you say you, your husband, and your, uh, brother were involved in?"

"We didn't, Doctor," Lydia answered calmly.

The doctor nodded, reaching into a small refrigerator and offering her a gel icepack wrapped in an Ace bandage pouch. She pressed it to the side of her head, the cold and the pain causing her to feel light-headed again. She lay back, hearing the crinkle of the sanitary paper over the vinyl table. The sound reminded her of childhood visits to the doctor, her mother, and how nice it was to feel cared for when you were sick.

"You do appear to have a mild concussion, Mrs. Smith. Now, I don't have the proper equipment here to check on the health of your baby. And I'm going to suggest that you get to your OB as soon as possible. But I will tell you that any type of trauma to the mother will put the fetus at risk. So my other suggestion is that you minimize your exposure to situations where you are vulnerable to, uh, accidents."

She turned to look at him and even though things were a bit on the fuzzy side, his eyes, the clearest blue she'd ever seen, were intelligent and a bit stern. She felt like he knew her, though they were strangers to each other. In him she recognized her own ability to intuit the truth about people, about who they truly were, by noticing small details, the things they said and didn't say. Everybody has a face they wear, the one they want people to see, to recognize as their true face. And for a few people, you get what you see. But usually there's something more beneath the surface, something hidden. The furtive gesture, the shifting glance, the tapping foot offered so much, revealed facets of personality that people tried to hide. Lydia had always possessed the ability to see quickly through façades. Tonight she wondered what this doctor saw when he looked at her. Someone careless, someone reckless, someone more concerned with chasing investigations than she was for the life of her child. Someone scared that she was not up to the responsibility about to be bestowed upon her. Someone running from her own problems by burying herself in nightmares that belonged to someone else.

"That's not always possible in my line of work," she said, feeling a little defensive.

He placed a hand on her arm. "Then take a vacation," he said gently.

His hand was big and warm, slightly callused. He looked like someone's daddy, someone's grandpa, the man who was always there for his family, the one everybody leaned on. She wondered what it would have been like to grow up with a man like that as your father. Life would be easier, she was sure. Decisions would be a lot less daunting. There would be fewer questions about what was right and wrong when you had someone like Dr. Wetterau to ask. Lydia fought the urge to cry; pregnancy was making her more emotional than she liked.

She managed a nod and sat up slowly. "You might be right," she admitted.

He kept watching her with those eyes and she started to feel a twinge of discomfort. When she returned his glance, her vision sharper than it had been a moment earlier, she saw he had the eyes of a combat soldier. There was a look a man got on his face when people had died at his hands. It was as if a piece of cosmic truth had been revealed to him that others never even glimpse, and as if that knowledge had come to rest in the color of his eyes. It's there even when he's laughing or looking on you with eyes of love. Her grandfather had eyes like that, as if the slightest trigger could start a cavalcade of images too awful to share with anyone who hadn't been there, who didn't know. But Lydia thought maybe if she looked deeply enough into the abyss of his pupils, she would see it all there playing like a movie on a screen, as if his eyes had a memory of their own. She saw it in Dr. Wetterau, clear as day.

"Did you know the Ross children?" Shot in the dark.

He rubbed the side of his face thoughtfully and looked at her as if deciding whether it was in either of their best interests to answer her question.

"I did," he answered, letting the sentence dangle.

"Julian and...," she said, hoping he'd finish the sentence for her.

"Is that why you and your friends are here? Are you looking for him?"

Lydia didn't answer, but cast her eyes down as if her clever ruse had been uncovered. "Do you know where he is?" she asked after a moment.

"James? I know where he belongs," he answered. "But he hasn't been there for over ten years."

"Where's that?"

"On my recommendation, his family committed him to Fishkill Facility, a psychiatric hospital not far from here."

"What for?"

"He tried to burn down his family home, his mother and sister along with it," said the doctor with a sad shake of his head. "A very disturbed young man."

"Did he say why he did it?"

"He claimed that his mother and sister had put a curse on him and that the only way to save himself was to burn them both and the house. The house, he believed, held all their negative energy."

"He thought they were witches?"

"Sometimes," said the doctor with a shrug. "There was that, and his bizarre obsession with Julian. He believed that her body housed the spirit of his true love from another life and that her soul could only be free if Julian died. He was later diagnosed as a paranoid schizophrenic. At first he was largely unresponsive to medication. But after many years of treatment, he graduated to a work release program. One night, after his shift at a library was over, he didn't return to the facility. That was ten years ago." The memory seemed to sadden the doctor. "He was the first person I thought of when I heard the news about Julian's husband."

"Which one?"

"Both. Tad was murdered just months after James disappeared."

"Did you go to the police?"

He sighed and shook his head. "No."

"Why not?"

Another heavy sigh. "The Ross family is like...a virus. If you want to preserve your health, you should just stay away. I learned that lesson a long time ago. I have a feeling you might benefit from learning that lesson as well, before it's too late."

"An innocent woman might have gone to jail," said Lydia.

"Let me tell you something: When it comes to the Rosses, there's not an innocent among them," he said, turning a joyless smile on her along with those eyes that had seen too much.

"What do you mean by that, Doctor?"

"Just stay away from them, Mrs. Smith. Take my advice."

She could tell by the firm line of his mouth and the flatness that had come to his eyes that he had said all he was going to say on the subject of the Ross family.

"You can keep the ice pack," he said, offering her a hand to help her off the table, which she accepted.

Jeffrey paid the bill in cash and they left the office. On the walkway, Lydia turned around and looked at the doctor, who stood in the doorway. The night had grown bitterly cold and Lydia wrapped her coat tightly around her. A harsh wind had crept up and a few stray snowflakes danced around them. The doctor's large frame filled the doorway.

"He's here, you know. In Haunted."

The doctor didn't seem surprised. "Some people claim he's been here all along, living in the woods. He's mythic in his way. Parents use him to warn their children to stay out of the woods at night."

"Be good or James Ross will get you?"

"That's right."

Back in the relative warmth of the Rover, Lydia told Jeff and Dax what the doctor had shared with her. Even with the heat blasting, the cold felt like a fourth presence in the car. Lydia was shivering, cupping her hands against one of the vents. She was grateful when the air grew warmer as the car heated up.

"Should we call Henry Clay?" she wondered aloud.

"And tell him what? That we broke into the Ross home and saw the bogeyman?" asked Jeff, driving carefully down the dark road, slick with the light snowfall.

"And that he kicked our asses," added Dax from the backseat.

"James Ross is not the bogeyman. He's a viable suspect for two murders and he's wandering around Haunted unchecked. He's dangerous," said Lydia.

"Sounds to me like he's only dangerous to his family."

"I beg to differ," said Dax. "I've got eight bloody stitches to make my argument."

“We don’t know that,” said Lydia, responding to Jeff. “He’s got to get picked up at some point for questioning at the very least.”

“But we’re not the people to do it at the moment. And I don’t feel like answering to the police about why we broke into the Ross home.”

“So, what? We just leave him out there?”

“No, we’ll call Ford, tell him what we’ve found. He can arrange something with the Haunted police.”

“What if it’s too late by then?”

“Lydia, the guy has been on the run for ten years and he’s still hanging around his own backyard. My guess is he’s not going to go far. In fact, if he’s mentally disturbed, I bet he even goes directly back to his tent in the basement. We’ll get him. Just not tonight.”

For once, Lydia was too tired to argue. Her head was pounding and fatigue made her limbs feel like they were filled with sand. Besides, Jeffrey’s logic, as usual, was irrefutable.

Lydia had wanted to stop at Maura Hodge’s again before leaving Haunted, but she didn’t even bother to broach the subject as Jeffrey pulled onto the highway going back to New York. The air between Lydia and Jeffrey was charged with a million things each of them wanted to say. But neither had the energy to say any of them. So after Jeff put in a call to Ford, letting him know about James Ross, they rode in silence until Lydia fell into an uneasy sleep, jerking awake every few miles, seeing alternately the face of her attacker and Jed McIntyre raging toward her over and over again.

NINETEEN

WCOU Bar on Second Avenue was slow on Monday nights. That, and the fact that the old bartender mixed a dangerous Manhattan and looked like as much a relic as the antique jukebox and the glowing neon art deco clock on the wall, was the reason Ford chose to stop there with Irma. The room was smoky and narrow, dim, with high tables and stools against the walls. It had atmosphere in that kind of nonchalant way that made it real. If the lights came up, you'd see cigarette butts on the floor, nicks in the wall, that the ceiling was mottled with water stains. But in the glow of low-wattage bulbs beneath glass shades, you felt like you were in a black and white movie and any second Humphrey Bogart was going to saunter through the door and bum a smoke.

So far, the forensics team had turned up nothing at the laundry room. He and Irma had stopped up after the interview with the twins to check in with the forensics scientist heading up the team. The Luminol had detected no blood traces. Because so many people had access to the laundry room, no one was optimistic that any of the prints, hairs, or fibers collected at the scene would have any relevance to the case. And no one was happy about how much work it was going to take to determine that.

Ford ordered their drinks from the bartender and then carried them back to the table Irma had chosen at the far back corner of the bar. Shedding his coat, he folded his arms and looked at her.

"So what are your thoughts on the twins?"

Irma sighed lightly and took a sip of her Cosmopolitan. "The children are deeply veiled," she said, keeping her voice low and her face close to Ford's. "Someone is exerting a lot of power over them. They're both very intelligent, especially Lola, so they have an instinct that something is wrong. But they feel powerless. And, of course, they are, in the context of their situation."

"So who's exerting this power?"

"Someone who frightens them, someone who in Nathaniel's mind has taken on the proportions of a monster, his bogeyman."

Irma took another sip of her cocktail, while Ford drank his Perrier with lime. Technically, he was still on duty, so the Manhattan was going to have to wait for another night.

Ford's mind jumped from Irma's comments, to the news Jeffrey had just given him about Julian's twin, to the picture he'd seen in the gallery, and then to the description of the man Jetty Murphy claimed he saw the night Tad was killed. Was James Ross the bogeyman Nathaniel claimed to have seen? Was he also guilty of the murder of Tad Jenson?

The fact that Julian had a twin brother was another crucial piece of information he hadn't had when investigating Tad's murder. The thought made him sick with frustration and anger—anger at himself for not digging deep enough. The knowledge threatened a cornerstone in his self-narrative. In his own mind, the excuse he gave himself for being a shitty father and husband was that he was a good cop. Tonight he didn't even feel like he was that. His mood was low and getting lower.

Efforts to calm Nathaniel Stratton-Ross had failed and Irma convinced Ford that pressing forward to find out why they were in the laundry that night would be pointless at best, traumatic at worst. So the interview with the twins had ended with both of the children in tears, Nathaniel screaming his head off, and Eleanor threatening Ford's job. Not that he cared much about that at the moment. The conversation he'd had with Lydia in the car kept coming back to him. I don't even know what I am if I'm not a cop, he'd told her. Maybe you should find out, she'd answered him. He was starting to wonder if she was right.

"Lola is clearly the dominant personality," Irma went on. "But I sense that she's just as afraid as Nathaniel is; she's just better at hiding it under a sullen façade."

"Do you think it's possible that they saw who killed their father?"

"I'm inclined to say that no, they didn't witness the murder. To be honest, there haven't been that many studies done on children who witness the death of their parents. But to watch their father murdered so brutally and to display no evidence of trauma or distress would be highly unusual."

"What if they're repressing the memory," said Ford.

Irma shook her head. "Repressed memory is far less common than you think. If anything emotionally charged events are the least forgettable of all memories."

"But it's possible."

She shrugged her assent. "It's possible. But say they had completely blocked out their memories of the event, there would be other indicators of repressed memory of the trauma. Probably any mention of that night would cause terror and panic. But they remember every detail happily until they went to bed."

"But Lola was down in that laundry room. We've got the videotape. And Piselli found Lola's nightgown back at the apartment. She didn't mention that."

"But that doesn't mean they've repressed the memory. It

will take more time to find out what happened at that point. They've been instructed not to discuss that with anyone. That much was clear. Lola tried to warn Nathaniel to be quiet. But he couldn't hold it in. He's afraid of someone. They both are."

"What about Nathaniel? If Lola went into the laundry room to move the washing machine..."

"Wait, she's just a little girl. How is she going to move that machine by herself?"

"It was on casters, very easy to move."

"Okay."

"Is Nathaniel smart enough to turn off that camera, wait till his sister and whoever have cleared the laundry room, and then turn the camera on again?"

She thought about it for a second. "It's hard to see Nathaniel acting like that on his own. He seems very dependent on Lola. He'd probably be able to follow instructions, but I doubt very much if he'd be able to carry out a task like that alone."

Ford took a sip from his Perrier and wished it was a Manhattan. He turned the pieces around in his mind, circling the edge of his glass with his fingertip, trying to fit everything together, what he knew, what Lydia and Jeffrey had come across.

Things weren't falling together, even with the possibility of James Ross as a suspect. There were just too many questions: Where had he been all these years? Why would he kill his sister's husbands when it was her he supposedly hated? And logistically, how would he have gotten from Haunted to New York City and back again? How did he know there was a tunnel leading to the building? How was he communicating with the children? It just seemed too far-fetched. Maybe Lydia and Jeffrey had time to play X-Files, but he needed a chain of hard evidence. He could only hope that, after taking James Ross in for questioning and analyzing the evidence Lydia and Jeffrey had collected, some tangible connection could be made, that answers would start to evolve from the tangled mass of questions in his mind.

He felt Irma's eyes on him and he looked up from his glass.

"Welcome back," she said, and gave him a smile that reminded him how pretty she was. There was concern in her eyes, and something more.

"I'm sorry," he said. "Lost in thought."

She put a warm hand on his arm and he looked down at her slender fingers, her perfectly manicured nails. Her blond hair looked like spun gold and framed her face in a delicate flattering way. He found himself remembering how long it had been since he'd been this close to a woman. It opened the hole in his heart that Rose had occupied, and for a moment he felt like putting his head down on his arm and sobbing. Luckily, his cell phone rang and he was spared the embarrassment.

"McKirdy," he answered, looking at Irma with apology in his eyes. She withdrew her hand and looked down at her Cosmo.

"Henry Clay here. This better be good."

Ford had put in a call to the Haunted PD and convinced the desk sergeant to rouse his chief from bed.

"Chief, you have someone residing in your town that I need to bring in for questioning. I'd like to send two of my detectives up to you tomorrow and I am hoping you can put some uniforms on this."

"Who exactly are we talking about here, Detective?"

"James Ross."

There was a leaden silence on the other end of the phone.

"Chief?"

"Are you fucking with me, Detective?" asked Clay, and Ford could hear an angry quaver in the man's voice.

"I don't have time to fuck around," said Ford, dropping the polite formality he'd employed up to this point and turning away from Irma. Ford was old school, and old school men don't swear in front of women, if they can help it.

"James Ross has not lived in this town for more than twenty years."

"I have good information that he's residing in his family home."

Silence again. Ford could hear Clay breathing on the line.

"Where did you get your information?" he asked finally.

"That's not important."

"The hell it isn't. We had reports of a break-in at the old Ross house tonight. Was that your people?"

"I don't know anything about that," Ford lied.

More silence.

"Look, are you going to help me or not?" said Ford, at the end of his patience. "I'll send someone up there either way. I was just giving you the respect of a phone call to let you know we'd be entering your jurisdiction to question a suspect in a murder investigation."

"Well, you won't get any of my men to go near that house."

"What are you talking about? Why not?"

"Because it's...not right, that house. It's evil."

Ford shook his head slowly in disbelief. He let out an uncertain laugh.

"Bad things happen to the people that go into that house," Clay continued, his voice low and serious.

Ford let a second pass before saying, "You're supposed to stop the bad things from happening, Chief. That's what cops do."

"Your men want to go up there, be my guest. But I guarantee you're not going to be bringing James Ross in for questioning."

"Why not?" Ford asked.

There was static on the line when Clay spoke, and Ford was sure he hadn't heard him correctly. "Can you repeat that?"

The man issued a mighty sigh.

"I said, because he's dead, McKirdy. James Ross is dead."

TWENTY

"When you love someone, I mean really love someone," she said, "it hurts so much. Even the pleasure can feel like a blade. It's all temporary and your heart recognizes that transience because it is temporary. Even the beauty of love is edged with the knowledge that an end will come—horribly, sadly, inevitably."

Marion Strong sat serene and beautiful at the edge of Lydia's bed. Jeffrey slept soundly beside Lydia, his breathing heavy and even. The angry words they'd spoken before bed still danced in the air.

"You look like an angel," Lydia told her mother.

"Only because you love me."

Marion's black hair streaked with gray flowed down over her shoulders to the small of her back. She wore a crisp white cotton nightgown that Lydia remembered from her childhood. Sitting there, the amber light from the street lamps outside leaking through the blinds, she seemed to glow.

Lydia observed every line on Marion's face, the way her strong veined hands rested in her lap, the arch of her dark eyebrows, the black of her eyes. She wanted every detail seared into her memory. Because that was all she would have of Marion to share with her own children. It was all she'd had for so long. Sometimes it seemed as if the sadness she felt over the loss of her mother was a well within her that could never be filled.

"I'm pregnant," Lydia said, feeling an odd longing, a kind of desperation, grow in her heart.

But Marion only smiled sadly and shook her head.

"People die," she said, as if she hadn't heard. "But love lives on, we carry it in our blood and our bones. When you lose someone, you've only lost the giver, not the gift."

When Lydia awoke she was already sitting up, her heart rate elevated, her breathing coming sharp and shallow. She reached for Jeffrey and shook him awake. He sat up quickly, startled.

"What's wrong?"

She didn't know what to say, so she moved to him, clung to him, feeling the soft skin and hard muscles of his chest against her cheek. He held on to her tightly. She needed to be as close as the boundaries of their bodies would allow so that she could feel his life and the warmth of blood flowing beneath his skin.

"It's okay. I promise," he said, not knowing what she was feeling but understanding that she needed him to comfort her. "I swear it's all okay."

She looked up at him and in her eyes he saw such a painful combination of fear and love that it awoke a powerful longing within him. He regretted deeply the lecture he'd delivered when they'd returned to the apartment about her carelessness for her health and safety. Even in the darkness of the room, he could see the purple and black of the bruise that dominated the right side of her face.

"I love you so much," he said. "I'm sorry."

"No, I'm sorry," she said quickly. "You were right... about everything."

He pressed his mouth to hers, wanting to be gentle but overwhelmed by a sudden hunger for her, which he felt returned in her kiss. She knelt before him on the bed now. He touched the slope of her shoulder and the curve of her bare breast. He touched the line of her jaw. She moved in closer, running her hand down his chest, over his tight abs, then stroking him as he grew hard in her hand. Then she leaned in to take him into her mouth. He lay back, her tongue, the wet walls of her mouth sending a shock of pleasure through him.

She slithered up his body and he felt every inch of her slide along every inch of him in a current of taut and silky flesh. Then she straddled him and took him inside of her with a moan. He placed his hands on the fullness of her hips and held her as she rocked, her movements slow, sensual. He felt weak with pleasure, as the rhythm of their bodies became more intense.

She threw her head back slightly as he pulled her closer, took her breast in his mouth and teased her nipple with his tongue. Her breath came in soft low moans. He knew her body so well, he could feel her coming to climax, every nerve ending in his body alive with the heat of wanting her. Then he came deep and hard inside of her.

"Lydia," he whispered, her name sounding like a prayer as she came for him, pulling him deeper inside of her.

She lay beside him, back to his front, her body curved into his, his arm draped over her. He breathed in the lavender scent of her hair.

"I need you to promise to take better care from now on," he whispered.

"I promise," she answered, trying to push away the memory of her dream and be in the present, feeling the warmth of him beside her.

He moved the hair off her face and touched the bruise there, then kissed it lightly.

She closed her eyes for a second, and when she opened them again, his breathing had sunk into the rhythm of sleep. She turned so that she could look at him. She observed every detail of his face, loving the tiny lines around his eyes, the fullness of his mouth, the small star-shaped scar on his right cheekbone. She watched him like this for she didn't know how long until sleep came for her as well.

To her obvious disappointment, Ford had dropped Irma off at her Central Park West apartment building. He was flattered by Irma's subtle advances and not a little attracted to her, but he was and maybe always would be in his heart still married to Rose. Still, Irma had awoken a terrible restlessness in him and he lay in bed, staring at the ceiling fan as it turned lazily above him. He thought of Rose, wondering where she was, how he might reach her, what he would say if he had her on the line.

He had the television turned on but the sound muted; it was something he did when he couldn't sleep, when he was missing his wife. It made him feel less alone. Something on the screen had attracted his attention and he turned his head to see Fran Drescher being interviewed by David Letterman. The Nanny, he remembered, was a show that Rose had liked. The thought brought Geneva Stout to his mind, reminded him that he'd wanted to have another conversation with her. Then it occurred to him that he hadn't seen Geneva the day they'd interviewed the twins.

He thought back to the night of the murder. After the paramedics had taken Julian Ross from the duplex, Ford had interviewed the live-in au pair. She was young, he remembered, twenty-one or twenty-two, soft-spoken, and very upset by the events of the evening. She'd been pretty in a dark, exotic way, with full lips and almond-shaped eyes. He remembered thinking the name sounded off, bringing to mind a busty Swedish girl with silky blond hair. Geneva clearly didn't have a Nordic bone in her body, with café au lait skin and a bolt of shiny black curls that spilled across her shoulders and down her back.

She'd been sleeping, she claimed that night, and had seen nothing. Ford had no reason to suspect otherwise, since her room was in the back of the first floor behind the kitchen, far from the entrance and master bedroom in the palatial duplex. He'd given her his card, asked her to call if she thought of anything that might help him, and told her she'd probably be hearing from him.

He leaned over, looked at the clock, hesitated, and then picked up the phone anyway.

"Where's the nanny, Ms. Ross?" asked Ford into the phone.

"Detective McKirdy, it's after midnight," said Eleanor, indignant.

"The nanny, Geneva Stout. She was there the night of the murder. But she wasn't with you when we interviewed the twins this evening."

"Well, naturally, she quit, Detective. Wouldn't you?"

"Where did she go?"

"How should I know? I didn't hire her. Only Julian would know that...and she doesn't even know who I am at this point."

"Do you know how long she worked for the family?"

"I'm not sure. A year, maybe eighteen months...Why is this relevant, Detective?"

"Thank you, Ms. Ross, sorry to disturb you.

"Huh," he said aloud after hanging up the phone.

Other than the name, nothing else about her had set off any alarms. He'd asked to see ID and she'd provided him with an NYU student ID and a New York State driver's license, both with the Rosses' address as her own. He knew he'd written down both her student ID and driver's license numbers. He'd run them through first thing in the morning. Even though she'd left the Rosses' employment—and

Eleanor was right about that, why wouldn't she?—he figured she'd be easy enough to find.

He'd need to check his notes again and then look through the papers at the Stratton-Ross home, see if there was another address for her. It was probably nothing, but now that the twins were part of the equation he had a strange feeling that maybe Geneva Stout, someone who'd been intimate with the children for more than a year, had more to contribute to his investigation than he'd originally thought.

After talking to Eleanor, he lay still for a few more minutes. Then with the remote he switched off the television and closed his eyes, hoping that sleep would come, that he wouldn't lie awake watching the hours pass, thinking of murder and lost love.

TWENTY-ONE

"Nice face," said Craig from his seat behind the reception desk as Lydia and Jeffrey pushed their way through the glass doors. As tall and thin as a reed, Craig slumped at the desk gripping a tattered copy of Neuromancer. He pushed aside the curly blond hair that fell over his round spectacle lenses and looked at Lydia quizzically.

"What happened to you?" he asked.

"You should see the other guy," answered Lydia with a half smile she didn't feel.

"Where's Rebecca?" asked Jeffrey.

"I'm filling in. She called in sick. Flu," he said. "She sounded like you look, Lydia." A boyish smile broke his long, narrow face and saved him from the barb she was about to toss back at him.

"Thanks. Thanks a lot," she answered as she stepped into her office. At the door, she paused a second. Something felt off. She looked around the room, saw nothing unusual, and decided she was just being paranoid. She shed her coat, though she knew they'd only be there for a short time, draped it over the sofa, and sat at her desk. She pulled a compact from her bag and gazed at herself in the mirror for the hundredth time since she'd gotten out of bed. A face only a prizefighter's mother could love, she thought. She snapped the compact closed and booted her computer.

"Was someone in my office?" she heard Jeffrey ask Craig over the intercom.

"Not that I know of," he answered. "Why?"

She got up and walked across the hall to Jeffrey's office. "What's wrong?"

"I don't know. My computer is on, my day planner is open. It's just not the way I left things," he said with a frown.

"Maybe Rebecca was looking for something?" she offered, knowing even as she spoke that it wasn't Rebecca's style. Everything would have been left exactly as she found it. Rebecca was precise, effective, and compulsively neat. Her appearance was always perfect; her work was always exceptional. In fact, Lydia couldn't remember a time when Rebecca had called in sick before today.

"Hm," said Lydia.

"What?"

"Let's get her on the phone."

"Why?"

"Because I had a feeling someone was in my office, as well."

"Something missing?"

"Nope. Just a weird feeling," she said thoughtfully. She walked back to her office and stood in the doorway. The space was pretty sterile because of Lydia's compulsive need to carry things with her everywhere she went and because she really considered her office at the loft to be her workspace. Still something seemed different.

"I got the machine. Left a message for her to call," said Jeffrey, coming up behind her. "I'm sure it's nothing."

Lydia nodded. "Yeah, you're probably right." The uneasy

feeling in her gut said something else. It was a feeling that stayed with her as they headed out the door, on their way to get some answers from Eleanor Ross.

When Lydia and Jeffrey reached the Waldorf, Eleanor and the twins appeared to be on their way out. Their luggage had been loaded onto a cart and a porter was leaving the room as Lydia and Jeffrey entered.

"Going somewhere, Ms. Ross?" asked Lydia.

"Back to the apartment. The children need to be in their home."

"But it's a crime scene," said Lydia, appalled that she would even consider moving the children back to the place where their father was murdered and wondering how she was even allowed access.

"Money talks," said Eleanor, drawing back her shoulders and jutting out her chin. "It's up to me to decide what's right for the children now, since there's no one to look after them."

"But to bring them back to the apartment where their father was—" Lydia stopped abruptly when the children entered the room.

They seemed to move as one, holding hands as they walked into the room. Their matching white blond heads of hair glowed golden in the sun that shone in from the window. Ivory skin and ice blue eyes, they looked as if they were made from light, luminous and ethereal.

"Grandma, Nathaniel can't find Pat the Bunny," said Lola, her voice light and musical.

"It's on the cart headed downstairs, Nathaniel. You'll have it before we get in the car. I promise."

Nathaniel nodded, but Lydia could see his anxiety. The kid wanted his bunny. Lydia felt an irrational wash of anger that Eleanor hadn't kept the bunny off the cart, knowing, as she must, that he would be looking for it.

"Who's that?" said Lola, eyeing Lydia suspiciously.

"These are friends of mine, children. Their helping us find out who hurt your father."

Lydia was surprised at the candor of Eleanor's answer and couldn't imagine what good could come of them knowing that. But the children didn't seem upset. Both Lola and Nathaniel turned their eyes on Lydia and Jeffrey with a kind of wonder. Lydia leaned down and offered her hand.

"I'm Lydia," she said, smiling. Each child shook her hand properly in turn. "And this is my partner, Jeffrey."

"Is he your boyfriend?" Lola wanted to know.

"He's my partner," she said again. It was really a more truthful answer anyway.

"Oh," said Lola with a little frown, as if sensing the complexity of the answer but too young to really understand.

"What happened to your face?" asked Nathaniel, pointing to her bruise. "It looks bad."

Lydia smiled at Nathaniel and then looked up at Eleanor. "Can we have a few minutes with you?"

Eleanor nodded and escorted the children from the room.

"Nice to meet you," Nathaniel tossed over his shoulder with a little smile. He had been taught to be polite and the lesson had stuck.

When Eleanor returned, Lydia didn't waste any more time.

"Why didn't you tell us you had a son, Eleanor? A son who'd been committed and escaped from a mental institution; a son who tried to kill you and Julian."

A stillness came over Eleanor. She moved over to the couch and sat unsteadily.

"My son is dead," she said quietly.

"No, I don't think so, Ms. Ross. I have this bruise on my face to prove it. He attacked me in the basement of your house in Haunted."

Eleanor shook her head firmly. "Whoever did that to you,

it wasn't my son. He was found dead last year in that same house. There's a death certificate to prove it."

Lydia was feeling a little unsteady herself suddenly. Her face had flushed with a rush of heat and she moved to the chair beside Eleanor.

"What about your brother, Eleanor? What about Paul? Where is he?"

Eleanor shook her head again, this time slowly. She cast her eyes to the floor. A deep sadness had come over her and for the first time since Lydia had met her, Eleanor seemed human.

"He's been missing for many years," she nearly whispered. "I've long believed him dead. He was my twin; I'd know if he were still alive."

"There are rumors, Eleanor. Ugly ones. About you and Paul, about James and Julian."

Eleanor slammed her hand suddenly down on the coffee table in a hard, flat slap.

"Goddammit!" she yelled. The lid that had opened in Lydia's office flew wide and all the demons flew out. "Why do you think I took Julian and left that place? Those rumors, the curse—they plagued us. Do you know what it's like to live beneath the shadows of others' fear and ignorance, their voyeurism? Everyone always whispering; thinking that they know you, your family. It is a nightmare."

She stopped and took a shuddering breath. Lydia and Jeffrey were silent, allowing her to collect her thoughts.

"When Jack was murdered, things became unbearable for us in that town. All they had was each other, James and Julian. None of the other children would play with them; at school they were taunted, bullied. James was fighting every week, defending himself and his sister. They became inseparable, united against the rest of the town. But then James started to change. I'd seen it before in Paul. The mental illness, the delusions, the terrible rages. That is the curse of our family, the shadow we live under."

Lydia imagined James and Julian, their father murdered, their mother accused, the people of the town treating them like pariahs. Adolescence is such a tortured time under the best of circumstances, there was no telling how additional pressures like that could damage a person.

"But there is no incest in our family, if those are the rumors you've heard. James and Julian loved each other, needed each other, were closer than other siblings because they were twins. That's it. Nothing more. The same was true for Paul and me. People in that town are so small and sick, so bored, they'll do anything, say anything to entertain themselves. God, I hated that place."

Eleanor was crying now. Silent tears streamed down her face and she looked old, frail, shattered. Her regal posture sagged, as though the truth had deflated her.

"What can you tell me about your relationship with Maura Hodge?"

Lydia saw Eleanor cringe at the sound of her name.

"Maura Hodge." She said the name as if it were sour on her tongue. "She hates us. Hates our family. Hates me most of all."

"Why?"

"She'll tell you it's because of years of injustice, starting with Hiram Ross. I'm sure you've heard about that curse. She's made sure that that legend never dies with that library of hers. She's been commissioning writers and historians for decades, making sure the history of Haunted is preserved forever. As if anyone cares but her."

"She claims not to believe in the curse, either," said Lydia, remembering what Maura had said about the Ross family cursing themselves.

"Whether she believes or not, she used it to turn the town against us when Jack was killed. A part of me holds her responsible for James losing his mind."

"How's that?"

"I just wonder if the people in the town hadn't been so

cruel, hadn't bought into all the rumors and made James and Julian feel like monsters, maybe James would have recovered. Maybe—" Eleanor stopped herself short. She looked past Lydia, rested her gaze on something far away.

"But Paul and James are dead now," she said after a moment, with a kind of relief in her voice, as if everything had been settled. "They're at peace."

"Great," said Lydia. "But that doesn't explain who killed your husband or who killed Tad Jenson and Richard Stratton. That doesn't help Julian."

Lydia waited for Eleanor to respond, but she didn't. The emotion she'd displayed earlier seemed to have drained from her and her former chilly demeanor returned. She wiped her eyes and straightened her back.

"Do you think Maura Hodge could be behind the murders?" asked Lydia, reaching now.

"I suppose it's possible," she said without conviction, almost without interest.

"Eleanor, you must have some idea. Some theory."

"Actually, dear," she said, "that's why I hired you."

The Eleanor who had raged about Haunted and the Eleanor who now sat cold and hard as an ice sculpture were two entirely different women.

"What are you hiding, Eleanor? What don't you want us to know?" asked Lydia.

"I have nothing else to say. I've told you all I can."

They had been dismissed.

TWENTY-TWO

“Dead men don’t eat Milky Way bars,” said Lydia, handing over to Ford the baggies of evidence she’d collected in the Ross basement.

They stood in Ford’s office, which was a little bigger, but not by much, than a broom closet. In the back of the main homicide office, a maze of busy cubicles and ringing phones, it was dank and dusty, but at least there was a door to pull closed. The blinds were pulled down over the only window and the room was lit by a flickering fluorescent overhead and a small desk halogen.

“Well,” he said, handing her a document, “Chief Clay had the hospital records department fax over his death certificate. Whoever it was did that to your face, it wasn’t James Ross.”

“I know what I saw,” Lydia said stubbornly, perusing the paper in her hand.

“You lost consciousness, right? You have a concussion? You can’t be sure of what you saw,” said Ford.

She looked at the document in her hand.

"You'd just seen the photograph of Julian's twin. It was a moment of intense stress. And it was very dark," said Jeff pragmatically. "Isn't it possible that you just imagined his face on whoever it was that attacked us?"

Lydia shook her head. She had been frightened in the moment and injured afterward, but she certainly wasn't going to let anyone convince her that she couldn't believe her own eyes.

"According to Chief Clay, his body was found in the Ross home last year by some kids who snuck in there to do some drinking, fool around," said Ford. "He'd hanged himself from the landing over the foyer."

"Jesus," said Jeffrey.

Lydia still hadn't taken her eyes off the paper Ford had handed her. According to the death certificate, James Ross had been found last April 16, dead over a week, cause of death determined as suicide by asphyxiation. He was positively identified by his dental records. She looked down at the signature. Dr. Franklin Wetterau.

"If James Ross was found dead, then why didn't Dr. Wetterau tell us that last night?" she said, showing Jeffrey the doctor's name on the document.

Jeffrey shrugged. "No idea," he said.

"Maura Hodge never mentioned that Julian even had a twin brother. Henry Clay didn't say anything about him when the two of you spoke yesterday. Eleanor never even mentioned him until we confronted her, and he's her son. Doesn't that seem odd to either one of you?"

"Maybe we just weren't asking the right questions," said Jeffrey.

"Anyway, what difference does it make? He's no good to me dead," said Ford. "If he's in the ground over a year, he didn't kill Richard Stratton."

"But he could have killed Tad Jenson."

"I suppose he could have. But that case is cold. I need to solve this one. You guys follow whatever leads you want."

"Just see if the hairs match the ones from the Jenson case, Ford. See if there's any DNA on the candy bar wrapper."

"And what if there is? How does that help this case? Even if the hairs match and the wrapper has the DNA from James Ross's ghost, what does that tell me about Richard Stratton?"

She looked at him and shook her head slightly, but didn't bother arguing. He had a case to solve and their investigation was becoming too far-fetched for him, she could see it in his eyes. It was like this when you were a private investigator; cops sometimes cooperated when they thought you might help. And Jeffrey had a lot of contacts, people who owed him favors, people he'd worked with in the past either with the FBI or as a private consultant, who gave them the kind of access of which other PIs could only dream. But when you started to get in the way, you got the official boot. She didn't blame him, that's just the way it was.

"Look," he said, "you guys are all over the board here... curses, ghosts, incest, family feuds. Sometimes, you know, the simplest solution is the right solution. Maybe someone hired a killer to do Richard Stratton. Maybe someone wants you to think James Ross is still alive, stalking his sister and murdering her husbands."

She nodded. "Maybe you're right," she said.

Ford and Jeffrey both looked at her with disbelief as she turned and walked out the door.

Outside the precinct, the air was cool, and that was exactly what she needed. A cold rain had fallen in the early morning, but now the sky was a bright blue with some light wisps of white clouds. The trees in the lot across the street were nearly bare and the wind blew the fallen leaves up to flutter into the sky, some of them sticking to the wet hoods of the crisp blue and white cruisers that lined the block.

Lydia took the cold air into her lungs and tried to breathe

against the pain she felt in her abdomen. But instead of subsiding the way it had the last few times, it seemed to grow hot and sharp inside her. She clutched her bag to her side, leaned against the concrete of the precinct building, and tried to keep herself together. Suddenly she wished she hadn't walked out of the building and away from Jeffrey, but the office had seemed so hot and close. She'd thought if she could just get some air, she would feel all right again. Now she was alone on the street and the pain grew even more intense. Somewhere in the distance, she heard a familiar voice, heard her name. Then there were hands on her. Everything around her pitched horribly, like she was on a boat in a storm. Then the street and the sky and her awareness of these things faded away.

PART TWO
TWENTY-THREE

It was a bright, clear day as Ford McKirdy pulled his Taurus up the sidewalk in front of the Sunnyvale Retirement Home on Broadway in the Bronx. It was a sad-looking place, as were all nursing homes, no matter how hard they tried. Really there was no escaping the fact that even the best of them were the antechamber to death. As he pushed open the white double doors and was assaulted by the odors of decay and disinfectant, he tried not to imagine himself in a place like this, nothing but a nuisance to his children, awake all day with his regrets, waiting to die.

Geneva Stout didn't exist. Well, she had existed, until two years ago when she'd died alone at the age of eighty-eight in a nursing home in Riverdale, leaving no children, no relatives at all. There was no one registered at NYU under that name. So the nanny, whatever her real name was, had disappeared.

But he had to wonder how the nanny had managed to

usurp Geneva's identity, and his wondering had led him to the place where the old women had died, looking for answers.

Nurse Jeremiah was about as pleasant and easy on the eyes as an old bulldog. With a pronounced underbite, and a head of gray hair that was clearly store-bought, her tremendous girth commanded about two-thirds of the counter behind which she sat. She turned an evil eye on Ford as soon as he'd put foot on the linoleum floor, her scowl seeming to deepen the closer he came.

"Good morning," he said with his most winning smile.

"If you say so," she answered, staring at him as if trying to figure out his game.

He took out his gold detective's shield and placed it on the counter in front of her, expecting her attitude to improve.

"I'm Detective Halford McKirdy from the New York City Police Department," he said.

She glanced at him, then down at his shield with cool distaste.

"That supposed to scare me?" she asked.

"Uh, no."

"What do you want, Officer?"

"Look, what's your problem? You get bonus pay for attitude?"

"I don't get bonus pay for nothin'. I see you walking in here and I know you're going to make my morning difficult. I can just see it in that cocky walk of yours."

Ford looked into her middle-aged face and saw that beneath the crust was a marshmallow center. There was a glitter to her brown eyes and just the slightest upturning of the corners of her thin pink lips. In the lines on her face, he saw a woman who had changed diapers, read stories, gone to graduations. He saw a woman who, in spite of her size, still got out on the dance floor at weddings, whose generous arms were a safe place for the people who loved her. He smiled and leaned in to her a little.

"Come on," he said. "Give me a break?"

She gave a little laugh, knowing somehow that he'd seen through her. "All right," she sighed. "What is it?"

"Does the name Geneva Stout mean anything to you?"

She looked past him as if running the name through her mental database.

"I do remember Geneva," she said finally. "A sweet, sweet old woman. She liked to play Scrabble. Never gave anyone a moment's trouble. She was all alone, I remember. No one to visit." She followed her sentence with a quick little cluck of her tongue, a noise that communicated sympathy and a little sadness. "What about her?"

"It's not her so much as who was working here when Geneva died that interests me."

She raised an eyebrow at him. "This place has a revolving door. It's gritty work, sad work. Reminds people of what the end could bring."

"She's a young woman, maybe in her late teens, early twenties when she was here. Exotic-looking, long dark curly hair. Pretty, petite. On the short side, maybe five-two, five-three."

She shrugged. "Like I said, a lot of people have been through here."

"What about employment records?"

The woman heaved a sigh. "See, now, there you go."

"What?"

"I knew you were gonna make me get up from this seat," she said, but she gave him a smile and hefted herself from the desk.

"Follow me," she said, buzzing him through a door to her left.

She asked another woman to watch the front for her and led Ford down a hallway, and through a door marked records.

"What's your name?" he asked her as they walked into the room.

"Katherine Jeremiah, my friends call me Cat. You can

call me Nurse Jeremiah," she said with a teasing smile.

When she flipped on the light switch, he expected to see rows of file cabinets; instead, he stood in a room filled with computers. The room was ice-cold and somewhere a vent rattled.

"Most everything is on computers these days. It took years to convert all our records. But we're mostly caught up. The older files got moved into the basement. And these machines hold all employee and patient files since, I think, 1980 or something."

Ford just nodded and smiled politely as if he cared. She pulled up a chair in front of one of the computers and began to type.

"Let's see, if she was that young, then she probably wasn't a nurse and definitely not a doctor," she muttered, thinking aloud. "I'm going to search for all females between the age of seventeen and twenty-five working here from 1998 to 2001, and that should cover it."

She typed a few things on the keyboard and then sat back. "Should take just a minute."

"You have photographs on there?" asked Ford after they'd waited for a minute.

"There should be a photograph for everyone who worked here."

She swiveled around in the chair and gave him a blatant once-over. "Wife left you?" she said out of nowhere.

"What?" Ford felt like she'd punched him in the gut.

"I'm just wondering because I see you're wearing a ring. But no wife would let her husband go out of the house looking all messy like you slept in your clothes. You have a five o'clock shadow and it isn't even noon."

"It's none of your business, Nurse Jeremiah," he said with a frown.

She shrugged and gave him a knowing smile.

"Get her back," she said, turning back to the computer. "All women who leave are hoping you'll beg them to come back."

"Thanks for the unsolicited advice," he said, a little angry, a little embarrassed, and a little bit wondering if she was right.

A soft bing from the computer announced that twenty-five matches had been found to the criterion she had entered. She motioned Ford over and he came to stand behind her as she scrolled through each of the entries, each record complete with driver's license photograph. She flipped slowly through and each face was unfamiliar to him, all of them young, most of them pretty, none of them the woman he was looking for.

He was starting to think he'd hit a dead end when she came to one of the last records. Her hair was much shorter, her face rounder. The picture didn't at all capture her fiery beauty, but there was the woman he knew as Geneva Stout.

"That's her," he said, moving in closer.

"I remember that one," said the nurse with a snort. "She walked around here like she owned the place. Lazy as the day is long. Then one day she didn't show up for her shift. Never came back again."

"Right after Geneva died?"

She thought about it a minute. "I guess that's right."

Ford leaned in to the record to read her name. "Oh, Lord," he said with a shake of his head. "I should have known."

"That sure is an odd name for a town," Nurse Jeremiah said, reading the young woman's address. "Haunted? I've never heard of such a place."

"Unfortunately," said Ford, "I have."

TWENTY-FOUR

In his hand Jeffrey held a sterling Tiffany baby rattle. He turned it and marveled at how small it looked in his hand. It made just the lightest tinkling as he played with it, watched it catch the light sneaking in through the slats of the drawn blinds. He'd bought the rattle for Lydia after he learned that she was pregnant and had been waiting for the right time to give it to her. That time wasn't going to come for a while.

Jeffrey hadn't really begun to conceive of the baby as a real person; he hadn't thought of whether it would be a girl or a boy, what he would look like, if she would have Lydia's eyes, her stubborn streak, his pragmatism. Jeffrey had only really thought of the baby as a happy concept rather than as a flesh-and-blood part of himself. But the loss was a crush on his heart. He didn't see it as a death, necessarily...maybe if Lydia had been further along, it would have felt more like that. But it was the death of a hope, a dream he'd had for their immediate future.

It wasn't to be for them, right now. He could accept that. All that mattered to him at the moment was that Lydia was all right. When he'd seen her fall on the street, he felt like the world was coming to end. It had seemed like miles between them as he ran to reach her, though it was only a few feet. And when he'd seen her face, pale and wan, her eyes half open, he'd felt fear on a level he didn't even know existed. Now she rested in their bed, her breathing heavy with painkillers and exhaustion.

Lydia had experienced an ectopic pregnancy, where the fetus had settled in her fallopian tube rather than in her uterus, causing a rupture that led to Lydia's collapse on the sidewalk outside Midtown North. He was more than a little thankful that the miscarriage was a result of circumstances beyond their control, rather than it being the result of the trauma she'd sustained the night before. He wasn't sure if he'd have been able to forgive himself for that. He was glad he didn't have to face anger and guilt, as well as grief.

These were the thoughts in his mind as he sat in the chair by the window of their bedroom and watched Lydia sleep. She looked small and fragile wrapped in their down comforter. But physically, she would be all right. With a laparoscopy, the doctor had managed to repair the ruptured tube. The rest of it would just take time.

It was amazing how the world can come grinding to a sudden halt. Everything that seemed so important three days ago couldn't mean less to him. When life is reduced to the survival of someone you love, everything else reveals itself as trivial. He hadn't even called in to the office since he called to tell them what had happened.

He replaced the rattle into its black velvet bag and stood to put it back in the drawer on the top of the dresser.

"Are you okay?" she asked groggily.

"Yeah," he said, closing the drawer and coming to sit beside her. He put a hand on her head and she looked up at him. "How are you?"

"I'm sorry," she said, for what must have been the hundredth time.

"There's nothing to be sorry for. It just wasn't meant to be right now. We have plenty of time," he answered, kissing her head. She nodded and then seemed to drift off again.

He stood and walked from the room, pulled the door closed behind him, and walked down the stairs. Before he reached the bottom level, the phone started ringing and he raced for it so that it wouldn't disturb Lydia.

"Hello?"

"Hey, it's Craig. How's Lydia?"

"On the mend," answered Jeff. "What's up?"

"I hate to bother you, man. But there's something you need to know." Craig's voice sounded strange to Jeff and it immediately made him alert, brought him back a little to life outside their loss.

"What's going on?"

"Rebecca's missing, Jeff."

"Missing?"

"Yeah," he said. He paused then as though he weren't sure how to go on. Finally, he blurted it out like what he had to say was burning his tongue. "Jed McIntyre's got her."

The words had the effect of a baseball bat to the stomach. "What?" was all Jeffrey could manage.

Craig started rambling out the details. He was talking fast.

"The day after I told you she called in sick? She didn't show up, and this time she didn't call. I left a message for her to make sure she was okay, but she never called back. Then the next morning her mother called, very worried, told me she normally speaks to Rebecca every day but hadn't been able to reach her at home. Christian headed over to Rebecca's place, convinced the doorman to let him into her apartment. From the mail the doorman had and the messages on her machine, it looked like she hadn't been there since Wednesday morning before work. Her coffee cup was still in the sink. We tried her cell phone, friends whose numbers we found in her home address book. Finally at the end of the day we filed a missing person's report."

"Why am I just finding out about this now?" said Jeff. His anger and fear were like a balled fist ready to fly.

"We didn't want to bother you," Craig said lamely. "I mean, we didn't know about Jed McIntyre until about an hour ago when we checked the surveillance tape from the lobby."

"It's been three days. Nobody thought to look at it sooner?"

"I guess we all just thought she'd show up. We never imagined..."

"What? What didn't you imagine?" he asked.

"That she'd been taken from the office."

He wouldn't have imagined it, either. They all thought of those offices as ultra-secure. Rebecca must have felt the same way. Jeffrey remembered now how both he and Lydia had felt that someone had been rifling though their offices. Now he knew why. He didn't even have time to think about what Jed might have learned about them, what kind of access he gained to their cell numbers, their security codes.

"How'd he get in?"

"He killed one of the Speedy Messenger guys, took his gear. Used the speed dial on his cell phone and called in a late route to the dispatcher. Christ," Craig said, his voice catching. "She was basically just sitting here waiting for him."

More silence.

"From what we saw on the camera as they left, she looked pretty out of it. He was holding her by the arm. We didn't know who it was at first. He was wearing a wig. Then he looked up to the camera and smiled."

"Oh, God," he said quietly. He said a silent prayer for Rebecca; one he was coldly sure would go unanswered. "Did you call the FBI?"

"They're here already."

"Okay...I'll be there as soon as I can," he said, looking up to the bedroom door. As sick as it was, part of him was glad to have something to think about other than his and Lydia's sadness. Of all the emotions, it was the hardest to deal with because there was an essential powerless to it, a lack of energy. It entered your system like a barbituate, slowing you down, making you weak, forcing you to feel its effects. Fear and anger were like speed, forcing you into action, pumping adrenaline through your veins. No reflection, just movement.

"Also," Craig said, "Ford McKirdy called a couple times today, said it's very important that he talk to you. And Eleanor Ross has called about a thousand times, she's threatening to fire you if she doesn't get a call back today."

"Okay, okay. I'll deal with it when I get there." He hung up the phone and released a sigh.

"Jesus," came Lydia's voice from the top of the stairs. She held the cordless extension in her hand. "You're outta commission for a few days and the whole world falls apart."

He recognized the tightness that her voice took on when she was trying not to sound afraid. She looked pale and weak, and seemed too wobbly to be standing at the top of the stairs.

"Don't even think about it," he said, sternly. "Get back into bed."

"But Rebecca—"

"You're no good to Rebecca or anyone else all hopped up on painkillers."

She headed tentatively down the stairs, her abdomen still painful from the laser surgery. She wore a pair of purple silk pajama bottoms and a gray oversized NYU sweatshirt, her black hair pulled back into a ponytail at the base of her neck. She walked over to the couch and sat down there as if the effort had drained her.

"I know," she admitted. She closed her eyes and seemed to squeeze back tears. "But Rebecca. Oh, God."

She tried to push away the visions of Jed McIntyre's

victims and pray instead that somehow Rebecca would manage to escape that fate. But she lacked the energy to control her thoughts, even to pray. Holding the phone to his ear with his shoulder, Jeffrey grabbed a chenille blanket off the couch and covered her with it.

"You need to get over here," Jeffrey said into the phone, presumably speaking to Dax. Without another word, he hung up.

"Naturally, you can't leave me here without my babysitter," she said. But she didn't have it in her to put up any kind of real protest. She was more just complaining out of habit.

"Please, Lydia," said Jeffrey with a sigh. "Spare me a little worry for the afternoon, will you? Just stay here with Dax. And when you're feeling stronger, we'll talk about getting back to work. In the meantime, I'll deal with the Ross case."

"I feel like I've been in bed for a month."

"You'll be on your feet again soon."

She nodded and looked away, out the window into the flat gray afternoon sky. He followed her eyes and saw tiny flurries of snow out the window. In the loft across the way, he saw a towering Christmas tree, lights glowing green, red, blue, tinsel glittering on the branches. He looked back at Lydia.

"You have to deal with this okay? Don't just bulldoze over it."

She nodded again and he saw the sadness in her eyes, how they were rimmed with dark smudges. He sat beside her and took her into his arms.

As if, she thought, resting her head on his shoulder, I had any choice but to deal with this. Even when her mind got up to its old tricks of pushing things she didn't want to deal with so far inside that she could almost forget them, the pain of her body was a harsh and constant reminder. She felt hollow and empty, as if something she didn't even know she wanted had been wrested from her. For all the ambivalence she'd felt about her pregnancy, she grieved the loss. She was trying hard not to feel like it was a punishment, a message from the universe that she wasn't worthy of motherhood. But the shadow of that belief hovered in her consciousness.

And the fatigue, physical, emotional, spiritual, was so powerful that it pushed everything else out...Julian Ross, Rebecca, even Jed McIntyre. If he were to come for her now, he wouldn't get much of a fight. She held on to Jeffrey, felt the strength of his body and his spirit, and it gave her comfort. She released him and lay back.

"I'm okay," she said, wiping the tears that had sprung to her eyes. "I'm going to be fine."

"I have no doubt," he said with a smile.

"It's Rebecca we should be worrying about now."

The buzzer for the door rang. "Was he waiting downstairs?" said Lydia with a roll of her eyes.

"Who is it?" said Jeff into the intercom.

"Land shark," said Dax.

"Very funny," said Jeffrey, pressing the buzzer.

As he hulked through the elevator door, Dax's head was not visible behind the gigantic bouquet of Stargazer lilies he'd brought for Lydia. The sight of them made her heart sink a little further. He placed the flowers down on the coffee table beside her, leaned in, and gave her a little kiss on the head. He smelled like musky cologne and snow, his cheek pink and cold against her own.

"How're you doing there, girl?" he asked, his green eyes sincere, concerned. No wisecracks, no insults. It was awful. If Dax felt like he had to be nice to her, things must be worse than she thought.

TWENTY-FIVE

Rebecca was a strong girl, with big, tight thighs. She may even have had some martial arts training and Jed McIntyre had some bruised ribs and a black eye to show for it. But in the end none of that had done her much good. Even the toughest women had throats with skin as soft and easily torn as silk. That had always been his favorite end for the women in his life. It was so intimate, so final. To feel their mortal struggle against his chest, panic radiating off their skin like a perfume, the pain as they tried to scratch at his arms, the music of the death rattle in their throats. Then the peaceful moments when life left them to sag into his arms. Then silence. Frankly, sex didn't even compare to the release. Yes, Rebecca was a strong girl. But he was stronger.

Nobody paid attention to the homeless man pushing his shopping cart up Central Park West, making a right at Eighty-sixth Street onto the path that led into park. Most people would rather stick their face in a public toilet than get too close to the man who shuffled, mumbling to himself, his clothes stiff with filth, his nails long and caked with dirt.

He'd piled his red hair into a stocking cap and pulled it down over his ears, wore an old pair of sunglasses he'd found in the tunnels. They were missing one plastic arm and hung crooked on his face. He'd found a pair of old scrubs in the Dumpster behind Mount Sinai Hospital and he wore those over thermal underwear and under a bright red bathrobe. Combat boots from the Salvation Army were a lovely finish to the ensemble. In his current capacity, he found it necessary to abandon vanity. It was truly liberating. And where else but New York City did you have to make an utter spectacle of yourself to disappear completely?

The right front wheel of his cart was making an irritating squeal and the temperature had dropped significantly in the last few minutes. His hands were going red in the cold and his load seemed to grow heavier with each passing second.

He wasn't exactly sure what he was going to do. He was waiting for inspiration, which he hoped would come soon, sometime after dark and sometime before rush hour when the park would fill with commuters and joggers. Then he'd be forced to wait outside for hours just to get a little privacy. This was another thing about New York: You could never find anyplace to be alone.

He'd developed a special affection for Rebecca over the last few days. She'd brought him closer to Lydia, and more important at this point to Jeffrey Mark, than he'd ever dreamed he would get. Of course, she struggled valiantly to keep the little details of their lives from him. It was the hydrochloric acid that had changed her mind. And then there was no shutting her up. Until he shut her up permanently.

He suspected she had known she was going to die whether she talked or not, even though he'd promised otherwise. He didn't like to lie, but sometimes it was necessary. He thought she was hoping not to be disfigured, for her family's sake. He found it so odd that people cared about things like that. But she was pretty in death. Prettier, he thought, than in life.

He looked out over the Great Lawn, the grand

Metropolitan Museum of Art white and stately across the park, took in the cold air and the aroma from a nearby hot dog vendor's cart. He watched as the short Mexican man bundled in a New York Yankees sweatshirt, scarf, and hat against the cold, handed a dog, lathered in mustard and kraut to a young rollerblader. The young man glided off down a slope, eating joyfully as he went.

"The devil is in the details," Jed said aloud, as he came to a bench, pulled his cart over, and sat heavily. None of the people moving past him on the path, not the businesswoman in her red wool coat and frumpy, well-used Coach briefcase, not the young mother pushing a stroller carting a baby so wrapped up that he resembled a cocktail wiener, not the old man and his little kerchiefed wife in their matching black coats and orthopedic shoes, turned to look at him when he spoke aloud. Persistent ignorance. He laughed out loud and noticed how people quickened their pace.

It's an acquaintance with the minutiae of a life that makes people truly intimate with each other, he thought. It's the knowing of preferences, habits, idiosyncrasies, the little quirks of personality that really allow you to get inside someone's head. When you know what someone loves, what someone fears, what turns someone on, what repulses him, and most important what hurts him, you have the lock, the full nelson. Nobody was going to give that to Jed McIntyre. He couldn't get close enough to Lydia and Jeffrey to figure it out for himself. So he'd had to hijack it.

Well, okay, maybe he hadn't exactly gotten into their heads via the information Rebecca had about them and what he could find in their offices. But what he did find was appointment books, cellular phone numbers, things he'd been lacking. The tunnels hadn't really given him the access for which he'd been hoping. They'd gotten him close, but not close enough. He'd fantasized that he'd find a way into Lydia's building through one of the mythic speakeasy tunnels he'd heard so much about. But it didn't work out that way.

So, he'd cased the offices of Mark, Striker and Strong and found easily the flaw in their security. The Speedy Messenger service, the one that came at the end of the day when most people had gone. It was easy enough to derail a few of the messengers...a flat tire here, a busted chain there. And then finally, grabbing the guy from his route, surprising him at the service exit of the CBS building with a pipe to the head. As far as Jed knew, no one ever found the naked body he'd left in the Dumpster. He took the kid's outfit, his bag, and his cellular phone. Called into the preprogrammed number on the phone to the Speedy dispatcher and told him he'd run into delays but would still make the stops. It was that simple. Rebecca had just been caught off guard.

Now, of course, the real question was how to use what he'd learned to its maximum effect. As darkness closed around him, he waited for inspiration.

"You cheating Aussie bastard," Lydia complained weakly as Dax destroyed her for the third time at the game of Go. He had a gift for pattern recognition and a strategy that was truly unsurpassed, and at the moment Lydia hated him for it.

"The least you could do is let me win," she said, feeling better for a few hours of thinking about nothing more serious than little black and white stones on a wooden board. Her nightmares had temporarily been put on hold and she was almost feeling normal again. Whatever that meant.

"Never. I have too much respect for you," he said. She looked at him for evidence of sarcasm, but his face was serious.

"Oh, please," she said with a laugh.

"And I'm sure you'd be even a worse winner than you are a loser."

"You're probably right about that," she said, leaning back on the couch. It was good to be with Dax, good to be with someone who didn't share her loss, whose face wasn't a mirror of her own sadness. The hurricane of emotions she'd experienced over the last few days had left her drained, too numb to feel anything at the moment. She knew the comfortable numbness wouldn't last. Grief wasn't linear, getting progressively better with time. It came in waves, in an ebb and flow. For a moment or a day, you'd feel almost whole, ready to begin the move forward. Then it came again out of nowhere like a tsunami, wiping you out with a crushing force. And then of course there was the Jed McIntyre nightmare looming, the innocent Rebecca in his clutches.

"So how long are you going to sit around in your pajamas?" asked Dax, regarding her with an open, honest face.

"Hi, I just had surgery?"

"Laser surgery," he said, as though it didn't count.

"Oh, yeah, I'm a real slug for lying around for two days after having a miscarriage," she said, getting a little pissed at him for being such an insensitive clod.

"Three days. And I think you should throw away those painkillers. Whatever pain you're in at this point is bearable. Those things will slow your recovery, and they make it easier for you to lie around here wallowing in depression."

"I'm not wallowing," she said defensively.

"Not yet," he said with a shrug, putting the Go pieces into their little wooden bowls.

"Why is everybody always telling me what to do?" she said, realizing that she sounded like a sullen teenager.

"Look. Jeff loves you. He wants to protect you from any pain or danger that might befall you. He'd be happy to keep you in a padded room under twenty-four-hour guard until Jed McIntyre is six feet under. But that's not you, you know? With everything going on, and now this," he said, pointing to her belly as if it were the offending party, "I think it would be easy for you to get really depressed. You need to pull yourself together and get back to work. Worry about someone else's messed-up life for a while."

She looked at Dax and wondered why she'd never realized he was so smart. Everything he'd said had been dead on and she added a new layer of respect to her concept of him.

"Fuck off, Dax," she said with a frown and a shrug. He just smiled and got up to put away the game. The phone rang.

"Can you get that?" she called as he disappeared upstairs.

"Get it yourself," he called back. She laughed and went over to the phone.

"Hello?" she answered.

"Is this Lydia Strong?" came a woman's voice, sounding edgy and fragile.

"Who's calling?" asked Lydia, trying to place the familiar voice.

"This is Julian Ross."

Lydia let a second pass as the information sank in. She could hear the sound of people talking in the background. She heard some laughter and then what sounded like a wail off in the distance.

"What's happening, Julian?"

"I need to see you. I need to talk."

"Where are you?"

"I'm at the Payne Whitney Clinic. Can you come? Can you come right away?" she asked. Her voice was desperate and Lydia could hear she was on the verge of tears.

"I'll be there in an hour," she answered without hesitation.

Forty minutes later they were in the Rover. There was something beautiful about a late fall dusk in New York City. The sky had taken on a kind of blue tinge, and Lydia watched as people hustled along the sidewalks, rushing to or from, carrying bags. Christmas was just a few weeks away and the shop windows were dressed to draw in holiday shoppers. She loved the energy this time of year, the excitement of tourists in the city to see the tree and look in the windows of the department stores on Fifth Avenue, the ringing bells of Salvation Army Santas outside Macy's. It reminded her of when she was a child, how thrilled she'd been when her mother took her into the city for these things, and for the museums and the theater, for the ballet and the Philharmonic. She'd never wanted to live anyplace else and she couldn't imagine her life without these things. She looked over to Dax, who was staring intently at the road ahead though traffic was thick and they were barely moving.

"It's an amazing city, isn't it?" she asked.

"New York City is a whore," said Dax with disgust. "It looks good enough from a distance, but there's disease at its core. It makes a lot of promises, but in the end you pay for what it gives you with your soul."

"That's nice, Dax," she said, not knowing quite how to respond to that.

A homeless man drifting up the street beside the Rover made her remember the tunnels that existed beneath the streets, made her think of the hole in the laundry room floor, and in turn of Ford McKirdy. She took her phone out of her purse and dialed his cell phone number.

"McKirdy," he answered.

"It's Lydia," she said.

"Hey, Lydia. How are you? You scared the shit out of me the other day."

"I'm okay," she said quickly, not wanting to be reminded that she should really still be in bed. "Listen, Julian Ross gave me a call. I'm on my way to talk to her."

"Good luck," he said with a laugh.

"You've been to see her?"

"Yeah, she seemed lucid enough at first, but she's fried," he answered. "I got nothing from her."

"What else has been happening? I'm a little behind," she said. There was a slide show in her mind of the events in the days before she'd collapsed. She saw Maura Hodge smoking her pipe in her Gothic drawing room, the monster attacking Dax in the basement of the Ross house, Dr. Wetterau shining his penlight into her eyes and telling her about James Ross but not the whole story. A thought was starting to take form in her mind, but she couldn't quite make out the shape.

"I've been trying to reach Jeff all day," said Ford, sounding a little exasperated. "I hated to bother you guys, knowing what you're going through. But I found something that makes me think you may have been on the right track after all."

"Why? What do you mean?"

He told her about the nanny and his visit to the Sunnyvale Retirement Home.

"So who was she?"

"The name on her employment record was Annabelle Hodge. She's from Haunted."

Lydia heard blood rushing in her ears and her heart did a little flutter. She was transported back to that night over a hundred years ago when Annabelle Taylor watched her five children die before her eyes because of Elizabeth Ross's cowardly heart. The vision was so vivid she smelled gunpowder.

"Annabelle Hodge. Who is she? Maura's sister?"

"Her daughter. Must be. She's only twenty-something. Looks like old Maura got a late start in the baby race."

Lydia remembered Maura telling her that all her children had been stillborn. More lies.

"I don't get it. Did Julian know that 'Geneva' was Maura Hodge's daughter? Or did Eleanor?"

"Eleanor says she had no idea. Says that she hasn't been to Haunted in twenty years, how could she have known. She and Maura weren't exactly on speaking terms. She didn't even know Maura had a daughter."

"Or so she says."

"Right."

"Hey, Ford," she said. "What are you doing tonight?"

"Funny you should ask. I was just about to take another little ride upstate. The address on Annabelle's employment record was a place you've visited recently. The residence of Maura Hodge."

She remembered then the noises she'd heard upstairs when they'd interviewed Maura, and the feeling she had that there was so much more going on than Maura was willing to reveal.

"Can you meet us at Payne Whitney in an hour? We'll go up with you."

"I never mind the company...unofficially, of course. You up to that?"

"Why not?" she said, her tone clipped, daring him to question her.

"Whatever you say, Lydia."

"That's an excellent philosophy."

TWENTY-SIX

Special Agent Charles Goban had a long, crooked nose set between small eyes so dark that his iris and pupil appeared to be one. His gray hair was close-cropped and Jeffrey could see his pink, slightly flaky scalp glowing under the overhead lights. A light sheen of sweat glistened on his wrinkled brow. Goban had the wiry build of a featherweight fighter and stood nearly three inches shorter than Jeffrey. Exuding a kind of pent-up nervous energy, he was a cork about to shoot off a champagne bottle. Although there was nothing to celebrate at the moment.

"I'm trying to get my head around why I didn't hear about this sooner," Goban said, wiping away the sweat from his forehead and looking at Jeffrey with some combination of suspicion and condescension.

"It was just a rumor," answered Jeff. "We were following up. We never found him. Or any real evidence that he'd ever been down there." It wasn't exactly a lie. Lying to the FBI was not high on his list of things to do. He'd done it before and he'd probably do it again. But he avoided it when possible.

On the train on his way to the office, he'd been staring out the window and saw a dark figure disappear into a hole in the tunnel wall. It had reminded him of Rain and that tomorrow was the deadline he and Dax had issued for the whereabouts of Jed McIntyre. But all bets were off now that Rebecca was missing. He was sorry to fuck with the order of things down there, recognizing it as a way for people who didn't belong to have a place in the world. But Jed McIntyre had Rebecca and the thought that she could be down there filled him with dread. He could only imagine her terror, and the thought of it caused a sharp pain behind his eyes. She was a good person, kind and hardworking, close to her mother. She didn't deserve to be drawn into this nightmare, a pawn for Jed McIntyre to cause Jeffrey and Lydia pain. Jeff felt an intense guilt and desperation to find her...alive. But there was also the voice in his head that whispered to him that it was already too late.

When he'd arrived at the office, it was crawling with agents. The space was being treated like a crime scene, with technicians scouring for evidence, photographers snapping shots of their offices. An agent stood behind Craig as Craig showed how their security systems worked. The whole thing made Jeffrey extremely uneasy; he didn't like other dogs on his turf. But it couldn't be avoided now and he was going to have to deal with whatever it took to help Rebecca.

Christian Striker looked pale and agitated as he paced the foyer.

"This is so fucked up, man," he said as Jeffrey approached.

"I know. What are we doing for Rebecca?"

"I've got ten of our guys visiting her friends and family, checking surveillance tapes from some of the other buildings on the block to see if we can get a handle on which way they went after they left. There's not much we can do, honestly. We know he took her, but no one's had a handle on Jed McIntyre in months. If we couldn't find him before, how're we going to find him now? It's not good. We're all too close to this, too worried to be thinking clearly and objectively."

"I think I know where he might have taken her."

"Christ, where, man?"

"Where's Goban?"

"He's in your office."

So he told the agent about their trip into the tunnel and how it had yielded nothing but a window into a world he never knew existed. Before he had even finished, Goban was mobilizing a team to head down beneath the streets.

"You're a fucking cowboy, Mark. You always have been. If you had told us about this sooner, Rebecca Helms wouldn't be in this situation at all."

Jeff didn't reply, just sat staring and wondering if Goban was right.

"What were you going to do when you found him?"

Jeff shrugged.

"Yeah, do me a favor and don't answer that. Just tell me one thing. Can you find your way around down there? Do you know where you're going?"

Before he could answer, a young agent walked into the room. With his slick black hair and bright blue eyes, he wore all the idealism and righteousness on his handsome face that Jeff had felt during the first few years on the job. The feeling had faded fast.

"Sir, a body's been found in Central Park matching the description of Rebecca Helms."

Dax watched Lydia disappear through the glass doors of the Payne Whitney Clinic and shifted the Rover into park. He sat with the engine idling and the heat blaring, keeping his eyes on the entrance to the hospital. No one would get in or out without his noticing. He knew Jeff was going to kick his ass for encouraging Lydia to be up and about. But aside from being a little sore, and a little broken inside, she was fine. Jeff wanted to treat her like she was made out of glass. That's why Dax never wanted to fall in love. From what he could see, it clouded your judgment terribly.

He could still see Lydia in the foyer trying to negotiate her way in, though only ten minutes remained for visiting hours. He was not surprised when he saw the guard relent and let her through. He wondered what she'd said to get her way.

When his cell phone sang inside his pocket, he had a feeling he knew who it was. He hadn't forgotten Rain's deadline, and he was sure Rain hadn't forgotten, either. With Rebecca missing now, the stakes were even higher.

"Dax-ie," said the husky voice on the other line. "How are you, darling?"

Danielle's voice was slurred and sloppy. There was a desperation to her mock-seductive tone. She was making Dax more and more uncomfortable every time they spoke. He could see that she had entered the downward spiral of booze, drugs, and dangerous sex that would likely end with her dead in an alley somewhere. He didn't want to feel badly about that when it happened. He needed to find a new street contact, someone not so high-risk, someone with better self-preservation instincts.

"What have you got, Danielle?" he said, trying to keep the disgust out of his voice.

"Can you come get me? I'm cold and hungry and I have some news for you," she said in a singsong voice that she must have imagined was enticing.

"Give me the news now and I'll come get you later. A woman is missing and I don't have time to play games with you."

There was a pause on the other line. And when Danielle spoke again, her voice had turned sharp and angry.

"Well, fuck you, too, Daxie." She hung up the phone with a loud slam. Dax just sat there, knowing she would call back in under a minute. She was jonesing and she needed him. The phone chirped and blinked in his hand.

"Let's try to be civilized, shall we?" he said as he answered.

"Come get me right now or I'm not going to give you Rain's message," she said, now pouting and sullen like a child. "I mean it, Dax."

Again the stab of pity in his heart for her. "Okay, okay. I'll be there. Where are you?"

She gave him her location and he hung up the line. "Bloody hell," he said, looking back at the glass doors through which Lydia had disappeared. He dialed Jeff's number and got voice mail, but didn't leave a message.

As he put the phone back in his pocket, Ford McKirdy's Taurus pulled up beside him and Dax rolled down the window. Ford got out of his car and walked over. Fatigue and stress radiated off him like an odor.

"Did you hear?" asked Ford.

"Hear what?"

"We found a body in Central Park that matches the description of Rebecca Helms."

"Christ," he said, feeling a wave of anger and sadness.

"I know," said Ford with a slow shake of his head.

"Listen," said Dax after a moment. "I have to go. I'll meet up with you two in Haunted. Ford, just watch out for Lydia. I'll be right behind you."

He didn't like leaving Lydia, especially since Ford had another agenda. But if Danielle had a line on Jed McIntyre, it couldn't wait. McIntyre had killed Rebecca and was moving closer to Lydia and Jeffrey. Dax could feel it, could smell it like a scent on the wind.

"Where are you going?" called Ford. But the Rover was already pulling down the street.

Julian Ross looked like one of the tortured figures in her paintings. She stood in the corner, huddled there as if protecting herself against some imagined assault. She had a white-knuckled grip on one of the room's orange plastic chairs, as if she might need to lift it and use it to ward off lions. Some of her color had returned, but her wild eyes spoke of a living nightmare. Her fear and confusion were palpable in the stale air of the room. Her hair looked grayer and she looked thinner than when Lydia had seen her last. So much had happened since then that it seemed like a month, but really it had been less than a week.

"They won't let me have any paper or paints," Julian said as the door closed behind Lydia. "I'm losing my mind in this place."

She laughed a little then at what she'd said. But then her face was a mask of sadness. "Are you going to help me? Or are you one of them?"

"One of who?"

"You know," said Julian with a sly smile and eyes that tried to bore into Lydia.

"I really don't know, Julian. But tell me and I'll try to help you."

Lydia seated herself in a chair by the wall, telling herself that a passive body posture would put Julian at ease. But really, she was just exhausted. Before she sat, she gave Julian an up and down, figured she had about thirty pounds on Julian and could definitely ward off an attack if it came to that. She felt comforted by that thought until it occurred to her that Tad Jenson and Richard Stratton probably would have thought the same thing.

She felt like she had used up every ounce of energy she had just by walking from the car to Julian's room. She wondered briefly if she should have listened to Jeffrey after all. She found herself wondering that a lot.

Julian was watching her carefully. "The destroyers, the takers, the damned," she whispered. "You're not one of them. I can tell."

Lydia's mind was racing with a thousand questions, but

Julian was skittish and jumpy; Lydia knew she had to be careful with words, careful not to frighten or upset Julian any more than she was or she ran the risk of losing her altogether. Julian finally released the chair and came around to sit in it, facing Lydia. She balanced on the edge, bouncing her knees up and down so quickly that she seemed to be trembling.

"The destroyers..." Lydia said, her tone leading.

"You know them?"

"Who doesn't?" she said, thinking of the forces that threatened to rip her own life apart at the seams.

Julian nodded solemnly. "All my life, they've been in the shadows, waiting to snatch away my soul, my life... everything. For a time, I thought I had eluded them. I should have known."

She thought about Julian's canvases, the small figures always in peril from the larger, dark, amorphous forms. She thought of the violence that Julian Ross had grown famous for painting. She wondered again whether Julian's demons were real or imagined.

"Why do they want to hurt you, Julian?"

"That's just it, you see. I have no idea," she said with a helpless shrug. Big tears filled her eyes and rolled down her cheeks; she made no sound, no move to wipe the moisture from her face. If she was an actress, she had real talent. Lydia felt a twinge of pity in her heart.

A sharp knock at the door startled them both. "Five minutes, Ms. Strong," said the guard from outside.

"You called me here, Julian. You said you wanted to talk."

Julian looked at Lydia closely, her eyes narrowing. Lydia observed her face, sought traces of Eleanor's cold and deceptive aura in the woman's daughter and saw none of it. The two woman sat looking at each other in silence, precious seconds passing. But Lydia didn't speak, sensing that Julian would only talk when she was ready.

"I am complicit in my own fate and in the fate of those I

have loved. I see that now," she said finally, speaking slowly, seeming more lucid for a moment. "We all are, you know. Other people, other forces may direct the orchestra, but each of us has the choice to pick up the violin and play—or not. I have played along all my life. Out of fear, out of need to please, out of something—who knows really why? Somehow you feel if you don't play the music that's written for you, then you're guilty of the chaos that ensues. None of the other players know how to proceed. It's so frightening for everyone."

Lydia had no idea what she was trying to say, but again she let silence do the coaxing.

"Especially when the queen doesn't get her way," she continued.

"The queen?" Lydia asked, but remembered that that's how she referred to her mother during their last visit.

"The Queen of the Damned," she said, with all the cool seriousness of a college professor.

"What happens when the queen doesn't get her way?" Lydia asked, even though it was pretty clear that Julian Ross was quite insane.

Julian smiled, a disturbing twisted grin. "Then off with your head," she said with a hard laugh. "Of course."

Julian's answer sent a chill through Lydia, as the images from the Richard Stratton crime scene came to her head.

"So Eleanor, your mother. She's one of the destroyers."

"I'd say so," Julian said indignantly.

"And your brother, James? What about him?"

"Oh, no," she said with gravity. "Not Jamey. He's one of the angels."

"But he tried to kill you, didn't he? He tried to burn you and your mother alive."

"No," she yelled suddenly, scaring the hell out of Lydia. "That was a lie. A fucking lie that they used to put him away, to keep him away from me."

The person before her had changed. She had transformed

from a meek, scared little waif into the very embodiment of rage. She jumped up from her perch and moved toward Lydia, who immediately stood. Julian's face had gone red, and the muscles in her arms and neck were taut and straining against her skin. A moment earlier she had looked like a strong wind would knock her down. Now she seemed to possess a kind of wiry strength, as though she were made of cord pulled tight, ready to snap. Her eyes were dark and unseeing, as her chest began to heave.

"Take it easy, Julian," said Lydia, trying to keep her voice calm as she edged toward the door. "I'm on your side."

But Julian, seeming not to have heard her, kept moving closer. In her face, which she'd pulled into a kind of grimace, Lydia could see the potential for all the things of which she hadn't believed Julian capable. Rage, violence, murder. Lydia felt the cold finger of fear poke her in the belly as her exhaustion was replaced by a burst of adrenaline.

"Guard!" Lydia called. Then, summoning her most authoritative voice and looking the other woman directly in the eye, "Julian, you need to calm down."

Julian laughed, and it was a frightening sound. The woman had turned into a ghoul; Lydia half expected to see that she had grown fangs. Lydia felt a surge of panic as she realized that she wasn't sure she could fend Julian off. She felt a physical weakness that was unfamiliar to her, as if her body were in rebellion after all the abuse it had suffered.

"Guard!" Lydia called again, this time louder.

Julian looked ready to lunge and Lydia flashed on the attack in the basement of the Ross home. She couldn't believe it. The bruise on her face hadn't even healed yet and she was going to get her ass kicked again.

The door opened suddenly and the young officer entered. Lydia sighed with relief, as Julian seemed to deflate like a blow-up doll. Julian sagged to the floor and started to cry, to sob like she was filled with all the grief and pain of the world. The guard shot Lydia an accusatory look as he helped

Julian to her feet. She looked about as menacing as a piece of string.

"Please help me," Lydia heard Julian call as she rushed down the hall, eager to get as far away from Julian Ross and her nightmare existence as possible.

TWENTY-SEVEN

Central Park was a postcard. A light snow fell, glimmering window lights from the buildings surrounding the park glowed against the blue black of the night sky. The air was crisp but not painfully cold against Jeffrey's skin as he stood, ignored by the throng of police officers and FBI agents swarming the crime scene. He felt helpless, useless, an outsider in the kind of situation where he was accustomed to being in control. But tonight he was a rogue private investigator, someone at least partially responsible for the dead woman lying naked and unprotected from the chill of winter and the eyes of a hundred agents of the law.

Jeffrey considered himself to have a particularly high threshold for stress. But standing behind the crime scene tape that surrounded Rebecca's body as it lay against a giant oak edging the Great Lawn in Central Park, he felt like he was pretty much at the edge of what he could endure. There had been too much loss, too much grief. He felt a kind of hollow space in his stomach, a heaviness in his heart, as though it were filled with stones.

Then there was the simmer of anger in the back of his mind, a nebulous area of negativity where thoughts of violence, revenge, and vigilantism dwelled. He wasn't proud of these feelings, which had grown stronger since he and Dax had followed Jed McIntyre into the tunnels below the city. He couldn't deny them, either. Unlike Lydia, in the cosmic scheme of things he didn't necessarily believe that these feelings were inherently wrong. But he did acknowledge that they felt like a kind of spiritual poison, a psychic hallucinogen that slipped through his veins igniting visions and desires that he wouldn't have thought himself capable of.

Over his grief ran a current of panic; Jed McIntyre had made an offensive strike. He was no longer on the run from them. He was moving in. And the only comfort Jeffrey had in this moment was that Lydia was safe at home with Dax.

Jeffrey was looking at a parody of Marion Strong's crime scene. No doubt that was McIntyre's agenda. Rebecca's throat had been cut, her legs bound, her arms bound and nailed above her head to the tree under which she rested. It was the way Marion and his twelve other upstate New York victims had been posed, albeit in their bedrooms, nearly seventeen years ago now. Sitting as yet untouched in Rebecca's lap was a white number ten envelope. In the glare of the flashbulbs from the crime scene photographers' cameras, he could see Lydia's name carefully printed in black. The forensics team would wait until the photographers had finished their work before dissecting the scene, hair by hair, fiber by fiber, print by print. Everyone was waiting to read the contents of that letter. Jeffrey only hoped that Goban wasn't going to be a prick and shut him out.

Jeffrey remembered the first letter Lydia had received from McIntyre, while he was still incarcerated, just after the release of her first book, With a Vengeance, which detailed McIntyre's murders and much of his life. Every month after that, he'd sent her a letter. Letters she received but never opened. It had been a recurring topic of argument between Lydia and Jeffrey. He thought that they should be returned;

but Lydia insisted that they be kept, locked away in a drawer. She said they were reminders to her that he was locked away forever, that he was just a mentally ill man who could only reach her by the U.S. mail and that she had the choice to read or not read his communications. His letters, she claimed, comforted her that he was mortal, caged away from society, and not a demon that could materialize from her nightmares. Jeffrey had eventually given up on arguing about the letters, came to understand the peace she had derived from them. This letter, however, proved just the opposite. That he was a demon, come to destroy them all.

Poor Rebecca. Her face was pale and calm like the face of an angel, her glassy eyes cast heavenward. He was glad to see that her face hadn't frozen in the mask of terror and pain that he had seen too often on murder victims. It made him think that she had found a moment of peace before she died. He held on to that hope as he turned away from her.

Jeffrey was about to approach Goban, who he could see pale beneath the spotlights, huddled with the other members of his team, when his cell phone chirped. He saw Dax's number on the caller ID display.

"What's up?"

"Hey. I've got big news. You have to meet me."

"Meet you. Where the fuck are you? Where's Lydia?"

"Jeff, man," said Dax, his voice excited, his accent thickening, "there's no time to explain. Just meet me as soon as you can." He gave Jeffrey his location.

"Dax, just tell me what you've got. Where's Lydia?"

But he was talking to dead air. He felt his stomach churn a bit, his heart getting in on the action, as well. He had a keen sense of danger and every nerve inside his body was tingling. He tried Lydia, first at the apartment, then on her cell. He got voice mail both places.

"Shit," he whispered to himself. He remembered the pale, exhausted, grief-stricken Lydia he'd left behind. If Dax had taken her from the apartment, there had to have been a good reason.

He hesitated a moment, turning his eyes back to Goban, who was looking in his direction now. He cast another glance at the letter on Rebecca's lap. If he left the apprehension of Jed McIntyre up to the FBI, played by their rules, there were no guarantees that he would ever be caught. And frankly, that wasn't exactly the outcome Jeffrey was looking for any longer. He turned from the scene and walked toward the car. The FBI could walk the grid, gather evidence for proper identification and prosecution, do what they had to do to tow the line. In the meantime, he was going to make sure Jed McIntyre never took another life.

Stupid, stupid, stupid, careless, fucking stupid, thought Dax through the cloud of his pain. He should have known when he saw that little dwarf with Danielle that there was something up. But who'd ever felt threatened by a midget, for fuck's sake?

Only as he'd pulled up to the doorway in the meatpacking district where Danielle had instructed him to meet her did he wonder: Why here? Usually he met her at her corner on Tenth Avenue. But he hadn't really thought much of it. For all her chronic neediness and her pathetic whining, he trusted her. Not in the way of friendship, exactly, but just that she was predictable. She had needs that their business transactions helped her to fulfill; it was a good arrangement. It was easy money for her. Why would she fuck with that?

She stood awkwardly beside a Dumpster. She was made up for work, this time in a wig of red curls, iridescent purple hot pants, thigh-high black boots, and a leather motorcycle jacket. Some weird kind of necklace glinted in the light from across the street. Her pink T-shirt that read you can't handle the truth! in red block letters. No shit, thought Dax. Danielle was a one-person Crying Game.

He hadn't even noticed the midget until he stopped the car. They made quite a pair. Dax had to turn away and suppress a laugh. Danielle, six feet of skanky chic, and then the little guy, who looked like a reject from a Ray Bradbury traveling carnival, barely reaching the seam of her hot pants; the street life encouraged some strange couplings, that was for certain. But this was the Twilight Zone.

He rolled down the window, smelled the snow and the stench of stale blood and raw meat. He was instantly alerted to a problem when Danielle didn't walk over to the Rover.

"So what's the fucking emergency, Danielle?" he said, sounding casual as he released the safety on the Desert Eagle wedged between the driver's seat and the center console.

"This here is Horatio," she said, motioning stiffly toward her small companion. "Says he's got word from Rain. But he wouldn't tell me. He only wants to talk to you." Her voice sounded different to Dax, thick and strained. He couldn't see her eyes in the darkness. He noticed then that a wall-mounted bulb above her head had been shattered.

"Well, let's have it, then, mate," he said, looking down at the dwarf. "What have you got?"

The dwarf shook his head. He hopped lightly from foot to foot, as if doing a strange ritualistic dance.

"He wants you to get out of the car. He's afraid of you," explained Danielle, as if she were Horatio's translator.

"He's going to have a lot more to fear if I get out of the car," he said with a smile that wasn't a smile at all. Then he gave a little laugh to break the tension that seemed to be building. "Come on, Danielle. The two of you get in and we'll go to McDonald's. Isn't that what you wanted?"

"You've got to come out here, Dax. Or Horatio's not going to give you the message."

"Well, fuck you both, then," he said, rolling up the window.

"Dax!" Danielle had a chance to yell before the razor wire that had been around her throat was pulled taught by a hand that appeared out of the darkness. She raised her hands to her throat and pulled them back bleeding; a horrible noise escaped from her mouth as blood spilled from the wound, from her lips, and down her shirt. Dax sprang from the car with the Desert Eagle in his hand. He fired a round into the dark from where the hand had come. Its roar bounced off the buildings surrounding the empty street and he heard the bullet connect with the concrete wall, sparks flying. In the fireworks he saw a dark form.

"Say hello to my little friend," came a voice from the darkness. As the words floated across the night air to Dax's ears, the little bastard dwarf slashed at the back of his calves with what must have been a straight razor. Achilles' tendons sliced, Dax fell straight to the ground, the pain like rockets up the backs of his legs, the gun launching from his hand and landing out of reach.

He looked to Danielle, who had slid down the wall to slump on the ground. Her glassy eyes had rolled back into her head and Dax could see that she had bled out already. On his forearms, he crawled after his gun, craning his neck to look behind him as he went but unable to see the midget now. As his fingers strained for the weapon, a combat boot came to rest on top of it. The midget appeared to his right, his straight razor gleaming like a shooting star, a ghoulish grin on his face. Dax fought for consciousness against the white pain that was nearly paralyzing and the weakness he imagined must be resulting from a loss of blood.

Jed McIntyre stepped out of the darkness.

"I should have killed you when I had the chance," groaned Dax, rolling over on his back.

"My thoughts exactly," said Jed as he brought his combat boot down hard onto Dax's face.

"The destroyers?"

"That's what she said before she went all Jekyll and Hyde on me."

Lydia was one with the upholstery of the Taurus, her

whole body sinking into its softness, the headrest the only thing actually holding up her head. Fatigue like this was a whole new thing to her.

"Lydia," said Ford, noting with concern the pallor of her skin, the dark circles under her eyes. "I hope you don't mind me saying, but you look like shit. Are you up to this?"

"What I'm not up to is lying around thinking about how fucked up my life is right now," she said, rolling her head over to meet his gaze and placing a hand on her stomach. He gave her a sad smile and a nod.

"I hear you," he said. "Still, you look like you belong on a gurney."

An ambulance wailed past them as though to make a point, its red and white lights flashing, siren screaming.

"She said something else, too," said Lydia, looking after the ambulance, which had stopped because the traffic was slow to give way. The wailing continued, seemed to get louder, and was joined by a cacophony of honking horns.

"What's that?"

"She calls Eleanor 'The queen'...'the Queen of the Damned.' "

"The mother-daughter relationship is very complicated," said Ford, pulling a bad Austrian accent.

"Eleanor Ross has done a lot of lying since she hired Jeffrey and me," Lydia continued, as if thinking aloud. "Really...she's done little else. She never told us about her murder trial or her missing son until confronted."

"Sins of omission...."

"And, if you think about it, she has a lot to gain. If Julian is declared incompetent, she's most likely to become Lola and Nathaniel's guardian."

"So you think it's about the kids."

"They'll be worth quite a bit. Daddy's dead; Mommy's in the nuthouse. If Julian doesn't recover, the family estate will likely go into trust for them. There will need to be an executor."

"Grandma."

Lydia shrugged. It was a theory she was trying on, something she and Jeffrey had begun to discuss during their last visit to Haunted. It didn't fit quite right, but it was something. She looked at her Movado watch.

"Maybe it's too late to head to Haunted?"

He shrugged. He was jonesing to head up there, find Annabelle Hodge, get her to answer a few questions. But he supposed it could wait until the morning. He'd be better off heading up there with Piselli or one of the other detectives on his team, rather than cowboy it, with Lydia Strong riding shotgun. If things got out of hand, there'd be hell to pay.

"What do you have in mind?" he asked.

"Let's see if we can't get an audience with the queen."

"As a matter of fact, I've got some questions for the court jester as well."

Anthony Donofrio didn't look happy to see Ford as he and Lydia walked through the front door of the Park Avenue apartment building. In fact, he looked downright pale. Apparently his fascination with the specifics of police work had come to an end.

In spite of Ford's vigorous objections, Eleanor and the twins had been allowed to move back into the duplex the day before yesterday. Money talks, apparently loudly enough that the order had been handed down directly from the chief of police. He had managed to keep sealed the bedroom where Stratton had been killed. Nobody seemed to think it was at all strange that Eleanor would feel comfortable moving the twins back into the apartment where their father had been brutally murdered.

"It's late, Detective. They're probably asleep," explained Anthony when no one answered his call, pulling himself up and squaring off his shoulders as if preparing himself for a fight.

Ford looked at him and noticed a light sheen of perspiration on his upper lip.

"That's okay, Anthony. I actually have a few questions for you, too," said Ford. "Did you know Geneva Stout?"

"Um, the name sounds vaguely fa-fa-familiar," he answered. He'd developed a stutter.

"The nanny for the Stratton-Ross children," said Ford calmly, looking around the foyer.

"Oh...yeah. I seen her around."

"You never spoke to her? She's a pretty girl," Ford said, turning his eyes on Anthony with a knowing smile. "I would've thought a stud like you would be putting the moves on."

"Uh, n-no. It wasn't like that."

"So you never talked to her? Never saw her outside the building?"

"No," he said with a shrug. The guy was lying, his eyes dancing all over the place, the sudden stutter. Ford decided to let him dangle a little.

"Sure about that, Anthony?"

"I'm sure," he said, his face coloring now.

"'Cause it wouldn't be a good idea to lie to me."

"I w-w-wouldn't," he said emphatically. "Let me try that buzzer for you again."

When there was still no answer, Ford and Lydia advanced toward the elevator.

"I can't let you go up there unannounced," said Anthony, a lilt of panic making his voice sound like a teenager's.

"Anthony," said Ford as they climbed into the elevator. "Whaddaya gonna do? Call the cops?"

The doors closed and Lydia and Ford were alone.

"What the hell was the matter with that guy?" asked Lydia as the elevator climbed slowly toward the top floor.

"I've been thinking about how the camera got turned off. The children's psychologist that I used to interview Lola and Nathaniel said that someone was exerting a lot of power over the kids, someone intimate."

"Yeah?"

"And that she couldn't see Nathaniel acting without Lola, or without someone giving orders."

"Okay..." she said, not quite sure where he was going.

"So, if Lola was down in the basement and Nathaniel was charged with turning off the camera and then turning it back on when she was done, something or someone had to distract Anthony long enough for him to do that. He couldn't have snuck into the office alone."

"And, to a loser like Anthony Donofrio, nothing is quite as distracting as a pretty girl?"

"Exactly. And a nanny would certainly exert plenty of power over the children."

"Interesting," said Lydia as they stepped off onto the floor. They walked down the hallway and paused at double doors to the duplex. The door stood ajar. Both Ford and Lydia drew their weapons. For once, Lydia was armed. Every other time she'd needed a gun in the last two months, it had been in her bag, in her car, somewhere out of reach. With the threat of Jed McIntyre on the loose, she had grown more cautious.

"Ms. Ross?" called Ford, looking at Lydia's Glock with disapproval. "Put that thing away, Lydia. You fire a round in this apartment and I've got serious trouble. I shouldn't even allow you to be here."

"I'm not even with you," she said. "I came here on my own with a separate agenda."

"Put it away," he said again, pushing the door open, moving in front of Lydia. Naturally, Lydia ignored him.

"Ms. Ross," he called again, this time louder.

They walked into the apartment, which was dark except for the embers of a fire still glowing in the fireplace of the drawing room to the right of the entryway. Lydia waited for her eyes to adjust to the darkness, keeping close to Ford. They both noticed at the same time that a form sat stiff and motionless in the overstuffed chair near

the fire. Lydia felt her heart start to do the rumba and her fingers tingled with adrenaline.

"Ms. Ross?" Ford said again, this time his voice a question. There was no movement, no response from the dark figure. Ford felt along the wall for a light switch and finally found one.

She sat upright and regal, her head tilted slightly back, the expression on her face one of cool disdain, the corners of her mouth turned down. Her long, thin hands gripped the arms of the chair to which she was bound with rope. Tresses of long gray hair cascaded down over her shoulders. She looked beautiful, except for the dark red bullet hole precisely between her blue eyes.

"Shit," said Lydia, all the answers she'd hoped to get from Eleanor disappearing up the chimney like the thin black smoke from the embers of the fire.

"Oh, God. Oh, Christ. I didn't know. I s-s-swear to G-G-God," cried Anthony Donofrio from behind them. He fell to his knees and started to weep.

Ford spun around to see Anthony in a crumpled mess on the floor, blubbering like a little girl. Ford's stomach fell out. Oh, God, he thought, if Eleanor's dead...where are the twins?

Lydia and Ford exchanged a glance, both of them of one mind, and together they ran through the living room. Ford pushed through the door and went down the long hallway that led to the children's bedrooms. The rooms were across the hall from each other, adjoined by a bathroom. Ford handed Lydia a pair of surgical gloves and pulled on a pair himself. They split up. Ford went into Nathaniel's room, characterized by a SpongeBob SquarePants motif. Lydia took Lola's room, filled, it seemed, with every Barbie and Barbie accessory ever made. Lydia could hear the sounds of Ford ripping back the covers on the bed, pushing aside the clothes in the closet, as she did the same.

"They're not here," said Ford, breathless, walking into Lola's room. He pulled out a cell phone and called in the Missing Children's Unit, as well as backup from the homicide department. While he talked, he and Lydia searched the rest of the apartment. The space was filled with the sounds of Lydia and Ford calling for the twins and with Anthony wailing in the foyer the entire time, pausing only to puke his guts up on two separate occasions.

TWENTY-EIGHT

"Where are the kids, Anthony?" asked Ford, remembering the days when no one cared about police brutality.

"I don't know. I don't know."

It seemed like a mantra he was using to calm himself. He'd said little else since Ford had grilled the truth out of him about the night Stratton was murdered. Apparently, while Richard Stratton was being disemboweled on the fourteenth floor, Anthony was getting the blow job of his life from the nanny formerly known as Geneva Stout. Anthony didn't know he was being duped, or so he claimed tearfully. He just thought Geneva liked him. He still didn't know how the camera got turned off, but Ford imagined that little Nathaniel snuck in while the couple were otherwise engaged and did the deed. He'd ask Nathaniel himself. But the twins were gone.

"Did it occur to you after the murder that maybe Geneva Stout had just been trying to distract you?" Ford had asked as he sat across from Anthony at the kitchen table.

Anthony shrugged, his face a mask of misery, his eyes

downcast. "Not really," he said sheepishly.

The guy was just too pathetic, too stupid. It had probably seemed just like the plot of every porn movie Anthony had ever seen. Doorman, just minding his own business, sexy nanny from upstairs comes to visit just dying to suck his dick. Anthony probably thought it happened all the time... to other guys.

"Jesus," said Ford now, shaking his head.

"Who came into this building tonight, Anthony. You're the fucking doorman. Who. Did. You. Let. In?"

"No one. I swear to God. No one was here."

"Oh, someone was here."

"Christ," Anthony sighed, lifting his eyes toward heaven. Ford thought he might actually be praying.

"So then, maybe you want me to conclude that you came up here, killed Eleanor Ross, and hid the twins, or handed them off to someone else, or maybe even killed them."

"Nonononono," he wailed. "God, no way. No fucking way."

"Then what kind of conclusion do you want me to draw?"

"I don't know." Back to his mantra. Ford sighed.

"Look, you're gonna ride down to Midtown North with one of the uniforms. We need to talk more and I don't have time right now."

"I told you everything I know," said Anthony, panicked.

"I don't think so," answered Ford. After a few hours to himself in an interrogation room, thinking things over, the thoughts and doubts would start turning like debris in the winds of a tornado: How did I get here...how did this happen...that bitch, I should've known she was up to something. People get talkative after a few hours in their own head.

"I want a lawyer," he said suddenly, looking up at Ford and crossing his arms across his chest.

"You're not under arrest," said Ford calmly.

"Then I don't have to go anywhere with you. I know my rights."

Ford brought his fist down hard on the kitchen table that stood between them. Anthony jumped and looked at him with fear and an uncertain anger in his eyes.

"Do not fuck with me, Anthony," said Ford, getting right in the kid's face and lowering his voice to a quiet menace. "You think you know how things go because you watch NYPD Blue? You have impeded the progress of my investigation by not being forthcoming with what you know. Cooperate with me, Anthony, and you could be home by midnight. Otherwise, man, I'll arrest you right now and you'll need a fucking lawyer. Do we understand each other?"

Anthony nodded and lowered his head. Ford thought the guy was going to start to bawl right there. "Good," he answered, clapping Anthony on the shoulder. "Stay here until I send someone to take you to the precinct."

Ford left him in the kitchen and walked out back toward the living room, where the crime scene technicians were starting to arrive. Detectives Piselli and Malone stood with their arms crossed by the door; they looked lost, like they didn't know what to do with their hands. He was reminded that they were young, new to the detective squad. Though they'd each been on the job nearly five years, they'd had mostly patrol, some "buy-and-bust." The crime scene was still new to them in this capacity.

"How's it going? Holding up the wall like that?" he said.

They looked embarrassed, both pushing themselves forward and glancing at him expectantly, waiting for orders. He shook his head.

"Jesus, start looking around. You know...for clues? Something that might help you figure out what went on here?"

Peter Rawls, the head of the Missing Children's Unit, had already arrived with his team and they seemed to be setting up shop in the room opposite from where Eleanor was found. He was grim-faced and barking orders. At well over six-foot-four with Popeye arms and a chest like a side of beef, no one argued with him.

"I'm trying not to trample on your scene McKirdy," he said with an apologetic nod. "But we got kids missing. Time is short."

Ford looked around him. It was pandemonium; even a first-year public defender would have a field day with evidence gathered in this circus.

"We'll work together. Find those babies, get the shooter." Ford's voice sounded sure even though he wasn't. Rawls nodded.

Ford briefed Rawls quickly on the family history and the homicide case he was working. Rawls listened with his eyes down and his arms crossed, nodding as Ford ticked off the facts as they stood so far.

"What a mess," Rawls said when Ford was done. Ford just nodded. It was a mess, all right.

"I need some time with that doorman when you're done with him," said Rawls.

"I am done for now. Take all the time you want with him and then have him sent to my precinct with a uniform. I'm going to take another go at him in less comfortable accommodations."

"I'll tell you what I get."

"I'll do the same."

They swapped cell numbers and Rawls stalked off, his face drawn and determined. Ford thought he looked like a man who didn't accept failure and he hoped that was good news for Lola and Nathaniel. Poor kids. He said a silent prayer for them, though he was not a religious man.

"Hey," Ford said, walking toward Piselli. "Where's Lydia Strong?"

"She left. She wasn't looking well. Said she needed to get home."

They walked off and Ford looked toward the door. “Crap,” he whispered to himself. Well, he thought, she’s a tough girl, with a big gun. She can take care of herself. Ford turned then to Eleanor Ross, whose corpse he thought seemed only slightly more cold and stiff than she had been in life.

She wasn’t being stubborn or reckless or any of the things she knew she’d be accused of once Jeffrey realized she’d left Ford McKirdy and headed home on her own. In fact, it was just the opposite. If she’d stayed at the scene or headed up to Haunted, she’d be hurting herself. She knew that. Her heart and mind had never felt more unwelcome in her body. What she wanted had been overridden unequivocally by pain and fatigue. Dax was wrong and she was stupid to have listened to him; she needed time to recover...mentally, physically, and emotionally. For once, she was going to do what was best for her, not what was best for her work. It was a lesson she had learned the hard way.

When the homicide guys arrived and then the Missing Children’s Unit showed up, she had felt as helpless, as useless there as she had been. Standing in the foyer looking at Eleanor’s corpse, Lydia had thought of her mother. Marion would have known which saint to pray to, which saint was charged with looking after children. Lydia couldn’t remember, so she just prayed to her mother. Prayed that Lola and Nathaniel were safe. That Nathaniel had his bunny. When her prayer was done, she knew that there was little else she could do in the state she was in, weak and ill, barely able to hold herself tall.

The energy of the loft embraced her as she stepped off the elevator and reset the alarm system. Home, she thought. And the thought sent waves of relief through her body. It was nice to be alone, too, without the watchful eyes of Dax or Jeffrey smothering her. She shed her coat and put a kettle on the stove. She could smell the warm scent of lavender mingling with the aroma of the Murphy's Oil Soap that Zel, their cleaning lady, used to wash the floors. She sat at the kitchen table and looked out at the city. The world was different to her than it had been before the miscarriage. Even the cityscape seemed to have changed.

The skyline had always fascinated her, each light representing a life lived, each window a mystery waiting to be solved. She was forever wondering who was doing what to whom, who within those lighted windows was laughing, crying, making love, mourning, celebrating. It was this curiosity that made her good at her work...actually, it was this curiosity that made her indivisible from her work. She had realized, during the days she'd spent in a drug-induced haze, that there was no separation between what she did and who she was. Was this a bad thing? she wondered.

It amazed her that, with all the demons she had battled since the death of her mother, both internal and external, there were still so many left to fight...Jed McIntyre not least among them.

Two days before Jed McIntyre murdered Marion Strong, Lydia saw him in a supermarket parking lot. She was waiting for her mother in the car while Marion ran into the A&P to get a quart of milk. Sitting in her mother's old Buick, the fifteen-year-old Lydia punched the hard plastic keys on the AM/FM radio, checking each preset station for acceptable listening, when she felt the hairs raise on the back of her neck. She felt heat that started at the base of her skull and moved like fire down her spine. A hollow of fear opened in her belly. She turned around and looked out the rear windshield.

The car's front windows were open and the already cool fall air seemed to chill. The man stood with his legs a little more than shoulder length apart, one hand in the pocket of his denim jacket and one resting on the sideview mirror of his red and white car, which reminded Lydia of the car in Starsky and Hutch. His flaming red hair was curly and disheveled, blowing into his eyes. She remembered that he did not move to keep it off his face. He just stared and rocked lightly back onto his heels and then forward onto the balls of his feet. Seeing him standing beside his car, his gaze locked on her, made her senses tingle. She detected his malice in his unyielding stare, his perversion in the way he began to caress the sideview mirror when their eyes met. She had reached to lock the doors and roll up the windows without taking her eyes off of him.

When her mother returned to the car, Lydia pointed out the man to her and he just stood there smiling. Marion tried to tell her it was nothing. But Lydia could see her mother was afraid in the hurried way she threw the milk into the backseat and got into the car, the way she fumbled to put the key in the ignition. They drove off and the man pulled out after them. But when Marion made a quick turn, he did not pursue them. They laughed; the threat, real or imagined, was gone. But Lydia would look back at that moment as the point at which she could have saved her mother's life. She had written down the license plate number with blue eyeliner on the back of a note a friend had passed to her in class. That information had led to the apprehension of Jed McIntyre, serial murderer of thirteen single mothers in the Nyack, New York, area. But only after he had killed Marion Strong, leaving her where Lydia would find her beaten and violated as she returned home from school.

She knew now, of course, that even if they had reported the parking lot incident to the police, they wouldn't have been able to do anything. But when she got that feeling, the feeling she and Jeffrey had come to know as "the buzz," she had never been able to walk away from it again. Wondering always who else would die if she did.

She had walked away from the missing twins, from Eleanor and Julian Ross tonight, not because this curiosity, the need to hunt the demons and save their victims, had died. It was not that she didn't care about the children, Julian's plight, or Eleanor's murder. She did very much; this drive was alive and well within her. It was just that the loss of her baby, the risk to her own life, and the damage done to her body had made clear things that had always been nebulous. She had realized for the first time how much her own life was worth, how much she cherished her time with Jeffrey, and how much, even though she hadn't realized it, she had wanted to be a mother. She rested her head on her arm and let a tear fall, as a hot wave of sadness swept over her.

There was a kind of peace to her grief, though. There was an irony to the situation that was not lost on her. Only the loss of her pregnancy could have made her see what it took to be a mother. And how she never could have taken care of her child when she wasn't even willing to take care of herself. Something in the fact that she had learned this lesson comforted her, made her believe that there would be another chance to do it right. She was reminded of the airplane safety rule stating that should the oxygen masks drop you should put on your own mask before putting it on your child. Something that seems so selfish, so backward, may be the ultimate selfless act. You can't help anyone until you've helped yourself.

The kettle on the stainless steel stovetop whistled and Lydia got up to make herself a cup of raspberry tea. She took the cup and placed it on the coffee table, pulled off her boots and lay on the couch. She pulled the chenille blanket over herself and sank into the plush furniture. She thought to turn on the television and watch the news, but she decided no. She thought briefly that she should check her messages. But she didn't do that, either. She never even had a chance to sip her tea because sleep came for her hard and fast and there was no resisting.

TWENTY-NINE

Sitting alone there, Anthony had indeed, as Ford suspected, whipped himself into a frenzy of worry, deciding confession and contrition were his only options. By the time Ford arrived, Anthony was barely holding it in. When Ford walked into the room, it wreaked of fear and body odor. Ford hadn't even taken his seat before Anthony started talking.

"She hated Julian Ross. And Eleanor, too. I mean hated their guts," said Anthony, wiping perspiration from his brow. He looked pale in the harsh fluorescents, with black smudges of fatigue and worry under his eyes. Anthony was a reasonably big guy with broad shoulders and thick arms, but behind the long table he looked deflated.

"Who did?"

"Geneva...or whatever her name was."

"Annabelle."

"Yeah."

"So you talked about Julian," said Ford, leaning his elbows on the table and folding his hands.

"And Eleanor. Yeah, we talked sometimes."

"So the whole dick-sucking incident wasn't your first encounter, is what you're telling me. Because before, you made it sound like—"

Anthony held up a hand and gave a nod. "We talked a couple of times. Nothing serious, you know. Not like we were dating or anything. I took her for coffee around the corner. But that's it. I swear."

"When did you talk?"

"She'd come down at night, after the kids were in bed. Sometimes she'd bring a couple of beers. She was lonely. I thought she was lonely," he said. His mouth had turned down at the corners and he shook his head a little bit. Anthony had been used and it was just starting to dawn on him. Ford felt for the guy, he really did.

"So what did you talk about?"

"About Julian and Eleanor Ross, mostly. She did most of the talking. I listened," he said, looking down at the table. "I guess, looking back, it always seemed like I could have been there, or not."

"So what kind of things did she say?"

"A lot of it didn't make sense. She would start off talking about what a bitch Ms. Ross was, how badly she treated her, Geneva—Annabelle, I mean. Then she would start on how Julian didn't deserve the life she had, her husband, the twins, all their money. But then she'd say things like, 'One day soon, that's all going to change.' When I asked her what she meant, she'd say that the past was bound to catch up with Julian and Eleanor Ross."

"You didn't think that was an odd thing to say?"

"I guess, to be honest, I wasn't really thinking too much about what she was saying," he said, looking at Ford sheepishly. "She was, you know, really hot. I was mostly just thinking about what it would be like to fuck her."

Ford nodded, not surprised.

"Did it sound like a threat to you? Like she was planning to hurt Julian Ross?"

"No...it sounded more like a prediction."

Ford cocked his head to the side and narrowed his eyes. "A prediction."

"Yeah, like she knew something bad was going to happen; not like she was threatening to make her pay for something. There's a difference, don't you think?"

Ford shrugged. "Did she ever talk about her home, her family? Did she ever mention Haunted?"

"She said she was part Haitian. Seemed pretty proud of it. She said, and I remember thinking this was weird, that she had the blood of a voodoo priestess in her veins. I was, like, You're not going to put a curse on me, are you? She didn't seem to think that was very funny."

"What did she say?"

"She said, 'Not if you're good.' But she didn't laugh or anything. She was a little freaky, I guess."

"I guess."

Back to the voodoo curses, thought Ford. Lydia Strong might not have been as far off base as he'd thought. He looked at Anthony, who instead of seeming less agitated after spilling his guts seemed to be getting more uncomfortable. He shifted up in his chair, rolled his neck and shoulders, releasing audible pops.

"What else, Anthony?"

He shrugged, looked around the room. He nodded to himself finally, as if coming to a decision after an internal conference.

"Tonight. She was there again tonight."

Ford shook his head in disbelief. "And you're just getting to this now?"

"I didn't know..." he said, his voice trailing off miserably.

"What did she want?"

"She didn't come to see me."

"Who'd she come to see?" asked Ford, feeling like he was going to have to wrestle every last bit of information from this kid.

"Eleanor Ross."

"And coincidentally, now Eleanor Ross is dead. And the twins missing."

Anthony nodded.

"What time did she come?"

"Around nine-thirty. Just after I came on duty."

"So you called up to Eleanor and told her Geneva was here."

"She said Eleanor was expecting her. That she was holding a paycheck for Geneva, and that she still had a key."

"So you didn't call up?"

Anthony hesitated a moment and then shook his head.

"And what time did she leave?"

"I never saw her leave. I thought she was still up there, maybe playing with the twins."

Ford turned it over in his mind. The basement entrance had been sealed and was no longer a way in or out. The back door, he knew, was attached to a fire alarm.

"Let me just ask you, Anthony," said Ford, reaching. "Did the fire alarm go off tonight for any reason?"

"Yeah, that thing is always acting up," he said with a laugh and a shake of his head like they were talking about a mischievous child. Then it dawned on him. "Oh...yeah."

"What time was that?"

"I guess about an hour before you arrived."

"Anything else, Anthony? And I mean anything."

Anthony shook his head slowly, his eyes telling Ford that he was searching the limited database of his brain. "Nope," he said finally. "Can I go now?"

"Did you tell any of this to Peter Rawls when he talked to you?"

Anthony shook his head. Ford glared at him and Anthony seemed to shrink into himself.

"With missing kids, every hour, shit, every minute counts. You may just cost those kids their lives. I hope you can live with that, Anthony."

Anthony started to blubber again. Ford was old school. He really hated it when men cried. He turned his back on the man and walked out the door.

"But—" Anthony was protesting as Ford closed the door behind him. He turned the camera and audio recorder off from the switch that looked like a thermostat outside the door.

Returning to his office, he called Peter Rawls and told him about Annabelle Hodge. Rawls sounded excited by the news of a suspect and he hung up the phone quickly. Then Ford called Piselli and told him to make sure that Rawls got anything from their files on Annabelle that he needed. He thought about the kids for a minute, remembering how they'd clasped hands during the interview with Irma Fox. And it made him think of his Katie and Jimmy. He thought about little Nicky Warren watching his mother shoot his father. He felt a rush of anger at the way kids get crushed when adults fail to protect them.

He leaned back in his chair, absently tapping an impatient staccato on the desk, trying to strategize his next move. His fingers touched manila.

Sitting on his desk was nothing short of a miracle. DNA evidence analysis takes weeks, sometimes months, especially in New York. Now, with all the cold cases being reopened, death row appeals, you're lucky to get your results at all. But Ford had a few friends, and the Ross case was a high priority. Still, he was surprised to see an envelope from the lab on his desk. In spite of the lecture he'd delivered to Lydia Strong, he had sent her Milky Way wrapper, with the hairs from the Tad Jenson murder scene, up to the lab.

"Well, goddamn," he said softly, scanning the report. "It's a match."

He'd sat there at his desk, working out what this might mean. It didn't mean James Ross was still alive, necessarily. They didn't have a DNA sample on him to compare to the hair and the wrapper. Legally, it only meant that someone at the scene of the Tad Jenson murder had also been in the basement of the Ross house in Haunted. Ford picked up the phone on his desk. When he didn't get Jeff, he left a message.

"Jeff, it's Ford. Listen, Lydia was right. That DNA evidence from the Milky Way bar links whoever attacked her in the Ross home with someone present at the Jenson scene. I'm not sure what it means, but I'm heading up to Haunted. This can't wait till tomorrow, especially with the twins missing. I'll keep you posted."

THIRTY

The ringing of her cell phone woke her finally. She glanced at the clock and saw that it was after two. It took her a few seconds to orient herself...home alone, Jeffrey not back, phone ringing...where's the phone? She found it in her jacket and saw on the caller ID that it was Jeffrey.

"Where are you?" she answered.

"Hello, Lydia."

She let silence be her answer as dread swelled within her. His voice had a nasal quality, a kind of raspy edge to it that she recognized even though she'd heard him speak only a few times. The room seemed to spin around her.

"You don't have to answer. I know you know who this is, old friend."

She didn't say anything because she couldn't. Fear had lodged itself in her throat like a chicken bone.

"It's been too long. We must get together, Lydia. It'll be a party. Your beloved Jeffrey and your friend and guardian Dax have already joined me. It wouldn't be the same without you. But, darling, it's a private party. Do not contact your friend Ford or Agent Goban. Come alone, come as you are, and come quickly."

"You don't have them," she managed, clinging to denial. This wasn't happening. It was too much like a nightmare. "I don't believe you."

Her mind raced. Wasn't this phone tapped? And then she remembered that no, only the land line was trapped. The cell transmissions weren't always monitored.

"We've been through so much together. Do you think I'd lie to you?"

When she said nothing, his voice changed from mocking, crooning, to razor-sharp.

"Think about it. Do you really think you'd be alone right now if I didn't? For such well-armed, well-trained men, it was really ridiculously easy."

"Where are you?" she said, suppressing a wave of nausea.

He told her where he wanted her to meet him.

"Remember, Lydia: One phone call from you to anyone and the party is over. Do you understand me?"

"I do."

The line went dead. Lydia waited, blood rushing in her ears, throat dry as sand, heart thumping. She waited to wake up in her bed, Jeffrey breathing beside her. When she didn't, she ran upstairs to their bedroom. She pulled off her shirt and pulled on a black ribbed Calvin Klein sweater of Jeffrey's. She traded the yoga pants she was wearing for comfort, since her abdomen was still swollen from surgery, for a pair of Levi's. She unlocked the safe in the floor and removed a Smith and Wesson .38 Special and a shoulder holster.

Downstairs, she took the Glock from her bag and stuffed it in the back of her jeans, donned her leather jacket and a pair of soft black leather motorcycle boots at the door, and she was gone. Adrenaline had taken care of her pain and fatigue, for the time being at least.

THIRTY-ONE

He recognized the smell, but he just couldn't see through the blackness that surrounded him; it was a copious dark in which not even a pinprick of light had survived. He could feel the space, cold and concrete, damp. As he fought to hold on to consciousness, his head nothing but a house of pain, he knew something was not as it should be. He just couldn't remember what. There was an odd tightness in his limbs. He was having difficulty breathing and he felt as if the room were spinning...or maybe his head was spinning. He tried to piece together the last events of his memory, but they eluded him, like the fading images of a dream.

There was a low groan to the left of him. And in hearing it, memory came rushing back like a kick in the teeth.

He'd taken the call from Dax and rushed to meet him, uneasiness buzzing in his subconscious. Something about Dax's voice, something about the way he'd said Jeff's name. Normally, his accent seemed to drag the word out, imbuing it with a rising and falling of tone, like Jay-eh-f. There was usually something pleasant about his tone, even when it was gruff, something musical and comforting about that Aussie accent. But that night, he'd seemed terse, his accent strained. If it hadn't been for the caller ID announcing his number, Jeffrey might not have recognized Dax's voice at all. But he'd ignored the alarm bells ringing, told himself that Dax was just excited and in a rush.

There are a few significant ways in which life is not like movies. Here, bound in the darkness, scared and disoriented, Jeffrey thought of one of those ways. In the real world, sometimes people disappear and no one who loves them ever knows what happened to them. Like the West Village couple who were expecting friends for dinner one fall evening a couple of years back. When their friends arrived and rang the buzzer, no answer. After waiting around for an hour or so, they figured that there had been a misunderstanding about date and time and left. But three days later, the superintendent lets NYPD into that apartment, after numerous calls from family and friends, and the table is set for entertaining, food is on the stove and in the oven; their shoes are by the door. It was as if something had sucked them from their life still in their stocking feet.

There was a dispute between the couple—middle-aged, childless, working good jobs, the woman in publishing, the man a public school teacher—and their landlord. They lived in a three-bedroom apartment that, if they vacated, could be rented for four times what they were paying for it, having lived there since the late seventies. For weeks there were news stories, posters all over the city. Then nothing; they faded from the city's memory. Jeffrey remembered the maddening feeling that they wouldn't ever be found, that no one would ever be certain if they were alive or dead, or what they might have endured in their last few hours on this planet. A life interrupted, no reason why.

Their disappearances coincided within a few weeks of police finding dismembered limbs on the Jersey side of the Henry Hudson. A couple of legs, some arms, a hand. Thought to be the work of the Russian mob, and in conjunction with allegations that the landlord had connections with the same organization, police thought initially that the mystery had been solved, as least as far as their end was concerned. Turns out the limbs belonged to someone else. Never identified. Another unsolved mystery...another miserable end.

He thought about Lydia now, feeling his heart begin pounding in his chest with fear for her, fear for himself. Where was she? Where was Jed McIntyre? Was this his plan, to keep Dax and Jeff locked up until he'd finished with her? He struggled against his bindings, which felt as if they must be duct tape. Panic was a swelling tide within him and he tried to keep it from choking him. He'd failed her so many times in the last few months, failed to protect her, failed to protect their child. He could barely stand the thoughts that were racing through his mind. Again the groan, bringing him back to himself.

"Dax?"

"Why the fuck did you come, man? That was the worst Australian accent I'd ever heard," said the darkness. "Christ, you're stupid."

"I saw your number on the caller ID," he said lamely, hating himself for ignoring his instincts. Fucked by technology.

"He took my phone," said Dax miserably, somewhere down and to the left.

The other way in which life differed significantly from the movies was that much of it is a series of stupid mistakes, unplotted, unplanned, reactionary.

When he'd pulled up to the warehouse in the meatpacking district, he first saw the Rover, parked, headlights on, driver's door standing open. Next, he'd seen Dax lying face down in a pool of blood. Forgetting every moment of training he'd ever had, not even thinking for a second who could be lurking in the darkness, he'd jumped from the Kompressor and ran to help his friend. He saw too late that Dax's mouth was gagged, his eyes open and wild with warning. Out of the corner of his vision, he saw a small form emerge from the darkness. In a surreal moment, a midget raised a blackjack and nailed him in the temple.

"Was there a midget?" Jeffrey asked Dax.

"Fucking midget," answered Dax. "I'm going to kill that little turd."

"What's your situation right now?"

"I'm in trouble, man," he said, his voice thick and slow, as if he were just barely holding on to consciousness. "That little dwarf sliced the back of my calves. I think I'm missing some teeth. I taste blood. I'm bound, can't move."

"Shit," said Jeff, his stomach hollowing out. "Hang in there, buddy. It's going to be okay." Panic was replaced by a lethargy, a feeling of desperate hopelessness.

That was the other way in which life was so different from fiction. Not everyone always gets out alive.

THIRTY-TWO

Lydia felt an odd calm as she walked down the cold empty street, a light snowfall crunching beneath her feet. The lamps created circles of light in a dark winter sky and the snowflakes that fell there glittered like stardust. On one level, she was scared—terrified, of course. That part of herself seemed to exist beneath a surface of soundproof glass, banging, screaming, but unheard. Mostly, she was numb. She had the sense that every moment of her life since the death of her mother had led her to this moment. She thought of what Julian Ross had said about the music written for her, the notes one chose to play or not. But Lydia wasn't quite as passive as that. She had written this symphony for all of them and she recognized it now. Hadn't she in a way forced the hand of fate? If she hadn't lived the life she had, chasing monsters, pulling back the curtain on evil, would she be here now? Would Dax and Jeffrey be in danger...or worse? She knew as a fact that they would all be somewhere else this moment. She couldn't say if it would be a better situation or a worse one, though it was a safe bet it couldn't be much worse. But they wouldn't be here.

If she hadn't written With a Vengeance, the book about Jed McIntyre and his crimes, he may never even have thought of her again while he rotted away in the New York State Facility for the Criminally Insane. If she and Jeffrey hadn't gotten into that mess in Miami, Jed McIntyre would still be locked away. She took a sharply cold breath of air into her lungs and stopped herself. This was a mental spiral that could only lead to a loss of focus. And she needed to be focused right now. She could self-flagellate later, when they were all safe.

She didn't have far to go. Just to the abandoned subway station

at Prince and Lafayette. She was to walk down the stairs and wait at the gate. She thought of the network of tunnels Dax and Jeffrey had described to her. She was about to see them for herself. She paused at the top of the stairs and wondered, not for the first time, if she should call Ford or Agent Goban. Somehow she didn't quite believe that McIntyre had the ability to know what she was doing, that he was watching her, or had some way to listen to her phone; but she was reluctant to take the chance. As if in answer to her musings, the phone in her pocket rang. She retrieved it and put it to her ear.

"Well," said Jed McIntyre. "What are we waiting for?"

Jeffrey was sitting on some kind of rickety wooden chair, each ankle bound to a chair leg, each wrist bound to its arms. Dax was gnawing at the binding on Jeffrey's ankle like a rat. Since Dax was tied and on his belly, that was the only binding he could reach. Occasionally he would stop and spit, make a noise of distaste. Jeffrey slowly moved his foot and ankle forward, trying to put stress on the tape. They didn't seem to be making much progress, until suddenly Jeffrey had more freedom of movement. The hope gave him strength and after a few minutes, he snapped the ankle free.

"Now what?" said Dax. "What are we going to do with this free ankle? Kick our way out?"

He had a point.

"Knock yourself over," suggested Dax. "And I'll try to get the bindings on your hands."

Jeffrey began to rock himself and eventually toppled to the side, landing hard on cold concrete.

"Does this type of thing really happen?" he asked.

"I heard that some people are actually hiring companies to kidnap them. I mean, like, attack them on the street, take them away in a van, and tie them up like this. They predetermine the number of days they'll be held, what kinds of things they want to happen to them. They try to get away. For fun. Can you imagine? There are too many idiots with money in this city."

"No shit."

Awkwardly, they snaked their bodies closer to one another, and after a few minutes of adjustment, Dax went to work on one of Jeffrey's wrists.

"You know," said Jeffrey, "in some cultures we'd have to get married now."

Dax spit. "Bloody homo."

Standing behind the gate was a homely midget. He was filthy, with a big face and a striped stocking cap; in his hand he held a key, which he passed through the gate to her. Lydia suppressed the urge to run screaming. When she leaned in to him, she saw that his beard was full of crumbs and that he gave off a strange odor, some combination of body odor, foot rot, and baked goods. He smiled a dirty smile at her, his teeth brown and filmy, as she swung open the gate. He took the key back from her and locked it behind them, then he jumped down on the tracks. She followed quickly, landing awkwardly and almost dropping to her knees. She'd never thought to carry a flashlight. The dwarf seemed comfortable with the darkness, so she kept her eyes on him and stayed close to the wall as the relative light from the abandoned station behind them faded, becoming smaller until it disappeared altogether.

The dwarf jumped though a hole in the concrete, and, pausing to look through, all Lydia could see was black. The darkness seemed alive with ugly possibilities and she was aware that her heart was pounding in her chest, every nerve ending in her body pulsing with fear and the desire to flee. She could hear the skittering of rats, but she couldn't see them. The sound of their tiny, clawed paws seemed to come from above and below her, all around. She steeled herself and followed the midget through the hole like Alice in some sick urban Underland.

They were making progress until Dax passed out. His head just kind of got heavier against Jeffrey's arm, and Jeffrey felt a wave of fear.

"Dax? Dax?" he said uselessly, his voice bouncing off the concrete that surrounded them. He forced his own breathing to quiet, and was relieved to hear Dax's. He couldn't begin to imagine how much blood Dax had lost.

For a second he almost believed that this was a nightmare, not real. He didn't want to believe they were going to die down here; thinking thoughts like that was suicide. But things were looking grim. He continued to turn his wrist, working it in circles and trying to stretch the tape and put stress on the tear Dax had made. He thought of Lydia, imagining that this piece of tape was the only thing that kept him from seeing her again, that kept him from holding her safe and warm in their apartment. He imagined that it was the only thing that kept them from putting an end to Jed McIntyre. Finally, he pulled his hand free. He had a moment of elation and relief. He reached out his hand to touch Dax's neck, feeling for a pulse. It was weak; but he was alive.

He went to work on the other hand, the left half of his body free now. He imagined that getting this hand loose was the only thing that was going to save Dax. And it wasn't far from the truth. Dax groaned next to him.

"Hang in there, Dax. Hold on."

It was then that he heard someone approaching in the darkness. Jeffrey held his breath, every nerve in his body on edge. There was silence again and he started pulling desperately on the other bindings. The sound of chains and a padlock coming undone made him freeze. He came as close to praying as he ever had. A door swung open and a large form stood in the doorway. It was lighter outside than it was in the room where they were being held, but he still couldn't see the face of the person standing before them.

"You boys are in a lot of trouble...again," said a voice Jeffrey recognized.

She didn't know how long they had been walking and the darkness was disorienting. She felt closed in and was having difficulty breathing in the dankness. Though she was trying to remember where they had turned by running her hands along the wall, feeling for abnormalities that she would remember if feeling her way out, it seemed fairly hopeless. She had no idea where she was, and if she turned and tried to leave, she might be wandering the tunnels forever.

She followed her guide more just by hearing him than actually seeing him. He shuffled his feet loudly, maybe on purpose so she could hear him. Or maybe that was just the way he walked...quickly, rushing, shuffling his little feet. He hadn't said a word and she wondered if he was mute. She started talking, mainly just to make herself feel better.

"Why are you doing this?" she asked him. "What's he giving you?"

He didn't answer her, just gave a little snort that was maybe meant to express disdain.

"Because he's using you, you know. When you've fulfilled your purpose he'll kill you and never think twice about it. So anything he's promised you is a lie."

"Shut up," came a small, whiny voice from in front of her.

Bull's-eye, she thought with an inner smile.

"It's true. He doesn't care about you. He's not your friend."

She had given it a little thought while feeling her way through the darkness. What would motivate someone to do the bidding of Jed McIntyre? The life of a homeless dwarf couldn't be an easy one. He was probably scared a lot of the time, lonely, a misfit even in a land of misfits. Money doesn't buy loyalty for very long, generally. But fear can, gratitude, maybe for a time. Maybe Jed was offering him protection.

"You think he's looking out for you. But as soon as he has what he wants, he won't need you anymore, Shorty."

"Don't call me that," he said, his voice defensive and angry.

She grinned at her victory. Even in moments of mortal danger and terrible fear, Lydia really had a knack for fucking with people's heads.

"Just tell me what he promised you. Is he protecting you? He's going to leave you here when he goes, trust me. He's not taking you with him. Besides, I'm going to kill him. Then you'll have to answer to me."

The midget laughed and it sounded at once childlike and sinister.

"Yeah, right. You're going to kill him."

"Watch me. Then we'll see who's laughing."

His giggling stopped abruptly. "When he's done with you, you're not even going to want to live."

The words sent an army of chills from her neck into her fingertips. She wanted to pull out her gun and make the dwarf wet his pants and weep for mercy. But if she killed him, she'd never find Jeffrey. If she never found Jeffrey, then the little bastard would be right after all.

“When this is over, I’m going to have mercy on you, Shorty.”

“Isn’t that generous?” came another voice out of the darkness. “You’re a better person than I am, Lydia Strong.”

Suddenly there was light and the darkness seemed to skitter away in the beam of the powerful flashlight. In the momentary blindness that followed, she heard Jed McIntyre laugh.

She struggled against arms that wrapped around her from behind, arms as cold and strong as lengths of chain. One impossibly powerful arm held her immobile across the chest and another wrapped tightly around her throat. She tried to twist away from him, feeling weak against his superior weight and the intensity of his grip on her. When she stomped down hard down on his foot, his grip loosened for just a moment and she managed to free an arm. Her hand flew to the shoulder holster but stopped dead when she felt the steel of a blade against her neck. It was so sharp that just the lightest touch nicked her skin and she felt a warm vein of blood trickle down her neck. Her breathing came harsh and ragged.

“This would be a good time to hand over your weapons, Lydia,” Jed McIntyre said reasonably. “I can feel one here at your back.”

Releasing her arms but keeping the knife pressed to her throat, he pulled the Glock from her waistband and handed it to the dwarf. “I dislike guns,” he said. “They’re so sloppy.”

The dwarf pointed it at her, his grin superior and malicious. She wondered if he realized she had the safety on. It was a piece of information she’d hold on to for the time being. Her mind was oddly clear in spite of the horror and unreality of the situation. Things seemed to be happening very slowly.

Jed McIntyre removed the Smith and Wesson from the holster and pushed her away from him; she hit a concrete wall hard. She raised a hand to her neck and felt the wet stickiness of her own blood. It looked black on her fingers.

Jed McIntyre picked up the flashlight that lay on the ground and shone it under his face. He looked ghoulish in the harsh white light, creating black circles under his eyes, his teeth yellow and shining. His red hair was a chaos of wild curls.

"You can't imagine how long I've been waiting for this moment, Lydia. Doesn't it feel like destiny?"

With that he pointed the revolver at the dwarf, whose malicious smile melted into uncertainty. He let go a little laugh, his eyes darting from Jed to Lydia and back to Jed. "What are you doing?" he asked, voice cracking. "Come on, Jed. It's not funny."

"I wouldn't shoot that in here if I were you," said Lydia, looking around at the concrete tunnel they were in. At such close range the bullet would pass through the dwarf and ricochet all over the tunnel.

"Sorry, Horatio. It's been great."

Horatio swung the gun he had pointed at Lydia toward Jed. It was too big for his hands, but he managed to reach the trigger. But the gun wouldn't fire. Those pesky safeties.

McIntyre fired the revolver and Lydia dropped to the ground, curled herself in a ball, and covered her head with her arms. The echoing bang must have been heard for miles.

Horatio issued a girlish scream that ended abruptly in a horrible gurgle. She heard him fall to the floor, heard him rasping and convulsing there on the ground for thirty seconds, maybe more. She heard the sharp scream of the bullet as it bounced off the walls, twice, maybe three times before losing momentum, all the while waiting to be struck by it. She leaned against the wall, feeling pity and revulsion, terror and rage come in flashes, competing with each other in intensity. Then there was silence.

"I hope I didn't act in haste," said McIntyre, musing.

Horatio's leg twitched horribly for a few seconds more as blood drained from a throat wound. Lydia felt pity for him as she got to her feet to stand face to face with Jed McIntyre.

THIRTY-THREE

"Ford?"

"Rose."

"How are you?"

"Can't complain." His throat felt as dry and his hands as shaky as a boy talking to his crush. An awkward silence fell between them. They were strangers to each other now. Strangers who shared a twenty-five-year past.

"Where are you?" he asked finally.

"With Katie in Houston."

"How is she?"

"She's doing well."

Again silence. He wasn't sure what she wanted, why she called. Was it guilt?

"I miss you, Ford."

He closed his eyes against the swell of emotions that rose in his chest. If he released all that he was feeling, he was sure that the wires on the phone would burst into flames. "I miss you, too," he said in a voice that croaked, one he barely recognized.

"Can we talk?"

"Aren't we talking?"

"In person."

"Come home," he said, and he tried not to sound like he was begging.

"Ford..."

"Just come home, Rose. We'll talk all you want."

"Things have to change."

"Okay—whatever you want," he said, and he meant it.

"No. It has to be what we want, Ford. If we don't want the same things, then there's no point in our being together anymore. Do you understand that?"

He paused, listening, really listening to her, maybe for the first time. He did know what she meant and he wondered if maybe it was hopeless after all.

"I can only be what I am, Rose," he admitted, expecting her to hang up.

"I wouldn't have it any other way." Her voice was soft, loving, sounding like she had when they were young.

"We'll talk, then. Figure it out."

"Yes. I'll come home in a few days. Friday."

"Okay."

"Ford?"

"Yeah?"

"I love you."

He cried then; he didn't care that she heard him sobbing like a baby. "I love you, Rose. So much," he managed to croak before he hung up the phone.

He played the conversation over in his mind as he drove the Taurus up to Haunted. He'd stopped home before heading upstate, to shower and change, more to keep himself awake than out of concern for hygiene, and had been there to take the call from Rose. Part of him was starting to believe he dreamt it, that she wasn't really coming back, that he was going to be forced to live out the rest of his life alone with only his unsolved cases to fill the empty hours and years.

Like a schoolgirl, he analyzed her words. Was she coming back to stay? If he didn't say the right things, would she leave again? Friday seemed impossibly far away. He pushed the conversation from his mind. He had to focus now. Two children were missing, two people were dead, three if you counted Tad.

He raced up the road that wound toward the outskirts of the town. Tall trees rose on either side of him and there was only the sliver of a moon in the sky. He should have waited for morning. But with the kids missing now, there wasn't a second to waste. He was a homicide detective, so finding out who killed Richard Stratton might be the only way he could help Lola and Nathaniel. Maybe he should have brought someone with him. But he needed Malone and Piselli working the crime scene, working with the task force assembled to find the twins. He reached for his cell phone to call Malone, let them know where he was headed. But the thing was dead. Goddamn things always ringing, never charged when you need them.

Anyway, he wasn't going to go breaking into the Ross house in the middle of the night, he wasn't going into the Hodge residence looking for Annabelle and Maura. He was just going to look around, absorb the situation, see who was coming and going. Before he made a move, he'd get some help, maybe stop by the precinct and get a hand from old Henry Clay's boys.

He found the drive leading to the Hodge house, then found a spot and pulled the car over, gave it some thought, and felt a little conspicuous beside the gate. So he drove a few yards farther until he found a place where he could move his vehicle slightly into the trees and out of the path of approaching headlights, giving him a little more cover. Then he cut the engine and settled in. It was going to be a long, cold night. But at least he could think about Rose and hope that this was going to be one of his last nights without her.

THIRTY-FOUR

How do you have a conversation with your worst nightmare? Lydia wondered. How do you do something as mundane as move your lips to talk when looking into the face that has become in your imaginings the embodiment of evil?

Since the murder of her mother, in Lydia's nightmares and daydreams Jed McIntyre had become Freddy Krueger and Jason and Charlie Manson in one horrible form. Standing across from him, she looked at his hands and knew that the bones within them bent to grip the knife that killed her mother, that part of him touched her in her last moments. It was almost too much for her mind to get around. She felt a part of herself shutting down, slipping into a kind of shock, a welcome emptiness.

But so close to him, seeing him in flesh and blood, seeing his chest rise and fall with his breath, smelling the stench of his body, in fact, took some of his power away. He was just a man with a beating heart, with skin, muscle, and bone. He was not a demon, a supernatural force the way he'd seemed to her since his mistaken release. He was just a man with an evil heart and a sick mind. Someone who would meet his end like the rest of them. Hopefully sooner.

"Where are they?" she forced the words from her mouth like they were children clinging to her coattails.

"We'll go to see them. Would you like that?"

She nodded.

"I wish I didn't see so much hatred in your eyes, Lydia. That's not what I'd hoped for," he said, and he really did sound disappointed.

She shook her head, reminded of how insane he was. He moved closer to her and she shrank from him. A look of hurt flashed in his eyes and she almost laughed.

"What did you expect?" she asked, not wanting to feel his name on her tongue, as if to say it would validate him in some way.

"I just thought maybe somewhere inside, you'd come to feel about me the same way I feel about you. That we are one mind, one heart. Sure, we have a complicated past. But can't we move beyond that?"

She had heard this tone of voice before. It was the tone of the manipulator, the controller, the tone of righteousness implying that all you think and all you feel, the things you believe, are wrong-headed. It was the tone of the angry and abusive man, the one who coaxes at first, then turns to violence when challenged. She'd heard it before, a couple of points lower on the Richter scale. It made him less frightening somehow, reducing him to his twisted psychology. She wondered how delusional he really was, how easily she could fool him. She forced herself to smile, though she wasn't sure she could make it reach her eyes. Pretending was not one of her strong suits.

"I don't hate you," she said softly. "Not at all."

He was a coil of energy, wound tight and ready to spring. She tried to look into his blue eyes but saw only a flat deadness reflected there. It was as if the thing within us that makes us human hadn't been granted to Jed McIntyre. Seeing him confirmed her long-held belief that evil was the absence of something, rather than the presence of something. He was a golem, a hideous creature in the tunnels below New York City, hated and reviled, hunted, made wretched and alone by his own terrible self. Even in his grasp, he was less terrifying to her than he had been in her imagination.

"I'm crazy, not stupid," he said, echoing exactly the words Jetty Murphy had said to Ford McKirdy. Funny how things came in circles.

He grabbed her arm and put the barrel of the gun to her temple. "We're in the endgame now. Let's not dawdle."

They came to a place where a rumble of trains could be heard far in the distance above their heads, a place where pieces of concrete fell fine and glittering like snow. Though Lydia couldn't imagine what their source could be, thin, very faint shafts of light came through the spaces between metal beams, revealing walls covered with graffiti, an old sagging couch, and other abandoned furniture. A school desk balancing on three legs, a toppled standing ashtray, a card table, its vinyl surface ripped and pouting like a mouth. A filthy pile of school lunch trays and milk cartons lay near the tracks. Unbelievably, a small tree stood in the dirt. It looked as though it had struggled in the dim light, then gave up the fight, its dead branches radiating an aura of abandonment and failure. Lydia tried to imagine the journey of each of these objects, how each of them had wound up in this place. It was something her mind was doing to distract her from the situation she was in; a kind of coping mechanism to keep the brain from being devoured by the chemicals of terror.

"Nice place you've got here," said Lydia, her flippant tone belying the fear that had burrowed a home in her belly.

"Mi casa, su casa," said McIntyre with a smile.

She hated him so much she felt like her heart would turn inside out. Death was too good for him, too easy, too quick a way out. She wanted to make him pay, not just for the things he had done, but for the way she had felt over the last sixteen years of her life. She had carried this hatred around with her for so long, it had poisoned nearly every experience she'd had, impacted nearly every decision, it had, in effect, changed the entire vector of her life. She hadn't realized the intensity of her pain and her anger she had carried on her back all these years until just this moment.

Again, she thought about the curse of Annabelle Taylor. She thought of how hatred and righteous anger had warped generation after generation of two families. And then she thought about her own lost child. She had to wonder if a child could survive in a body so consumed by pain; what child would want to be born to such a woman, whose whole life had been directed by vengeance? She looked at Jed McIntyre and for a second she wondered if she was any better than he. Maybe the only difference between them was that she didn't kill others to mitigate her own suffering. Maybe that was the only thing that separated them. That we are one heart, one mind. Maybe he was right.

Just let it go, a voice inside her head whispered. Be calm, focus.

"We're here," he said as they stopped in front of a metal door locked by chains. "I'm going to let go of your arm right now to unlock this door. Remember, if you try anything, I'll kill them both and let you live. Remember that—life will be your punishment."

She nodded and looked expectantly at the metal door, praying that when it swung open she'd see Jeffrey and Dax safe and sound. She closed her eyes, unable to bear the waiting, the awful desperate feeling of hopeful expectancy that bloomed inside her.

But when the beam of the flashlight filled the room, there was only a toppled chair and scattered pieces of duct tape. Inside, she smiled. They got away...but how? she wondered. The door had been locked from the outside.

Jed McIntyre stood staring into the room, his mouth agape. He squeezed his eyes shut once and then opened them again as if willing his vision to obey his expectations.

It took about a half a second for Lydia to realize that she didn't have a reason to cooperate anymore, and another half a second to decide whether to stay and try to end this twisted match of theirs or run. Then another second to assess her odds, unarmed and physically smaller than her opponent. She ran.

Any athlete will tell you that mental edge is what it takes to win when it comes to physical exertion. You can be the strongest or the fastest or the most talented athlete in any competition, but when focus is replaced by doubt, you might as well go home. The other thing is—and athletes don't necessarily know this in the same way that, say, antelope do—that fear, the terror of being pursued, is like a shot of nitro in your engine. You'll never be faster than when you're running for your life.

Lydia ran into darkness, back the way she came. She ran without seeing into a labyrinth that she didn't know her way out of. She summoned every ounce of strength left in her battered body, knowing she only had to stay an inch out of the grasp of the man behind her.

It took Jed McIntyre a few seconds to give chase. He chased her with a powerful flashlight in his hand, and its beam cast her shadow long in front of her and lit her way a bit, though the light shifted and pitched as he ran. Shadows and shapes of light and dark danced in front of her and she felt like she was in a house of horrors. She could feel him right behind her, not feet but inches, as her heart tried to beat its way out of her chest and her throat went dry with exertion. Her breathing came ragged now, every intake of air like sandpaper on her lungs.

She took a tight corner quickly and was running into blackness again, back the way they came but in another tunnel. It took him longer to get around the corner, but soon his beam filled the narrow tunnel ahead of her. It was so dark that the light only reached a few feet in front of her; she never knew what lay just ahead of the beam. It could be a wall, it could be a ten-story drop. But she had no choice...in this case, the devil she didn't know was better than the one at her back. She heard him stumble behind her and it gave her an extra push forward. As the light came up again, she saw what looked to be a hole in the concrete, a makeshift doorway with planks of wood slanted across.

Heading for that doorway, she saw something that glinted on the ground. As she drew closer, she saw it was a wrench. She bent as she ran and picked it up, slowing only a little. She took a chance; turning as she ran, she threw the wrench with a hard flick of her wrist and sent it sailing through the air. He ducked out of its way and it landed harmlessly on the ground behind him. He laughed and then she stumbled, tried to catch herself, but fell fully to the ground hard onto her abdomen. Waves of pain turned the world red and white and threatened to take her consciousness. He slowed and stood over her, breathing heavily. She tried to crawl away from him, but he put his foot hard on her back. More fireworks of pain. He put the flashlight down beside her.

"Silly girl," he gasped. "I could have shot you in the back anytime I chose. Ask yourself why I didn't."

"Fuck off," she said, her mouth full of dirt.

"Kiss your mother with that mouth?" he said. "Oh, that's right. I killed her."

She struggled against his foot and got nowhere; it felt like a lead weight on her back.

"You're not an easy woman to love, Lydia."

"I'd have to disagree with that," said Jeffrey, somewhere in the dark around them.

She felt the barrel of her own Smith and Wesson at her temple. Did you know that you're forty times more likely to be the victim of a violent crime if you own a gun? her inner voice quipped. Hysteria was setting in.

Jed crouched and stretched out an arm to pick up the flashlight, never moving the gun from her head. He swung the beam around. Lydia could see that they had spilled from the narrow tunnel into an open space where five track lines lay next to each other. Around them and above them were metal stairways, ledges, and catwalks. The beam of his flashlight didn't reveal where Jeffrey was standing.

"Jeffrey," she said, her voice sounding desperate and scared even to her own ears.

"Jeeefffreey," Jed mimicked. "I know you're not armed, G-man."

"You also thought I was tied up and locked behind a metal door. It's time for you to start questioning your assumptions."

"If you shoot me, I'll make sure my last action on this earth is to put a bullet in her brain," he said, but Lydia could hear the nervousness in his voice.

A loud bang sounded from the left, like metal falling on metal. Jed swung his gun and fired. He had four rounds left.

"I'm over here," said a voice Lydia didn't recognize from above them and to the right. Jed fired again.

"Just put the gun down, McIntyre," came Jeffrey's voice again.

"I can't even believe you would waste your breath by saying that. It's such a cliché. Of course I'm not going to put the fucking gun down."

He spun madly, shining the light above him and all around. A shot rang out of the darkness, but missed its mark, hitting the dirt next to his feet. He let out a scream and moved for cover, dragging Lydia with him by the collar of her jacket. Lydia clawed at his wrist and kicked her legs, resisting him as best she could, but it didn't seem to be of much use. They were right next to the doorway she had seen before.

Lydia craned her head to try to look around her, but she could see nothing in the pitch-black outside the flashlight beam, which was starting to flicker and dim. She felt the barrel of the gun leave her temple and looked up to see Jed moving toward the doorway. He kept the gun pointed at her, and backed away slowly.

"Another day, Lydia," he said, and disappeared. She heard him clanging down a stairway.

THIRTY-FIVE

The time was passing slowly and the car was getting cold. Ford could feel the tip of his nose and his toes going numb. The night was silent, the sky riven with stars. Somewhere in the woods around him he could hear the low calling of an owl, slow and mournful. It was giving him the creeps. In all the time he'd been sitting by the side of the road, not one car had passed him. He turned the key in the ignition and pulled out onto the street.

The more he thought about it, Maura Hodge's residence was probably the last place Annabelle would go. Sitting, freezing his ass, he'd recalled the conversation he'd had with Chief Clay, how the old man had told him the cops wouldn't go near the Ross home, how they thought it was haunted. He thought of the old house, sitting gated and avoided by the police, and wondered if maybe, were he Annabelle Hodge, it might not be a half-bad place to hide temporarily.

Ford had never heard such silence. Maybe if it had been summer there would have been crickets singing or something. But as he pulled the car onto the side of the road across from the gate leading to the Ross estate and killed the engine, the silence was so loud it felt like a presence. He looked longingly at his cell phone. He even had one of those things that you plug into the cigarette lighter to power it. Malone had given him one after the last time his phone had died. But he'd never used it. It sat still in its stiff plastic packaging in his desk. It just seemed so self-important to have a cell phone, to be so concerned about it and who might be calling you or who you should be calling that you'd have a little rig in your car. But it didn't seem quite as foolish right now.

He got out of the car and shut the door. Even though he'd tried to do it quietly, the click of the door closing and the crunching gravel beneath his feet seemed to echo through the night. He crossed the street and stood before the gate, noting that it was unlocked and, in fact, ajar. He pushed it open and it emitted a long, slow screech.

As he walked up the long narrow drive, the house rose out of the trees. As he grew closer, he saw that it was completely dark, no sign of life or movement. But he drew his gun anyway. Something about it, its black windows and towering copulas, its shutters hanging askew, its sagging eaves, the great dead oak beside it communicated menace to him. The house seemed to be regarding him with disdain, seemed to bear its teeth. Ford felt the thump of adrenaline in his chest, felt it drain the moisture from the back of his throat.

What the hell are you doing, old man? he thought. You shouldn't be here alone. What are you trying to prove? That you're a good cop after all? That it will all have been worth it, everything you threw away for the job, if you can just prove to yourself that you were a good cop?

He heard the conversation he had with Lydia play in his head again.

I don't even know what I am if I'm not a cop.

Maybe it's time you figure that out.

He stood at the bottom of the stairs leading to the house

and the silence around him grew louder. The moonlight dappled the porch, cast the spindly shadow of the dead oak across the shingles.

Inside that door, he might find the answers to the Tad Jenson and Richard Stratton murders. Jenson, one of his cold cases, and Stratton, maybe his last case. The thought of solving them both felt like closure to him. Maybe then he could walk away from the job, from that basement office, and feel like everything he'd forced Jimmy, Katie, and most of all Rose to endure might have some meaning after all. Justice had meaning, didn't it? It was worth a lifetime of hard work and sacrifice, if it was truly served.

Then he heard a child crying. It was soft and low, just like the owl, but without the peaceful, mournful rhythm. He looked around him and the sound seemed to come from the sky and the trees, not from inside the house. He walked around back, slowly, gun in his hand, staying close to the house. He could see in the moonlight that a path cut into the trees and again heard the sobs of a child. He thought of Nathaniel and how he'd cried that day about the bogeyman. It sounded like him, but Ford couldn't be sure. With his gun drawn and his heart in his throat, he headed toward the sound.

THIRTY-SIX

"Jeffrey," Lydia yelled, struggling to her feet. "He's getting away."

The echo of Jed McIntyre's footsteps had faded. She ran to the doorway and saw that it led to a stairway into nothingness. She could still just barely hear his footfalls on the metal steps and started to head down after him when Jeffrey emerged from the darkness and came to her side.

"I thought I was never going to see you again," he said, putting what looked like her Glock in his waistband and taking her into his arms. Relief washed over her, as she let it sink in for a second that they were both safe. But then she pushed herself away from him, as relief was replaced with panic.

"He can't get away, Jeffrey," she said, listening to his footfalls fading. "I can't live like this anymore. Not for one more day."

"All right," he said simply. He didn't offer the usual arguments for why he should go and she should stay, seemed to recognize that they needed to go after him together.

“Where does this staircase come out?” he said.

“How should I know?” she answered. But then she realized he wasn’t talking to her.

Jeffrey motioned with his head behind her and she turned to see what amounted to a small army of men and women. Maybe twenty or thirty people had gathered around them. She remembered what Jetty had called them, the mole people. They were the most beautiful sight Lydia had ever seen. One man stood apart, ahead of them, looking

at once regal and strong, in spite of his torn and tattered clothes, the dirt on his face. His gray hair was like a dusting of snow on dark earth and in his eyes Lydia saw wisdom and an inherent goodness.

“This is Rain,” said Jeffrey.

Lydia reached out a hand to Rain, and when he shook it, his hand was callused and rough.

“The staircase leads to other, smaller tunnels, other catwalks beneath the electric wires, there are maybe twenty offshoots from the main stairwell,” said Rain. “But as far as I know, this doorway is the only way back into the main tunnel system. He’s trapped. I’ll take you down. The others will stay here and watch the entrance.”

“All right, let’s go,” said Jeffrey. They stood aside and let Rain pass in front of them.

THIRTY-SEVEN

Ford moved into the trees and the darkness seemed to come alive around him, the shadows and dark spaces in the woods seemed to shift and move, seemed to have life and substance. The ground beneath his feet was soft, covered with dead leaves still wet from the last rain or snow, and it allowed him to move quietly toward the sound. He felt like he'd been walking forever and the sound never seemed to grow louder. Then it ended abruptly. The silence that followed was more frightening than the cries and Ford picked up his pace to a light jog. Up ahead he saw a dancing orange light and smelled the scent of wood burning.

He came to a clearing where he saw several ruined structures, shacks with tin roofs, all but one of which had toppled, grown over with weeds and moss. A wood fence sagged around the area, most of it rotted, eaten by termites. The shacks were arranged in a half circle and in the center was a fire, crackling and smoking. Trees stood all around like an army of dark soldiers. Ford paused, not seeing any movement. He thought of the story Lydia had told him about Annabelle

Taylor, about her murdered children, about the curse she'd cast on the Ross family. Standing in the silent, wooded night alone watching the fire burn, looking at the tumbled shacks, he could almost believe it. He was gripping his Smith and Wesson service revolver so hard his hand was starting to hurt.

"Nathaniel!" he yelled suddenly, shattering the silence like a thunderclap. "Lola!"

He felt better, like he'd taken control of the night. Until a dark form appeared in the door of the only shack still standing. He took a step back, unlatching the safety on his gun. The figure stepped into the light.

"Put down the gun, Detective," she said.

Ford McKirdy sighed, strangely comforted by the sight of the gun in her hand. At least she was human.

"I can't do that," he said. "Where are the children?"

"The gun or the children die," she said, her voice dead and flat. She reached into the darkness and pulled Lola out of the shack by the hair. The little girl shrieked, her face a mask of fear. Nathaniel leapt out after her, clinging to her legs.

"No-no-no-no-no-no," he cried, his little voice broken by sobs.

She thrust the gun to Lola's temple. "You think I don't mean it? You think I give a shit about either one of these brats?"

Lola shrieked again and Ford felt like someone had a hand over his heart and was squeezing without mercy. He inched closer to Annabelle and saw that she was as frightened as the kids; Ford could see it in her shifting eyes, hear it in the quaver of her voice. Lola started a quiet whimper and Nathaniel joined in. He could see tears in Annabelle's eyes, too. Christ, he thought, they're all children.

"Annabelle, listen to me," Ford said, his voice soft and coaxing. "It doesn't have to be this way." His voice was steady, but his mind was racing, turning over his options. If he didn't put the gun down, Lola could be dead. If he put the gun down, they all could be.

"Yes, it does. Don't you see that? It always had to be this way. Before I was even born she had this whole thing planned. I never even had a choice.

"It's my destiny," she went on, practically spitting the word. "You think the Rosses are cursed? They got nothing on me."

"You have a choice now," he said rationally. "Let's all walk away from this together. I can help you, Annabelle. I wouldn't say that if I didn't mean it."

He wanted her to see a way out, but he wasn't sure she could hear it. She was in a black place and he could see something dark in her expression; he was afraid it was a loss of hope. More than menace, more than terror, it was the most dangerous thing you could see in an adversary's eyes.

"You can't help me. No one can," she said. His heart pumped, hearing the echo of Julian Ross's words. "He's come for all of us."

"Who has, Annabelle? Tell me and I can make it all stop."

The night was filled now with the sound of the children crying. The three of them were before him, lit by the orange glow of the fire, the fear in each of their eyes burning bright and wet. There was a moment when he saw her expression shift, when he thought he'd reached her. It was the last thing he saw before he felt a terrible pressure on the back of his head and a curtain of darkness fell before his eyes.

THIRTY-EIGHT

Jed could hear them coming for him, hear their clumsy steps on the metal stairs he had just descended. So he crouched in the darkness and waited. He'd left his flashlight up above, not that he could use it. His eyes had adjusted to the new level of blackness and he felt comfortable in the cold air. Light did, unbelievably, travel down here and the eye found it after a few moments of adjustment.

He sighed and his voice echoed throughout the cavernous space, a maze of walkways below electric mains and who knew what else. A giant mess of veins hung suspended from the ceiling, stories of ledges and narrow walkways connected by ladders. He had gone as far as he could go before he realized that there was no other exit. Now he hid at the uppermost level of the final chamber connecting to the stairway. There was a ten-story drop below him. He was trapped, but he was in the catbird seat. He'd see them before they saw him and he had three bullets left.

He was disappointed in Lydia Strong. He never imagined her to be such a foul-mouthed bitch. When he'd looked into her eyes he'd seen only hatred and anger, not the connection he'd imagined them to have all these years. His plan had been thwarted, but it might not have worked anyway. He'd wanted her to see him kill her love and her only friend. He'd hoped that in her grief, she'd turn to him. But he had the sense now that she might still have rejected him even if she'd had nothing left. There was that defiance to her. It was not an attractive quality in a woman.

He was uncomfortable and shifted. In doing so, he knocked some unseen piece of debris and it fell loudly, bouncing off metal, clanging, and then hitting the floor. A silence followed and Jed McIntyre held his breath.

The three of them stopped in their tracks on the stairway at the sound. The flashlight Lydia held in her hand flickered dramatically and recovered, though the light was dimmer still. Figures.

Lydia opened her mouth to talk, but Rain put a silencing hand on her shoulder. He motioned for them to follow; they tried to be as quiet as possible moving toward the sound. After a moment, he took the flashlight from Lydia and turned it off, laying it on the stairs beside them. They were plunged into blackness and it took a few minutes for their eyes to adjust.

Following Rain, they turned off the stairwell into a cavernous chamber, a maze of walkways crisscrossing across the height of it, some ten stories tall or more. Lydia's eyes scanned the catwalks.

"I can hear you breathing," said Rain suddenly, loudly, and his voice echoed off the concrete. They were answered by silence. Rain moved in close to Jeffrey and whispered, "I'm going to draw his fire. When he shoots, you'll be able to see where he is." Jeffrey nodded and Rain moved toward one of the ladders and started to climb. He moved quickly with grace and strength.

"You better stay where you are," came a voice from high above them. But Rain kept moving; he was already at the third level.

A shot rang out and the blast from the gun revealed Jed's position, high and in the far corner of the room. He was trapped like a rat, and from the tone in his voice, he was starting to realize it. He was not getting out of this room a free man.

"You're trapped, McIntyre," said Lydia. "And you only have two rounds left."

Lydia surmised that Rain was still out of Jed's range, but he wouldn't be for long. Jeffrey and Lydia started up after him. When Rain was on the fourth level, Jeffrey opened fire in the direction from which Jed's shot had come. He let three rounds go. Judging by the sparks and the sharp sound of the ricochet, it sounded like two of the bullets hit concrete or metal. But the third shot...she couldn't be sure. The darkness around them seemed to hold its breath, and all three of them crouched low in their positions waiting for return fire. But none came. For a brief second hope bloomed in Lydia's heart that Jed McIntyre was dead. It was an ugly feeling and she was ashamed of it; but she felt it nonetheless. After what seemed like an eternity of waiting, a low groan came from above them.

"Hold your fire," McIntyre said. "I'm hit. I give up."

Lydia and Jeffrey exchanged a skeptical look.

"Throw down the gun, McIntyre," said Jeffrey. "Then we'll talk."

"I can't move," he said, his voice rasping and just a little too pathetic.

Rain had reached the top level and was approaching the prostrate form they could now see above them, as they, too, drew closer.

"Be careful, Rain," said Jeffrey.

His words were drowned out by the firing of the Smith and Wesson. Lydia and Jeffrey watched, helpless, as Rain staggered back toward the railing before falling over the side and landing with a sickening thud on the next level.

"Oh, God," Lydia screamed, feeling a wash of helplessness as Jeffrey opened fire on Jed McIntyre. The darkness came alive with the explosion of gunshots and Lydia wished she could cover her ears as she raced up the ladder and across the landing to Rain, Jeffrey right behind her. In the flashes of light that came each time Jeffrey fired, she could see Rain's milky, desperate eyes, McIntyre running on the landing above them, Jeffrey's gaze intent on his target, and finally, McIntyre's body jerk hard as it absorbed one of Jeffrey's bullets. Then there was silence and darkness again.

They could hear as he gasped above them. It was a sound they both recognized, something known as the death rattle, the sound of breath passing through mucus in the moments before death. They heard the gun drop from his hand as it clattered down, hitting metal and then landing in the dirt below them.

Lydia climbed up the final ladder, shaking off Jeffrey's grasp on her arm. She wanted to see him die. She wanted to see life pass from his body.

He stood still, leaning against the railing, his hand at the wound on his chest, his mouth agape, his eyes shocked. He looked ghostly and weak, and as she approached he turned his eyes on her. They were cold and soulless, revealing nothing even in the final moments of his life. She searched her heart for compassion for this twisted man; she searched herself for one human emotion. And the only one she could come up with was stone-cold hatred. There was no forgiveness in her heart for Jed McIntyre, there was nothing inside her that was right or good or evolved in this moment. In this moment, she was everything he had made her. No better than him.

He seemed to teeter against the railing and she thought he might fall, but she didn't reach out to grab him. She just watched as his life seemed to drain from the wound in his chest, the ground around him slick with his blood. He whispered something then, a wet sound. And she leaned in to hear him. When she did, he grabbed her wrist, held it hard. She struggled to pull it back, but he wouldn't let go of her. Panic welled within her as a wide smile bloomed on his face and a wicked look glittered in his eyes. She braced herself against his pull, but her feet couldn't find purchase on the bloody metal beneath her feet and they slipped as he pulled her closer, whispering something to her that she couldn't hear.

She felt hypnotized, pulled in by his powerful gaze. He drew her closer and she fought the irrational fear that he could take her into hell with him just by holding her eyes as he died. They were locked like that for she didn't know how long.

Then Jeffrey's arm snaked around her from behind, pulling at her waist. She saw the Glock come around and Jeffrey emptied it into Jed McIntyre. The hand that had grabbed her wrist flew open and the force of the blast pushed him over the railing. They watched as he sailed down ten stories and landed in a heap on the ground below, his arms and legs spread apart as if he were trying to make an angel in the snow.

PART THREE
THIRTY-NINE

"Rebecca Helms had a great deal of love in her life, it's clear to see," said the young preacher at the graveside. "She'll be deeply, grievously missed by friends and colleagues, and most especially by her younger brother Peter, by her mother and father, Ruth and Gregory. In that love, part of her will live on."

The preacher was thin and pale, with light blond hair and blue eyes that glowed with his faith. His strident voice carried through the cold and over the heads of the mourners gathered to say good-bye to a woman whose life was over far too soon. Jed McIntyre's last casualty, the last person destroyed by a man who had been destroyed long ago. Lydia leaned into Jeffrey, hanging back behind the crowd of Rebecca's close family and intimate friends. One hand rested on the back of Dax's wheelchair, where he'd be until his Achilles' tendons healed. He looked up at her with grim green eyes, his face solemn and drawn from sadness and physical pain.

He had a bit of a stunned look to him. She moved her hand to his shoulder and he patted it.

Jeffrey shivered beside her and Lydia couldn't tell if it was the chill or the pall that had settled over all of them. She tightened the arm she held around his waist and pressed down the feeling of helplessness, the useless parade of "if only's" and "why her's" that marched around in her conscience. Did she hold herself responsible? No. Jed McIntyre and no one else was responsible for the murder of Rebecca Helms and the others. But did she feel as though she had inadvertently written a part for Rebecca in the twisted, morose symphony of her life? Absolutely. She'd have to live with it, that and so many things.

"Ashes to ashes, dust to dust."

No real sense of relief had come since the death of Jed McIntyre. It didn't feel as though a burden had been released. The world didn't seem like a better, safer place, and the loss of her mother was no less with her. None of the things that she imagined would happen if the world were suddenly free of her bogeyman had happened. Maybe it was too soon. Or maybe, as was her fear, the damage had already been done. That she wouldn't heal the way Dax would heal, or Rain would heal. Maybe she was so altered by the events of her life, so damaged, that part of her was as dead as Rebecca or Marion, buried and gone for good. She was trying not to believe that, but a funeral was a difficult place to cultivate a positive attitude.

Lydia watched as Rebecca's mother and father approached the graveside, each with a white rose in hand. They were quiet, brave. Lydia knew they were enduring the most awful possible moment, the last second of physical connection to their daughter. She knew that when the roses dropped from their fingers and landed on the casket, it was the last time anything they touched would have contact with anything she touched. That each of them was screaming, raging inside with grief and fury, pain that would cause them to wish for death more than once over the next months, maybe years. But they were stoic. Lydia wanted to scream for them. Maybe they were the last victims of Jed McIntyre.

The crowd began to thin, as people stopped at the graveside and then moved along to waiting cars and limos. The day was cruelly clear and bright, a light blue sky with a round white winter sun. Better to rain. God didn't seem so oblivious then to the pain of His children.

The three of them came to stop at the edge of Rebecca's grave and they looked down onto her gleaming silver casket littered with the roses dropped by the people who loved her. Jeffrey dropped the three white orchids he had been holding for them. And Lydia said quietly, "I'm sorry, Rebecca."

After all, what else was left to say?

At the Rover, Jeffrey and Lydia helped Dax into the backseat and he bore the assistance like a rectal exam, uncomfortable and humiliated. Jeffrey put the wheelchair in the back of the car and Lydia reached to help him settle and strap in.

"I'm not a child," said Dax, grabbing the seat belt from Lydia's hand. He didn't look at her and his face was flushed with embarrassment.

"Well, then stop acting like one, you big baby."

She patted him on the head and he glared at her, but there was no heat in it. He was just tired and crabby and hurting. She understood and he knew she did. She was about to open the front passenger door for herself when she was aware of someone standing behind her. She turned to see Detectives Malone and Piselli.

"Ms. Strong," said Malone. "We need to talk."

"What's up, guys?" she asked, Jeffrey walking up beside her.

The two of them looked uncomfortable, worried. They exchanged a glance and then Piselli spoke up.

"When's the last time you heard from Detective McKirdy?"

The events of the last few days came rushing back in a wave as Lydia tried to remember the last time she'd talked to Ford.

Slowly they'd filed into the underground chamber, Rain's legions. Quietly, shuffling and unspeaking, they'd carried Rain and Jed McIntyre up the long metal staircase and eventually out of the tunnels, Lydia and Jeffrey following in a kind of haze. The surreal quality of the whole ordeal made it easy for Lydia to pretend she was participating in an incredibly vivid lucid dream. When they emerged into the city night, the cold air snapped her back a bit and the events that had just transpired began to sink in. At the corner of Prince Street and Lafayette, they were greeted by the stone-faced Special Agent Goban and the rest of the FBI team, as well as some NYPD uniforms.

Dax had been taken from the tunnels hours earlier, Lydia later learned, and was rushed to the hospital. Before the emergency surgery to repair his injured legs, he managed to explain to one of the hospital staff that they needed to contact the FBI and tell them where Lydia and Jeffrey were. The man, whom Dax couldn't name and probably wouldn't recognize, had done that, hence the greeting committee.

A waiting ambulance rushed Rain to Bellevue, where he was recovering from a gunshot wound to the chest. And Lydia had the grim satisfaction of watching the coroner's office team zip Jed McIntyre into a body bag. He lay white, his eyes staring, a thin line of blood dripping from the corner of his mouth. She watched as he was swallowed by black plastic and loaded into the back of the van, the doors slamming hard and final behind him.

"Where will you bury him?" she asked one of the men. "No one will claim him."

He shrugged, not looking at her. "Depends."

"How do I find out?" Something in her voice must have

caught his attention because he turned his eyes on her. He was an older Hispanic man, with deep lines etched around his eyes and a receding hairline. In his face she saw the reflection of a thousand ugly, anonymous deaths.

"Call the office tomorrow," he said, with something like sympathy in his voice. "Ask for Hector, that's me. I'll let you know."

"Thanks," she said, offering her hand. But he didn't see it and walked off.

"Time to let go," said Jeffrey from behind her. "You don't need to know where the body goes."

She nodded but knew she would call to find out anyway. Why? She didn't really understand, herself.

The next two days, they'd barely talked, left the house only to go to the hospital to be with Dax. They walked around each other in a kind of daze of pain and loss, touching more than speaking. That had always been the way with them in times of trouble; they communicated better with their bodies than with words. Everything that had happened before the tunnels had become a distant memory. Everything, of course, except the loss of the pregnancy. Lydia carried that with her like an arm in a cast. The physical pain was subsiding; she imagined the emotional pain would fade eventually, as well.

Julian and Eleanor Ross, the missing twins, their drama, all seemed to exist on a distant planet in another galaxy. Their client was dead. The questions were still out there, floating in the outer edges of Lydia's consciousness, her curiosity, but she didn't have the energy to acknowledge them again yet. She hadn't even thought about Ford.

This morning Dax had insisted on coming to Rebecca's funeral. He didn't have insurance, so the hospital was looking to unload him anyway. Lydia believed that he needed to stay another few days, just to assure he'd stay off his injured legs. Against their better judgment, they wheeled him out and here they were.

"I haven't seen Ford since we discovered Eleanor Ross's body at the duplex," she answered finally.

"That's the thing," said Piselli, lighting a cigarette. "Neither have we."

"It's not like him. He's not going to just take off," said Piselli, sitting in the pub where they'd decided to meet at on Astoria Boulevard in Queens. It was a dump of a place called Cranky's. Every inch of the wall had a beer-bottle cap nailed to it like some alcoholic mosaic. The jukebox played "Love Me Do" by the Beatles. A couple of old men hunched in the corner, nursing pints and arguing about Giuliani. The typical bar aroma of booze and cigarettes was accented by a subtle but definite hint of vomit.

Piselli and Malone sat across from Lydia and Jeffrey in a red vinyl booth; they'd parked Dax's wheelchair at the end of the table.

Lydia really looked at them for the first time. They were both pretty good-looking guys, Piselli with slicked black hair and dark eyes that observed sharply and missed nothing. He had a fashionable bit of stubble on his square jaw and a slight hook in his nose didn't detract from his face but made it almost aquiline, at once sexy and regal. They were both young, but Malone had more of a boyish look to him, a soft innocence around the corners of his eyes. The acne scarring she'd noticed when she'd met him the first time didn't seem as angry or red as it had. His skin was unlined, shaven, and clean. He smelled of Ivory soap.

Lydia and Jeffrey ordered Amstels from the bartender; Malone ordered a Coke. And Piselli drank coffee from a white ceramic mug that read one day at a time. Dax sulked.

"This is what we know," said Piselli, lighting the fourth cigarette he'd smoked since approaching them at the Rover. Lydia fantasized about asking for one but didn't.

"He had a uniform take Anthony Donofrio down to the

station while he hung around the scene for awhile with us. He poked around the apartment, then headed down after them. We know that he spent about forty-five minutes with Donofrio; he taped the conversation. During this conversation he learned that Annabelle Hodge had entered the building just hours before you and Ford found Eleanor Ross dead."

"I talked to him right after he learned about Annabelle Hodge," interjected Piselli. "He wanted me to cooperate with Rawls, the head of MCU. Make sure he got anything he needed from our files. But I didn't ask him where he was going and he didn't say."

"We know he spoke to his wife briefly that evening late, after midnight. She called from Houston," Piselli said.

"Did you talk to Donofrio?" asked Jeffrey.

"We can't find him."

"What do you mean?" asked Lydia, taking a sip from her beer.

"Rawls headed back there and spent some more time with him, but he basically just went over and over the same stuff he'd told Ford. Rawls had nothing to hold him on, so they had to let him go. He never made it home after he left the precinct."

"You think he fled?" asked Jeffrey.

"With no money, no change of clothes, no call to his mother? No," said Piselli with a shake of his head.

"Do you have the videotape of their conversation?" asked Lydia.

Piselli pulled a videotape from the inside pocket of his coat and handed it to her. "I didn't know if it would help you, but I thought I'd bring you a copy.

"They talked about Annabelle Hodge, mostly," he said, and then ran down the general content of the conversation. "How much she hated Julian Ross and a bunch of other crap about how she was a voodoo priestess or some shit."

Lydia and Jeffrey exchanged a look.

"You think she's the shooter? That she took the twins?"

"She's suspect number one as far as the Missing Children's Unit is concerned."

"Have you been up to Haunted?" asked Lydia.

"We been up there, looking for Ford and Geneva Stout, a.k.a. Annabelle Hodge. No sign of either of them. But we got a warrant and with the help of the locals up there, we took the Hodge residence apart. They're still watching the place."

"What did you find?"

"We found a knife that was consistent with the injuries incurred by Richard Stratton. But it had been thoroughly cleaned, no prints, no blood evidence."

"You talked to Maura Hodge?" asked Jeffrey.

Malone and Piselli shook their heads.

"Can't find her, either?"

"She's gone, too," said Malone.

"The Missing Children's Unit is working around the clock. Julian Ross's attorneys are riding them like you wouldn't believe. Those kids are worth millions."

"No leads?"

"Nothing, and I mean nothing. They're taking tips from a hotline. They've been canvassing the neighborhood and Haunted, too. The lawyers posted a reward, we've got sketches of Annabelle and Maura Hodge all over the television, newspapers, the streets. Rawls won't admit it, but he's feeling desperate. You can see it in him."

Lydia felt a flutter of panic and a little guilt. She'd been so overwhelmed with the events of her own life that she hadn't even thought about the kids since she'd left Eleanor's apartment that night. Lydia thought of their sweet faces, remembering shaking each of their little hands that day at the hotel. She felt a little ache in her chest, wondering what had happened to Lola and Nathaniel, their father and grandmother dead, their mother locked away.

"It's cold and getting colder. The case is at a dead end. Two bodies, two missing children, one missing detective, the only survivor whose whereabouts we know of," said Piselli, showing the palms of his hands, "in the nuthouse. Crazy, talking about 'destroyers' and monsters eating her young."

"Eating her young..." said Lydia. "She's been saying that from the beginning."

"She has, hasn't she?" said Jeffrey.

"A cop disappears like that," said Malone, apparently not listening to the conversation but thinking about Ford, "people figure he turns up somewhere having parked with a bottle and his service revolver. You know what I mean?"

There was a look of worry and sadness on his face; the job hadn't yet taught him how to hide his emotions better, hadn't desensitized him to the ugliness of a cop's life. Lydia found herself hoping that maybe he'd get out before it did. There was something refreshing about a young man whose feelings you could read on his face. Even Jeffrey had learned a game face; Lydia couldn't always tell what he was feeling by looking into his eyes.

They were all quiet for a minute. "We been to Ford's place in Brooklyn," said Piselli. "Rose came back; she's worried sick, of course."

"Though maybe if she was so worried she wouldn't have left in the first place," said Malone with a disapproving snort.

"Not your business," said Piselli, giving him a look.

"You said he talked to Rose the night he disappeared. What was that conversation about?" she asked.

"She told him she was coming back so that they could talk."

"He would have been happy about that; the conversation would have made him hopeful," said Lydia. She remembered her conversation with Ford when they'd driven upstate. He'd seemed very depressed then, unsure about the future and doubting the way he'd lived his life. Those things and the pressures of the job, the lack of an outlet for his emotions and a viable support system...well, it led a lot of cops to the end Malone feared. But not with Rose coming back. Unless that added a whole other set of pressures that he couldn't handle.

"Ford wouldn't go out like that," said Jeffrey, sounding certain. "Especially not with Rose coming back. It doesn't make sense."

"So what can we do, guys?" said Lydia.

Now that they were talking about the case again, she was infused with a sense of urgency. It gave her a jolt of energy that she hadn't felt in a while. Her fear for Ford and the twins and the itch of curiosity awoke a familiar fire within her. She felt a little guilty, but part of her was relieved to have a problem to solve. Her work had always helped her keep her mind off of her life...for better or for worse.

"Nothing," said Piselli with a shrug and a sideways glance. "We're just following up with you, Lydia, since you were one of the last people to see him."

"Nothing?"

"Yeah, since you know, legally we got no reason to go back up to Haunted and take another look around," he said, looking pointedly at Lydia. "The Richard Stratton case takes precedence over Ford, since there's no evidence of foul play in Ford's case. MCU is handling the twins and our help is not exactly welcome. We have no chain of evidence that leads us back to Haunted, with Maura and Annabelle Hodge nowhere to be found. We're stuck."

"Well," she said, leaning back and looking at Jeffrey, unable to keep the edge out of her voice. She was hoping that he wasn't going to try to stop her from getting involved. "We should be getting back to work on the Ross case, anyway."

"Even though our client is dead, we have a responsibility to Julian Ross to follow through," agreed Jeffrey. "Maybe we can come up with something on Ford while we're up there."

Lydia observed the same combination of concern and energy in Jeffrey's face, in the way he was so quick to agree.

Distractions could not be overrated when the options were sitting around grieving and reliving nightmares.

"Of course, you'll let us know how it goes," said Piselli with a satisfied nod.

"Naturally," answered Lydia.

They all looked at each other for a minute, the questions and possibilities turning in front of each of their eyes.

"Why doesn't anybody in this country just say what they mean?" said Dax sourly.

FORTY

Back at the apartment, they watched the tape of Ford's interview with Anthony Donofrio. Jeffrey and Lydia sat next to each other on the couch and Dax had asked to be parked by the window. Lydia had a pad on her lap and a Montblanc pen in her hand. She tapped the pen quickly on the arm of the couch, turning things over in her mind as the tape played.

"So Annabelle—" said Jeffrey when the taped had ended, getting up and flipping off the VCR, "why would she hate Eleanor and Julian so much?"

"Maybe it's inherited hatred. Passed from mother to daughter, like the curse?" answered Lydia, speculating.

"As far as we know, she was the last person to see Eleanor, the last person to enter that apartment before the twins went missing," Jeffrey said.

"But why? Why kill Eleanor in cold blood and take the twins? What does she have to gain?"

There was no answer for that question that Lydia could get her brain around. She knew the facts, that Annabelle was the obvious person to be looking at for the murder of Eleanor

Ross and the disappearance of the twins. But the motive seemed weak to her: Kill Eleanor because Maura hated her. And even if that were the case, why take the twins?

"So we go back to the basic question: Who has the most to gain now that Richard Stratton and Eleanor Ross are dead and Julian is locked away?" said Jeffrey, sitting beside Lydia. "I mean, it looked for a while like Eleanor had the most to gain."

"But now she's dead."

"So presumably the Stratton-Ross estate will go to the twins."

"But they're only children. So right now probably those lawyers Piselli was talking about would be in charge of their trust."

"So the lawyers have the most to gain."

"Assuming that all of this comes down to money."

"Doesn't it usually?" said Dax.

Someone had said to Lydia not very long ago that it was not money but the love of money that was the root of all evil. She didn't want to believe that...there was something so cheap about the concept that the human soul could be corrupted by something so fleeting, so ultimately unsatisfying as monetary wealth.

"Maybe it's not about money. Maybe it's about revenge," said Lydia.

"The curse, you mean?" said Jeffrey.

"Yeah." The quest for justice, no matter how twisted, was something that Lydia could understand better.

"So who's invested in the fulfillment of the curse?" asked Jeffrey.

"Maura and Annabelle Hodge. The daughters of the daughters of Annabelle Taylor. Cops found that knife at the scene."

Jeffrey shrugged. "Without prints or blood evidence. I mean, you could probably find a knife in our kitchen that was consistent with the knife that killed Richard Stratton."

Lydia nodded. "But still, it's something."

They were quiet for a minute.

"If you ask me—" said Dax sullenly, "and you didn't—whether it's about the money or it's about the curse, whether it's Annabelle or Maura Hodge, or the goddamn ghost of whoever, there's only one person left to get any answers from."

They both looked at him.

"Julian Ross."

Sitting on an orange plastic chair in the Payne Whitney waiting room, Lydia, in spite of everything, felt a strange lightness, like the relief that comes after the blinding pain of a migraine subsides.

She had come to Payne Whitney unaccompanied. And though it was a grim errand, the fact that she had traveled here not stalked by Jed McIntyre, not watched by the FBI, and not guarded by Dax and Jeffrey gave her a sense of freedom she didn't remember feeling for years.

As she'd stepped off the train, moved through the platform, and jogged up the concrete steps to the street, she had the sudden thought: Jed McIntyre is dead. And something inside her shifted. She had the powerful sense that a high justice had been served. The grief and numbness she'd been feeling wasn't gone exactly, but she could see thin fingers of light splitting the gray she'd been dwelling beneath. Then she wondered, was it the satisfaction of a vengeance that made her feel this good—vengeance for her mother, for herself, for all his victims living and dead—or was it just relief? She looked into her own heart and didn't find the answer. But she did realize that, for her, revenge had been a powerful motivator—love, even greater. And, sitting in the sterile clinic waiting room, that thought led her to draw the conclusion that love, revenge, and money were probably the most powerful drives she could think of, outside of survival. It applied to everyone she could think of, including Jed McIntyre. She wondered which of those things were at play in the Ross case; she was starting to suspect all three.

Every time Lydia had come to see Julian Ross, she seemed smaller and grayer. Her lips were cracked and her eyes were dull, side effects, Lydia imagined, of her medications. The woman who had turned into a demon before her eyes just days earlier seemed incapable of even sitting up straight. Still, a burly orderly stayed in the room during their interview this time.

"What do you want?" asked Julian, looking at her with darting, paranoid eyes.

Lydia sat down so that they were eye-level. She held eye contact and made sure her voice was clear and strong. "Listen, Julian. This is your last chance to play straight with me."

Julian narrowed her eyes. "They sent you, didn't they?"

"No, Julian, they didn't. Listen to me," she said, using the voice she would use to speak to a child. "The destroyers have your children. You need to tell me how to help them. Right now, before it's too late."

Dax was right. Julian was their only hope for answers, their only hope for a direction that might lead to Ford and the twins. Maybe, by speaking Julian's language, she might get something that they could use.

But Julian stared blankly at Lydia, blinked her eyelids heavily, slowly, as though they were filled with sand. A long minute passed and Lydia wondered if she'd made a mistake. She looked into Julian's eyes, searching for something there that she might appeal to, but they were flat and glassy.

"Your mother is dead and the twins are gone," she said finally. "If you don't help me, I can't help find your children."

She didn't seem moved by the information, but something flickered on Julian's face and then she rose and walked over to her bed, casting a glance at the guard by the door. She reached beneath her mattress and withdrew a large sketchpad. Some black ink pens clattered to the floor.

"She's not allowed to have that," said the orderly quickly, moving toward Julian.

"It's okay," said Lydia, reaching her hands out to Julian. "I'll take it. Please."

Julian handed it to her. "Now get out," she whispered venomously. "I have nothing left to say."

Remembering their last encounter, Lydia didn't have to be told twice.

"I wondered when you'd find your way back to me," he said, with just a hint of smugness. The gallery was empty and Orlando DiMarco was alone in his office. He'd risen to greet her, but she'd made it to his office before he'd reached the gallery floor. Lydia noticed that Julian Ross's last canvas still leaned against the wall where she and Jeffrey had viewed it on their first visit.

"I thought it might be gone by now," she said.

"No, there will be an auction when it goes on sale."

"It's not on sale yet?"

"No. Not yet."

"What are you waiting for?"

He shrugged. "I'm not sure. Maybe I'm having trouble parting with it. Afraid it might be her last. Believe me, I'm not very popular right now. There are a lot of very wealthy people who are dying to get their hands on this canvas. But—I just..." His voice trailed off.

Lydia regarded him carefully. He was expensively dressed in a beautifully cut black suit, with a white collarless shirt. His dark, thick hair hung loose around his shoulders. In his handsome face, tanned dark brown, with a strong nose and thick red lips, she saw the lines of grief. It was a tightness at the corners of his mouth, a slight upturn of the tips of his eyebrows. She wondered, of the three major motivators she had recently been contemplating, which was his.

Lydia held up the sketchpad Julian had given her. He looked at her blankly for a moment and then seemed to recognize what she held.

"Where did you get that?" he asked, moving toward her quickly.

"Julian Ross gave it to me."

"Why would she do that?" he said, and he looked hurt.

"Did you bring this to her?"

"Yes," he admitted. "I smuggled it in the back of my jacket. They wouldn't let her have any paper or pens. She was miserable. I brought her that and some charcoal pencils and some fine artists' pens. I thought, at least then she could draw. You cannot separate an artist from her art. It's the cruelest punishment, like cutting out someone's tongue."

"Because this is how she communicates."

"Of course," he said, as if she were some kind of philistine.

"I'm glad you see it that way. I was hoping you might have some insight into what she was trying to tell me in giving me these drawings."

He looked at her and then down at the sketchpad as though it were an infant he believed Lydia might drop on its head.

"An artist's paintings are like dreams...the symbols often mean something only to her," he said with a shake of his head. "Especially Julian's work. Even she wasn't always sure where those images came from."

Lydia looked at him for a second and their eyes locked. In his face, she saw the same love she had seen when she first visited his gallery. Unrequited, she thought now. Maybe they'd been lovers once, as Ford had claimed. But Julian had never loved Orlando the way he loved her. Lydia could see the longing and the pain and she appealed to that part of him.

"But you know her, don't you, Orlando? You've loved her for years."

He looked at her, the exposure seeming to shame him. He lowered his eyes.

"It's true," he said slowly. "But even in love we don't always know each other. Sometimes even less so."

She walked over to a long table that stood covered with neatly kept bottles of paint, a jar of brushes, some folded tarps, a stack of palettes. The surface of the table was covered with thousands of drops of dried paint, leaving behind a multicolored pattern that was at once bumpy and smooth as glass. She lay the sketchpad down and opened the cover.

Outside Payne Whitney, she'd flipped through the sketchpad and saw a chaotic collection of nightmares, intricate and insane, a window into Julian Ross's twisted psyche. But she also had the powerful sense that somewhere inside what she saw were the messages of a sane woman trying to escape her own diseased mind. She wanted to talk to someone who'd known Julian before she'd lost her mind. And she could only think of one place to go.

"Tell me what you see here, Orlando," she said. "Tell me what you know. For Julian."

He walked to stand beside her and she could smell the light aroma of his expensive cologne. He moved his hand and ran light fingers over the sketch. His nails were perfectly manicured. The delicate bones and thick veins of his hand danced beneath skin the color of caramel.

A naked woman lay sprawled in a sea of blackness, her hands reaching out to the image of two children who huddled together beneath a giant set of jaws. The woman's eyes and face showed a kind of resignation, a hopelessness.

"She's been stripped bare, left in the darkness. She's lost her children to some danger and she feels sure she'll never see them again. She's never painted them before, the twins. She's never painted anything that gives her joy, anything that she's loved."

He flipped the page to the image of a house. Lydia recognized it as the house in Haunted, twisted and bleeding, with fire leaping from its windows. It had the personality of pain, seemed to reach out as the fire consumed it. Drawn into the flames, the twins clung to each other, surrounded by a vast, living darkness writhing with demons. In their eyes was the reflection of the burning house.

"Hmm," said Orlando.

"What?"

"This house has come up again and again in her work," he said. Lydia tried to call to mind others of Julian's paintings with which she was familiar and couldn't remember seeing it.

"Nothing that has ever been sold or published," said Orlando, as if reading her expression. "I've asked her about it. She said, 'The past is immortal. It might be forgotten, but it never dies. It lives in us. It can live in the structures we build, in the children we bear.' The house symbolized that idea for her."

On the next page was the image of a man hanging by the neck from the landing above the foyer at the house in Haunted. He was young and beautiful, seemed to float in the air, the noose hanging just loosely about his neck like a scarf. His eyes were closed, his expression serene. Lydia recognized him as James Ross, the young man she'd seen in the photograph, not the monster in the large portrait that stood behind them. On the ground looking up at him was the image of a demon with wild eyes and claws, head thrown back in a violent roar. The demon's scaled hands reached out toward James, but he was just out of reach.

"Her twin," said Lydia.

"You know about her twin?" asked Orlando.

Lydia nodded.

"Then you know that's him, too," he said, using his eyes to gesture to the portrait behind them.

"Yes," she said, thinking back to the night she came across his photograph in Haunted. "I figured it out eventually."

"She never accepted his death," he said, his voice

sounding far away, contemplative. "She always believed she'd been lied to."

"Why would anyone lie about that?" she asked.

"That's what I asked her."

"And what did she say?"

"She said she was sure she would feel it when he died," he said with a mystified laugh. "And she never felt it. She believed he was still out there waiting for her."

"She may have been right," said Lydia. "I think I may have seen him."

There was something then that came over Orlando. It was a kind of stillness, a waiting. Lydia saw him almost visibly stiffen. "Is that possible?" he asked, his voice almost a whisper.

"Anything's possible, isn't it?"

"But the body they found last year in Haunted. It was positively identified," he said. He had the look suddenly of someone trying to appear nonchalant. She watched as a tiny muscle started to dance involuntarily at the corner of his eye.

Lydia shrugged. "Records can be falsified."

"Could he be responsible for all of this?" he said, looking at Lydia with alarm.

"If he's alive, it seems like a highly likely possibility."

He seemed to turn the possibility over in his mind. He closed his eyes for a second. "It's her worst nightmare realized," he said.

"She's afraid of him?"

"He tried to kill her and her mother when they were teenagers," Orlando said, turning to look at her. "They put him away, but he escaped. She always believed that her brother was responsible for the murder of Tad Jenson."

"But she never implicated him?"

"In spite of her terror of him, there's a bond there that I could never understand," he said.

She remembered what Julian had said about her brother,

that he was her "angel," always trying to protect her. You can never be sure with crazy people if what they said was the deepest truth or the most outrageous fantasy.

"Did she ever have any contact with him? Did she know where he was?"

He shook his head. "Not that I know of. She always said that she believed he was lying in wait for her to be happy again, and then he was going to tear her life apart. He's like her bogeyman, you know. The embodiment of all her worst fears...about the world and about herself."

"About herself?"

"That's what she said. She never explained except to say that they were one...what he was, she was."

Lydia shuddered as his words reminded her of Jed McIntyre. One mind, one heart.

They flipped through the rest of the images slowly, the burning house, the huddled children, the naked woman, the young beautiful James, and the monster were images that repeated over and over. Then, on the last page of the sketchpad, Lydia was surprised to see a drawing she'd missed the first time. Filling the page was a mass of curls, and the malicious stare of giant eyes. Smoke danced upward

in rings from the bowl of a pipe. Delicately drawn into one of the smoke rings was the scene of the murder of Annabelle Taylor's children that the librarian Marilyn Woods had described to Lydia. Five small corpses lay on the ground in a field of fire, as the figure of a man stood with a gun drawn. In another of the rings was an image

of the twins lying lifeless on the ground before the burning house. Half the face on the page was that of Maura Hodge, the other half was Eleanor Ross. Julian had written, "Behold the Queens of the Damned and the havoc they have wrought on all of us."

"Jeff, it's Ford. Listen, Lydia was right. That DNA evidence from the Milky Way bar links whoever attacked her in the Ross home with someone present at the Jenson scene. I'm not sure what it means, but I'm heading up to Haunted. This can't wait till tomorrow, especially with the twins missing. I'll keep you posted."

As he'd listened to the message, Jeffrey had felt a surge of dread. He was relieved to have a lead on Ford, where he'd gone, and why; but it had been more than seventy-two hours since Ford had left that message. Jeffrey had lost the phone to Jed McIntyre and for all he knew it was lying somewhere in the tunnels. He hadn't even missed it until he'd been wracking his brain, trying to figure out what Ford's move would have been after leaving Donofrio, wondering what would have led him to take off, not letting anyone know where he was going. Out of desperation he'd called his own cell phone, hoping maybe there was a message there.

Jeffrey was certain now, as Lydia had been all along, that the answers to Richard Stratton's and now Eleanor Ross's murders, as well as the disappearance of the twins and Ford McKirdy, would all be found in Haunted.

"Don't leave me here like this, man," begged Dax, and it wasn't a pretty sight. He sat on Lydia and Jeffrey's couch, legs up on the ottoman, phone and remote control within easy reach. He looked pale and anxious, as if Jeff were leaving him on the battlefield to die.

"We're only going to be a few hours, Dax."

"Look," he said, "I can help you."

"You can't walk, Dax," Jeffrey said gently.

"I can walk," he insisted.

Really, the truth was that he could hobble. With enough painkillers, Dax could get himself around a small area. But he had been instructed to stay off his feet to allow the partially severed tendons to heal properly. So Lydia had insisted that he stay with them in their downstairs bedroom until he could get around his house in Riverdale a little better. Dax had grudgingly agreed, though Jeffrey thought he was secretly glad for the offer. The three of them were close now, more so than they had been before everything went down. The things they had endured together had bonded them.

"Besides, you don't need legs to fire a gun. Just prop me up in the backseat and I'm good to go."

"It's not going to be like that," said Jeffrey, pulling on his leather coat. "You'd just be sitting uncomfortable in the car when you could be here resting. And there aren't going to be any shootouts."

"I've heard that before," Dax said with a snort. "That's why you have the Desert Eagle, then?"

"Seriously, we'll be back in a couple of hours. We'll call if we're going to be late."

Dax turned on the television and tuned Jeffrey out. He really wasn't handling his recovery period very well.

"Do you need anything before I go?" asked Jeffrey, starting to feel like the nanny to a difficult child. "I have to meet Lydia."

"I'm fine," Dax said sullenly. "I'll just sit here like a completely useless turd until you get back."

"Cheer up, man," said Jeffrey, patting Dax on the shoulder. "We'll be back before you know we're gone."

He put in a quick call to Malone and Piselli to let them know about Ford's last message and headed out the door.

FORTY-ONE

Maybe it was because snow threatened, turning the sky a moody gray and black. Or maybe it was the time Lydia spent with Orlando probing the depths of Julian Ross's twisted psyche. But on crossing into the Haunted city limits, the town felt unwelcoming to the point of menace. It seemed emptier, almost deserted, not that it had been a bustle of activity before. But something about it now had the air of abandonment. The depressed little Main Street, which on their first visit had been more or less innocuous, if approaching dilapidation, seemed...haunted. As they pulled off of Main and up the winding roads to the outskirts of town, the black dead trees rising up on either side warned them away with branches reaching like witch's fingers into the sky.

They pulled the Kompressor off the main road and through the open gate that led to the Hodge house. At the end of the drive, they came to a stop behind a black and white prowler that sat in front of the porch where they'd first seen Maura Hodge with her shotgun and Dobermans. They climbed out of the car and Lydia could see by the tilt of his head that the cop sitting in the car was dozing.

"I'm not sure this is what Malone and Piselli had in mind when they said the Hodge residence was under surveillance," Lydia said as they approached the driver's side of the squad car.

Jeffrey tapped on the window and the cop awoke with a startled snort. He looked around for a few seconds, disoriented, and then rolled down the window. A mingling scent of body odor and stale coffee wafted out into the cold air.

"This is a crime scene," said the cop. He was young, red-faced, with a bristle of strawberry blond hair on his head. He had a sleep crease on his cheek where he'd obviously rested it against the door as he napped. His gold nameplate read reed.

"NYPD Detective Malone was supposed to call with clearance," said Jeffrey, holding out his identification.

The cop looked from Jeffrey to Lydia with suspicion but then reluctantly pulled the radio from its hook on the dash and muttered into the mouthpiece unintelligibly. He waited, silent, not looking at them, while the radio crackled with static and other communications.

Lydia looked up at the house and remembered the last time they'd been there. She remembered the noises upstairs she'd heard when they'd interviewed Maura, how Dax had seen a figure in the upstairs window. The thought made her skin tingle. The windows were dark now, had that air of desertion like the rest of the town.

"Forty-one, forty-one," the radio yelled.

Reed grabbed the radio and seemed to puff up with self-importance. Lydia noticed that his fingers were long and girlish in their shape and apparent softness.

"Forty-one," he said into the mike.

"Clearance granted for Mark and Strong."

"Ten-four."

"You can go in," he said, friendlier now that they had

been cleared. "Holler if you need anything."

"Thanks," said Jeffrey.

The smell that Lydia remembered from their first visit seemed to have staled and solidified. She felt the same swelling of her sinuses just seconds after stepping though the door. A staircase to her left led into darkness.

"Let's split up," she said. "I'll head upstairs."

Jeffrey looked at her and flashed on the attack in the basement of the Ross house. The habits of the last few months, the feeling that someone always had to be with her because of Jed McIntyre, were dying hard.

"Okay," he said with effort.

Lydia smiled at him, squeezed his hand. "I'll holler if I need anything."

The stairs groaned beneath her weight and the wood felt like it had a bit too much give. But she made it to the top of the stairs without falling through. She pushed the door open to the immediate right of the landing and flipped on the light. It was totally bare, the windows boarded up. She walked across to a closet and saw only a single wire hanger lonely on a mauve tension rod.

Two other rooms she entered were identically empty, though the rest of the windows were free of plywood. Lydia walked down the hallway over sagging wood floors, her footfalls sounding loud to her own ears. At the end of the hall, she turned the brass knob of one of the two remaining bedrooms. Here the smell was more powerful than anywhere else in the house, some combination of mold and dust, maybe wood rot.

The room was full of junk. A blue bicycle with rusted handlebars and a missing front wheel leaned against the wall. A Singer sewing machine, its plastic case yellowed and cracked, sat atop a rickety wood table. The fading light outside struggled in through windows that were opaque with grime. Lydia flipped the light switch and a bulb hanging from a wire, naked of fixtures, sizzled to life, albeit dimly. It flickered as she moved through the stacks of junk. Ripped and soiled clothes—a man's gray wool overcoat with the pockets torn out, a flowered housedress covered with dark red stains, a child's red corduroy jumpsuit cut with scissors—were piled randomly about the space. A tower of old record albums teetered in a corner. It was a big room, maybe four or five hundred square feet, and Lydia moved through the maze of junk.

One of the major principles of good Feng Shui is to clear all spaces of clutter. Clutter represents stale energy. A person who feels comfortable in clutter is the kind of person who holds on to the past, can't let go. Lydia was not surprised to see a room like this in Maura Hodge's home. Maura could hold a grudge...even one that wasn't necessarily her own. Righteous anger like that was addictive; it allowed a person to stagnate, wallow in her contemplation of injustice, spend all her energy seeking revenge and never for a second thinking that there might be another way to live. Lydia herself had been guilty of this for many years.

Something in the far corner of the room was covered with a white sheet. As she approached, a gust of wind traveled through the house with a low groan. Lydia felt a little flutter of fear and was glad when a second later she heard Jeffrey's footfalls on the stairs. She'd had too many people leaping out of the dark at her in the last several days; she was getting a bit skittish.

"Where are you?" he called.

"The room at the end of the hall."

"Find anything?" he said as he entered.

"Not yet," she said, walking over to the sheet and yanking it.

The sheet came down in a cloud of dust to reveal a bookcase filled with the same leather-bound volumes Lydia remembered seeing at the Haunted Library. She scanned the titles embossed in gold on the bindings.

"Christ," said Jeffrey. "How many volumes could you fill with the history of Haunted?"

"Looks like about thirty. Three centuries' worth."

The books, all titled History of Haunted, New York, were shelved in order by decade dating back to the 1700s and ending in the early 1900s. Some of them were slim, no thicker than a hundred pages.

"Fascinating."

"You know," Lydia said, "all these books have exactly the same binding. So did all the books in the Haunted Library."

"So?"

"When's the last time you were in a library and all the books were the same?"

"I haven't been in a library since Quantico," he said with a shrug. "In fact, I'm not sure I even remember how to read."

She picked a book off the shelf at random and turned to the title page.

The History of Haunted, New York
1800–1810
by
Maura Hodge

"Voodoo priestess-slash-author," said Jeffrey, leaning over Lydia's shoulder.

"Looks self-published."

"Didn't Eleanor say that Maura had been commissioning writers and historians to document the history of Haunted?" said Jeffrey.

"Yeah, I guess she's been publishing the work as well. Or at least binding it. That must be why all the books have the same package."

Lydia grabbed another volume and saw that it, too, was written by Maura Hodge. In fact, after a few minutes of inspection it appeared that Maura had written them all.

"Wow, that's stamina for you," said Jeffrey.

"No. That's obsession."

"She's obsessed with Haunted? Doesn't seem like much of an obsession."

"With the past. Remember how Ford said that the person who killed Tad Jenson and Richard Stratton was enraged? And how Maura's grudge was over one hundred and fifty years and had nothing really to do with her immediate world so she couldn't muster the rage it took to commit those crimes?"

"Yeah...."

"Well, look at this. I mean, to write all these books, she must have lived for this town and everything that happened here. She must think about it every day. For Maura Hodge, the past is right now. It's more present for her than the present, living in this place, isolated from

the world, harboring her grudge against Eleanor and the Ross bloodline, planning her vengeance for Annabelle Taylor. For Christ's sake, she named her daughter after Annabelle."

"So...what? Because she wrote a few books that means she killed Tad Jenson, Richard Stratton, Eleanor Ross, and took Lola and Nathaniel?"

"Or her daughter did. She must have been fed that hatred like mother's milk."

Jeffrey could hear that edge in Lydia's voice that brooked no argument.

"I don't know," he said anyway. "It seems weak."

Lydia shrugged and crouched down, looking at the books on the bottom shelf. She slipped one out and stood, flipping it open to the title page:

"'The Legend of Haunted, New York: The Murder of Innocents, by Maura Hodge,'" she read out loud. She turned the page and saw the dedication: "To Paul, the only pure soul."

"Who's Paul?" asked Jeffrey.

"When we were here last, we talked to her about Paul—Eleanor's brother, remember? She said something like: 'He was the only one of them that was any good.' Remember that? Remember how soft and wistful her voice became?"

It was a fairly light volume and Lydia flipped through, scanning the pages, with Jeffrey looking over her shoulder.

She read over the legend as Marilyn Woods had told it to her. Much of the text was rambling, clearly unedited, with poor grammar, fraught with typos. There were some crude line drawings of Hiram and Elizabeth, of the Ross house, of the shack where Annabelle had lived with her five children. There was a striking drawing of Annabelle Taylor and Austin Steward, the lines dark and dramatic, Annabelle's hair a wild mane of black curls much like Maura's. Lydia came to the final chapter, called "The Curse."

The curse of Annabelle Taylor is alive and flowing through my veins. For years, I was electric with the purpose of continuing Annabelle's quest for vengeance. But I grew weak when J left me. I thought that they had won and I had lost everything. I felt the cold disapproval of Annabelle herself, felt her anger in my blood. She hated me and my weakness so much that she took my only child from me. I wanted to die in my failure. Then a miracle occurred.

On a night in the fall when the harvest moon hung bloated in the sky, much like the night that Annabelle lost her children, Austin Steward came to me. And he made love to me as he had made love to Annabelle; he said her name over and over. Nine months later I gave birth to my only daughter. I named her Annabelle.

"Okay," said Jeffrey. "So Maura thinks that the ghost of Austin Steward visited her and impregnated her with Annabelle."

"It would appear that way," said Lydia.

"There must be something in the water in this town. These people are nuts."

"Who do you think she's talking about when she writes, 'when J left me'?"

Jeffrey considered it. "I have no idea, and unfortunately, everyone who might be able to tell us is either dead, missing, or nuts."

"Not quite everyone."

"I very nearly lost my job after your last visit, Ms. Strong. I'm afraid I have nothing left to say to you."

"Ms. Woods, with two dead bodies, a missing detective, and two missing children, I'm afraid you don't have much of a choice."

"You've come to the wrong place," said the librarian. "I don't know anything that's going to help you."

"Then tell me who does."

The librarian shook her head hard from side to side and pressed her mouth into a thin, hard line.

"Where's your boss?" probed Lydia. "Where's Maura Hodge?"

"I have no idea."

"You are aware, Ms. Woods, that if you try to impede the prog-ress of this investigation and we later learn that you knew some-

thing that you didn't reveal, you could be charged as an accessory to murder?"

Jeffrey turned so that Marilyn Woods wouldn't see him roll his eyes. Lydia's statement, of course, was a lie. It would probably have been a lie even if she was a cop. It had sounded pretty convincing, though; he'd give her that.

"Don't give me that crap," said Marilyn. "I watch television. I know my rights."

Jeffrey heard Lydia sigh. She was dwarfed by the large desk that Marilyn sat behind, which elevated her by about two feet above Lydia. The librarian stared down at Lydia behind thick glasses and a hard expression that seemed as immovable as stone. She looked more like a judge than a bookworm.

"I thought if anyone could be counted on to help us find the truth, it would be you, Marilyn."

She'd shifted flawlessly from intimidation to manipulation, but it hadn't chiseled even a chip from Marilyn's expression.

"You're more worried about your job than you are about

the lives of two innocent children?" Lydia pressed, her voice a combination of disgust and disapproval.

The first crack in her indifferent façade appeared as Marilyn's face flushed red.

"I don't know anything. I told you," she said, her tone somewhat less emphatic and her voice catching at the end.

But Lydia backed off. She placed a business card on top of the desk.

"When your conscience catches up with you, give me a call on my cell," she said. "In the meantime, we'll be giving your name to the NYPD. Expect a visit."

This was another lie, but it hit its mark. As Lydia and Jeffrey walked toward the door, the librarian called them back.

"Wait," she said.

They stopped and turned to face her.

"What I know...it's just gossip."

"Let us decide," said Lydia, walking back. The librarian walked to the door and locked it, turning around a sign that read back in five minutes though it was well after dark and there didn't appear to be an especially high patronage of the Haunted Library. She went to her office, beckoning Lydia and Jeffrey to follow.

"Well, no one knows where Maura has gone. I'll tell you that much," said Marilyn, seating herself behind the desk. Lydia sat on the sofa, and as was his habit, Jeffrey stood by the door.

"It's about Maura and Eleanor. There's a bit more to the hatred between them than just the curse. I heard that Eleanor had been killed and it made me think about the past."

Lydia waited while the woman seemed to be composing herself. Marilyn sighed heavily and seemed unsure as to whether she should go on.

"And..." said Lydia.

"Jack Proctor and Maura Hodge were lovers," she finally said in a whisper, as if someone might overhear.

"So that was the 'J' she referred to in her book?" asked Lydia.

Marilyn nodded. "They were high school sweethearts and everyone thought they would get married. But in the end, he succumbed to pressures from his family and married Eleanor Ross instead. Maura, because she had Haitian blood in her veins, was thought to be an inappropriate wife for Jack, who was the sole heir to his family's considerable fortune."

"That would be another reason for Maura to hate Eleanor. A more contemporary reason," said Lydia, looking at Jeffrey.

"Yes. And it didn't end there. After Jack and Eleanor were married, he continued his affair with Maura," she said. Then she shook her head and added with a cluck of her tongue, "Everybody knew.

"But when Eleanor became pregnant, Jack ended the affair with Maura. Unfortunately, Maura was pregnant, as well. She paraded about town, telling anyone who would listen that she was having Jack Proctor's child. It was a humiliation for everyone. But Maura's child was stillborn. Eleanor gave birth to Julian and James. Jack never saw Maura again. And five years later, he was murdered.

"Everyone suspected Maura," said Marilyn. "Even after Eleanor was accused and went to trial, people still believed it was Maura, that it had something to do with the curse."

"Eleanor said that Maura wanted people to believe that," said Lydia, remembering her last conversation with Eleanor. "That she used it to hurt Eleanor and the children even after Eleanor had been acquitted."

"She told anyone that would listen that it was the curse of Annabelle Taylor," said Marilyn. "Even though it made her an outcast, as well. She didn't care, anything to hurt Eleanor."

"And all that money...from the Proctor estate?"

"Went to Eleanor, James, and Julian, I assume. Now just Julian, I guess. James Ross's body was found at the Ross house last year."

"Combine that with the Jenson and Stratton money, not

to mention Julian's own fortune, and we're talking about a huge pile of cash," said Jeffrey.

"But none of it has ever bought that family a moment's peace," said Marilyn with a slight smile. "Even now."

"And what about Annabelle Hodge?"

Marilyn shrugged and shook her head. Lydia saw a quick shift of her eyes, though. She registered it but said nothing.

"Why didn't you mention her the last time I was here?"

"You didn't ask."

Lydia looked hard at the librarian. "What do you know about her?"

"Nothing, really. Maura got pregnant late in life. She'd never married but had the child anyway. Annabelle was home-schooled, went off to college a couple of years ago."

"So who's her father?"

"No one knows, really."

"A town this small, a woman bears a child out of wedlock, and usually there are rumors, at least."

"Well, if there were, I didn't hear any of them," she said primly, straightening her back.

"Seems like there's not much you don't know about this town," said Jeffrey gently.

"Maura is not—well," said Marilyn.

"We were just at the Hodge house and saw the book she'd written about the curse," said Lydia. "Seems like she believed that the ghost of Austin Steward impregnated her."

Marilyn lifted her frail shoulders and nodded. "That's what she believes."

"Still?"

"Still. Or so she says."

"What about Annabelle? What does she believe?"

"If you ask me, Annabelle doesn't know what to believe. She's a puppet, more or less, to Maura's whims. Maura totally isolated that child; she never even went to the school here. Maura educated her at home."

"I can only imagine what that lesson plan looked like,"

Jeffrey said from the door.

"And you, Marilyn," coaxed Lydia. "Who do you think might be Annabelle's father? Any thoughts at all?"

"Honestly, Miss Strong, when it comes to those families, the less you know, the better."

"Okay," said Jeffrey back at the wheel of the Kompressor. "So I get why Maura hated Eleanor Ross, why she might have been motivated to kill Jack Proctor, and even Eleanor, though why she'd wait all this time to kill her is beyond me. I also get the whole curse thing, and why that might motivate someone to kill Julian's husbands, you know, if they believed it was their ancestral duty or whatever. And there's a lot of money at stake, we know that. But how these things fit together...it doesn't make sense."

"If it was just about revenge, about the 'curse,' why take the children? They're not part of it."

"What if it's about the money?"

"Yeah, but the kidnapper isn't going to inherit the money if Julian is declared incompetent. We talked about who had the most to gain and how it seemed like Eleanor."

"But now Eleanor is dead."

"Maybe it's not about money; maybe it's just about hatred pure and simple. Maybe someone just hates Julian Ross."

"Then why not just kill her?"

"When you hate someone enough, maybe death seems like an easy way out."

Jed McIntyre's face flashed in front of Lydia's eyes and she heard his threat to her, Life will be your punishment. She'd given a lot of thought to something else he'd said, as well. When she ran from him in the tunnels and he'd finally caught her, he'd said, I could have shot you in the back anytime I chose. Ask me why I didn't. She hadn't asked him, because she already knew the answer. He didn't want to kill her because he wanted to possess her. That's why he'd gone after her grandparents, why he'd taken Dax and Jeff. He wanted to destroy everything she loved so that she'd have nothing left; he wanted to strip her bare. Imagining that when she was a shell of herself, he would be able to control her, own her. Insanity had a way of making the ridiculous seem possible.

She thought then of Julian Ross, about the image in her drawing of the naked woman sprawled in the darkness.

"Julian Ross has been stripped bare," she said, turning to look at Jeffrey, who had his eyes on the road. "She's nothing but a ghost of herself, her life in shambles."

"Yeah...."

"So maybe it's not about the money, or about the curse, or even about hatred and revenge. Maybe someone just wants to destroy Julian's life," she said, shifting forward in her seat.

"But why?"

"Because when you've lost everything, what do you become?"

Jeffrey shrugged.

"Whatever you have to be to survive," Lydia said.

"So who hates her that much?"

"I think the better question is: Who loves her that much?"

"Let me guess where you're going with this," said Jeff.

"James Ross is alive."

He paused a second. "I thought we were looking at Maura and Annabelle."

"They might be a part of it. But look at who is the real victim here. It's Julian. She's the one who's lost everything. Her husband, her mother, her children, her sanity. Maura and Annabelle hated Eleanor enough to kill her. But did they hate Julian enough to wreak such havoc on her life? It had to be someone else, someone intimate to Julian. And I think that's James Ross."

"Did you forget that we have a death certificate on him?"

"None of this makes sense without him."

He released a sigh at her stubbornness.

"What about the DNA evidence?" she said.

"The DNA evidence only proves that someone who was at the scene of the Tad Jenson murder was also in the basement of the Ross home."

"And how many candidates do you think there are for that?"

Jeffrey considered the question for a minute, then shrugged. "The police chief, the hospital records, and Eleanor, even the librarian, all say James Ross is dead."

"But the man who signed his death certificate, Dr. Wetterau, he could have told us that when we were in his office. But he didn't. Why?"

"I don't know," Jeffrey admitted.

"Well, I think we'd better find out. Because when we find James Ross, we're going to find Ford and the twins."

In an investigation, Lydia noticed, no one was ever as friendly or cooperative on your second visit. And even though they'd visited him for a completely different reason the first time, Dr. Wetterau looked like he'd seen a vision of the Headless Horseman himself when he entered his waiting room to find Lydia looking over Jeffrey's shoulder as he flipped through the December issue of Cosmopolitan.

"What are you doing here?" he asked. He looked over at the door that led to the outside. "Wasn't that door locked?"

"Not well," said Jeffrey pleasantly.

"I'm calling the police," he said, reaching for the phone that stood on the reception desk.

"No need," said Lydia, standing. "I've already called them."

"What? Why?"

"Because you falsified a death certificate for James Ross when you know fully well that he's alive. And I want to know why. I doubted you'd tell me, so I figured I'd see if the police have any luck when they take you in for questioning regarding the murder of Eleanor Ross and the disappearance of her grandchildren."

Jeffrey had always admired that Lydia could lie with such complete self-righteousness.

"That's ridiculous," said the doctor, who suddenly seemed to need the doorjamb for support. "I've done no such thing."

"Then explain how I was attacked by James Ross just a week ago when I have this document," she said, pulling a copy of James Ross's death certificate from the pocket of her coat. "With your signature

on it."

"You can't prove that the man who attacked you was James Ross."

"I have the DNA evidence to prove it. I recovered a candy wrapper from the basement with his saliva all over it."

This half lie hit the doctor right between the eyes. He caved like a good man who'd done a wrong thing and worried every day since that it might catch up with him. What Lydia said was nothing less than his worse fears realized.

"Oh, Christ," said the doctor, his giant shoulders sagging as he put his head to his hand.

"Now tell me what you know and you just might keep your medical license."

The lighting in his office was dim and the room smelled of bandages and antiseptic. He leaned on the edge of his desk, which was covered with files, pictures of people she assumed were his kids and grandkids. Predictably, there was the Norman Rockwell print that every doctor has hanging on the dark-paneled wall of his office. His computer screen saver had turned on and a galaxy sped past.

"Eleanor Ross wanted her son declared dead," he said,

sitting down in one of the chairs across from Lydia and Jeffrey.

"Why?" asked Lydia.

"Because there were funds and properties held in trust for him that she couldn't touch until he'd been declared dead."

"Did she have money problems?"

"Not really. More than the money I think it was a matter of her wanting to put the past behind them. And also because of Julian."

"What about Julian?"

"She dreaded him. He was her worst nightmare. Her fear of him led her to periods of deep depression. And Eleanor believed that if she thought he was dead, it might alleviate some of her suffering."

"So how did it work out?"

"A drifter hung himself in the Ross home last year and there was suspicion that it was James Ross; he was about the same size and build. The body was so decayed as to be unidentifiable. Eleanor was informed and she came to me with her request."

"And why would you oblige?"

The doctor shrugged and gave a sad shake of his head.

"She offered to pay you?"

"It wasn't just the money. I wanted to give some peace to an old..."

"Flame?"

"Friend," he said, glancing toward the door that led to his house. "And I thought, if it helped Julian, more the better. She'd suffered so much."

"Part mercenary, part altruist. You're a complex man, Doctor," said Lydia.

"When Richard Stratton was murdered, did you think about coming clean?" asked Jeffrey.

"I thought about it. But that's why Eleanor hired you."

"What?"

"She and I agreed that if the evidence indicated that

James was still alive and responsible for Richard's murder, we'd come clean about what we did. Hopefully, you or the police would catch him and put him away for good. And we'd bear the consequences of our actions."

"But when we came to you the first time, you could have lied. You could have said he was dead, but I noticed you stopped short of that."

He shrugged. "Maybe part of me wanted the truth to come out."

"And if we found someone else to be guilty?"

"The secret would die with us."

"Good plan. You're halfway there."

He nodded his head slowly and he looked someplace inside himself.

"What can you tell us about Maura and Annabelle Hodge?" Lydia asked.

"I can tell you that they are two women with a lot of hatred in their hearts for the Ross bloodline."

"How do you know that?"

He gave her a flat look that she couldn't read and lifted his hands. "It's common knowledge."

"Or is it just a myth, like James Ross haunting the woods?"

"I guess it's not as easy to tell the difference as one might think. Anyway, as far as their involvement in any of this, I don't have the first idea."

Lydia didn't know whether to believe him or not, but she did believe he'd said all he was going to. He looked at her with tired, resigned eyes. But there was relief there, too. He'd unloaded a burden, and for better or for worse, at least he wouldn't have to carry it around on his back any longer.

"So, who's Annabelle's father?"

The doctor shook his head. "Now, that's something that only Maura Hodge knows for sure. I asked her that question many times."

"And she told you Austin Steward."

“That’s right...the ghost of Austin Steward. Tell you what, she was so adamant about it that I started to believe it myself.”

“I guess ghost stories are like that. Part of us wants to believe in the fantastic, no matter how frightening and horrible it might be.”

The doctor walked around to the seat behind his desk and sank into the leather chair. He was pale, and dark circles had appeared under his eyes.

“I noticed the police haven’t arrived,” he said after they’d all been silent for a long moment, realizing maybe that Lydia hadn’t quite told him the truth.

“Must be caught in traffic,” said Jeffrey, looking at his watch.

Lydia got up and moved toward the door. Jeffrey followed.

“That DNA evidence you mentioned?”

Lydia just smiled. “Might be a good time to start considering retirement, Doctor.”

“I was just thinking that.”

They stepped out of the office and into the cold, Lydia pulling the door closed behind them.

“You’re an accomplished liar,” said Jeffrey as they got into the Kompressor and pulled to the end of the drive. They paused there as a pair of headlights approached from the right.

“Thank you,” she answered.

“I’m not sure I meant it as a compliment.”

“There are lots of different ways to get to the truth. Lying is just one of them.”

“Well, when you’re right, you’re right.”

“So where to?”

“To the only place we’ve ever seen James Ross.”

Jeffrey didn’t pull out into the road right away. Instead he put the car in park.

“What’s wrong?” asked Lydia.

"I'm just afraid of what we're going to find up there."

Jeffrey sighed and rested his head on the steering wheel. Cold air blew from the vents but started to warm as the car heated up. They sat in the darkness, with only the glow from the dashboard lights. Mick Jagger and the Stones sang "Start Me Up" softly from the radio. Lydia reached over and turned it off. She wasn't sure what to say.

"There's so much loss," Jeffrey said quietly into the steering wheel. "How much more of this can we take?"

Lydia didn't have the answer to that question so she said nothing, just moved her hand from his arm to the back of his head. The air coming from the vents had gone from frigid to lukewarm; still Lydia shivered.

"The pregnancy, Rebecca, now Ford," he said. He turned to look at her then, his head still resting on his arm draped over the steering wheel. "I really wanted that baby."

His words felt like a blow to her solar plexus and tears sprang to her eyes, more from the surprise and the pain than from sadness. "I know," she managed.

Lydia had never seen Jeffrey like this. He was a man of action, believing that motion was the way to deal with fear, anger, sadness. Tonight he seemed to buckle under the weight of everything.

"It will be better when we try again," she said, withdrawing her hand and looking away from him. "We won't be living with the worry of Jed McIntyre, where he is, what he's planning. Won't it be better to bring a child into a life that isn't controlled by fear?"

The car was filled with their breath and their sadness, quiet except for the vents blowing the slowly warming air. Lydia's toes felt cold, and her heart ached, but she knew with an odd certainty that what she said was not just hopeful but true.

"You're right," he said, reaching out to touch her face and wipe the tear that trailed down her cheek. She turned back to him. "You're right," he said again. Jeffrey sat up and took a deep breath, seemed to shake off the mood.

“Good,” she said with a nod. She didn’t want to think about any of this anymore tonight. “People need us right now, Jeffrey. We can worry about ourselves when they’re safe.”

He leaned in to kiss her softly on the lips. He put the car into gear and they moved toward the road.

“Ford, where the hell are you, man?”

With the moon behind thick cloud cover, the night was eerily black. No streetlights lit the road ahead of them.

FORTY-TWO

They drove about half a mile past the Ross house and parked the car at the side of the road. From where they parked, they could see the outline of the dark house. The place had a definite presence and Lydia thought again back to Julian's drawings. The home where Julian grew up had become a symbol of terror for her, her father had been murdered there, her brother allegedly tried to kill her by burning it down. Maybe she was right, maybe the past did live in the structures we build, radiated off them like an aura.

A deep sense of unease had taken hold of Jeffrey. He didn't like that no one knew where they were or what they were doing.

"Call Dax," he said. "Tell him what we're doing."

Before he'd finished the sentence, Lydia's phone was chirping. She pressed the button on the dash that answered the phone.

"Do you want the good news or the bad news?" said Dax.

"The bad news," answered Jeff.

“I just heard on the news that the Haunted police found Ford’s car in a river over there in Haunted.”

“Shit,” said Jeffrey, feeling a brew of fear, adrenaline, and sadness boil in his stomach. “What’s the good news?”

“The good news is he wasn’t in it.”

Lydia sighed in relief. “Well, that’s something.” Hope was always something.

“Where are you two?”

“We’re at the Ross house. We think James Ross is alive. We’re going to check it out.”

“I thought you were just going to be asking questions,” said Dax, sounding like the kid picked last for the dodgeball team.

“Listen, Dax. If you don’t hear from us in an hour, call the Haunted police. Okay?” asked Lydia, trying to keep him involved.

“Right,” he said sullenly. “Be careful.”

When they reached the bottom of the drive, the tall iron gate that had stood unlocked during their last visit was now shut tight, a new lock in place where the old one had rusted away. Jeffrey removed the picklock from his pocket and tried to work the lock, but he couldn’t get it. After a few minutes, he sighed and stood back, looking up at the gate, which was supported on either side by high brick posts. It hadn’t been designed with any real security in mind; it was probably partly for show and partly to keep curious or lost people from driving up to the house.

“We can get in,” he said, bending down and cupping his hands. “I’ll give you a leg up to the top of the post, and you just lower yourself down on the other side. I’ll be right behind you,” he whispered.

“Great.” Jeffrey was always assuming that she had more grace and physical prowess than she actually did.

She placed her foot in his hand and he hoisted her while

she clumsily clawed her way to the top of the post, using every last ounce of upper body strength to push herself up and lift her butt to the top. She was breathless by the time she came to sit on top of the struc-ture. She looked down the other side.

"I can't jump. It's too far," she said, feeling a little panicked. She was glad she had worn her black stretch Emmanuel jeans and her soft black leather motorcycle boots and matching leather jacket. The front of her gray sweatshirt was now lined with dirt from her climb. She looked over and saw that Jeffrey had already scaled the other post and was lowering himself onto the ground on the other side. He landed with a light thump and walked over to her.

"Just turn over on your belly and lower your legs first. You're not that high up," he instructed.

She remembered him saying almost exactly the same words to her in Miami not long ago. That little maneuver hadn't ended well and she had a feeling this one was going to end up the same way. But she managed to lower herself and land on both feet without falling on her ass, though the impact was a bit jarring to her damaged insides.

"Hey," said Jeffrey. "You're getting better at this."

"Practice makes perfect," she said, holding her abdomen for a minute.

"You okay?"

"I'm fantastic," she said.

They moved quickly and quietly up the drive toward the house, staying to the side under cover of the trees. The winter woods that surrounded them were silent and the air was sharp with cold. Lydia peered in through the trees and saw nothing but pitch-black in the moonless night. She shivered involuntarily.

A black late-model Lexus was parked near the front door and Lydia and Jeffrey stood at the edge of the house, waiting for a moment to be sure no one was in the car. They stood like that, still and listening, when they heard a voice from inside the house. It was a man's voice, speaking in light, comforting tones.

Lydia and Jeffrey moved onto the veranda, Jeffrey drawing his gun, and they both peered into the window beside the door.

The man was tall and thin, with slick blond hair. He was expensively dressed in royal blue oxford, sleek black pants, with a Gucci belt around his waist. His back was to them, but Lydia could see that he moved with grace, gesticulating grandly with his hands. A fire crackled in the hearth and on a couch that had been pushed beside the fire, Lola and Nathaniel Stratton-Ross huddled together beneath a blanket, their eyes wide and trained on the man before them. Lydia felt flooded with relief to see them; they looked terrified but otherwise unharmed.

He turned suddenly as if he sensed eyes on him, and Jeffrey and Lydia moved away from the window. But not before she recognized his face. It was James Ross. They heard footsteps coming closer and managed to get off the veranda and hide themselves before James Ross exited the house with a twin on each hand. They were stiff and silent, both of them looking pale and tired, as though they had been drained from fear and sleeplessness. He put them in the backseat, made sure they were strapped in, and shut the door.

"We'll be with Mommy soon," he said sweetly before locking the car with a remote he held in his hand. From the truck, he then unloaded five red gallon containers marked gasoline and walked back into the house with one in each hand, leaving the other three on the ground by the car. Lydia and Jeffrey exchanged a look. Lydia shrugged and they followed Ross into the house.

They stood in the foyer watching as James Ross doused the living room with gasoline. It was a full minute before he felt their eyes on him and turned to see them. Instead of startling, he smiled. His face was so strikingly like Julian's face, the face from her drawings and the portrait at DiMarco's gallery, that Lydia almost gasped. His eyes were the searing blue of a crystal-clear sky, and in them she saw the same glitter of insanity she'd viewed in his sister. He may have cut his hair and changed his clothes, but she could see the maniac alive and well inside him.

"You clean up pretty good for a dead guy, Mr. Ross," said Lydia, trying through humor to trick her heart out of her stomach.

He laughed good-naturedly. "It's funny how the things people do to destroy you can wind up working out to your advantage. It's like I always say, you can't control the things that happen to you in your life. All you can control is your attitude."

He didn't seem at all surprised to see them, seemed to know who they were. Lydia wondered how, somewhere in the periphery of her consciousness.

"We're looking for a friend of ours. Hoping maybe you can help us," said Jeffrey.

"You've come to the right place," he said. "And maybe when I'm done with this, I can help you out."

"So...what are you up to?" asked Lydia, matching his casual tone.

"I'm reclaiming what's mine, Ms. Strong."

"Looks to me like you're getting ready to set it on fire," said Jeffrey, clicking the safety off his gun.

James Ross looked at Jeffrey's gun and then at the house around him. "Time for a fresh start," he said brightly, clapping his hands together. "Our past is so ugly, ugly, ugly. I want my family to move forward from here. The twins deserve better than we had."

"That's why you killed their father?"

He blinked at Lydia as if she were an apparition that he wished would disappear. And she wondered for a second if he thought they were real or a product of his diseased mind.

"I am their father," he said slowly. "Julian's husband may have been their sire, but those children belong to me."

"How do you figure?"

"Because Julian and I are one person," he said with a sympathetic smile. "We come from the same seed; what she is, I am. What comes from her body, comes from mine. Can you understand that?"

"What about Julian?"

"Julian had her chance for us all to be together. I offered her freedom from a marriage to a man she could never love. But she couldn't see that. She'd wanted this normal life that she could never have. That's why she's lost touch with reality, why she's locked away in that hellhole. She can't accept who she is, who we are. So the twins and I will just have to go on without her. Now I really have to be going."

Lydia nodded. "I understand how you feel, James. I do. Do you understand that we can't let you burn this place down? And we can't let you have the twins?"

"What business is it of yours, anyway? My mother hired you, right? She's dead. I'll pay your fee and this can stay between us," he said, like it was the most logical thought in the world.

"That's not the way it works, James," said Jeffrey.

"I'm not armed," James said to Jeffrey, nodding toward his gun.

"You've got a can of gasoline and, I'm assuming, a lighter in your pocket. I call that armed."

James shrugged. He paced a bit and then turned to them.

"You're looking for justice, right? Bring the murderer, the kidnapper, to justice. That's noble. I respect that. But," he said, and here his face changed, went from cool and reasonable to angry, "you don't understand any of this. Don't you know what they did to me?"

His brow furrowed and his face flushed.

"They locked me away from Julian. Said I tried to burn

down this house, kill my sister and my mother. But it was a lie." He spat the last word out like it burned his tongue.

"Was it?"

"Yes," he yelled, and then composed himself. "Because Eleanor wanted to keep Julian and me apart. She thought we had something dirty. But it was never like that. Never. It was the purest love two people could share.

"We loved each other, we belonged together. Even Eleanor could see that. Jealous old cow. She said I was evil, afraid that I was the manifestation of that stupid curse she obsessed about every fucking day. So she had her lover lock me away. Dr. Wetterau. They were lovers. Did you know that? She always went on and on about how my father had been her one true love, that there would never be another. But it didn't stop her from fucking around like a whore."

"So they sent you away. To keep you from Julian," said Lydia.

"But I escaped," he said, and laughed.

"And where did you go?"

"Julian was at Chapin by then, in New York. So I went to her. But she didn't love me anymore," he said, and his eyes filled with tears. He turned away from them and stood before the hearth.

"They'd brainwashed her, convinced her that I was evil. She turned me away, told me she wanted a normal life, a natural love. I was ruined, destroyed. Started to believe that I was evil. I was never far from her, always shadowing her, watching over her.

"I lived like an animal for a lifetime. But now, as you can see, I've had a rebirth. I've claimed my children."

"Did you kill Tad Jenson?"

"I didn't mean to," he said, and appeared truly remorseful. "I just wanted to see her, to touch her. And he wouldn't let me. Things just got out of hand. You know how it goes... don't you? The rage, that monster inside, just takes over."

"And Richard Stratton?"

"The rage..." he said, and didn't go on. He looked off in the distance now, into the past, a gallery of all his regrets and mistakes.

"The past is so unforgiving," he went on. "But the future is a blank slate. We can make anything of it. That's what I'm going to do for the twins. They represent everything I have lost...my love, my fortune, my family. In them, all things will be made right."

"What about the curse? Where do Maura and Annabelle Hodge fit into this?"

"Oh, they were happy for the opportunity to destroy Eleanor and Julian. When I finally found the courage to return to this place," he said, looking around him. "You know, to set the past right. I went to see Maura. Because we had a common enemy, Eleanor, we became allies. We both got what we wanted. Maura and Annabelle got to see Eleanor's worse nightmares come true and then they got to watch her die. It wasn't really about the curse, you know. That's just a myth. It was hatred pure and simple. Now Maura and Annabelle are long gone. Maura has her vengeance after all these years."

"What did Annabelle get out of all of this?"

"I think Annabelle was more motivated by the payoff than anything. That and fear of her mother. Poor kid. And who wouldn't be afraid of Maura? She's fucking insane."

In her zeal to classify all human motivation, Lydia had neglected maybe the most powerful of all...hatred. It had been the food Maura ate most of her life and apparently had fed to her daughter. In a way, Lydia felt bad for Annabelle; she was as much a victim as Lola and Nathaniel, used in the same way.

"Have you satisfied your curiosity, Ms. Strong? Do you know everything you want to know?"

"There's just one thing. Our friend, Ford McKirdy."

"Your nosey little friend almost ruined everything. Let's make a deal, shall we? I'll give you your friend, and you let me walk out of here. We'll just pretend this little meeting never happened."

"How about you tell us where Ford McKirdy is and I don't blow your head off?" said Jeffrey, losing his patience. It was then that from somewhere deep in the house they heard a pounding, the sound of a voice shouting through layers of wood and concrete. They both turned to look in the direction of the noise, and when they looked back, James was gone, the gas cans with him.

Lydia took off in the direction of the noise, heading toward the basement. In the distance she heard the wail of sirens, but remembered the locked gate at the bottom of the drive and wondered how anyone could get up to the house. She pushed down panic as she moved through the long hallway. Suddenly she caught the scent of smoke.

She stopped in her tracks. "Jeffrey," she yelled. "There's fire!"

But he didn't answer her. She'd drawn the .38 she'd had in the pocket of her leather jacket and was watchful of the dark corners, not sure where James lurked or what his agenda was. The pounding grew louder as she drew closer to the basement door, but when she turned the knob, it was locked.

"Stand back," she yelled to whoever could hear her. She gave it ten seconds and then she fired a round at the doorknob. The latch gave way and the door swung open and a dark stairway yawned below her.

"Ford," she yelled. But there was no answer and the pounding had stopped. A horrible moment passed during which Lydia feared that Ford had been standing behind the heavy door and she had just shot him. She reached in for a light switch and found one. But when she flipped it, no lights came on...naturally. Then she heard a croaking voice in the darkness. "Lydia."

"Ford?"

She heard a weak groan.

She ran down the stairs to find him bound to a chair. He'd knocked himself to the floor and had apparently gotten one leg free and was kicking at the wall. That was the pounding they'd heard. He was dirty and looked awful but seemed unharmed.

"Ford. Thank God."

"I thought I was going to die down here," he said.

"Not if I can help it," said Lydia, dropping to her knees and starting to work the knots in the ropes that bound him.

"I smell smoke," said Ford.

"I think there's a fire," said Lydia, glancing up the stairs and wondering where Jeffrey was. Then she heard the sound of a gun firing. Her stomach twisted as she pulled on the bindings. The ropes were damp from the moisture in the basement and Lydia struggled with the tight knots, but was finally able to get him free.

"Can you walk?" she asked as she helped him to his feet.

"Yeah...."

"Let's go."

By the time they reached the top of the stairs, the house was starting to fill with smoke. They turned the corner and were headed toward the door when Jeffrey jumped out at them through the black cloud that was gathering. He had his shirt pulled up over his nose. Ford and Lydia quickly did the same.

"Where's James?" asked Lydia.

"I shot him, but he got away from me. He went deeper into the house. I tried to follow him, but this place is going up like kindling. We have to get out of here. He's still in here. The Lexus is still parked outside with the twins in it."

Jeffrey grabbed Ford and dragged him the rest of the

way out of the house, as Ford seemed to lose strength. Lydia paused before exiting, looked at the grand home being eaten by flames, and she wondered if this was James Ross's funeral pyre. Then she ran out the front door.

Outside, police and fire vehicles were moving up the drive, their blue and red lights casting the night in a bizarre strobe.

Jeffrey helped Ford away from the house. Lydia, smashing in with the butt of her gun the front passenger side window, unlocked the Lexus and took the terrified, screaming twins from the car. She picked them up, one on each hip, and moved quickly behind Jeffrey and Ford. Though they'd only met her once, the twins clung to her. The five of them made quite a sight to Henry Clay as he stepped out of his prowler. And he would remember that as they passed him and moved toward the waiting ambulance, there seemed to be a moment of silence, when the house and the woods around them took a deep breath before an explosion blasted them all back at least ten feet. It was an explosion of such force that Henry Clay had his eyebrows and what was left of his hair singed to ash.

The house burned for hours. Every time it seemed that the flames might be dying, the fire appeared to reignite itself. The firefighters could only struggle to keep it under control as much as possible, keep it from spreading to the surrounding trees.

Lydia watched from an ambulance, where she sat on a stiff white seat, the twins lying against her. They had collapsed on her like puppies seeking warmth and comfort from her body heat. And she had draped an arm around each of them. They probably didn't realize it, but they were comforting her, as well.

Jeffrey had ridden in another ambulance with Ford, and Lydia had chosen to stay with the twins until someone could come for them. They didn't really know her, but she was more familiar to them than anyone else on the scene and they seemed calmed by that.

"My daddy used to take me to see the penguins at the zoo," said Nathaniel solemnly.

"He used to take us to the zoo," corrected Lola. "He took both of us."

"Your daddy loves you very much," said Lydia, using the present tense without really thinking.

"He loved us," said Lola. "He's dead now. Dead people can't love you."

"Lola," said Lydia, thinking of the dream she'd had recently about her mother, "that's not true. It's not true at all."

FORTY-THREE

When Lydia and Jeffrey walked into his broom closet of an office, Ford McKirdy was cleaning out his desk. And though it was a bright cold day, he wore a festive Hawaiian shirt and a pair of khakis. A big down parka rested on the chair by the door.

"So you're finally getting a life," said Lydia with a smile.

He stopped what he was doing and looked at them. "Thanks to you two, yeah," he said. He walked over and embraced each of them.

"Have a seat," he said, hanging his parka on a hook behind the door.

"We're going to Europe," he said, with the excitement of a kid on his way to Disneyland. "Me and Rose. Can you believe it?"

"That's great, Ford," said Jeffrey, smiling broadly. "We're happy for you, man."

"Hey, I'm happy for you guys, too. Dax says you're finally getting hitched. I know you'll do a better job at it than I did. But I'm going to make up for it now."

Jeffrey put his arm around Lydia and smiled into her eyes. Lydia had never seen Ford so animated, and it made her happy; it also made her think twice about why they'd come to see him.

"Hey, speaking of Europe, you guys'll be happy to know this," he said, sitting behind his desk. "Interpol picked up Maura and Annabelle Hodge in Paris yesterday. They had a palatial apartment and a big fat bank account. Anyway, they're bringing them back to face conspiracy-to-murder charges. James Ross might be dead, but someone's going to pay for all of this."

The explosion and fire had consumed the Ross house so totally that James Ross's body had not yet been recovered in the debris. The explosion had come from a rudimentary bomb in the kitchen and had been so powerful that the house was completely leveled. It had been three weeks and investigators were still sifting through debris. The remains of Anthony Donofrio had been recovered, investigators believing that his body had been on one of the top floors of the house. But they had yet to find James Ross. This detail hadn't rested well with Lydia, and in thinking of it, a couple of other details weren't sitting so well, either. That's why they had come today to talk to Ford.

"So when's your last day?" asked Lydia, looking at him guiltily.

"Tomorrow," he said, turning his cop's eyes on them, his voice shading suspicious. "Why?"

"There are just a couple of things nagging at us," said Jeffrey, giving Ford an apologetic look.

"Man, you guys need to learn how to let things go. He confessed to you...didn't he?"

"Yeah...but there are just a few things that don't add up," answered Lydia, sitting down. "If you can put them to bed for us, we're on our way to Hawaii to meet my grandparents and to get married."

He leaned back and looked at them, scowling, but Lydia could see the gleam of curiosity in his eyes.

"Like what?"

"Like where did he get all that money? The money to buy the Lexus and the new clothes? Presumably, now that you mention it, to pay Maura and Annabelle Hodge for their services. Remember he'd been declared dead. He had no funds, no assets."

Ford nodded, seemed to consider the question. "What else?"

"Don't you think it's an awfully big coincidence that Julian Ross would wind up living in a building that had one of those Prohibition tunnels, convenient to her crazy tunnel-dwelling twin who happens to be stalking her?"

Ford shrugged. "What else?"

"That night in the house," said Jeffrey. "I shot James in the foyer. He had a choice to run from the burning house, hop in his Lexus, and take off with the twins. But instead, he turned and ran up the stairs...into the flames. Why didn't he just take off? Our car was all the way down on the street; he knew I wouldn't leave you and Lydia in the house to chase after him. He would have had a clean getaway."

Ford seemed to think about it. He leaned back in his chair and looked up at the ceiling. "Well, the police were heading up the drive at that point, right?" said Ford, hopeful.

"And the other thing," said Lydia, "may be the most important. James told us he took the twins so that he could reclaim his family and his fortune. But how would kidnapping the twins accomplish the recovery of his fortune? There was no way for him to claim their money when he was their kidnapper. We already know that Orlando DiMarco was named legal guardian of the twins. It doesn't make sense."

"So what are you getting at?"

"Now Julian, miraculously recovered, her evil twin dead, is cleared of her husband's murder and reunited with her children," said Lydia, mimicking a society column entry. "Even more fabulously wealthy than ever before, she's about to embark on a new life, in a new country. She leaves for Switzerland next week, where her dear friend Orlando has a villa where she'll stay until she and her children have found appropriately luxurious accommodations."

They were all quiet, listening to the bustle of the busy precinct outside the office. Lydia looked at Ford and saw that none of what she'd said surprised him, that he'd been turning over the same questions in his mind. He shook his head slowly and closed his eyes.

"You remember Julian's shrink, Dr. Barnes?" Lydia said. "Something she said keeps coming back to me. She said about a year before Stratton was murdered, Julian ended her therapy. She told the doctor that she'd decided to 'surrender' to her true self. And that fits with something James told us. He said that he'd been sent to Fishkill because Eleanor believed they had an incestuous relationship. Not because he'd tried to set the house on fire. When he found Julian again, he said she didn't love him anymore. And that all this time, he'd been stalking her trying to convince her that they belonged together."

She stopped and looked at Ford as he tried to connect the dots.

"Lydia, just what are you thinking?"

"I'm thinking," said Lydia, "maybe after all these years of being apart, maybe after all these years of 'trying to have a normal life,' Julian gave in to James. Maybe Julian and James finally found a way to be together."

The Park Avenue duplex was a bustle of workers, covering furniture and carrying boxes out the doors and to a waiting freight elevator. Some of the windows were open, Lydia assumed to air out the place, but she shivered against the cold. Julian Ross didn't seem to notice the temperature, even though she wore only jeans and a thin white silk turtleneck. Looking fit and healthy, her cheeks a robust pink, her eyes clear, Julian greeted Lydia at the door with an embrace. Lydia regarded her and thought that she looked truly happy, that it radiated from the inside out.

"The children have gone on ahead to Switzerland with Orlando," she said, leading Lydia into the parlor, which was still relatively intact. "They've come to love and trust him so much."

They sat together on a red velvet sofa that was still uncovered.

"How are they holding up?"

"Young children are resilient," she said calmly. "They'll have the best counselors when we're settled."

"What about you?"

"For me," she said, her expression darkening just slightly, "it might take longer. But I'm getting there." A brightness came back to her, but this time it seemed forced.

"There were just some loose ends I wanted to tie up...."

"Oh, your fee!" she said, hopping up as if to rush off for her checkbook. "Of course. How much did my mother agree to pay you?"

"It's not the fee, Julian."

The other woman must have heard something in Lydia's voice, because the color drained from her cheeks. She sat back down and was suddenly wary. "What is it, then? As you can see, I'm quite busy."

"It won't take long," Lydia said with a smile. She rose and walked over to one of the open windows and looked down the fourteen stories to the street below. It was a busy midafternoon, with cabs rushing by, people swiftly walking along the sidewalk. From the window, Lydia could see the top of the Chrysler Building gleaming in the bright afternoon sun, smell the wood burning from fireplaces.

"We looked into the ownership of the Lexus James was driving and found something interesting. We found that it was registered to you, purchased just a week before Richard was killed."

The words hung in the air between them.

"That's not possible," Julian said with a shake of her head. But she diverted her eyes to look out the window behind Lydia.

"We also discovered that on the same day, you opened a small checking account for Nathaniel and Lola and placed ten thousand dollars there."

"So?"

"So...someone was using a bank card to draw on that money. We've managed to get a surveillance photo from one of the ATM machines. And guess who it was."

"I have no idea," she said, drawing herself up in the same way Lydia had seen Eleanor do.

"Your brother."

Everything Lydia had said was true except for the part about the surveillance photo. That was a lie.

After Lydia and Jeffrey had posed their questions to Ford, he'd immediately contacted the DMV and the banking institutions where Julian Ross and Richard Stratton had kept their liquid assets. It had taken them less than an hour to come up with the vehicle ownership and the information about the small checking account. It had been a small enough withdrawal not to arouse suspicion during the initial investigation into Richard Stratton's murder, as Julian and Richard regularly made purchases and withdrawals in that ballpark, and the police weren't really working a murder-for-hire angle.

"He could have stolen that bank card. How should I know?" Julian said, a kind of calm seeming to come over her. "I'm going to ask you to leave now."

Ford and Jeffrey, along with Detectives Malone and Piselli, walked in through the front door. The moving men paused in their activities, sensing that something was going down. Julian looked over at them, and then back to Lydia. She seemed to deflate a bit.

"Where is he, Julian? Where's James?"

"This is crazy," she said simply. "I want my attorney."

"With Ford McKirdy missing, I think you knew it was a good bet that we'd head back up to Haunted and the trail would eventually lead us to the house. I think James wanted to confess his whole plot to us and then allow us to see him die. This way, he could take the rap for everything, you'd be cleared of all charges, and he'd be 'dead.' You could go to a country where no one would know him and finally, Julian, you would be reunited after all these years apart."

Lydia wasn't positive that she had it exactly right, but she was confident that all the elements were there. How had James recognized them? How had he known they would eventually come back to the house? These were questions for which she didn't have answers. But she knew that she and Jeffrey were meant to hear his confession and see him die that night. Her gut told her this with cold certainty.

Looking now into Julian's eyes, she could see that she had hit her target.

"Why did you decide to give in to him, Julian? You'd fought so hard to have a normal life. First with Tad, then, even when your mother begged you not to marry, you tried again with Richard."

Julian sat stone-faced.

"You watched him kill Tad, didn't you? Jetty heard you scream. What was it you said to him? 'I never loved you. Not like that.' But it wasn't the truth, was it? You did love him. You were so afraid that your love for your twin was the unnatural love of the curse, the threat of which your mother tortured you with all your life. The thought repulsed you, terrified you, but you couldn't help it. You loved him so much that even when you could have implicated him in Tad's murder, you didn't. Even when you might have gone to jail for a murder you didn't commit, you didn't implicate James."

Lydia let silence fill the room.

"Your mother must have made you feel so sick, so dirty. How she must have punished and tortured you just to make you see how wrong it was. In her own way, just to save you from the curse she was so afraid of."

Julian looked at her with surprise. Tears filled her eyes and trailed down her face.

"But it had been the same with her, hadn't it? She loved her brother. And he killed Jack Proctor. What happened to Paul, Julian?"

Julian spoke for the first time.

"She killed him. He came for her again. After my father was dead and my brother sent away. She shot him dead. Even though she loved him, she killed him. I helped her bury the body behind the house. Then we left Haunted and never went back. She thought she'd ended it for us. She really believed that. Then James escaped."

"Why didn't she tell the police about him when Tad was murdered?"

"She loved him, too. He was her son, don't forget. She thought I would be exonerated. If it looked like I might be convicted, she would have come forward. I promised her that I would never marry again. And she thought that was enough to keep him away. But I broke my word."

"Why? Why would you take that risk?"

She shrugged and looked down in shame. "I was lonely. I was afraid. I felt him always right behind me, shadowing my life. Richard was strong, safe. And..." She paused. "I didn't really love him. I thought it would be safe if I didn't love him. But then I got pregnant. It was an accident, but I got pregnant with the twins. He came for me again. He wanted the twins."

"When did you decide to give in?"

"I didn't," she said weakly. "He did this to my life. Now he's dead. And we are finally free, Lola, Nathaniel, and I."

"No, Julian. You ended your therapy with Dr. Barnes. You moved your family into this building with access to the tunnels beneath the street. You hired Geneva Stout."

"I didn't know who she was when I hired her. I hadn't been to Haunted in over twenty years."

"I don't believe you, Julian. Maybe you were James's victim once. But I believe you're his accomplice now. Your breakdown...maybe it was real, maybe it was an act. But it seems like you helped him orchestrate all of this so you could look like the victim, so that he could take the rap and then fake his own death. I think you're planning on meeting him in Switzerland."

Everyone, Jeffrey, Ford, the other officers and the moving men, stood silently looking at Julian.

"Maybe Maura Hodge was right," said Lydia. "She said, 'The Ross family doesn't even need a curse. They are fucked up in so many ways that they curse themselves.'"

It happened so fast, Lydia barely knew what hit her. Julian went from the calm woman sitting before her to the demon Lydia had met once before at Payne Whitney. She lunged at Lydia like a wildcat and Lydia went staggering back toward the open window behind her with Julian at her throat. All Lydia could think was that the other woman's strength was phenomenal, and try as she did she couldn't pull herself from Julian's grip. In the periphery of her consciousness, she heard Ford shouting as her waist hit the sill, Julian on top of her. Lydia felt the cold of the outside air and heard the street noise below her as she and Julian leaned out the window, the upper halves of their bodies dangling over a straight drop to the sidewalk. Somewhere on the street, a woman screamed.

"You won't keep us apart," Julian whispered fiercely. Lydia felt herself tip toward the ground, the sky tilting around her, the buildings dancing. And she felt an odd lightness as gravity pulled on her. She felt the fragile thread that connected her soul to her body stretch to the point of snapping and she wondered, Am I going to die here? She reached out and held on hard to Julian. The woman had a death grip on Lydia's throat, and she felt like she was breathing though a straw.

White stars had started to dance before her eyes.

Things seemed to be happening so slowly as Lydia felt the balance shift from most of their weight being in the building to most of their weight being out. And in the next second, she felt her feet lift from the floor and her body tilt more steeply toward the ground. Julian must have felt it, too, because her expression morphed from malice to surprise and fear. She loosed her grip on Lydia's throat. It was then that Lydia felt strong hands on her ankles. Julian's body started to slip over hers. Lydia tried to hold on, but the momentum of Julian's fall was too great. Julian flipped over her like an acrobat, Ford getting to the window a millisecond too late. There was a shocked silence among them, as Julian fell, her scream like a siren ending abruptly as she hit the sidewalk. It was a gruesome sound; everyone who heard it felt the shattering of bones. Screeching tires, the sound of metal on metal, yelling voices from the street below carried up and filled the room.

Jeffrey pulled Lydia in the rest of the way and she sank to the floor, feeling every nerve ending in her body pulse with the relief of mortal terror. He held on to her as she buried her head in his shoulder, taking in the scent of his skin, the strength of his muscles, the sound of his breath. She'd never been so glad to be alive.

FORTY-FOUR

The ferry ride was grim and it was a journey she made alone. Jeffrey thought she was having her run and then going on to Central Park West, visiting her doctor for an early morning follow-up visit after her laparoscopy. And she would do that today, as well. But later.

It was six-thirty and the sky was a flat dead gray. The air was cold, and coming off the water it was downright frigid, but Lydia stood at the bow away from the cargo and near the workers, who were bundled in layers and drinking coffee from thermoses. Hector approached her.

"I don't know why anyone would want to be here if they didn't have to be," he said, his Dominican accent heavy.

Hector, the morgue worker she'd met the night Jed McIntyre died, had been true to his word when she called to ask where the city would bury him. When a week later she'd called again and offered him a thousand dollars cash to take her to his grave, he'd said, "Lady, are you nuts? Go back to your life."

"That's just it," she'd told him. "I can't do that until I've seen the grave."

He'd reluctantly agreed and told her to meet him at City Island in the Bronx and that he'd take her over to Potter's Field on Harts Island when he took over that day's Jane and John Does. She stood and watched as twenty anonymous pine coffins, branded only with serial numbers, were loaded from a van onto the waiting ferry. An old priest stood by waiting and she wondered if he started every morning like this, watching as workers loaded the bodies of God's forsaken children onto a boat that would take them to their unmarked graves. She wondered how it didn't shake his faith. But she didn't ask. She had her own faith to worry about.

"I do have to be here," she said.

And Hector just nodded at her. He had a thick brown face with wide features and sharp eyes. He was looking at her with those eyes that were neither warm nor cold, neither kind nor cruel. They were eyes that saw things the way they were and didn't judge. She turned away from him and watched as the island approached, looking into the murky choppy water of the Long Island Sound. And she thought about her recent breakdown of motivations. She thought about Julian and James and their twisted love for each other. A love they thought excused them from moral behavior, a love that made it okay to lie and scheme and murder to be together. And how it had ended with Julian a broken mess of herself on a city sidewalk. James Ross was still at large.

She thought about Maura and Annabelle Hodge, so warped by a legacy of revenge and hatred, by jealousy and greed, that they allowed themselves to be drawn into a plot that would end lives they considered less worthy than their own and children to grow up without parents. The righteous anger of their ancestor so many years ago, thwarted and used for their own selfish means. Lydia still wondered about Annabelle's father, who he was, why he had disappeared. Lydia had her suspicions, thinking perhaps it was Paul, Eleanor's brother. It was the way Maura had talked of him, the dedication in her book. Maybe she knew Eleanor had killed him, maybe she knew no one would ever believe her even if she told. Maybe all of this gave her a nudge a little further down the road to insanity. But it was just a guess and Lydia would probably never know the truth.

She thought about Orlando DiMarco. Of all of them, he was the one who confused her the most. When he returned from Switzerland with the children for Julian's funeral, Lydia had visited him at his gallery. He was in the process of closing it down and moving to Switzerland permanently with Nathaniel and Lola, of whom now he was guardian.

"I think part of me always knew it would end like this for them," he said when he saw her.

"You knew," she said.

"I had an idea."

"But you never implicated her...or him."

"I loved her," he said simply. "And they were one. Anything I'd done to harm him would have harmed her. Did you ever love anyone that much...that you'd do anything, no matter how wrong it was? Even if you knew they could never love you the same way?"

She didn't want to judge him or say to him that she didn't consider that love. That when love asked you to betray yourself and betray others, it was only need or fear in a clever masquerade. She only shook her head.

Lola and Nathaniel were chasing each other around the empty gallery space, their laughter echoing against the walls. To look at them, one would never know what they had endured over the last several weeks of their young lives. They seemed happy, normal.

"Do they ever talk about that night?"

"They told their therapist that they were playing a game with their nanny that night. I don't know that they've quite connected that event with the death of their father. They don't blame themselves. Anyway, they'll be in therapy for a while."

"Why did Julian ask you to take the twins?"

"I don't know, really. She came to the gallery a couple of months ago and asked me if I would take the twins should anything happen to her and Richard. I told her yes, of course. I thought it was odd, but I wouldn't have considered turning her down," he said, looking past Lydia at the memory of that day.

"I think part of her suspected that all this would end in tragedy," he went on. "She wanted to be sure that they'd be cared for. That's as close as I can come to a guess."

"And what about James? Do you think he'll come for them?"

"It would be suicide. They'll be watched by Interpol for a little while and then by a security team I've hired in Switzerland. If he comes near them, he'll be arrested and charged with murder."

Lydia nodded.

"It's funny," he said as she began to leave. "In Lola and Nathaniel, I have more of her in death than I did while she was alive. They are so much like her...it's a joy and torture. I think they'll bring me great pleasure and great sadness for the rest of my life, just like their mother before them."

There was something beautiful and something ugly about what he'd said, something almost Gothic in its romance, its utter selflessness, and something sick about it, too.

As she left the gallery, she saw the twins peeking around a wall to look at her. They were beautiful children, but there was something old in their eyes. She knelt down and they came to her, each of them hugging her in turn.

"Remember what I told you, Lola," Lydia said, releasing her. "You, too, Nathaniel."

"You lose the giver, not the gift," said Lola obediently. And Nathaniel nodded uncertainly. Lydia wasn't sure that they understood yet the meaning of what she'd told them that night, but she believed that they might one day. She knew what it was like to go through life without parents; she hoped that her words would come back to them on the tough days and give them comfort.

When the ferry had docked and the gate opened, Hector handed her a piece of paper with a number on it and pointed toward the east.

"You got ten minutes. Don't hold us up. You'll get me in trouble," he said. The other men, on the boat and on the shore, even the priest, all had their eyes on her. They were all curious, but no one asked any questions.

It was a dead place. There were no shading branches or grassy lanes lined with flowers, only black dirt paths and anemic trees scattered among the graves. She made her way on a rough walkway, through the maze of small white stone markers. No names, only numbers. And Lydia couldn't believe how many there were. Hector had told her that were between 750,000 and a million graves here. There were layers of them—the workers buried coffin on top of coffin—and Lydia felt unspeakably sad. Prisoners, indigents, orphans, and unknowns...all these lost souls. She thought of Rain and all the people below the subways who had helped them and wondered if most of them wouldn't end up here like this. What path do you take that leads you to this end? She only knew the answer for one of them.

Across a vista of open grass, Lydia could see the ruins of old abandoned buildings, a hospital, a reformatory, a house. All once served a function for the city, now nameless and abandoned like the dead surrounding them.

She came upon the fresh grave with Jed McIntyre's serial number on it and she reflected on why she'd come. It wasn't to see him dead in the ground, as one might imagine. It wasn't even for a sense of closure to the reign of terror he'd had over her life. She did not come to cry for her mother or for herself.

From a pocket of her long black cashmere coat, she removed the letter that Agent Goban had given her from Rebecca Helms's crime scene. It had been opened and read by the people at the scene. But Lydia had never opened it. The letters she had received from him over the years had been like missives of reassurance that he was locked away. She didn't need them anymore. She removed that pile now from another pocket and placed his most recent letter on top. She bent to pick up a rock she found by the path and she laid the letters on the earth, placed the rock on top to weight them down, and stood again.

She was here to give him back everything he had given her, all his pain, all his hatred, all his terror, all his letters. All the ugly parts of himself that she had allowed to become parts of her, she wanted him to have. For good. That was all. She turned away and walked back down the path toward the ferry.

When the ferry returned to the pier, Lydia saw Jeffrey standing on the dock. A gull screamed above her and a bell clanged in the wind as she approached him. He wore faded jeans and a gray hooded sweatshirt underneath his distressed leather jacket. His nose and cheeks were pink, as though he'd been standing in the cold for a while.

"You followed me," she said, trying to sound disapproving.

"You lied to me," he answered simply.

She shrugged. It was true. She couldn't argue.

"I had to come alone."

He nodded his understanding. "Did you get what you wanted?"

"I have what I want," she said, reaching for his hand. "I just left some things I didn't need behind."

She turned to look as though she might see those things waving there at her like flags, but there was nothing. Just the murky water and the flat, dead island.

He raised her hand to his cheek and held it there. And she knew with clarity in that moment that the past was dead, the future just a fantasy. It was only the present that lived and breathed. It was all they had. And it was all they needed.

Author's Notes

The following texts and Web sites were invaluable in the writing of this novel: The Mole People: Life in the Tunnels Beneath New York City (Chicago Review Press) by Jennifer Toth; The Tunnel: The Underground Homeless of New York City (Yale University Press) by Margaret Morton; The Making of New York (www.nysl.nysed.gov); The New York Geneological and Biological Society (www.nygbs.org); Forgotten New York (www.forgotten-ny.com); and Ectopic Pregnancy Trust (www.ectopic.org).

Special thanks to Larry Labriola, New York City Police Department Narcotics Detective (ret.) for his patient answers to my million questions on NYPD policy and procedures and to Dr. Thomas Walter M.D., F.A.C.O.G., for his invaluable insights on ectopic pregnancy.

However, in spite of my careful research, I'm sure I've gotten something wrong along the way and I know I've taken artistic license as the narrative dictates. Either way, don't blame my sources! All mistakes, intentional or otherwise, are mine.

Keep reading for an excerpt from Lisa Miscione's next mystery, *Smoke*, available in paperback from Snowbooks in June

SMOKE

Lydia Strong wanted a cigarette to celebrate the defeat of her enemy. She leaned back in her chair and looked at the manuscript that sat fat and neat on her desk beside her computer. She felt like a prizefighter who had finally, after a brutal showdown, sent her opponent to the mat. The Lost Girl had taken her nearly a year to write and every page had been a battle. It was a first for her. Words were her tools, sometimes her weapons. Either way, she'd always wielded them with ease. But this book didn't want to be written. Every day the blank page had seemed like a taunt, a dare, a bully on the playground looking for her lunch money.

Maybe it was because in the writing of it, she had to let go of things she'd been clinging to for years. Maybe because, as painful as those things were, they were comfortable, familiar, and a part of her didn't really want to see them exorcised. But now they were safely incarcerated in the pages of her manuscript. Soon they'd be edited and revised, edited and revised again. Then they'd be exposed to the light of the world. And, like all demons, in the sun they'd turn to piles of dust.

She laughed a little, just because of the lightness of her relief. She got up from her desk and tossed around the idea of going out for a pack of cigarettes. Maybe if Jeffrey wasn't lying on the couch reading the Sunday Times, she'd go down to the bodega on the corner of Lafayette and Great Jones, smoke a cigarette on the street and then throw away the rest of the pack. But he'd be able to tell and then he'd give her a hard time. It wasn't worth it.

"I'm done," she called, walking out of her office and through the loft. But he wasn't on the couch; he was standing at the counter that divided the kitchen from the living room, talking on the phone.

"Oops, sorry," she said when she saw him.

He looked at her strangely when she walked in. She hadn't heard the phone ring. She took a frosty bottle of Ketel One vodka from the freezer and poured herself a lowball, trying and failing to be quiet as she put some ice in the glass and squirted some lime juice from one of those little plastic bottles shaped cutely like a lime.

"I see," he said, lowering his eyes to the floor beneath his feet, tapping a pen on the countertop. "No, I'd rather tell her, David, if you don't mind."

"Is that my grandfather?" Lydia asked, looking at him now. She could tell there was something wrong, but she sipped at the drink in her hand and pretended she couldn't. She needed a few minutes to enjoy the completion of her manuscript before life leaked in and started demanding attention.

Jeffrey put the phone back in the cradle and didn't look at her right away.

"Did you hear me? I'm finished. I finished The Lost Girl."

"That's fantastic. Congratulations," he said softly, moving toward her and taking her into his arms.

"Want a drink?" she asked.

"Not right now," he said. She pulled away from him after a second and then walked over to the living room. The fire they'd made earlier in the afternoon was low, just a few flames danced. Outside, a light snow tapped against the windows and their view of lower Manhattan was obscured by frost.

She sat on the couch and curled her legs up beneath her. Something in her chest was thumping. She didn't like the look on Jeffrey's face or the careful way he was moving toward her.

"There's some news," he said, sitting beside her.

"Are they all right?" she asked, bracing herself. Her maternal grandparents, David and Eleanor Strong, were the only living family members to whom she had any connection. She thought of them, both hearty, young-minded, still traveling, enjoying their lives and each other. It seemed like they would always be there. But with both of them in their early seventies, she knew she'd have to deal with their mortality at some point. But she hadn't done that yet. And she wasn't ready.

"Oh, yeah," he said quickly. "Yeah, they're both fine."

She felt a wash of relief. "Okay," she said, releasing a breath she'd been holding.

"Then what?" she said, sitting up, leaning into him as he sat beside her. He took her hand in his and cast his eyes down.

"Your father..." he said, letting the sentence trail.

The phrase sounded so strange. She never thought of herself as having a father. Most times she forgot he even existed.

"What about him?" she asked, frowning.

"He's dead, Lydia," he said. "I'm sorry."

Something shifted inside of her. "Dead?" she said, like it was a word that didn't have any meaning to her.

"I'm sorry," he said again, releasing her hand and taking hold of her shoulder. She looked at his face, saw worry there, sadness for her.

"How?" she asked after a moment where she searched herself for feeling and came up with nothing. She wanted to feel something, but there was only a cool numbness.

"Your grandfather didn't have the details."

She'd met her father only once, when she was fifteen years old, on the day after her mother's funeral. It was a lifetime ago, and she found that she remembered everything about that time like a lucid dream. Some details were vivid but a strange fog seemed to hang over the events.

She remembered the door ajar on the day she discovered her mother's body, the blaring stereo that greeted her as she arrived home. But the terrible discovery of her mother's body and the grim investigation that followed was a jumble of isolated events with no real timeline in her memory. She remembered the crowded funeral service and the hushed sobbing and the somber voice of the priest, the burial on a day that was too bright and sunny, too beautiful. She remembered identifying Jed McIntyre as the man who'd been following her and her mother for days. She remembered the single garnet earring missing from her mother's jewelry box. And she remembered her father's visit. The one and only time she'd seen him in the flesh.

She had sat alone in the living room staring out the bay window at the woods behind her house. The leaves were turning, a riot of orange, red, and gold. The day was cool and sun washed, and she remembered wishing for rain. She wanted thunder and gale-force winds, hail and lightning.

She'd heard the doorbell but paid no attention, sure it was another neighbor come to offer their condolences. She pulled herself into a tight ball and closed her eyes, dreading having to smile politely, having to say she would be all right. Then she heard her grandfather's voice as he opened the door, then a soft murmuring, then silence. Her grandfather's voice sounded angry, but she thought she must be mistaken. Then she saw him at the door, his face tight and ashen.

Hovering behind her grandfather, there was a stranger with her storm-cloud gray eyes. Tall and slouching, poorly dressed, he held flowers and had a hangdog look about him, an aura of shame. He shifted uncomfortably from foot to foot. He was a tall, lean man, blondish, faded looking, like a bad copy of himself. Even though she'd never met him, she knew him immediately.

"You're my father?" she asked, getting up.

"You don't have to see him, Lydia," her grandfather said.

But her curiosity had been great. It was the first feeling she'd had other than grief and horror since her mother died.

"No," she said. "It's okay, Grandpa."

She stood up and her father walked toward her. He held the flowers out to her. She took them, her eyes fixed on him. Struggling in her relationship with her mother, she'd thought about her missing father often. None of the fantasies she'd had about him in her life had even come close to predicting the ordinary man who stood before her. She had imagined him as a great lover, dark and handsome; a motorcycle daredevil, reckless and brave; an international spy, suave and sophisticated. What other kind of man, she concluded, could have stolen her strong, beautiful mother's heart and then left her broken and forever sad? Surely, some great danger or some irresistible intrigue had lured him from his family. In spite of what her mother said.

"Don't fantasize about your father, Lydia," her mother had told her numerous times. "He was just an irresponsible man, living for get-rich-quick schemes, always looking for something more than he had."

She had never believed her mother, until the moment he stood before her, eyes begging, hands quivering. It had felt like another death for her.

She let the flowers drop to the floor, turned her back on him, and walked back to her perch by the window. She might have forgiven him for leaving them, for breaking her mother's heart, but she could never forgive him for being so unremarkable. She could never forgive that he had obviously left them for nothing.

"It's time for you to go," her grandfather had said. He'd

stood like a sentry in the corner of the room. He had always been a big man, with strong, imposing shoulders and hands as big as oven mitts, a strong, angular face that looked like it should be carved in a mountain somewhere.

"You've made her a cold bitch, just like her mother," her father said then. For all this size, David Strong moved on him like a cat.

Up until the day they moved from the house where Lydia's mother had been murdered, the stain left by her father bleeding into the carpet after her grandfather had belted him remained, a faint reminder of a small man. She remembered thinking that the house was full of her parents' blood, and the thought made her stomach turn. That was the only memory she had of her father.

"Lydia," said Jeffrey.

"I'm okay," she said, snapping back to the present. And she was. She was shocked and there was something churning in her stomach. But she felt strong, stable. She could hardly be grief stricken for a man she'd barely known.

"I guess I'm not sure how to feel."

Jeffrey shook his head slowly, looked at her as if he were wondering if she would cry. He didn't say anything.

"Is there a funeral?" she asked, leaning back on the couch.

"There was. Last week. Your grandfather only found out because an old buddy of his who still lives in Nyack saw the obit."

Lydia's grandparents had recently moved from Nyack to a two-bedroom apartment on the Upper West Side, partly to be closer to Lydia and partly because they were unable to sleep in a house where Jed McIntyre, the man who'd murdered their daughter, had come for them as well.

Lydia nodded, placed her drink on the coffee table, and laid her head in Jeffrey's lap.

"I'm sorry, Lydia," he said quietly, putting a hand on her head.

"It's a strange feeling," she said after a few minutes of quiet. "To lose something you never had. I don't know how to explain it. I don't know how to feel it."

But she knew she didn't have to explain herself to him. He understood her; he always did. She turned around, took his hand in hers, played absently with the thick platinum band he wore on his left hand. Inscribed on the underside of it were her name and the date of their wedding. She wore a matching band, studded randomly with tiny star-cut sapphires.

They'd been married in a simple ceremony on Hanalei Bay in Kauai nearly a year ago. She'd worn a simple white linen shift and traditional plumeria lei and stood barefoot with him on the sand at sunset. Their ceremony, officiated by an old Hawaiian priestess, had been witnessed by David and Eleanor Strong and Dax Chicago, a man who'd become their closest friend.

"I can't believe you'd have the nerve to wear white," Dax had whispered to her after she and Jeffrey had exchanged rings. She'd laughed out loud. In all her life, she'd never felt as light and happy as she had that day. The long and treacherous journey they'd taken to the altar had ended well and she was grateful.

"What do we need to do?" Jeffrey asked her now. "You know—to observe this?"

She closed her eyes. "I don't know. I'll get back to you."

It was after ten when the phone rang. Jeff was still reading and Lydia was half asleep, her head still in his lap. She'd managed to push thoughts of her father away enough to doze but not enough to actually fall asleep; a kind of low-grade sadness and uneasiness had taken hold of her. She hopped up to get the phone.

"Who'd call so late?" asked Jeff, not looking up from his book on New York State gun law. He had his glasses on, which Lydia thought made him look sexy and intellectual.

He thought they just made him look old but he couldn't read without them so he endured.

"Must be more good news," said Lydia. She was thinking to herself that it was probably Dax, king of trampling boundaries.

The caller ID read "unavailable."

"Hello?"

"This is Detective Matt Stenopolis, NYPD Missing Persons Unit. I need to speak to Lydia Strong."

His voice sounded youngish but there was a gravity and deep timbre to it that told Lydia he took himself seriously and expected others to do the same.

"This is."

"Ms. Strong, you left a message for Lily Samuels about two weeks ago indicating that you were returning a call she made to you." She could hear street noise on the other end of the phone.

"That's right," she said, concern and curiosity aroused.

He cleared his throat. "Ms. Samuels has been missing now for over two weeks and I'm wondering if we can talk."

"Sure," she said. "Of course."

"I'm calling from my car. I know it's late but would it be inconvenient if I came by?"

"Um, no," she said glancing at the clock. "Come on by."

She gave him the address and hung up the phone.

"Who was that?" said Jeffrey, putting down his book and looking at her.

"A detective. Lily Samuels is missing," she said leaning against the counter.

"Who?"

"Remember that journalism class I taught at NYU as a visiting professor a couple of years ago? She was one of my students. She started at the Post last year on the crime desk."

Lydia had felt a special affinity for Lily from the day she had walked into the large, over-warm classroom and sat in the front row. There was an earnestness, an honesty to her that Lydia could see in her deep brown eyes. And she had a belly full of fire. Lydia could always recognize it, that love of the hunt, that drive for the heart of a story. Lily's talent had set her apart from the rest of the class; the kindness and compassion in her interview style and in her writing put her head and shoulders above most of the professional writers Lydia knew. In the past two years, Lydia had given her advice on pursuing stories she was working on for her degree, and eventually a reference that got her a foot in the door at the Post.

It wasn't long before the buzzer rang. She checked the video monitor. A very tall, well-dressed, youngish man in a leather coat lifted his shield to the video monitor. Lydia pressed the button that allowed entry to the elevator bank downstairs. She watched as he stepped out of view and into the elevator that would lift directly into the apartment.

It was the little things like this which reminded her that she was free; she didn't have to feel the cold fingers of fear tugging at her every time the buzzer rang late, didn't have to wonder if the person she saw at the door was a threat. It was like a grip had been released from her heart. Jed McIntyre, the man who murdered her mother and then last year came for her after his erroneous release from a maximum-security mental hospital, was dead. Unlike incarceration, death was a securely permanent condition. And Lydia found she could breathe again.

As she waited by the elevator door, she heard Jeffrey in the kitchen making coffee.

"How long has she been missing?" he called from the kitchen.

"Two weeks," said Lydia grimly. In a missing persons investigation it was the first thirty-six hours that were critical. After that time period had passed, the odds of anyone being found alive decreased exponentially. For Lily, that window had closed.

"And the guy is still working into the night," said Jeffrey.

"Must have its hooks in him."

Lydia nodded to herself. They both knew what that was like.

Detective Matt Stenopolis was, simply put, gigantic. He ducked his head slightly as he stepped from the elevator and Lydia's hand disappeared into his when he took it in greeting. He had pale white skin, a chaos of blue-black hair and a dark shadow of stubble to match. He smelled like snow and cigarettes.

He's bigger than Dax, thought Lydia, as he and Jeffrey introduced themselves. It was a different kind of big, though. Dax was big by design. The detective was big by genetics. His shoulders, wide as a refrigerator, slouched the way the shoulders of all extremely tall people seem to, as if protecting themselves against the jeers and taunts that have been hurled at them all their lives.

"Thanks for letting me stop by so late, Ms. Strong."

"No problem. Lily's a friend," she said. "Anything I can do."

He followed her into the living room and she encouraged him to have a seat on the couch. When he sat on it, the large sofa looked as if it had been made for Barbie Dolls. She thought she heard it groan in protest.

"Coffee?" she asked.

"Please," he answered gratefully.

"Three weeks ago today," began the detective, as Lydia handed him a cup of coffee, "Lily Samuels' brother Mickey committed suicide in his car in an Office Depot parking lot in Riverdale."

"Oh, no," said Lydia. She remembered thinking that Lily had sounded strained and worried in her message. But she hadn't mentioned Mickey's suicide. Not that anyone would leave that kind of news on someone's voicemail.

The detective nodded slowly, took a sip of his coffee, and continued.

"The police ruled it a suicide right away. The guy was

alone in his car with all the doors locked. He had a half-finished bottle of Jack Daniels between his legs. There was gunshot residue on his right hand. He left a note for his sister. He put his gun in his mouth and pulled the trigger."

They were all silent for a second, as if out of respect.

"What did the note say?" asked Lydia.

"It said: 'Dear Lily, I'm so sorry to leave you all alone here. But I just can't do it anymore. You're the strong one. It's too much for me."

He said it like he'd played the note over and over in his mind and the words had ceased to have meaning for him. But Lydia could hear the crushing sadness in them.

"Lily was totally devastated, of course. And apparently she refused to believe he would kill himself. I mean, she wasn't just doubtful. She was positive that he couldn't have done it."

"That's pretty common with family members of a suicide," said Jeffrey.

"An initial phase of denial is common. But, according to friends she was certain, and after the funeral she set out to prove it. She took a week off from her job and went up to Riverdale." Detective Stenopolis took a sip of his coffee.

"I remember her telling me that she and her brother were close, more like best friends than siblings," said Lydia. "She didn't have any indication that he was depressed or in some kind of trouble?"

"Apparently not. Friends got the sense that there had been some kind of conflict between them. But she never said what specifically, just that he was 'acting like a jerk.' He had moved from the city up to Riverdale about six months ago, apparently wanting to open some kind of café and performance space, leaving a mega-money job in banking. Sounded to me like he was burned out."

He was quiet a second, then he went on.

"Lily Samuels went up to Riverdale on October 15th. She was in touch with her friends for the first week. Then nothing.

Her cell phone voicemail, which we accessed with the help of her mobile service provider, was full of worried messages from her friends. One of those messages was from you. Do you remember what she said on her message to you?"

"I can do better than that, Detective. I'm sure I saved it because I didn't hear back from her. I tend to save email messages and phone messages until I connect with the person involved, otherwise I just forget."

"There are messages on there from 1995," said Jeffrey with a small smile. He considered her system of keeping track of messages somewhat disorganized. Ever since he'd read Clear Your Clutter with Feng Shui, he'd been nearly impossible to live with on such matters. She ignored him as she grabbed the cordless phone. She entered her codes and after she skipped about twelve messages, she put the phone on its speaker setting.

"This message was left on October 22nd at 7:04 p.m.," said the electronic voice.

Then, "Ms. Strong, it's Lily Samuels." She released a heavy sigh. "I really need your help. I am out of my league. Big time. I—I just really need to talk to you. Can you call me back? As soon as possible? Thanks. Bye."

Lydia felt a twist of guilt in her stomach. Listening to the message now she heard the fear, the anxiety in Lily's voice. When she'd heard it the first time, Lily had just seemed really stressed to her. It had taken Lydia until the next day to return the call because she'd been stressed out herself, wrestling with her own work.

"I've never heard her voice before," said Detective Stenopolis, an expression on his face that Lydia couldn't read. "She sounds so young."

"She is young," said Lydia. "Twenty-five or twenty-six, I think."

"Twenty-six," he said. "Under what circumstances did she generally contact you? Did you talk often? Would you say you were friends?"

"It was really more of mentoring relationship. She was a student of mine when I taught a journalism class at NYU. She was special, really talented. At the end of the class, I encouraged her to keep in touch if she needed anything. She'd call for advice on stories, references, stuff like that."

"So when you got the call you thought she was probably calling about work?"

"Yes. That was generally what we talked about. Sometimes we chatted about personal things briefly but mainly not."

"When was the last time you saw her?"

"I think we had drinks about a year and a half ago. She wanted to thank me for getting her in for her interview at the Post."

Detective Stenopolis was scribbling notes as she spoke and continued writing for a minute after she'd gone silent.

She remembered that Lily was radiant that night with excitement. The interview had gone well and she felt like she was on her way to fulfilling the only dream she'd ever had, to be a journalist. She was dating someone new—a banker, if Lydia remembered right—and Lily seemed smitten with him. At the time, things in Lydia's life had been pretty hairy, so her time with Lily had seemed like a little oasis of cocktails and girl talk in a sea of madness.

"Who reported her missing?" asked Lydia. Curiosity was tapping her on the shoulder.

"Her mother. When Lily missed her mother's fiftieth birthday everyone knew there was something wrong. Apparently, it was not unlike Lily to be incommunicado for a week or so when she was working on something. But she was a loving daughter and a good friend. No matter how busy she was, she wouldn't miss her mother's birthday, especially knowing what a hard time it would be for her on the heels of Mickey's death."

"Her mother must be a wreck," said Lydia. What a nightmare it must be to lose a child to suicide and then for the other to go missing. It was hard to imagine.

"She's heavily medicated right now. Major valium just to get through the day, the husband says."

"Lily's father?" asked Lydia, reaching for something Lily had told her about her family.

"Her stepfather. Raised both kids from the time Lily was two and Mickey was four."

"What happened to their father?" asked Lydia.

Detective Stenopolis paused for a second, seemed to consider whether he should say. "Suicide," he said, finally. "Shot himself in a car, drunk on JD. Just like his son Mickey."

Lydia felt her heart thump. It was strange to be having this conversation after just hearing about her father's own death. It seemed surreal and Lydia felt a familiar nervousness, a slight anxiety.

"That's pretty odd," said Jeffrey, narrowing his eyes.

The detective rubbed his hands together as if he were warming them, seemed to consider it for a moment, whether it was odd or not. Then, "Depression runs in families often. I'm not sure how uncommon it is. Suicide. I don't know... maybe it's easier to do it if you know someone who has."

Lydia wouldn't have thought of it that way but it made an odd kind of sense to her. As if the idea of suicide was a contagion; the more closely exposed to it you were, the easier it was to catch.

"So you said you've been working on the case for two weeks?" said Lydia.

The detective nodded. "Today is the fourteenth day. I think she's been missing since October 23rd, though, because no one who called her on or after that day heard back from her. Which means that the thirty-six hours where it would be most likely for us to find her passed before we ever knew she was gone."

Lydia looked down at the floor. If I'd called her back on the 22nd, could I have helped her? Lydia thought. It wasn't a healthy way to think but that was the way her mind worked.

There was little point in considering the answer.

"So what have you got so far?" asked Jeffrey.

Detective Stenopolis gave him a look. "Thanks so much for your time," he said, politely. "Ms. Strong, would you mind if I sent a tech over to record that message from your voicemail?"

"We can take care of that, if you want, Detective," said Jeffrey. "One of the communication techs from my firm can do it tomorrow and we'll email you the digital file."

"That would be great," he said, rising and handing Jeffrey his card. "It could take a week to get someone from the department over here on such a low priority."

"Low priority?" said Lydia with a frown. "I'd think something like this would be big news. A pretty young reporter goes missing while trying to prove her brother didn't kill himself. In fact, I'm surprised I haven't heard anything about this earlier in the media."

Lydia was usually a news junkie, but admittedly she had been a bit of a hermit in the last few weeks while she struggled to finish her manuscript. She had tried to keep outside input at a bare minimum.

"The Post did a piece. And there's been some coverage in Riverdale. But there's absolutely no evidence of foul play. She had clothes and a good deal of cash with her; we know that. Her car is gone. She easily could have just taken off."

"But you don't think she did."

"No. I don't."

"What do you think happened?" Lydia said, knowing she was pushing.

"All due respect, Ms. Strong, but I'm not going to discuss this with you."

She nodded to indicate she understood. They'd been fortunate with access in the past because of Jeffrey's connections to the FBI and the NYPD. But cops generally didn't like writers or private investigators. Since she was a true crime writer and a partner in Jeffrey's private detective firm, Mark, Striker and Strong, she was a little of both.

"I understand," she said, following him toward the elevator.

"I appreciate your cooperation, both of you," he said, shaking each of their hands. "If you think of anything else, call anytime."

He stooped back into the elevator and gave them a little wave as the door closed in front of him.

"Lydia," said Jeffrey, his voice a warning and a question.

"What?" she said defensively. The buzz was so intense that her hands were shaking a little.

To read more, look out for *Smoke* by Lisa Miscione - out in June, or visit www.snowbooks.com for more information.